Praise for *USA TODAY* bestselling author Penny Jordan

"Women everywhere will find pieces of themselves in Jordan's characters."
—*Publishers Weekly*

"[Penny Jordan's novels]...touch every emotion."
—*RT Book Reviews*

Praise for *USA TODAY* bestselling author Lynne Graham

"Another keeper...
a mesmerizing blend of wonderful characters, powerful emotion and sensational scenes."
—*RT Book Reviews* on *The Winter Bride*

"Lynne Graham doesn't disappoint readers with her trademark alpha hero, powerful sensuality and compelling story line."
—*RT Book Reviews* on *The Stephanides Pregnancy*

PENNY JORDAN

has been writing for more than twenty-five years and has an outstanding record—more than 165 novels published. She says she hopes to go on writing until she has passed the 200 mark, and maybe even the 250 mark.

Although Penny was born in Preston, Lancashire, U.K., where she spent her childhood, she moved to Cheshire as a teenager and has continued to live there. She lives with a hairy Birman cat, Posh, who assists her with her writing.

Penny is a member and supporter of both the Romantic Novelists' Association and Romance Writers of America—two organizations dedicated to providing support for both published and yet-to-be-published authors.

LYNNE GRAHAM

has lived in Northern Ireland all her life. She grew up in a seaside village and now lives in a country house surrounded by a woodland garden, which is wonderfully private.

Lynne wrote her first book at fifteen, and it was rejected everywhere. She started writing again when she was home with her first child. It took several attempts before she sold her first book, and the delight of seeing that book for sale at the local newsagents has never been forgotten.

Lynne loves gardening and cooking, collects everything from old toys to rock specimens and is crazy about every aspect of Christmas.

USA TODAY Bestselling Author
PENNY JORDAN

Her Christmas Fantasy

USA TODAY Bestselling Author
LYNNE GRAHAM

The Winter Bride

TORONTO • NEW YORK • LONDON
AMSTERDAM • PARIS • SYDNEY • HAMBURG
STOCKHOLM • ATHENS • TOKYO • MILAN • MADRID
PRAGUE • WARSAW • BUDAPEST • AUCKLAND

Recycling programs
for this product may
not exist in your area.

ISBN-13: 978-0-373-68814-2

HER CHRISTMAS FANTASY & THE WINTER BRIDE

Copyright © 2010 by Harlequin Books S.A.

The publisher acknowledges the copyright holders of the individual works as follows:

HER CHRISTMAS FANTASY
Copyright © 1996 by Penny Jordan

THE WINTER BRIDE
Copyright © 1997 by Lynne Graham

This edition published by arrangement with Harlequin Books S.A.

For questions and comments about the quality of this book please contact us at Customer_eCare@Harlequin.ca.

www.eHarlequin.com

Printed in U.S.A.

CONTENTS

HER CHRISTMAS FANTASY

USA TODAY Bestselling Author

Penny Jordan

CHAPTER ONE

LISA PAUSED HESITANTLY outside the shop, studying the very obviously designer-label and expensive outfits in the window doubtfully.

She had been given the address by a friend who had told her that the shop was one of the most exclusive 'nearly new' designer-clothes outlets in the city, where outfits could be picked up for less than a third of their original price.

Lisa was no fashion victim—normally she was quite happy with her small wardrobe of good-quality chain-store clothes—but Henry had seemed so anxious that she create a good impression on his family and their friends, and most particularly his mother, during their Christmas visit to his parents' home in the north that Lisa had felt obliged to take the hints he had been dropping and add something rather more up-market to her wardrobe. Especially since Henry had already indicated that he wanted to put their relationship on a more formal basis, with an official announcement to his family of their plans to marry.

Lisa knew that many of her friends found Henry slightly stuffy and old-fashioned, but she liked those aspects of his personality. They indicated a reliability, a dependability in him which, so far as she was concerned, outweighed his admitted tendency to fuss and find fault over minor details.

When the more outspoken of her closest friends had asked her what she saw in him she'd told them quietly that she saw a dependable husband and a good father.

'But what about romance?' they had asked her. 'What about falling desperately and passionately in love?'

Lisa had laughed, genuinely amused.

'I'm not the type of woman who falls desperately or passionately in love,' she had responded, 'and nor do I want to be!'

'But doesn't it annoy you that Henry's so chauvinistically old-fashioned?' Her friends had persisted. 'Look at the way he's fussing over you meeting his parents and family—telling you how he wants you to dress.'

'He's just anxious for me to make a good impression,' Lisa had argued back on Henry's behalf. 'He obviously values his parents' opinion and—'

'And he's still tied to his mother's apron strings,' one of her friends had scoffed. 'I know the type.' She had paused a little before adding more seriously, 'You know, don't you, that he was on the point of becoming engaged to someone else shortly before he met you and that he broke off the relationship because he wasn't sure that his family would approve of her? Apparently they're very old-fashioned and strait-laced, and Janey had been living with someone else when she'd first met Henry—'

'Yes, I do know,' Lisa had retorted firmly. 'But the reason that they broke up was not Janey's past history but that Henry realised that they didn't, simply *didn't* have enough in common.'

'And you and he do?' her friend had asked drily.

'We both want the same things out of life, yes,' Lisa had asserted defensively.

And it was, after all, true. She might not have fallen deeply in love with Henry the night they were introduced by a mutual friend, but she had certainly liked him enough to accept his invitation to dinner, and their relationship had grown steadily from that date to the point where they both felt that their future lay together.

She might not be entirely comfortable with Henry's insistence that she buy herself a new wardrobe in order to impress his wealthy parents and their circle of friends, but she could sympathise with the emotion which had led to him making such a suggestion.

Her own parents would, she knew, be slightly bemused by her choice of a husband; her mother was a gifted and acclaimed potter whose work was internationally praised, whilst her father's stylish, modern furniture designs meant that he was constantly in demand, not just as a designer but as a lecturer as well.

Both her parents were currently in Japan, and were not due to return for another two months.

It would have been a lonely Christmas for her this year if Henry had not invited her to go north with him to the Yorkshire Dales to visit his parents, Lisa acknowledged.

He had already warned her that his parents might consider her work as a PA to the owner of a small, London-based antique business rather too bohemian and arty. Had she worked in industry, been a teacher or a nurse, they would have found it more acceptable.

'In fact they'd probably prefer it if you didn't work at all,' he had told Lisa carefully when they had been discussing the subject.

'Not work? But that's—' Hastily she had bitten back the words she had been about to say, responding mildly instead, 'Most women these days expect to have a career.'

'My mother doesn't approve of married women working, especially when they have children,' Henry had told her stiffly.

Firmly suppressing her instinctive response that his mother was very obviously rather out of touch with modern life, Lisa had said placatingly instead, 'A lot of women tend to put their career on hold or work part-time when their children are young.'

She had hesitated outside the shop for long enough, she decided now, pushing open the door and walking in.

The young girl who came forward to help her explained that she was actually standing in for the owner of the shop, who had been called away unexpectedly.

The clothes on offer were unexpectedly wearable, Lisa acknowledged, and not too over-the-top as she had half dreaded. One outfit in particular caught her eye—a trouser suit in fine cream wool crêpe which comprised trousers, waistcoat and jacket.

'It's an Armani,' the salesgirl enthused as Lisa picked it off the rail. 'A real bargain… I was tempted to buy it myself,' she admitted, 'but it's only a size ten and I take a twelve. It's this season's stock—a real bargain.'

'This season's.' A small frown puckered Lisa's forehead. Who on earth these days could afford to buy a designer outfit and then get rid of it within a few months of buying it— especially something like this in such a classical design that it wasn't going to date?

'If you like it, we've got several other things in from the same per…the same source,' the girl was telling her. 'Would you like to see them?'

Lisa paused and then smiled her agreement. She was beginning to enjoy this rather more than she had expected. The feel of the cream crêpe beneath her fingertips was sensuously luxurious. She had always loved fabrics, their textures, differing weights.

An hour later, her normally immaculate long bob of silky blonde hair slightly tousled from all her trying on, she grimaced ruefully at the pile of clothes that she had put to one side as impossible to resist.

What woman, having bought such a luxuriously expensive and elegantly wearable wardrobe, could bear to part with it after so short a period of time?

If she had been given free rein to choose from new herself, she could not have chosen better, Lisa recognised as she sighingly acknowledged that the buttermilk-coloured silk, wool and cashmere coat she had just tried on was an absolute must.

She was, she admitted ten minutes later as she took a deep breath and signed her credit-card bill, buying these clothes not so much for Henry and his family as for herself.

'You've got an absolute bargain,' the salesgirl told her unnecessarily as she carefully wrapped Lisa's purchases in tissue-paper and put them into several large, glossy carrier bags.

'I think these are the nicest things we've had in in a long time. Personally I don't think I could have brought myself to part with them... That coat...' She gave a small sigh and then told Lisa half enviously, 'They fitted you perfectly as well. I envy you being so tall and slim.'

'So tall.' Lisa winced slightly. She wasn't excessively tall, being five feet nine, but she was aware that with Henry being a rather stocky five feet ten or so he preferred her not to wear high-heeled shoes, and he had on occasion made rather irritated comments to her about her height.

She was just on her way out of the shop when a car drew up outside, its owner double parking in flagrant disregard for the law.

He looked extremely irritable and ill-tempered, Lisa decided as she watched him stride towards the shop, and wondered idly who he was.

Not a prospective customer, even on behalf of a woman friend. No, he was quite definitely the type who, if he did buy clothes for a woman, would not need to exercise financial restraint by buying them second-hand.

Lisa was aware of his frown deepening as he glanced almost dismissively at her.

Well, she was equally unimpressed by him, she decided critically. Stunningly, almost overpoweringly male he might look, with that tall, broad-shouldered body and that hawkish, arrogant profile, but he was simply not her type.

She had no doubt that the more romantic of her friends would consider him ideal 'swoon over' material, with those frowning, overtly sexual, strongly drawn male features and his dominant masterful manner. But she merely thought him arrogantly over-confident. Look at the way he had dismissed her with the briefest of irritable glances, stalking past her. Even the silky gleam of his thick dark hair possessed a strong air of male sexuality.

He would be the kind of man who looked almost too hirsute with his clothes off, she decided unkindly, sternly suppressing the impish little demon of rebellion within her that immediately produced a very clear and highly erotic mental image of him thus unclad and, to her exasperation, not overly hirsute at all... In fact...

Stop it, she warned herself as she flagged down a cruising taxi and gave the driver the address of the friend who had recommended the shop to her.

She had promised her that she would call round and let her know how she had fared, but for some reason, once her purchases had been duly displayed and enviously approved, she discovered that Alison was more interested in hearing about the man she had passed in the street than discussing the likelihood of her forthcoming introduction to Henry's parents going well.

'He wasn't my type at all,' she declared firmly to Alison.

'He was far too arrogant. I don't imagine he would have the first idea of how to treat a modern woman—'

'You mean that Henry does...?' Alison asked drily, stopping Lisa in her tracks for a moment before she valiantly responded.

'Of course he does.'

'You just wait,' Alison warned her. 'The moment he gets that ring on your finger, he's going to start nagging you to conform. He'll want you to stop working, for a start. Look at the way he goes on about what a perfect mother his own mother was...how she devoted her life to his father and himself...'

'I think it's rather touching that he's so devoted to her, so loyal and loving...' Lisa defended.

'Mmm... What's he like in bed?' Alison asked her curiously.

Even though Lisa was used to her friend's forthrightness, she was a little taken aback by her question, caught too off guard to do anything other than answer honestly.

'I...I don't know... We...we haven't... We don't...'

'You don't *know*. Are you crazy? You're planning to *marry* the man and you don't know yet what he's like in bed. How long have you two known one another?'

'Almost eight months,' Lisa replied slightly stiffly.

'Mmm... Hardly the type to be overwhelmed by passion, then, is he, our Henry?'

'Henry believes in old-fashioned courtship, that couples should get to know one another as...as people. He doesn't... he doesn't care for the modern approach to casual sex...'

'Very laudable,' Alison told her sardonically.

'Look, the fact that we haven't...that we don't...that we haven't been to bed together yet isn't a problem for *me*,' Lisa told her vehemently.

'No? Then it should be,' Alison returned forthrightly. 'How

on earth can you think of marrying a man when you don't even know if the two of you are sexually compatible yet?'

'Easily,' Lisa replied promptly. 'After all, our grandparents did.'

Alison rolled her eyes and mocked, 'And you claim that you aren't romantic.'

'It takes more to build a good marriage than just sex,' Lisa told her quietly. 'I'm tired of men who take you out for dinner and then expect you to take them to bed as a thank-you... I want stability in a relationship, Alison. Someone I can rely on, depend on. Someone who respects and values me as a *person*... Yes, all right, Henry might be slightly old-fashioned and...and...'

'Sexless?' her friend came back, but Lisa shook her head and continued determinedly.

'But he's very loyal...very faithful...very trustworthy... and...'

'If that's what you're looking for you'd be better off with a dog,' Alison suggested critically, but Lisa wasn't prepared to argue the matter any further.

'I'm just not the type for excitement and passion,' she told her friend. 'I like stability. Marriage isn't just for now, Alison; it's for the future too. Look, I'd better go,' she announced, glancing at her watch. 'Henry's taking me out for dinner this evening.' As she got up and headed for the door, she added gratefully, 'Thanks for recommending that shop to me.'

'Yes, I'm really envious. You've got some lovely things and at a knock-down price. All current season's stuff too... Lucky you.'

As she made her way home to her own flat Lisa was ruefully aware of how difficult her friends found it to understand her relationship with Henry, but then they had not had her upbring-

ing and did not possess her desire—her craving in a sense—
for emotional tranquillity, for roots and permanence.

Her parents were both by nature not just extremely artis-
tic—and because of that at times wholly absorbed by their
work—they were also gypsies, nomads, who enjoyed travelling
and moving on. The thought of basing themselves somewhere
permanently was anathema to them.

During her childhood Lisa couldn't remember having spent
a whole year at any one school; she knew her parents loved
her, and she certainly loved them dearly, but she had a different nature from theirs.

All right, so she knew that it would be difficult persuading
Henry to accept that there was no reason why she should not
still pursue her career as well as being a mother, but she was
sure that she would be able to make him understand that her
work was important to her. At the moment Henry worked for
a prestigious firm of insurance brokers, but they had both
agreed that once they were married they would move out of
London and into the country.

She let herself into her small flat and carefully carried her
new purchases into her bedroom.

After she had had a shower she intended to try them all
on again, if she had time before Henry arrived. However,
when she replayed her answering-machine tape there was a
message on it from Henry, cancelling their date because he
had an important business dinner that he had to attend and
reminding her that they still had to shop for suitable Christmas
presents to take for his family.

She had already made several suggestions based on what
Henry had told her about his family, and specifically his
parents—a very pretty petit point antique footstool for his
grandmother, some elegant tulip vases for his mother, who,
he had told her, was a keen gardener. But Henry had pursed
his lips and dismissed her ideas.

She had been tempted to suggest that it might be better if he chose their Christmas presents on his own, but she had warned herself that she was being unfair and even slightly petty. He, after all, knew their tastes far better than she did.

She had just put on her favourite of all the outfits she had bought—the cream wool crêpe trouser suit—when her door-bell rang.

Assuming that it must be Henry after all, she went automatically to open the door, and then stood staring in total shock as she realised that her visitor wasn't Henry but the man she had last seen striding past her and storming into the dress agency as she'd left it.

'Lisa Phillips?' he demanded curtly as he stepped past her and into her hall.

Dumbly Lisa nodded her head, too taken aback by the unexpectedness of his arrival to think to question his right to walk uninvited into her home.

'My name's Oliver Davenport,' he told her curtly, handing her a card, barely giving her time to glance at it before he continued, 'I believe you purchased several items of clothing from Second Time Around earlier today.'

'Er...yes,' Lisa agreed. 'But—'

'Good. This shouldn't take long then. Unfortunately the clothes that you bought should not have been put on sale. Technically, in fact, the shop sold them without the permission of their true owner, and in such circumstances, as with the innocent purchase of a stolen car or indeed any stolen goods, you have no legal right to—'

'Just a minute,' she interrupted him in disbelief. Completely taken aback by his unexpected arrival and his infuriatingly arrogant manner, Lisa could feel herself becoming thoroughly angry. 'Are you accusing the shop of selling stolen clothes? Because if so it should be the police you are informing and not me.'

'Not exactly. Look, I'm prepared to refund you the full amount of what you spent plus an extra hundred pounds for any inconvenience. So if you'll just—'

'That's very generous of you,' Lisa told him sarcastically. 'But I bought these clothes for a specific purpose and I have no intention of selling them back to you. I bought them in good faith and—'

'Look, I've just explained to you, those clothes should never have been sold in the first place,' he cut across her harshly, giving her an impatiently angry look.

Lisa didn't like the way he was filling her small hall, looming almost menacingly over her, but there was no way she was going to give in to him. Why should she?

'If that's true, then why hasn't the shop been in touch with me?' Lisa challenged him.

She could see that he didn't like her question from the way his mouth tightened and hardened before he replied bitingly, 'Probably because the idiotic woman who runs the place refuses to listen to reason.'

'Really?' Lisa asked him scathingly. 'You seem to have a way with women. Has it ever occurred to you that a little less aggression and a good deal more persuasion might produce better results? Not that any amount of persuasion will change my mind,' she added firmly. 'I bought those clothes in good faith, and since the shop hasn't seen fit to get in touch with me concerning their supposedly wrongful sale I don't see why—'

'Oh, for God's sake.' She was interrupted furiously. 'Look, if you must know, the clothes belong to my cousin's girl-friend. They had a quarrel—it's a very volatile relationship. She walked out on him, vowing never to come back—they'd had an argument about her decision to go on holiday with a girlfriend, without him apparently—and in a fit of retalia-tory anger he gave her clothes to the dress agency. It was an impulse…something he regretted virtually as soon as he'd done it, and when Emma rang him from Italy to make things up he asked me to help him get her things back before she comes home and discovers what he's done.'

'He asked *you* for help?'

There was very little doubt in Lisa's mind about whose girlfriend the absent Emma actually was, and it wasn't Oliver Davenport's fictitious cousin.

The look he gave her in response to her question wasn't very friendly, Lisa recognised; in fact it wasn't very friendly at all, but even though, concealed beneath the sensual elegance of her newly acquired trousers, her knees were knocking slightly, she refused to give in to her natural apprehension.

It wasn't like her to be so stubborn or so unsympathetic, but something about him just seemed to rub her up the wrong way and make her uncharacteristically antagonistic towards him.

It wasn't just the fact that he was demanding that she part with her newly acquired wardrobe that was making her combative, she admitted; it was something about the man himself, something about his arrogance, his…his maleness that was setting her nerves slightly on edge, challenging her into a mode of behaviour that was really quite foreign to her.

She knew that Henry would have been shocked to see her displaying so much stubbornness and anger—she was a little bit shocked herself.

'He was about to go away on business. Emma's due back at the end of the week. He didn't want her walking into the flat and discovering that half her clothes are missing…'

'No, I'm sure you…he…' Lisa corrected herself tauntingly '…doesn't…'

She saw from the dark burn of angry colour etching his cheekbones that he wasn't pleased by her deliberate 'mistake', nor the tone of voice she had delivered it in.

'You have no legal claim over those clothes,' he told her grimly. 'The shop sold them without the owner's permission.'

'If that's true, then it's up to the shop to get in touch with me,' Lisa pointed out. 'After all, for all I know, you could want them for yourself...' She paused. His temper was set on a hair-trigger already and although she doubted that he would actually physically harm her...

'Don't be ridiculous,' she heard him breathe softly, as though he had read her mind.

Inexplicably she realised that she was blushing slightly as, for no logical reason at all, she remembered exactly what she had been thinking about him—and his body—earlier in the day. Just as well he hadn't second guessed her private thoughts *then*!

'So you're not prepared to be reasonable about this?'

She be reasonable? Lisa could feel her own temper starting to rise.

'Doesn't it mean anything to you that you could be putting someone's whole relationship at risk by your refusal?'

'*Me* putting a relationship at risk?' Lisa gasped at the unfairness of it. 'If you ask me, I'm not the one who's doing that. If your relationship is so important to you, you should have thought of that before you lost your temper and decided to punish your girlfriend by selling her clothes—'

'Emma is not *my* girlfriend,' he told her with ominous calm. 'As I've already explained to you, I am simply acting as an intermediary in all of this for my cousin. But then I suppose it's par for the course that you should think otherwise. It goes with all the rest of your illogical behaviour,' he told her scathingly.

'If you ask me,' she told him, thoroughly incensed now, 'I think that Emma...whoever's girlfriend she is—yours or your cousin's...is better off without you. What kind of man does something like that…? Those clothes were virtually new and—'

'Exactly. New and expensive and paid for by my cousin, who is a rather jealous young man who objects to his girlfriend wearing the clothes he bought her to attract the attentions of other men…'

'And because of that he stole them from her wardrobe and sold them? It sounds to me as though she's better off without you…without him,' Lisa corrected herself fiercely, her eyes showing her contempt of a man—any man—jealous or otherwise, who could behave in such a petty and revengeful way.

'Well, I'm sorry,' she continued, patently anything but. 'But explaining to Emma just exactly what's happened to her clothes is your problem and not mine. I bought them in good faith—'

'And you'll be able to buy some more with the money I'm willing to refund you for them, especially since… Oh, I get it,' he said softly, his eyes suddenly narrowing.

'You get what?' Lisa demanded suspiciously, not liking the cynicism she could see in his eyes. 'Those clothes were virtually brand-new, this season's stock, and I'd be very lucky indeed to pick up anything else like them at such a bargain price, especially at this time of year, and—'

'Oh, yes, I can see what you're after. All right then, I don't like blackmailers and I wouldn't normally give in to someone who plainly thinks she's onto a good thing, but I haven't got time to waste negotiating with you. What would you guess was the full, brand-new value of the clothes you bought today?'

'The full value?' A small frown puckered Lisa's forehead. She had no idea at all of what he was getting at. 'I have no idea. I don't normally buy exclusive designer-label clothes, especially not Armani…but I imagine it would have to be several thousand pounds…'

'Several thousand pounds.' A thin, dangerous smile curled

his mouth, his eyes so coldly contemptuous that Lisa actually felt a small, icy shiver race down her spine.

'Why don't we settle for a round figure and make it five thousand pounds? I'll write you a cheque for five thousand here and now and you'll give me back Emma's clothes.'

Lisa stared at him in disbelief.

'But that's crazy,' she protested. 'Why on earth should you pay me five thousand pounds when you could go out and buy a whole new wardrobe for her for that amount...?' She shook her head in disbelief. 'I don't—'

'Oh, come on,' he interrupted her cuttingly. 'Don't give me that. You understand perfectly well. Even *I* understand how impossible and time-wasting an exercise it would be for me to go out and replace every single item with its exact replica... even if I knew what it was I was supposed to be buying. Don't overplay your hand,' he warned her. 'All that mock innocence doesn't suit you.'

Mock innocence!

As she suddenly recognised just what he was accusing her of, Lisa's face flushed a brilliant, furious scarlet.

'Get out... Get out of my flat right now,' she demanded shakily. 'Otherwise I'm going to call the police. How dare you accuse me of...of...?' She couldn't even say the word, she felt such a sense of outrage and disgust.

'I wouldn't give you those clothes now if you offered to pay me ten thousand...twenty thousand,' she told him passionately. 'You deserve to lose Emma... In fact, I think I'm probably doing her a favour by letting her see just what kind of a man you are. I suppose you thought that just because you bought her clothes for her you had a right to...to take them back... If I were her... If I were her...'

'Yes? If you were her, what?' he goaded her, just as furious as she was herself, Lisa recognised as she saw the small pulse beating fiercely in his jaw and the banked-down fury in his eyes.

'I wouldn't have let you buy them for me in the first place,' she threw emotionally at him, adding, 'I'd rather—'

'Rather what?' he challenged her, his voice dropping suddenly and becoming dangerously, sensually soft as he raked her from head to foot in such a sexually predatory and searching way that it left her virtually shaking, trembling, her body overreacting wildly to the male sexuality in the way he was looking at her, the sensual challenge in the way his eyes deliberately stripped her of her clothes, leaving her body vulnerable...exposed...naked.

'You'd rather what?' he repeated triumphantly. 'Go naked?'

Lisa couldn't speak; she was too shocked, too outraged, too aware of her feminine vulnerability to the blazing heat of his sexuality to risk saying anything.

'But then in actual fact, according to you—since you refuse to believe the truth and accept that I am acting for my cousin and not for myself—you are wearing clothes that I have chosen...bought...' he added softly, his glance slipping suggestively over her body for a second time, but this time more slowly, more lingeringly...more...more seductively, Lisa recognised as she felt herself responding helplessly to the sheer force of the magnetic spell he seemed to have cast over her.

From somewhere she managed to find the strength to break free. Stepping back from him, putting a safer distance between them, averting her eyes and her over-flushed face from his powerful gaze, she demanded huskily, 'I want you to leave. Now. Otherwise...'

'You'll call the police. I know,' he agreed drily. 'Very well, since it's obvious I can't make you see reason... I won't forget how co-operative you've been,' he added, sending a small shiver down her spine as she saw the look in his eyes. 'Although I can understand why you're so loath to part with your borrowed finery.

'The suit looks good on you,' he added unexpectedly as he turned towards the door, pausing to look at her before lifting his hand and outrageously tracing a line with the tip of his index finger all the way along the deep V of the neckline of the waistcoat just where the upper curves of her breasts, naked underneath it, pressed against the creamy fabric.

'It's a bit tighter here on you than it was on Emma, though,' he told her. 'She's probably only a 34B whereas you must be a 34C. Nice—especially worn the way you're wearing it now, without anything underneath it...'

Lisa swallowed back all of the agitated, defensive remarks that sprang to her lips, knowing that none of them could do anything to wipe out what he had just said to her, or the effect his words had had on her.

Why, she wondered wretchedly as he opened her front door and left her flat far more calmly than he had entered it, did her body have to react so...so...idiotically and erotically to his touch? Even without looking down she knew how betrayingly her nipples were still pressing against the fine fabric of her waistcoat—as they certainly hadn't been doing when he'd first arrived. As they had, in fact, only humiliatingly done when he had reached out and touched her with that lazily mocking fingertip which had had such a devastating effect on her senses.

It was because she was so overwrought, that was all, she tried to comfort herself half an hour later, the front door securely bolted as she hugged a comforting mug of freshly made coffee.

She would have to ring the shop, of course, and find out exactly what was going on, and if they asked her to return the clothes then morally she would have no option other than to do so.

How dared he accuse her of trying to blackmail him…? *Her*. The coffee slopped out of the mug as her hands started to shake. As if she would ever…ever do any such thing. She felt desperately sorry for the unknown Emma. It was bad enough that he should have sold her clothes, but how would she feel, knowing that he had touched her, another woman, so…so…? No, in her view Emma was better off without him. Much better off.

How dared he touch her like that…as though…as though…? And he had known exactly what he was doing as well. She had seen it in those shockingly knowing steel-grey eyes as she'd read the message of male triumph and awareness that they'd been giving her. He had known that he was arousing her—had known it and had enjoyed knowing it.

Unlike her. She had hated it and she hated him. Emma was quite definitely better off without him and she certainly wasn't going to be the one to help him make up their quarrel by returning her clothes.

At least he was not likely to be able to carry out that subtle threat of future retribution against her—thank goodness.

CHAPTER TWO

LISA STOOD IN FRONT of the guest-bedroom window of Henry's parents' large Victorian house looking out across the wintry countryside.

They had arrived considerably later than expected the previous evening, due, in the main, to the fact that Henry's car had been so badly damaged whilst parked in a client's car park that their departure had been delayed and they had had to use her small—much smaller—model, much to Henry's disgust.

They had arrived shortly after eleven o'clock, and whilst Henry had been greeted with a good deal of maternal anxiety and concern Lisa had received a considerably more frosty reception, Henry's mother giving her a chilly smile and presenting a cool cheek for her to kiss before commenting, 'I'm afraid we couldn't put back supper any longer. You know what your father's like about meal times, Henry.'

'It was Lisa's fault,' Henry had grumbled untruthfully, adding to Lisa, 'You really should get a decent car, you know. Oh, and by the way, you need petrol.'

Lisa had gritted her teeth and smiled, reminding herself that she had already guessed from Henry's comments about his family that, as an only child and a son, he was the apple of his mother's eye.

Whilst Henry had been despatched to his father's study, Lisa had been quizzed by Henry's mother about her family and background. It had subtly been made plain to Lisa that so far as Henry's mother was concerned the jury was still out on the subject of her suitability as Henry's intended wife.

Normally she would have enjoyed the chance to visit the Yorkshire Dales, Lisa acknowledged—especially at this time of the year. Last night she had been enchanted to discover that snow was expected on the high ground.

Henry had been less impressed. In fact, he had been in an edgy, difficult mood throughout the entire journey—and not just, Lisa suspected, because of the damage to his precious car.

It had struck her, over the previous weekend, when they'd been doing the last of their Christmas shopping together, that he was obviously having doubts about her ability to make the right impression on his parents. There had been several small lectures and clumsy hints on what his family would expect, and one particularly embarrassing moment when Alison had called round to the flat just as Henry had been explaining that he wasn't sure that the Armani trouser suit was going to be quite the thing for his parents' annual pre-Christmas supper party.

'What century are Henry's parents living in?' Alison had exploded after Henry had left the room. 'Honestly, Lisa, I can't—'

She had stopped when Lisa had shaken her head, changing the subject to ask instead, 'Any more repercussions about the clothes you bought from Second Time Around, by the way?'

Lisa had told Alison all about her run-in with Oliver Davenport, asking her friend's advice as to what she ought to do.

'Ring the shop and find out what they've got to say,' had been Alison's prompt response.

'I've already done that,' Lisa had told her. 'And there was just a message on the answering machine saying that the owner has had to close the shop down indefinitely because her father has been taken seriously ill.'

'Well, if you want my opinion, you bought those clothes in all good faith, and I feel that their original owner deserves to know exactly what kind of miserable rat her boyfriend is... I mean...selling her clothes... It's...it's... Well, I'd certainly never forgive any man who tried to pull that one on me. I think you did exactly the right thing in refusing to give them back,' Alison had said comfortingly.

'No. No further repercussions,' Lisa had told her in response to her latest question. 'Which I find surprising. I suppose I did overreact a little bit, but when he virtually accused me of trying to blackmail him into paying almost more for them than they had originally cost...'

Her voice had quivered with remembered indignation as she recalled how shocked and insulted she had felt to be confronted with such a contemptuous assessment of her character.

'You overreacting—and to a man... Now that's something I *would* like to see,' Alison had told her.

'Who are you discussing?' Henry had asked, coming back into the room.

'Oh, no one special,' Lisa had told him, hastily and untruthfully, hoping that he wouldn't question the sudden surge of hot, guilty colour flooding her face as she remembered the shocking unexpectedness and intimacy of the way Oliver Davenport had reached out and touched her, and her even more shocking and intimate reaction to his touch.

The whole incident was something that was best forgotten she told herself firmly now as she craned her neck to watch a shepherd manoeuvring his flock on the distant hillside. She felt very sorry for Emma, of course, in the loss of her clothes, but hopefully it would teach Oliver Davenport not to behave so arrogantly in future. It was certainly a lesson he needed to learn.

Lisa glanced at her watch.

Henry's mother had announced last night that they sat down for breakfast at eight o'clock sharp, the implication being that she suspected that Lisa lived too decadent and lazy a lifestyle to manage to get up early enough to join them.

She couldn't have been more wrong, Lisa acknowledged. She was normally a very early riser.

The build-up to Christmas, and most especially the week before it, was normally one of her favourite times of the year. Her parents might live a rather unconventional lifestyle by Henry's parents' standards, but wherever they had lived when she'd been a child they had always made a point of following as many Christmas traditions as they could—buying and dressing a specially chosen Christmas tree, cooking certain favourite Christmas treats, shopping for presents and wrapping them. But Lisa had always yearned for the trappings of a real British Christmas. She had been looking forward to seeing such a traditional scenario of events taking place in Henry's childhood home, but it had become apparent to her the previous evening that Henry's parents, and more specifically Henry's mother, did not view Christmas in the same way she did herself.

'The whole thing has become so dreadfully commercialised that I simply don't see the point nowadays,' she had commented when Lisa had been describing the fun she had had shopping for gifts for the several small and *not* so small children who featured on her Christmas present list.

Her father in particular delighted in receiving anything toy-like, and had a special weakness for magic tricks. Lisa had posted her gifts to her parents to Japan weeks ago, and had, in turn, received hers from them. She had brought the presents north with her, intending to add them to the pile she had assumed would accumulate beneath the Christmas tree, which in her imagination she had visualised as tall and wonderfully

bushy, dominating the large hallway that Henry had described
to her, warmed by the firelight of its open hearth and scent-
ing the whole room with the delicious aroma of fresh pine
needles.

Alas for her imaginings. Henry's mother did not, apparently, like real Christmas trees. They caused too much mess
with their needles. And as for an open fire! They had had that
boarded up years ago, she had informed Lisa, adding that it
had caused far too much mess and nuisance.

So much for her hazy thoughts of establishing the beginnings of their own family traditions, her plans of one day
telling her own children how she and their father had spent
their first Christmas together, going out to choose the family
Christmas tree.

'You're far too romantic and impractical,' Henry had criticised her. 'I agree with Mother. Real Christmas trees are
nothing but a nuisance.'

As she turned away from the window Lisa was uncomfortably aware not only of Henry's mother's reluctance to accept
her, but also of her own unexpectedly rebellious feeling that
Henry was letting her down in not being more supportive of
her.

She hadn't spent one full day with Henry's family yet, and
already she was beginning to regret the extended length of
their Christmas stay with them.

Reluctantly she walked towards the bedroom door. It was
ten to eight, and the last thing she wanted to do now was arrive
late for breakfast.

'Off-white wool… Don't you think that's rather impractical?'
Henry's mother asked Lisa critically.

Taking a deep breath and counting to ten, Lisa forced herself to smile as she responded politely to Mary Hanford's
criticism.

'Perhaps a little, but then—'

'I never wear cream or white. I think they can be so draining to the pale English complexion,' her prospective mother-in-law continued. 'Navy is always so much more serviceable, I think.'

Lisa had arrived downstairs half an hour ago, all her offers to help with the preparation of the pre-Christmas buffet supper having been firmly refused.

So much for creating the right impression on Henry's parents with her new clothes, Lisa reflected wryly, wishing that Alison was with her to appreciate the ironic humour of the situation.

She could, of course, have shared the joke with Henry, but somehow she doubted that he would have found it funny... He had, no doubt, inherited his sense of humour, or rather his lack of it, from his mother, she decided sourly, and was immediately ashamed of her own mean-spiritedness.

Of course, it was only natural that Henry's mother should be slightly distant with her. Naturally she was protective of Henry—he was her only son, her only child...

He was also a man of thirty-one, a sharp inner voice reminded Lisa, and surely capable of making his own mind up about who he wanted to marry? Or was he?

It hadn't escaped Lisa's notice during the day how Henry consistently and illuminatingly agreed with whatever opinion his mother chose to voice, but she dismissed the tiny niggling doubts that were beginning to undermine her confidence in her belief that she and Henry had a future together as natural uncertainties raised by seeing him in an unfamiliar setting and with people, moreover, who knew him far better than she did.

In the hallway the grandfather clock chimed the hour. In a few minutes the Hanfords' supper guests would be arriving.

Henry had already explained to her that his family had

lived in the area for several generations and that they had a large extended family, most of whom would be at the supper party, along with a handful of his parents' friends.

Lisa was slightly apprehensive, aware that she would be very much on show, which was one of the reasons why she had chosen to wear the cream trouser suit.

Henry, however, hadn't been any more approving of her outfit than his mother, telling her severely that he thought that a skirt would have been more appropriate than trousers.

Lisa had no doubt that Oliver Davenport would have been both highly amused and contemptuous of her failure to achieve the desired effect with her acquired plumage.

Oliver Davenport. Now what on earth was she doing thinking about such a disagreeable subject, such a contentious person, when by rights she ought to be concentrating on the evening ahead of her?

'Ah, Lisa, there you are!' she heard Henry exclaiming. 'Everyone will be arriving soon, and Mother likes us all to be in the hall to welcome them when they do.

'I see you didn't change after all,' he added, frowning at her.

'An Armani suit is a perfectly acceptable outfit to wear for a supper party, Henry,' Lisa pointed out mildly, and couldn't help adding a touch more robustly, 'And, to be honest, I think I would have felt rather cold in a skirt. Your parents—'

'Mother doesn't think an overheated house is healthy,' Henry interrupted her quickly—so quickly that Lisa suspected that she wasn't the first person to comment on the chilliness of his parents' house.

'I expect I'm feeling the cold because we're so much further north here,' she offered diplomatically as she followed him into the hallway.

Cars could be heard pulling up outside, their doors opening and closing.

'That's good!' Henry exclaimed. 'Mother likes everyone to be on time.'

Mother would, Lisa thought rebelliously, but wisely she kept the words to herself.

Henry's aunt and her family were the first to arrive. A smaller, quieter edition of her elder sister, she was, nevertheless, far warmer in her manner towards Lisa than Henry's mother had been, and Lisa didn't miss the looks exchanged by her three teenage children as they were subjected to Mary Hanford's critical inspection.

Fifteen minutes later the hallway was virtually full, and Lisa was beginning to lose track of just who everyone was. The doorbell rang again and Henry went to answer it. As Lisa turned to look at the newcomers her heart suddenly stood still and then gave a single shocked bound followed by a flurry of too fast, disbelieving, nervous beats.

Oliver Davenport! What on earth was he doing here? He couldn't have followed her here to pursue his demand for her to return Emma's clothes, could he?

At the thought of what Henry's mother was likely to say if Oliver Davenport caused the same kind of scene here in public as he had staged in the privacy of her own flat, Lisa closed her eyes in helpless dismay, and then heard Henry saying tensely to her, 'Lisa, I'd like to introduce you to one of my parents' neighbours. Oliver—'

'Lisa and I already know one another.'

Lisa's eyes widened in bemused incomprehension.

Oliver Davenport was a neighbour of Henry's parents! And what did he mean by implying that they knew one another… by saying her name in that grossly deceptive, softly sensual way, which seemed to imply that he…that she…?

'You do? You never said anything about knowing Oliver to me, Lisa,' Henry said almost hectoringly.

But before Lisa could make any attempt to defend herself

or explain, Oliver Davenport was doing it for her, addressing Henry in a tone that left Lisa in no doubt as to just what kind of opinion the other man had of her husband-to-be, as he announced cuttingly, 'No doubt she had more important things on her mind. Or perhaps she simply didn't think it was important...'

'I...I...I didn't realise you two knew one another,' was the only response Lisa could come up with, and she saw from Henry's face that it was not really one that satisfied him.

She nibbled worriedly at her bottom lip, cast Oliver Davenport a bitter look and then was forced to listen helplessly whilst Oliver, who still quite obviously bore her a grudge over the clothes, commented judiciously, 'I like the outfit... It suits you... But then I thought so the first time I saw you wearing it, didn't I?'

Lisa knew that she was blushing. Blushing...? She was turning a vivid and unconcealable shade of deep scarlet, she acknowledged miserably as she saw the suspicious look that Henry was giving her and recognised from the narrow, pursed-lip glare that Henry's mother must have also overheard Oliver's comment.

'Oliver, let me get you a drink,' Henry's father offered, thankfully coming up to usher him away, but not before Oliver managed to murmur softly to Lisa,

'Saved by the cavalry...'

'How on earth do you come to know Oliver Davenport?' Henry demanded angrily as soon as Oliver was out of earshot.

'I don't *know* him,' Lisa admitted wearily. 'At least not—'

'What do you mean? Of course you *know* him...and well enough for him to be able to comment on your clothes...'

'He's... Henry...this isn't the time for me to explain...' Lisa told him quietly.

'So there *is* something to explain, then.' Henry was refusing to be appeased. 'Where did you meet him? In London, I suppose. His business might be based up here at the Hall, but he still spends quite a considerable amount of time in London... His cousin works for him down there—'

'His cousin...?' Lisa couldn't quite keep the note of nervous apprehension out of her voice.

'Yes, Piers Davenport, Oliver's cousin. He's several years younger than Oliver and he lives in London with his girl-friend—some model or other...Emily...or Emma...I can't remember which...'

'Emma,' Lisa supplied hollowly.

So Oliver hadn't been lying, after all, when he had told her that he was acting on behalf of his cousin. She glanced uneasily over her shoulder, remembering just exactly how scathingly she had denounced him, practically accusing him of being a liar and worse.

No wonder he had given her that look this evening which had said that he hadn't finished with her and that he fully intended to make her pay for her angry insults, to exact retribution on her.

Apprehensively she wondered exactly what form that silently promised retribution was going to take. What was he going to do? Reveal to Henry and his parents that she had bought her clothes second-hand? She could just imagine how Mary Hanford would react to that information. At the thought of her impending humiliation, Lisa felt her stomach muscles tighten defensively.

It wasn't all her fault. Hers had been a natural enough mistake to make, she reminded herself. Alison had agreed with her. And Oliver had to share some of the blame for her error himself. If he had only been a little more conciliatory in his manner towards her, a little less arrogant in demanding that she return the clothes back to him...

'I do wish you had told me that you knew Oliver,' Henry was continuing fussily. 'Especially in view of his position locally.'

'What position locally?' Lisa asked him warily, but she suspected she could guess the answer. To judge from Mary Hanford's deferential manner towards him, Oliver Davenport was quite obviously someone of importance in the area. Her heart started to sink even further as Henry explained in a hushed, almost awed voice.

'Oliver is an extremely wealthy man. He owns and runs one of the north of England's largest financial consultancy businesses and he recently took over another firm based in London, giving him a countrywide network. But why are you asking me? Surely if you know him you must—?'

'I don't know him,' Lisa protested tiredly. 'Henry, there's something I have to tell you.' She took a deep breath. There was nothing else for it; she was going to have to tell Henry the truth.

'But you evidently do know him,' Henry protested, ignoring her and cutting across what she was trying to say. 'And rather well by the sound of it... Lisa, what exactly's going on?'

Henry could look remarkably like his mother when he pursed his lips and narrowed his eyes like that, Lisa decided. She suddenly had a mental image of the children they might have together—little replicas of their grandmother. Quickly she banished the unwelcome vision.

'Henry, nothing is going on. If you would just let me explain—' Lisa began.

But once again she was interrupted, this time by Henry's mother, who bore down on them, placing a proprietorial hand on Henry's arm as she told him, 'Henry, dear, Aunt Elspeth wants to talk to you. She's over there by the French windows. She's brought her god-daughter with her. You remember Louise. You used to play together when you were children—such a sweet girl…'

To Lisa's chagrin, Henry was borne off by his mother, leaving her standing alone, nursing an unwanted glass of too sweet sherry.

What should have been the happiest Christmas Eve of her adult life was turning out to be anything but, she admitted gloomily as she watched a petite, doe-eyed brunette, presumably Aunt Elspeth's god-daughter, simpering up at a Henry who was quite plainly wallowing in her dewy-eyed, fascinated attention.

It was a good thirty minutes before Henry returned to her side, during which time she had had ample opportunity to watch Oliver's progress amongst the guests and to wonder why on earth he had accepted the Hanfords' invitation, since he was quite obviously both bored and irritated by the almost fawning attention of Henry's mother.

He really was the most arrogantly supercilious man she had ever had the misfortune to meet, Lisa decided critically as he caught her watching him and lifted one derogatory, darkly interrogative eyebrow in her direction.

Flushing, she turned away, but not, she noticed, before Henry's mother had seen the brief, silent exchange between them.

'You still haven't explained to us just how you come to know… You really should have told us that you know Oliver,' she told Lisa, arriving at her side virtually at the same time as Henry, so that Lisa was once again prevented from explaining to him what had happened.

What was it about some people that made everything they said sound like either a reproach or a criticism? Lisa wondered grimly, but before she could answer she heard Mary Hanford adding, in an unfamiliar, almost arch and flattering voice, 'Ah, Oliver, we were just talking about you.'

'Really.'

He was looking at them contemptuously, as though they were creatures from another planet—some kind of subspecies provided for his entertainment, Lisa decided resentfully as he looked from Mary to Henry and then to her.

'Yes,' Mary continued, undeterred. 'I was just asking Lisa how she comes to know you…'

'Well, I think that's probably best left for Lisa herself to explain to you,' he responded smoothly. 'I should hate to embarrass her by making any unwelcome revelations…'

Lisa glared angrily at him.

'That suit looks good on you,' he added softly.

'So you've already said,' she reminded him through gritted teeth, all too aware of Henry's and his mother's silently suspicious watchfulness at her side.

'Yes,' Oliver continued, as though she hadn't spoken. 'You can always tell when a woman's wearing an outfit bought by a man for his lover.' As he spoke he reached out and touched her jacket-clad arm—a brief touch, nothing more, but it made the hot colour burn in Lisa's face, and she was not at all surprised to hear Henry's mother's outraged indrawn breath or to see the fury in Henry's eyes.

This was retribution with a vengeance. This wasn't just victory, she acknowledged helplessly; it was total annihilation.

'Have you worn any of the other things yet?' he added casually.

'Lisa…' she heard Henry demanding ominously at her side, but she couldn't answer him. She was too mortified, too furiously angry to dare to risk saying anything whilst Oliver Davenport was still standing there listening.

To her relief, he didn't linger long. Aunt Elspeth's goddaughter, the same one who had so determinedly flirted with Henry half an hour earlier, came up and very professionally broke up their quartet, insisting that Oliver had promised to get her a fresh drink.

He was barely out of earshot before Henry was insisting, 'I want to know what's going on, Lisa... What was all that about your clothes...?'

'I think we know exactly what's going on, Henry,' Lisa heard his mother answering coolly for him as she gave Lisa a look of virulent hostility edged with triumph. So much for pretending to welcome her into the family, Lisa thought tiredly.

'I can see what you're *both* thinking,' she announced. 'But you are wrong.'

'Wrong? How can we be wrong when Oliver more or less announced openly that the pair of you have been lovers?' Mary intoned.

'He did not announce that we had been lovers,' Lisa defended herself. 'And if you would just let me explain—'

'Henry, it's almost time for supper. You know how hopeless your father is at getting people organised. I'm going to need you to help me...'

'Henry, we need to talk.' Lisa tried to override his mother, but Henry was already turning away from her and going obediently to his mother's side.

If they married it would always be like this, Lisa suddenly recognised on a wave of helpless anger. He would always place his mother's needs and wants above her own, and presumably above those of their children. They would always come a very poor second best to his loyalty to his mother. Was that really what she wanted for herself...for her children?

Lisa knew it wasn't.

It was as though the scales had suddenly fallen from her eyes, as though she were looking at a picture of exactly how and what her life with Henry would be—and she didn't like it. She didn't like it one little bit.

In the handful of seconds it took her to recognise the fact, she knew irrevocably that she couldn't marry him, but she still owed him an explanation of what had happened, and from her own point of view. For the sake of her pride and self-respect she wanted to make sure that he and his precious mother knew exactly how she had come to meet Oliver and exactly how he had manipulated them into believing his deliberately skewed view of the situation.

Still seething with anger against Oliver, she refused Henry's father's offer of another drink and some supper. She would choke rather than eat any of Mary Hanford's food, she decided angrily.

Just the thought of the kind of life she would have had as Henry's wife made her shudder and acknowledge that she had had a lucky escape, but knowing that did not lessen her overwhelming fury at the man who had accidently brought it about.

How would she have been feeling right now had she been deeply in love with Henry and he with her? Instead of stalking angrily around the Hanfords' drawing room like an angry tigress, she would probably have been upstairs in her bedroom sobbing her heart out.

Some Christmas this was going to be.

She had been so looking forward to being here, to being part of the family, to sharing the simple, traditional pleasures of Christmas with the man she intended to marry, and now it was all spoiled, ruined… And why? Why? Because Oliver Davenport was too arrogant, too proud…too…too devious and hateful to allow someone whom he obviously saw as way, way beneath him to get the better of him.

Well, she didn't care. She didn't care what he did or what he said. He could tell the whole room, the whole house, the whole world that she had bought her clothes second-hand and that they had belonged to his cousin's girlfriend for all she cared now. In fact, she almost wished he would. That way at least she would be vindicated. That way she could walk away from here...from Henry and his precious mother...with her head held high.

'An outfit bought by a man for his lover...' How dared he...? Oh, how dared he...? She was, she suddenly realised, almost audibly grinding her teeth. Hastily she stopped. Dental fees were notoriously, hideously expensive.

She couldn't leave matters as they were, she decided fiercely. She would have to say something to Oliver Daven-port—even if it was to challenge him over the implications he had made.

She got her chance ten minutes later, when she saw Oliver leaving the drawing room alone.

Quickly, before she could change her mind, she followed him. As he heard her footsteps crossing the hallway, he stopped and turned round.

'Ah, the blushing bride-to-be and her borrowed raiment,' he commented sardonically.

'I bought in good faith my second-hand raiment,' Lisa cor-rected him bitingly, adding, 'You do realise what impression you gave Henry and his mother back there, don't you?' she challenged him, adding scornfully before he could answer, 'Of course you knew. You knew perfectly well what you were doing, what you were implying...'

'Did I?' he responded calmly.

'Yes, you did,' Lisa responded, her anger intensifying. 'You knew they would assume that you meant that you and I had been lovers...that *you* had bought my clothes—'

'Surely Henry knows you far better than that?' Oliver interrupted her smoothly. 'After all, according to the local grapevine, the pair of you are intending to marry—'

'Of course Henry knows me...' Lisa began, and then

stopped, her face flushing in angry mortification. But it was too late.

Swift as a hawk to the lure, her tormentor responded softly, 'Ah, I see. It's because he knows you so well that he made the unfortunate and mistaken assumption that—'

'No… He doesn't… I don't…' Lisa tried to fight back gamely, but it was still too late, and infuriatingly she knew it and, even worse, so did Oliver.

He wasn't smirking precisely—he was far too arrogant for that, Lisa decided bitterly—but there was certainly mockery in his eyes, and if she hadn't known better she could almost have sworn that his mouth was about to curl into a smile. But how could it? She was sure that he was incapable of doing anything so human. He was the kind of man who just didn't know what human emotions were, she decided savagely—who had no idea what it meant to suffer insecurity or…or any of the things that made people like herself feel so vulnerable.

'Have you any idea what you've done?' she challenged him, changing tack, her voice shaking under the weight of her suppressed emotion. 'I came here—'

'I know why you came here,' he interrupted her with unexpected sternness. 'You came to be looked over as a potential wife for Mary Hanford's precious son.

'Where's your pride?' he demanded scornfully. 'However, a potential bride is all you will ever be. Mary Hanford knows quite well who she wants Henry to marry, and I'm afraid it isn't going to be you…'

'Not now,' Lisa agreed shortly. 'Not—'

'Not ever,' Oliver told her. 'Mary won't allow Henry to marry any woman who she thinks might have the slightest chance of threatening her own superior position in Henry's life. His wife will not only have to take second place to her but to covertly acknowledge and accept that fact before she's allowed to marry him. And besides, the two of you are so obviously unsuited to one another that the whole thing's almost a farce. You're far too emotionally turbulent and uncontrolled for Henry... He wouldn't have a clue how to handle you...'

Lisa couldn't believe her ears.

'You, of course, would,' she challenged him with acid sweetness, too carried away by her anger and the heat of the moment to realise what she was doing, the challenge she was issuing him, the risks she was taking.

Then it was too late and he was cutting the ground from beneath her feet and making a shock as icy-cold as the snow melting on the tops of the Yorkshire hills that were his home run down her spine as he told her silkily, 'Certainly,' and then added before she could draw breath to speak, 'And, for openers, there are two things I most certainly would do that Henry obviously has not.'

'Oh, yes, and what exactly would they be?' Lisa demanded furiously.

'Well, I certainly wouldn't have the kind of relationship with you—or with any woman who I had the slightest degree of mild affection for, never mind being on the point of contemplating marrying—which would necessitate you feeling that you had to conceal anything about yourself from me, or that you needed to impress my family and friends with borrowed plumes, with the contents of another woman's wardrobe. And the second...' he continued, ignoring Lisa's quick, indrawn breath of mingled chagrin and rage.

He paused and looked at her whilst Lisa, driven well beyond the point of no return by the whole farce of her ruined Christmas in general and his part in it in particular, prompted wildly, 'Yes, the second is...?'

'This,' he told her softly, taking the breath from her lungs, the strength from her muscles and, along with them, the will-power from her brain as he stepped forward and took her in his arms and then bent his head and kissed her as Henry had

never kissed her in all the eight months of their relationship—
as no man had ever kissed her in the whole history of her
admittedly modest sexual experience, she recognised dizzily
as his mouth moved with unbelievable, unbeatable, unbearable
sensual expertise on hers.

Ordinary mortal men did not kiss like this. Ordinary mortal
men did not behave like this. Ordinary mortal men did not
have the power, did not cup one's face with such tender mastery. They did not look deep into your eyes whilst they caressed your mouth with their own. They did not compel you,
by some mastery you could not understand, to look back at
them. They did not, by some unspoken command, cause you
to open your mouth beneath theirs on a whispered ecstatic
sigh of pure female pleasure. They did not lift their mouths
from yours and look from your eyes to your half-parted lips
and then back to your eyes again, their own warming in a
smile of complicit understanding before starting to kiss you
all over again.

Film stars in impossibly extravagant and highly acclaimed,
Oscar-winning romantic movies might mimic such behaviour. Heroes in stomach-churning, body-aching, romantically
sensual novels might sweep their heroines off their feet with
similar embraces. God-like creatures from Greek mythology
might come down to earth and wantonly seduce frolicking
nymphs with such devastating experience and sensuality, but
mere mortal men...? Never!

Lisa gave a small, blissful sigh and closed her eyes, only to
open them again as she heard Henry exclaiming wrathfully,
'Lisa...what on earth do you think you're doing?'

Guiltily she watched him approaching as Oliver released
her.

'Henry, I can explain,' she told him urgently, but he obviously didn't intend to let her speak.

Ignoring Oliver's quiet voice mocking, 'To Henry, maybe,

but to Mary, never,' she flushed defensively as his taunting comment was borne out by Henry's furious declaration.

'Mother was right about you all along. She warned me that you weren't—'

'Henry, you don't understand.' She managed to interrupt him, turning to appeal to Oliver, who was standing watching them in contemptuous amusement.

'Tell him what really happened... Tell him...'

'Do you really expect me to give you my help?' he goaded her softly. 'I don't recall you being similarly sympathetic when I asked you for yours.'

Whilst Lisa stood and stared at him in disbelief he started to walk towards the door, pausing only to tell Henry, 'Your mother is quite right, Henry. She wouldn't be the right wife for you at all... If I were you I should heed her advice—now, before it's too late.'

'Henry,' Lisa began to protest, but she could see from the way that he was refusing to meet her eyes that she had lost what little chance she might have had of persuading him to listen to her.

'It's too late now for us to change our plans for Christmas,' he told her stiffly, still avoiding looking directly at her. 'It is, after all, Christmas Eve, and we can hardly ask you to... However, once we return to London I feel that it would be as well if we didn't see one another any more...'

Lisa could scarcely believe her ears. Was this really the man she had thought she loved, or had at least liked and admired enough to be her husband...the man she had wanted as the father of her children? This pompous, stuffy creature who preferred to take his mother's advice on whom he should and should not marry than to listen to her, the woman he had proclaimed he loved?

Only he had not—not really, had he? Lisa made herself admit honestly. Neither of them had really truly been in love.

Oh, they had liked one another well enough. But liking wasn't love, and if she was honest with herself there was a strong chord of relief mixed up in the turbulent anger and resentment churning her insides.

Stay here now, over Christmas, after what had happened...? No way.

Without trusting herself to speak to Henry, she turned on her heel and headed for the stairs and her bedroom, where she threw open the wardrobe doors and started to remove her clothes—her borrowed clothes, not her clothes, she acknowledged grimly as she opened her suitcase; they hadn't been hers when she had bought them and they certainly weren't hers now.

Eyeing them with loathing, her attention was momentarily distracted by the damp chilliness of her bedroom. Thank goodness they had driven north in her car. At least she wasn't going to have the added humiliation of depending on Henry to get her back to London.

The temperature seemed to have dropped since she had left the bedroom earlier, even taking into account Mary Hanford's parsimony.

There had been another warning of snow on high ground locally earlier in the evening, and Lisa had been enchanted by it, wondering out loud if they might actually have a white Christmas—a long-held childhood wish of hers which she had so far never had fulfilled. Mary Hanford had been scornful of her excitement.

As she gathered up her belongings Lisa suddenly paused; the clothes she had bought with such pleasure and which she had held onto with such determination lay on the bed in an untidy heap.

Beautiful though they were, she suddenly felt that she knew now that she could never wear them. They were tainted. Some things were just not meant to be, she decided regretfully as she stroked the silk fabric of one of the shirts with tender fingers.

She might have paid for them, bought them in all good faith, but somehow she had never actually felt as though they were hers.

But it was her borrowed clothes, like the borrowed persona she had perhaps unwittingly tried to assume to impress Henry's family, which had proved her downfall, and she was, she decided firmly, better off without both of them.

Ten minutes later, wearing her own jeans, she lifted the carefully folded clothes into her suitcase. Once the Christmas holiday was over she would telephone the dress agency and explain that she no longer had any use for the clothes. Hopefully they would be prepared to take them back and refund most, if not all of her money.

It was too late to regret now that she had not accepted Alison's suggestion that she join her and some other friends on a Christmas holiday and skiing trip to Colorado. Christmas was going to be very lonely for her alone in her flat with all her friends and her parents away. A sadly wistful smile curved the generous softness of her mouth as she contemplated how very different from her rosy daydreams the reality of her Christmas was going to be.

'You're going to the north of England—Yorkshire. I know it has a reputation for being much colder up there than it is here in London, but that doesn't mean you'll get snow,' Alison had warned her, adding more gently, 'Don't invest too much in this visit to Henry's family, Lisa. I know how important it is to you but things don't always work out the way you plan. The Yorkshire Dales are a beautiful part of the world, but people are still people and—well, let's face it, from what Henry has said about his family, especially his mother, it's obvious that she's inclined to be a little on the possessive side.'

'I know you don't really like Henry…' Lisa had begun defensively.

But Alison had shaken her head and told her firmly, 'It isn't that I don't care for Henry, rather that I *do* care about you. He isn't right for you, Lisa. Oh, I know what you're going to say: he's solid and dependable, and with him you can put down the roots that are so important to you. But, to be honest—well, if you want the truth, I see Henry more as a rather spoiled little boy than the kind of man a woman can rely on.'

It looked as if Alison was a much better judge of character than she, Lisa acknowledged as she zipped her case shut and picked it up.

CHAPTER THREE

LISA WAS HALFWAY down the stairs when Henry walked into the hallway and saw her.

'Lisa, why are you dressed like that? Where are you going?' he demanded as he looked anxiously back over his shoulder, obviously not wanting anyone else to witness what was going on.

'I'm leaving,' she told him calmly. It was odd that she should be able to remain so calm with Henry who, after all, until this evening's debacle had been the man she had intended to marry, the man she had planned to spend the rest of her life with, and yet with Oliver, a complete stranger, a man she had seen only twice before and whom she expected…hoped…she would never see again, her emotions became inflamed into a rage of gargantuan proportions.

'Leaving? But you can't… What will people think?' Henry protested. 'Mother's got the whole family coming for Christmas dinner tomorrow and they'll all expect you to be there. We were, after all, planning to announce our engagement,' he reminded her seriously.

As she listened to him in disbelief Lisa was shocked to realise that she badly wanted to laugh—or cry.

'Henry, I can't stay here now,' she told him. 'Not after what's happened. You must see that. After all you were the one—'

'You're leaving to go to him, aren't you?' Henry accused her angrily. 'Well, don't expect Oliver to offer to marry you,

Lisa. He might want to take you to bed but, as Mother says, Oliver isn't the kind of man to marry a woman who—'

That was it. Suddenly Lisa had had enough. Her face flushing with the full force of her emotions, she descended the last few stairs and confronted Henry.

'I don't care what your mother says, Henry,' she told him through gritted teeth. 'And if you were half the man I thought you were *you* wouldn't care either. Neither would you let her make up your mind or your decisions for you... And as for Oliver—'

'Yes, as for me...what?'

To her consternation Lisa realised that at some point Oliver had walked into the hall and was now standing watching them both, an infuriatingly superior, mocking contempt curling his mouth as he broke into her angry tirade.

'I've had enough of this... I've had enough of both of you,' Lisa announced. 'This is all your fault. All of it,' she added passionately to Oliver, ignoring Henry's attempts to silence her.

'And don't think I haven't guessed why you've done it,' she added furiously, her fingers tugging at the strap of her suitcase. She wrenched the case open and cried out angrily to him, 'You want your precious clothes back? Well, you can have them...all of them...'

Fiercely she wrenched the carefully packed clothes from her case and hurled them across the small space that lay between them, where they landed in an untidy heap at Oliver's feet.

She ignored Henry's anguished, shocked, 'Lisa...what on earth are you doing...? Lisa, please...stop; someone might see... Mother...'

'Oh, and we mustn't forget this, must we?' Lisa continued, ignoring Henry, an almost orgasmic feeling of release drowning out all her normal level-headedness and common sense.

For the first time in her life she could understand why it was some people actually seemed to enjoy losing their temper, giving up their self-control…causing a scene…all things that were normally completely foreign to her.

Triumphantly she threw the beautiful Armani suit which she had bought with such pleasure at Oliver's feet whilst he watched her impassively.

'There! I hope you're satisfied,' she told him as the last garment headed his way.

'Lisa,' Henry was still bleating protestingly, but she ignored him. Now that the sudden, unfamiliar surge of anger was retreating she felt oddly weak and shaky, almost vulnerably light-headed and dangerously close to tears.

In the distance she was aware that Henry was still protesting, but for some reason it was Oliver whom her attention was concentrated on, who filled her vision and her prickly, wary senses as she deliberately skirted around him, clutching her still half-open but now much lighter suitcase, and headed for the front door.

There had been a look in his eyes as she had flung that trouser suit at him which she had not totally understood—a gleam of an emotion which in another man she could almost have felt was humour mixed with a certain rueful respect, but of course she must have been imagining it.

As she tugged open the front door and stepped outside a shock of ice-cold air hit her. She hadn't realised how much the temperature had dropped, how overcast the sky had become.

Frost crunched beneath her feet as she hurried towards her car. Faithful and reliable as ever, it started at the second turn of the key.

As Lisa negotiated the other cars parked in the drive she told herself grimly that she had no need to try to work out whom that gleaming, shiny Aston Martin sports car belonged to. It just had to be Oliver Davenport's.

As she turned onto the main road she switched on her car radio, her heart giving a small forlorn thud of regret as she heard the announcer forecasting that the north of England was due to have snow.

Snow for Christmas and she was going to miss it.

It was half past eleven; another half an hour and it would be Christmas Day, and she would be spending it alone.

Stop snivelling, she told herself as she felt her throat start to ache with emotional tears. You've had a lucky escape.

She knew she had a fairly long drive ahead of her before she reached the motorway. As she and Henry had driven north she had remarked on how beautiful the countryside was as they drove through it. Now, however, as she drove along the empty, dark country road she was conscious of how remote the area was and how alone she felt.

She frowned as the car engine started to splutter and lose power, anxiety tensing her body as she wondered what on earth was wrong. Her small car had always been so reliable, and she was very careful about having it properly serviced and keeping the tank full of petrol.

Petrol. Lisa knew what had happened from the sharp sinking sensation in her stomach even before she looked fearfully at the petrol gauge.

Henry had not bothered to replace the petrol they had used on the journey north and now, it seemed, the tank was empty.

Lisa closed her eyes in mute despair. What on earth was she going to do? She was stranded on an empty country road miles from anywhere in the dark on Christmas Eve, with no idea where the nearest garage was, no means of contacting anyone to ask, dressed in jeans and a thin sweater on a freezing cold night.

And she knew exactly who she had to blame for her sorry plight, she decided wrathfully ten minutes later as the air inside her car turned colder and colder with ominous speed. Oliver Davenport. If it hadn't been for him and his cynical and deliberate manipulation of the truth to cast her in a bad light in front of Henry and his parents, none of this would have happened.

Even now she still couldn't quite believe what she had done in the full force of that final, unexpected burst of temper, when she had thrown her clothes at him.

Lisa hugged her arms tightly around her body as she started to shiver. It was too late to regret her hasty departure from Henry's parents' home now, or the fact that she had brought nothing with her that she could use to keep her warm.

Just how far was it to the nearest house? Her teeth were chattering now and the windscreen had started to freeze over.

Perhaps she ought to start walking back in the direction she had come. At least then the physical activity might help to keep her warm, but her heart sank at the thought. So far as she could remember, she had been driving for a good fifteen minutes after she had passed through the last small hamlet, and she hadn't seen any houses since then.

Reluctantly she opened the car door, and then closed it again with a gasp of shock as the ice-cold wind knifed into her unprotected body.

What on earth was she going to do? Her earlier frustration and irritation had started to give way to a far more ominous and much deeper sense of panicky fear.

One read about people being found dying from exposure and hypothermia, but it always seemed such an unreal fate somehow in a country like Britain. Now, though, it suddenly seemed horribly plausible.

Her panic intensified as she realised that unless she either managed to walk to the nearest inhabited building, wherever that might be, or was spotted by a passing motorist, it would be days before anyone realised that she was missing. There was, after all, no one waiting at home in London for her. Her parents had agreed not to telephone on Christmas Day because they knew she would be staying with Henry's family. Henry would assume—if indeed he gave her any thought at all—that she was back in London.

As she fought down the emotions threatening to overwhelm her Lisa happened to glance at her watch.

It was almost half past twelve...Christmas Day.

Now she couldn't stop the tears.

Christmas Day and she was stuck in a car miles from anywhere and probably about to freeze to death.

She gave a small, protesting moan as she sneezed and then sneezed again, blinking her eyes against the dazzling glare of headlights she could see in her driving mirror.

The dazzling glare of headlights... Another car...

Frantically Lisa pushed on her frozen car door, terrified that her unwitting rescuer might drive past her without realising her plight.

The approaching car was only yards behind her when she finally managed to shove open the door. As she half fell into the icy road in her haste to advertise her predicament any thoughts of the danger of flagging down a stranger were completely forgotten in the more overriding urgency of her plight.

The dazzle of the oncoming headlights was so powerful that she couldn't distinguish the shape of the car or see its driver, but she knew he or she had seen her because the car suddenly started to lose speed, swerving to a halt in front of her.

Now that the car was stationary Lisa recognised that there was something vaguely familiar about it, but her relief overrode that awareness as she ran towards it on legs which suddenly seemed as stiff and wobbly as those of a newborn colt.

However, before she could reach it, the driver's door was flung open and a pair of long male legs appeared, followed by an equally imposing and stomach-churningly recognisable male torso and face.

As she stared disbelievingly into the frowning, impatient face of Oliver Davenport, Lisa protested fatalistically, 'Oh, no, not you...'

'Who were you hoping it was—Henry?' he retorted sardonically. 'If this is your idea of staging a reconciliation scene, I have to tell you that you're wasting your time. When I left him you were the last thing on Henry's mind.'

'Of course I'm not staging a reconciliation scene,' Lisa snapped back at him. 'I'm not staging a scene of any kind... I—it isn't something I do...'

The effect of her cool speech was unfairly spoiled by the sudden fit of shivering that overtook her, but it was plain that Oliver Davenport wouldn't have been very impressed with it anyway because he drawled, 'Oh, no? Then what was all that highly theatrical piece of overacting in the Hanfords' hall all about?'

'That wasn't overacting,' Lisa gritted at him. 'That was...'

She shivered again, this time so violently that her teeth chattered audibly.

'For God's sake, put a coat on. Have you any idea what the temperature is tonight? I know you're from the south and a city, but surely common sense—?'

'I don't have a coat,' Lisa told him, adding bitterly, 'Because of you.'

The look he gave her was incredulously contemptuous.

'Are you crazy? You come north in the middle of December and you don't even bother to bring a coat—'

'Oh, I brought a coat all right,' Lisa corrected him between shivers. 'Only I don't have it now...'

She gritted her teeth and tried not to think about the warmth of the lovely, heavenly cream cashmere coat which had been amongst the things she had thrown at his feet so recklessly.

'You don't... Ah... I see... What are you doing, anyway? Why have you stopped?'

'Why do you think I've stopped? Not to admire the view' Lisa told him bitterly. 'The car's run out of petrol.'

'The car's run out of petrol?'

Lisa felt herself flushing as she heard the disbelieving male scorn in his voice.

'It wasn't my fault,' she defended herself. 'We were supposed to be coming north in Henry's car, only it was involved in an accident and couldn't be driven so we had to use mine, and Henry was so anxious to get...not to be late that he didn't want to stop and refill the tank...'

Lisa hated the way he was just standing silently looking at her. He was determined to make things as hard for her as he could. She could see that... He was positively enjoying making her look small...humiliating her.

In any other circumstances but these she would have been tempted simply to turn her back on him, get back in her car and wait for the next driver to come by, but common sense warned her that she couldn't afford to take that kind of risk.

Her unprotected fingers had already turned white and were almost numb. She couldn't feel her toes, and the rest of her body felt so cold that the sensation was almost a physical pain.

Taking a deep breath and fixing her gaze on a point just beyond his left shoulder, she said shakily, 'I'd be very grateful if you could give me a lift to the nearest garage...'

Tensely she waited for his response, knowing that he was bound to make the most of the opportunity which she had given him to exercise his obvious dislike of her. But when it came the blow was one of such magnitude and such force that she physically winced beneath the cruelty of it, the breath escaping from her lungs in a soft, shocked gasp as he told her ruthlessly, 'No way.'

It must be the cold that was making her feel so dizzy and light-headed, Lisa thought despairingly—that and her panicky fear that he was going to walk away and simply leave her here to meet her fate.

Whatever the cause, it propelled her into instinctive action, making her dart forward and catch hold of the fabric of his jacket as she told him jerkily, 'It wasn't *my* fault that your cousin sold his girlfriend's clothes without her permission. All *I* did was buy them in good faith... He's the one you should be punishing, not me. If you leave me here—'

'*Leave* you here...?'

Somehow or other he had detached her hand from his jacket and was now holding it in his own. Dizzily Lisa marvelled at how warm and comforting, how strong and safe it felt to have that large male hand enclosing hers. She could almost feel the warmth from his touch—his body—flooding up through her arm like an infusion of life-giving blood into a vein.

'Leave you *here* in this temperature?' he said, adding roughly, 'Are you crazy...?'

She couldn't see him properly any more, Lisa realised, and she thought it must be because the tears that had threatened her eyes had frozen in the intense cold. She had no idea that she had actually spoken her sentiments out loud until she heard him respond, 'Tears don't freeze; they're saline... salty.'

He had let go of her hand and as Lisa watched him he stripped off his jacket and then, to her shock, took hold of her and bundled her up in it like an adult wrapping up a small child.

'I can't walk,' she protested, her voice muffled by the thickness of the over-large wrapping.

'You're not going to,' she was told peremptorily, and then, before she knew what was happening, he was picking her up and carrying her the short distance to his car, opening the passenger door and depositing her on the seat.

The car smelled of leather and warmth and something much more intangible—something elusive and yet oddly familiar... Muzzily Lisa sniffed, trying to work out what it was and why it should inexplicably make her want to cry and yet at the same time feel oddly elated.

Oliver had gone over to her car, and as he returned Lisa saw that he was carrying her case and her handbag.

'I've locked it...your car,' he told her as he slid into the driver's seat alongside her. 'Not that anyone would be likely to take it.'

'Not unless they had some petrol with them,' Lisa agreed drowsily, opening her mouth to give a yawn which suddenly turned into a volley of bone-aching sneezes.

'Here.' Oliver handed her a wad of clean tissues from a pack in the glove compartment, telling her, 'It's just as well I happened to be passing when I did. If you're lucky the worst you'll suffer is a bad cold; another hour in these temperatures and it could have been a very different story. This road is never very heavily trafficked, and on Christmas Eve, with snow forecast, the locals who do use it have more sense than to...'

He went on talking but Lisa had heard enough. Did he think she had wanted to run out of petrol on a remote Yorkshire road? Had he forgotten whose fault it was that she had been there in the first place instead of warmly tucked up in bed at Henry's parents' home?

Tears of unfamiliar and unexpected self-pity suddenly filled her eyes. 'It isn't Christmas Eve,' she told him aggressively, fighting to hold them back. 'It's Christmas Day.'

It was the wrong thing to say, bringing back her earlier awareness of how very fragile were the brightly coloured, delicate daydreams that she had cherished of how this Christmas would be—as fragile and vulnerable as the glass baubles with which she had so foolishly imagined herself decorating that huge, freshly cut, pine-smelling Christmas tree with Henry.

It was too much. One tear fell and then another. She tried to stop them, dabbing surreptitiously at her eyes, and she averted her face from Oliver's as he started the engine and set the car in motion. But it was no use. He had obviously witnessed her distress.

'Now what's wrong?' he demanded grimly.

'It's Christmas Day,' Lisa wept.

'Christmas Day.' He repeated the words as though he had never heard them before. 'Where would you have been spending it if your car hadn't run out of petrol?' he asked her. 'Where were you going?'

'Home to London, to my flat,' Lisa told him wearily. Despite the fact that at some point, without her being aware of it, he had obviously noticed that she was shivering and had turned the heater on full, she still felt frighteningly cold.

'My parents are both working away in Japan so I can't go to them, and my friends have made other plans. I could have gone with them, but...'

'But you chose to subject yourself to Henry's mother's inspection instead,' he taunted her unkindly.

'Henry and I were planning to get engaged,' Lisa fought back angrily. 'Of course he wanted me to meet his parents, his family. There was no question of there being any "inspection".'

'No? Then why the urgent necessity for a new wardrobe?'

Lisa flushed defensively.

'I just wanted to make a good impression on them, that's all,' she muttered.

'Well, you certainly did that all right,' he mocked her wryly. 'Especially—'

'I would have done if it hadn't been for your interference,' she interrupted him hotly. 'You had no right to imply that you and I had been...that those clothes...' She paused, her voice trailing away into silence as she saw the way he lifted one eyebrow and glanced unkindly at her.

'I spoke nothing but the truth. Those clothes were bought by my cousin for his girlfriend—his lover...'

'It might have been the truth, but you twisted it so that it seemed...so that it sounded...so that...'

Lisa floundered, her face flushing betrayingly as he invited helpfully, 'So that what?'

'So that people would think that you and I...that you had bought those clothes for me and that you and I were lovers,' she told him fiercely.

'But surely anyone who really knows you...a prospective fiancé, an established lover, for instance...would automatically know that it was impossible for us to be lovers?' he pointed out to her.

'Henry and I are not lovers.'

Lisa bit her lip in vexation. Now what on earth had prompted her to tell him that? It was hardly the sort of thing she would normally discuss with someone who was virtually a stranger.

Again the dark eyebrows rose—both of them this time—his response to her admission almost brutally comprehensive as he asked her crisply, 'You're not? Then what on earth were you doing thinking of getting engaged to him?'

Lisa opened her mouth but the words she wanted to say simply wouldn't come. How could she say them now? How could she tell him, I loved him, when she knew irrevocably and blindingly that it simply wasn't true, that it had possibly and shamingly never been true and that, just as shamingly, she had somehow managed to delude herself that it might be and to convince herself that she and Henry had a future together?

In the end she had to settle for a stiff and totally unconvincing, 'It seemed a good idea at the time. We had a lot in common. We were both ready to settle down, to commit ourselves. To—' She stopped speaking as the sound of his laughter suddenly filled the car, drowning out the sound of her own voice.

He had a very full, deep, rich-bodied and very male laugh, she acknowledged—a very…a very…a very sensual, sexy sort of laugh…if you cared for that sort of thing…and of course she didn't, she reminded herself firmly.

'Why are you laughing?' she demanded angrily, her cheeks flying hot banners of scorching colour as she turned in her seat to glare furiously at him. 'It isn't…there isn't anything to laugh at…'

'No, there isn't,' he agreed soberly. 'You're right… By rights I— How old are you? What century are you living in? "We had a lot in common. We were both ready to settle down…"' he mimicked her. 'Even if that was true, which it quite patently is not—in fact, I doubt I've ever seen a couple more obviously totally unsuited to one another—I have never heard of a less convincing reason for wanting to get married.

'Why haven't you been to bed with him?' he demanded, the unexpectedness of the question shocking her, taking her breath away.

'I don't think that's any of your business,' she told him primly.

'Which one of you was it who didn't want to—you or him?'

Lisa gasped, outraged. 'Not everyone has…has a high sex drive…or wants a…a relationship that's based on…on physical lust,' she told him angrily. 'And just because…'

Whilst they had been talking Oliver had been driving, and now unexpectedly he turned off the main road and in between two stone pillars into what was obviously the drive to a private house—a very long drive, Lisa noted, before turning towards him and demanding, 'What are you doing? Where are you taking me? This isn't a garage.'

'No, it isn't,' he agreed calmly. 'It's my home.'

'Your home? But—'

'Calm down,' Oliver advised her drily. 'Look, it's gone one in the morning, Christmas morning,' he emphasised. 'This isn't London; the nearest large petrol station is on the motorway, nearly thirty miles away, *if* it's open—and personally what I think you need right now more than anything else is a hot bath and a good night's sleep.'

'I want to go home,' Lisa insisted stubbornly.

'Why?' he challenged her brutally, and reminded her, 'You've already said yourself that there's no one there. Look,' he told her, 'since it is Christmas, why don't we declare a cease-fire in our…er…hostilities? Although by choice neither of us might have wanted to spend Christmas together, since we are both on our own and since it's patently obvious that you're in no physical state to go anywhere, never mind drive a car—'

'You're spending Christmas on your own?' Lisa interrupted him, too astonished to hold the question back.

'Yes,' he agreed, explaining, 'I was to have spent it entertaining my cousin and his girlfriend, but since they've made up their quarrel their plans have changed and they flew to the

Caribbean yesterday morning. Like you, I'd left it too late to make alternative plans and so—'

'I can't stay with you,' Lisa protested. She was, she recognised, already starting to shiver as the now stationary car started to cool down, and she was also unpleasantly and weakly aware of how very unappealing the thought of driving all the way back to London actually was—and not just unappealing either, she admitted. She was uncomfortably conscious that Oliver had spoken the truth when he had claimed that she was not physically capable of making the journey at present.

'We're strangers...'

'You've already accepted a lift in my car,' he reminded her drily, adding pithily, 'And besides, where else can you go?'

All at once Lisa gave in. She really didn't have the energy to argue with him, she admitted—she was too cold, too tired, too muzzily aware of how dangerously light-headed and weak she was beginning to feel.

'Very well, then,' she said, adding warningly, 'But only until tomorrow...until I can get some petrol.'

'Only until tomorrow,' he agreed.

CHAPTER FOUR

'YOU LIVE HERE ALL ALONE?' Lisa questioned Oliver, breaking into his conversation as she curled up in one corner of the vast, deep sofa where he had taken her and told her sternly she was to remain until he returned with a hot drink for her.

'Yes,' he said. 'I prefer it that way. A gardener comes twice a week and his wife does the cleaning for me, but other than that—'

'But it's such a big house. Don't you...?'

'Don't I what?' Oliver challenged her. 'Don't I feel lonely?' He shook his head. 'Not really. I was an only child. My mother died when I was in my teens and my father was away a lot on business. I'm used to being on my own. In fact I prefer it in many ways. Other people's company, their presence in one's life isn't always a pleasure—especially not when one has to become responsible for their emotional and financial welfare.'

Lisa guessed that he was referring obliquely to his cousin, and she sensed that he was, by nature, the kind of man who would always naturally assume responsibility for others, even if that responsibility was slightly irritably cynical rather than humanely compassionate. It also probably explained why he wasn't married. He was by nature a loner—a man, she suspected, who enjoyed women's company but who did not want to burden himself with a wife or children.

And yet a house like this cried out for children. It had that kind of ambience about it, that kind of warmth; it was a real family home for all its obviously priceless antiques. It had a lived-in, welcoming feel to it, Lisa acknowledged—a sense of having been well used and well loved, a slightly worn air which, to her, gave it a richness that far surpassed the sterile, elegant perfection of a house like Henry's parents'.

It didn't surprise Lisa to learn that the house had been in Oliver's family for several generations but what did surprise her was how at ease, how at home she actually felt here, how unexpectedly easy it was to talk to Oliver after he had returned from the kitchen with a huge mug of piping-hot chocolate which he insisted she drink, virtually standing over her until she had done so.

She had suspected from the taste of it that something very much more alcoholic than mere milk had been added to it, but by that stage she had been so grateful for the warmth of her comfortable niche in the deep sofa, so drowsily content and relaxed that there hadn't seemed to be any point in mentioning it, never mind protesting about it.

Now, as she yawned sleepily, blinking owlishly, her forehead pleating in a muzzy frown as she tried to focus on the fireplace and discovered that she couldn't, she was vaguely aware of Oliver getting up from his own chair and coming over to her, leaning down towards her as he firmly relieved her of the now empty mug.

'Bath for you, and then bed, I think,' he told her firmly, sounding so much as her father had when she had been a little girl that Lisa turned her head to look at him.

She hadn't realised that he was quite so close to her, nor that his grey eyes had a darker outer rim to them and were not flat, dead grey at all but rather a mystical mingling of so many silvers and pewters that she caught her breath a little at the male beauty of them.

'You've got beautiful eyes,' she heard herself telling him

in a soft, slightly slurred…almost sexy voice that she barely recognised as her own.

She was unaware that her own eyes were registering the shock of what she had said as Oliver responded gravely, 'Thank you.'

She was, she recognised, still holding onto her mug, even though his own fingers were now wrapped securely around it—so securely in fact that they were actually touching her own.

Some of that molten silver heat from his eyes must have somehow entered his skin, his blood, she decided dizzily. There could be no other reason for those tiny, darting, fiery sensations of heat that she could feel where her own flesh rested against his.

'So are yours…'

'So are yours'? Uncomprehendingly, Lisa looked at him and watched as he smiled a slow, curling, sensual smile that made her heart soar and turn over and do a bellyflop that left her as shocked and winded as though her whole body had actually fielded a blow.

'Your eyes,' Oliver told her softly. 'Your eyes are beautiful too. Do you always keep them open when you kiss?'

'Why?' Lisa heard herself croak shakily. 'Do you?'

As she spoke her glance was already drifting down to his mouth, as though drawn there by some potent force that she couldn't control.

'That depends,' Oliver was drawling, 'on who I'm kissing…'

He was looking at her mouth now, and a panicky, unfamiliar feeling of mingled excitement and shock kicked into life inside her, bringing with it some much needed sobering sanity, bringing her back to reality.

Lisa gulped and turned her head away, quickly withdrawing her hand from the mug.

'I...I...'

As she fought to find the words to explain away her totally uncharacteristic behaviour and conversation, she was overcome by a sudden fit of sneezing.

Quickly reaching for the box of tissues that Oliver had brought her, she hoped that he would put her flushed complexion down to the fever or the cold that she had obviously caught rather than to her self-conscious embarrassment at what she had said.

What on earth had come over her? She had practically been flirting with him...asking him...inviting him...

Thankfully, Lisa buried her face in another tissue as she sneezed again.

When she had finished, determined to dispel any erroneous ideas that he might have gained from her unguarded and totally foolish comments, she said quickly, 'It must have been wonderful here at Christmas when you were young—your family...this house...'

'Yes, it was,' he agreed, before asking, far too perceptively for Lisa's peace of mind, 'Weren't your childhood Christmases good?'

'Yes, of course they were,' Lisa responded hastily.

'But?' he challenged her.

'My parents travelled a lot with their work. They still do. Whilst I dreamed of traditional Christmases in a house with log fires and a huge tree surrounded by aunts and uncles and cousins, going to church on Christmas morning and doing all the traditional British Christmas things, the reality was normally not roast turkey with all the trimmings but ice cream on an Australian beach or sunshine in Japan.

'My parents did their best, of course. There were always mounds of presents, and they always made sure that we spent Christmas and Boxing Days together, but somehow it just wasn't the same as it would have been if we'd been here...

It's silly of me, really, but I suppose a part of me still is that little girl who—'

She stopped, embarrassed by how much of herself she had inadvertently revealed. It must be whatever it was he had obviously added to her hot chocolate that was making her so loquacious and communicative, she thought. She certainly wasn't normally so open or confiding with people she barely knew, although in some odd way it felt as though she had actually known Oliver for a very long time.

She was still frowning over this absurdity when he handed her a glass of amber liquid that he had just poured.

'Drink it,' he told her when she looked at it doubtfully. 'It's pure malt whisky and the best antidote for a heavy cold that I know.'

Reluctantly, Lisa took the glass he handed her. Her head was already swimming slightly, and she felt that the last thing she needed was any more alcohol, but her father was also a great believer in a hot toddy as a cure for colds and so hesitantly she began to sip the tawny golden liquid, closing her eyes as it slid smoothly down her throat, spreading the most delicious sense of beatific warmth throughout her body.

There was something so comforting, so safe, so…so pleasurable about being curled up cosily here in this house…with this man… With this man? What did that mean? Where had that thought come from?

Anxiously Lisa opened her eyes and started to sit up.

'Was that why you wanted to marry Henry, because you thought he could provide you with the traditional lifestyle you felt you'd missed out on?' she heard Oliver asking her.

'Yes…yes, I suppose it was,' she agreed huskily, caught too off guard to think of prevaricating or avoiding the question, and then flushing slightly as she saw the way Oliver was looking at her.

'It would have been a good marriage,' she defended herself.

'We both wanted the same things...' As she saw the way his eyebrows rose, she amended herself shakily, 'Well, I thought that we did.'

'I've heard of some odd reasons for getting married,' she heard Oliver telling her drily, 'but marrying someone because you think he'll provide you with a traditional Christmas has to be the oddest...'

'I wasn't marrying him for that—' Lisa began indignantly, stopping when another volley of sneezing mercifully prevented her from having to make any further response or explanation.

'Come on,' Oliver told her. 'I think it's time you were in bed.'

The whisky that she had drunk was even more potent than she had realised, Lisa acknowledged as Oliver led the way back into the warm, panelled entrance hall and up the stairs.

Just where the stairs started to return towards the galleried landing, Lisa paused to study two large oil paintings hung side by side.

'My grandparents,' Oliver explained, adding informatively, 'My grandfather commissioned the artist to paint them as a first wedding-anniversary present for my grandmother.'

'You look very like him,' Lisa told him. And it was the truth, only the man in the portrait somehow looked less acerbic and much happier than Oliver—much happier and obviously very much in love with his young wife. In the portrait his face was turned slightly towards her matching portrait, so that for a moment it seemed as though the two of them were actually looking at one another.

'It's this way,' Oliver told Lisa, touching her briefly on her arm as he directed her across the landing and towards one of the bedrooms.

'Since my cousin Piers and his girlfriend were supposed to

be spending Christmas here a room had already been made up for them and you may as well sleep there.' As he spoke he pushed open one of the seven wooden doors leading off the landing. Lisa blinked dizzily as she stepped inside the room.

It seemed huge—almost as large, she was sure, as the entire floor space of her own small flat. It was so large, in fact, that in addition to the high, king-sized bed there was also a desk and chair and a small two-seater sofa drawn up close to the open fireplace.

'The bathroom's through that door,' Oliver told her, indicating one of a pair of doors set into the wall. 'The other door opens into a walk-in wardrobe.'

A walk-in wardrobe. Lisa blinked owlishly before reminding him, 'Well, that's something I shan't be needing.' When he frowned she explained, 'I don't have any other clothes with me. The others are the ones I—'

'Hurled at me in a fit of temper,' Oliver finished for her.

She had started to shiver again, Lisa noticed, hugging her arms around herself despite the warmth of the bedroom, with its soft fitted carpet and heavy damask curtains.

That whisky really had gone to her head, she acknowledged as a wave of dizziness swept over her, making her sway and reach out instinctively for the nearest solid object to cling onto—the nearest solid object being Oliver himself.

As he detached her hand from his arm she looked up at him muzzily, only to gasp in startled surprise as she was suddenly swung very firmly up into his arms.

'What…what are you doing?' she managed to stammer as he strode towards the bed, carrying her.

'Saving us both a lot of time,' he told her drily as he deposited her with unexpected gentleness on the mattress before asking her, 'Can you manage to get undressed or…?'

'Yes, of course I can,' Lisa responded in a flurry of mingled indignation and flushed self-consciousness, adding defensively, 'I…I just felt a little bit dizzy, that's all…I'm all right now…'

He didn't look totally convinced, and Lisa discovered that she was holding her breath as she watched him walk towards the bedroom door, unable to expel it until she was sure that he had walked through it and closed it behind him.

He really was the most extraordinary man, she decided ten minutes later as she lay in a huge bath of heavenly, deep hot water.

At Henry's parents' house both baths and hot water had been rationed and now it was sheer bliss to ease her aching limbs into the soothing heat, even if something about the steamy atmosphere of the bathroom did somehow seem to increase the dizzying effect that the whisky had had on her system. She felt, she recognised when she eventually reluctantly climbed out of the bath and wrapped herself in one of the huge, warm, fluffy towels on the heated rail, not just physically affected by the alcohol but mentally and emotionally affected by it as well, as though she was on some sort of slightly euphoric high, free of the burden of her normal, cautious, self-imposed restraints.

Shaking her head, she towelled herself dry, remembering only when she had finished that she had no night-clothes.

Shrugging fatalistically, she wrapped herself in another towel instead and padded towards the bed, discarding it as she climbed into the bed's welcoming warmth.

The bedlinen was cotton and deliciously soft against her skin. It smelled faintly of lavender. She breathed in the scent blissfully as she closed her eyes. After the austere regime of Henry's parents' home this was luxury indeed.

She was just on the point of falling asleep when she heard the bedroom door open. In the half-light from the landing she could see Oliver walking towards the bed carrying something.

As he reached the bed she struggled to sit up.

'I've brought you a hot-water bottle,' he told her. 'Just in case you get cold during the night.'

His thoughtfulness surprised her. He was the last person she would have expected to show such consideration, such concern.

Tears filled her eyes as she took it from him, and on some impulse, which when she later tried to rationalise it she could only put down to the effects of the whisky on her system, she reached out and lifted her face towards his, kissing him.

He must have moved, done something...turned his head, because she had never intended to kiss him so intimately, only to brush her lips against his cheek in a small gesture of gratitude for his care of her. She had certainly never planned to do anything so bold as kiss him on the lips, but oddly, even though her brain had registered her error, her body seemed to be having trouble responding to its frantic message to remove her mouth from the male one which confusingly, instead of withdrawing from her touch, seemed to be not merely accepting it but actually actively...

Lisa swallowed, panicked, swallowed again and jerked her head back, only to find that somehow or other Oliver's hand was resting on her nape, preventing her from doing anything other than lift her lips a mere breath away from his.

'If that's the way you kissed Henry, I'm not surprised the two of you never went to bed together,' she heard him telling her sardonically. 'If you want to kiss a man you should do it properly,' he added reprovingly, and then before she could explain or even object he had closed the small distance between them and his mouth was back on hers, only this time it wasn't merely resting there against her unintended caress but slowly moving on hers, slowly caressing hers, slowly and then not so slowly arousing her, so that...

It must be the drink, Lisa decided giddily. There could be no other reason why she was virtually clinging to Oliver with both her hands, straining towards him almost as though there was nothing she wanted more than the feel of his mouth against her own.

It *had* to be the drink. There could be no other explanation for the way her lips were parting, positively inviting the masterful male thrust of his tongue. And it had to be the drink as well that was causing her to make those small, keening, soft sounds of pleasure as their tongues meshed.

And then abruptly and shockingly erotically Oliver's mouth hardened on her own, so that it was no longer possible for her to deceive herself that what they were sharing was simply a kiss of polite gratitude. No longer possible at all, especially when the rest of her body was suddenly, urgently waking up to the fact that it actively liked what Oliver was doing and that in fact it would very much like to prolong the sensual, drugging pleasure of the way his mouth was moving on hers and, if at all possible, to feel it moving not just on her mouth but on her...

Shocked by her own reactions, Lisa sobered up enough to push Oliver away, her eyes over-bright and her mouth trembling—not, she admitted inwardly, because he had kissed her, but because he had stopped doing it.

'I never meant that to happen,' she told him huskily, anxious to make sure that he understood that even though she might have responded to him she had not deliberately set out to encourage such intimacy between them.

'I just wanted to say thank you for—'

'For making Henry think you're having an affair with me,' he mocked her as he sat back from her. 'Go to sleep,' he advised her, adding softly, 'unless you want me to take up the invitation these have been offering me…' As he spoke he reached out and very lightly touched one of her exposed breasts.

The bedclothes must have slipped down whilst he'd been kissing her, revealing her body to him, even though she herself hadn't realised it, Lisa recognised. And they hadn't just revealed her body, either, she admitted as her face flushed to a pink as deep as that of her tight, hard nipples.

Quickly she pulled the bedclothes up over herself, clutching them defensively in front of her, her face still flushed, and flushing even deeper as she saw the fleeting but very comprehensive and male glance that Oliver gave her now fully covered body.

'Forget about Henry,' he advised her as he turned to leave. 'You're better off without him.'

He had gone before Lisa could think of anything to say—which in the circumstances was probably just as well, she decided as she settled back into the warmth of the bed. After all, what was there she possibly could have said? Her body grew hot as she remembered the way he had kissed her, her toes curling protestingly as she fought down the memory of her own far from reluctant reaction.

No wonder there had been that male gleam of sensual triumph in his eyes as he'd looked at her body—a look which had told her quite plainly that he enjoyed the knowledge that he had been responsible for that unmistakable sexual arousal of her body—his touch…his kiss…*him*.

It had been an accident, that was all, Lisa reassured herself. A fluke, an unfortunate sequence of events which, of course, would never be repeated. Her toes had relaxed but there was a worrying sensual ache deep within her body—a sense of… of deprivation and yearning which she tried very firmly to ignore as she closed her eyes and told herself sternly to go to sleep.

CHAPTER FIVE

LISA OPENED HER EYES, confused by her unfamiliar surroundings, until the events of the previous evening came rushing back.

Some of those events were quite definitely ones that she did not want to dwell on and which had to be pushed very firmly back where they belonged—in a sealed box marked 'very dangerous'. And some of those events, and in particular the ones involving that unexpectedly passionate kiss she had shared with Oliver, were, quite simply, far too potentially explosive to be touched at all.

Instead she focused on her surroundings, her eyes widening in disbelief as she looked towards the fireplace. She rubbed them and then studied it again. No, they were not deceiving her; there was quite definitely a long woollen stocking hanging from the fireplace—a long woollen stocking bulging with all sorts of odd shapes, with a notice pinned to it reading, 'Open me.'

Her curiosity overcoming her natural caution, Lisa hopped out of bed and hurried towards the fireplace, removed the stocking and then returned to the sanctuary of her bed with it.

As she turned it upside down on the coverlet to dislodge its contents, a huge smile curled her mouth, her eyes dancing with a mixture of almost childlike disbelief and a rather more adult amusement.

Wrapped in coloured tissue-paper, a dozen or more small

objects lay on the bed around her. Some of them she could recognise without unwrapping them: the two tangerines, the nuts, the apple…

There could, of course, only be one person who had done this; the identity of her unexpected Father Christmas could not be in doubt, but his motivation was.

Her fingers trembled slightly as she removed the wrapping from what turned out to be a tube of thick white paper. As she unrolled it she began to frown, her frown turning to a soft gasp as she read what had been written on it in impressive copperplate handwriting.

In this year of our Sovereign Queen Elizabeth it is hereby agreed that there shall be a formal truce and a cessation of hostilities between Mistress Lisa and Oliver Esquire in order that the two aforenamed may celebrate the Festival of Christmas in true Christian spirit.

Beneath the space that he had left for her to sign her own name Oliver had signed his.

Lisa couldn't help it. She started to laugh softly, her laugh turning into a husky cough and a fit of sneezes that told her that she had not, as she had first hoped, escaped the heavy cold Oliver had warned likely the previous evening.

At least, though, her head was clear this morning, she told herself severely as she scrabbled around amongst the other packages on the bed, guessing that somewhere amongst them there must be a pen for her to sign their truce.

It touched her to think of Oliver going to so much trouble on her behalf. If only Henry had been half as thoughtful… But Henry would never have done anything like this. Henry would never have kissed her the way Oliver had done last night. Henry would never…

Her fingers started to tremble as she finally found the parcel containing the pen.

It hurt to think that the future that she had believed she and Henry could have together had been nothing more than a chimera…as childish in its way as her daydreams of a perfect Christmas which she had revealed to Oliver last night, under the effects and influence of his malt whisky.

Her eyes misted slightly with fresh tears, but they were not, this time, caused by the knowledge that she had made a mistake in believing that she and Henry had a good relationship.

After she had signed the truce she noticed that her signature was slightly wobbly and off balance—a reflection of the way she herself had felt ever since Oliver had thrust his way into her life, demanding the return of his cousin's girlfriend's clothes.

Thinking of clothes reminded Lisa that she had nothing to wear other than the things she had discarded the previous evening. Hardly the kind of outfit she had planned to spend Christmas Day in, she acknowledged as she mourned the loss of the simply cut cream wool dress that she had flung at Oliver's feet before her departure from Henry's parents' house.

Still, clothes did not make Christmas, she told herself, and neither did Christmas stockings—but they certainly went a long way to help, she admitted, a rueful smile curling her mouth as she pictured Oliver painstakingly wrapping the small traditional gifts which for generations children had delighted to find waiting for them on Christmas morning.

It was a pity that after such an unexpected and pleasurable start the rest of her Christmas looked so unappealingly bleak. She wasn't looking forward to her return to her empty flat. She glanced at her watch. She had slept much later than usual and it was already nine o'clock—time for her to get up and dressed if she was going to be able to retrieve her car, fill it with petrol and make her return journey to London before dark.

She had just put one foot on the floor when she heard Oliver knocking on the bedroom door. Hastily she put her foot back under the bedclothes and made sure that the latter were secured firmly around her naked body as she called out to Oliver to come in. She didn't want there to be any repeat of last night's still blush-inducing *faux pas* of not realising that her breasts were clearly on view.

The sight of him carrying a tea-tray complete with a china teapot, two cups and a plate of wholemeal toast made her eyes widen slightly.

'So you found it, then. How are you feeling?' he asked her as he placed the tray on the empty half of her bed, half smiling as he saw the clutter of small objects still surrounding her and the evidence of her excitement as she had unwrapped them in the small, shredded pieces of paper torn by her impatient fingers.

'Much better,' Lisa assured him. 'Just as soon as I can get my car sorted out I should be off your hands and on my way back to London. I still haven't thanked you properly for what you did,' she added, half-shyly. Last night the intimacy between them had seemed so natural that she hadn't even questioned it. This morning she was acutely conscious of the fact that he was, after all, a man she barely knew.

His soft, 'Oh, I wouldn't say that,' as he looked directly at her mouth made her flush, but there was more amusement in his eyes than any kind of sexual threat, she acknowledged.

'I haven't thanked you for the stocking either,' she hurried on. 'That was… I… You must think me very childish to want… I'm not used to drinking, and your whisky… I've signed this, by the way.' She tried to excuse herself, diving amongst her spoils to produce the now rerolled truce.

As she did so she suddenly started to sneeze, and had to reach out for the box of tissues beside the bed.

'I thought you said you were feeling all right,' Oliver reminded her sardonically.

'I am,' Lisa defended herself, but now that she was fully awake she had to acknowledge that her throat felt uncomfortably raw and her head ached slightly, whilst yet another volley of sneezes threatened to disprove her claim to good health.

'You're full of a cold,' Oliver corrected her, 'and in no fit state to drive back to London—even if we could arrange for someone to collect your car.'

'But I have to... I must...' Lisa protested.

'Why...in case Henry calls?'

'No,' Lisa denied vehemently, her face flushing again as she suddenly realised how little thought she had actually given to Henry and the end of their romance.

But it was obvious that Oliver had mistaken the cause of her hot face because he gave her an ironic look and told her, 'It will never work. He'll always be tied to his mother's apron strings and you'll always have to take second place to her...

'It's half past nine now,' he told her, changing the subject. 'The village is only ten minutes away by car and we've got time to make it for morning service. I've put the turkey in the oven but it won't be ready until around three...'

Lisa gaped at him.

'But I can't stay here,' she protested.

'Why not?' he asked her calmly. 'What reason have you to go? You've already said that you'll be alone in your flat, and since I'll be alone up here—if you discount a fifteen-pound turkey and enough food to feed the pair of us several times over—it makes sense for you to stay...'

'You want me to stay?' Lisa asked him, astonished. 'But...'

'It will be a hell of a lot easier having you to stay than

trying to find a reputable mechanic to sort out and make arrangements for a garage to collect your car, check it over and refuel it. And having one guest instead of two is hardly going to cause me any hardship...' He gave a small shrug.

It was a tempting prospect, Lisa knew. If she was honest with herself she hadn't been looking forward to returning to her empty flat, and even though she and Oliver were virtually strangers there was something about him that... Severely she gave herself a small mental shake.

All right, so maybe last night her body *had* reacted to him in a way that it had certainly never reacted to Henry... Maybe when he had kissed her she *had* felt a certain...need...a response...but that had only been the effect of the whisky... nothing more.

She opened her mouth to decline his invitation, to do the sensible thing and tell him firmly that she had to return home, and instead, to her chagrin, heard herself saying in a small voice, 'Could we really go to church...?' As she realised what she was saying she shook her head, telling him hastily, 'Oh, no, I can't... I haven't anything to wear. My clothes...your cousin's girlfriend's clothes...'

'Are hanging in the closet,' Oliver informed her wryly.

Lisa looked at him. 'What? But they can't be... I left them at Henry's parents'.'

'I didn't,' Oliver informed her succinctly.

'But...but you wanted to give them back to Emma.'

'Originally, yes, but only because Piers was so convinced that the moment she knew what he had done she'd walk out again. However, it transpires that she's off Armani and onto Versace so Piers was allowed to make his peace with her by taking her out and buying her a new wardrobe.'

'So you went to all that trouble for nothing,' Lisa sympathised, knowing how she would have felt in his shoes.

The look he gave her in response made her heart start to

beat rather too fast, and for some reason she found it impossible to hold his gaze and had to look quickly away from him.

His slightly hoarse, 'You'd have been wasted on a man like Henry,' made her want to curl her toes in much the same way as his kiss had done last night, and the small shiver that touched her skin had nothing to do with any drop in temperature.

'I'll meet you downstairs in half an hour,' Oliver was saying to her as he moved away from the bed.

Silently, Lisa nodded her agreement. What had she done, committing herself to spend Christmas with him? She gave a small, fatalistic shrug. It was too late to worry about the wisdom of her impulsive decision now.

Thirty-five minutes later, having nervously studied her reflection in the bedroom mirror for a good two minutes, Lisa walked hesitantly onto the landing.

The cream wool dress looked every bit as good on as she had remembered; the cashmere coat would keep her warm in church.

Her hair, freshly washed and dried, shone silkily, and as yet the only physical sign of her cold was a slight pinky tinge to her nose, easily disguised with foundation.

At the head of the stairs she paused, and then determinedly started to descend, coming to an abrupt halt as she reached the turn in the stairs that looked down on the hallway below.

In the middle of the large room, dominating it, stood the largest and most wondrous Christmas tree that Lisa had ever seen.

She gazed at it in rapt awe, unaware that the shine of pleasure in her eyes rivalled that of the myriad decorations fastened to the tree.

As excited as any child, she positively ran down the remaining stairs and into the hall.

'How on earth…?' she began as she stood and marvelled at the tree, shaking her head as she was unable to find the words to convey her feelings.

'I take it you approve,' she heard Oliver saying wryly beside her.

'Yes. Yes. It's wonderful,' she breathed, without taking her eyes off it to turn and look at him. 'But when… How…?'

'Well, I'm afraid I can't claim to have gone out last night and cut it down. It had actually been delivered yesterday. Piers and I were supposed to be putting it up… It's a bit of a family tradition. He and I both used to spend Christmas here as children with our grandparents, and it was our job to "do the tree". It's a tradition we've kept up ever since, although this year…

'I brought it in last night after you'd gone to bed. Mrs Green had already brought the decorations down from the attic, so it was just a matter of hanging them up.'

'Just a matter…' Lisa's eyebrows rose slightly as she studied the rows and rows of tiny lights, the beautiful and, she was nearly sure, very valuable antique baubles combined with much newer but equally attractive modern ones.

'It must have taken you hours,' she objected.

Oliver shrugged.

'Not really.'

'It's beautiful,' she told him, her throat suddenly closing with emotion. He hadn't done it for her, of course. He had already told her that it was a family tradition, something he and his cousin did together. But, even so, to come down and find it there after confiding in him last night how much she longed for a traditional family Christmas…suddenly seemed a good omen for her decision to stay on with him.

'It hasn't got a fairy,' she told him, hoping he wouldn't notice the idiotic emotional thickening in her voice.

As he glanced towards the top of the tree Oliver shook his

head and told her, 'Our fairy is a star, and it's normally the responsibility of the woman of the house to put it on the tree, so I left it—'

'You want me to do it?' Fresh emotion swept her. 'But I'm not... I don't belong here,' she reminded him.

'But you are a woman,' he told her softly, and there was something in the way he said the words, something in the way he looked at her that warned Lisa that the kiss they had shared last night wasn't something he had forgotten.

'We'll have to leave it for now, though,' he told her. 'Otherwise we'll be late for church.'

It had been a cold night, and a heavy frost still lay over the countryside, lending it a magical quality of silvered stillness that made Lisa catch her breath in pleasure.

The village, as Oliver had said, was ten minutes' drive away—a collection of small stone houses huddled together on one side of the river and reached by a narrow stone bridge.

The church was at the furthest end of the village and set slightly apart from it, small and weathered and so old that it looked almost as though it had grown out of the craggy landscape around it.

The bells were ringing as Oliver parked the car and then led her towards the narrow lych-gate and along the stone-flagged path through a graveyard so peaceful that there was no sense of pain or sorrow about it.

Just inside the church, the vicar was waiting.

The church was already almost full, but when Lisa would have slipped into one of the rear pews Oliver touched her arm and directed her to one at the front. A family pew, Lisa recognised, half in awe and half in envy.

The service was short and simple, the carols traditional, the crib quite obviously decorated by very young hands, and yet

.o Lisa the whole experience was more movingly intense than f they had been in one of the world's grandest cathedrals.

Afterwards the vicar was waiting to shake hands and exchange a few words with all his congregation, including them, and as they ambled back to where Oliver had parked the car the final magical seal of wonderment was put on the day when the first flakes of the forecast snow started to fall.

'I don't believe it,' Lisa whispered breathlessly as Oliver unlocked the car doors. 'I just don't believe it.'

As she whirled round, her whole face alight, Oliver laughed. The sound, so spontaneous and warmly masculine, had the oddest effect on Lisa's body. Her heart seemed to flip helplessly, her breathing quickening, her gaze drawn unerringly to Oliver's mouth.

She shouldn't be feeling like this. It wasn't fair and it certainly wasn't sensible. They barely knew one another. Yesterday they had been enemies, and but for an odd quirk of fate they still would be today.

Shakily she walked towards the car, the still falling snowflakes forgotten as she tried to come to terms with what was happening to her.

What exactly *was* happening to her? Something she didn't want to give a name to... Not yet... Perhaps not ever. She shivered as she pulled on her seat belt.

'Cold?' Oliver questioned her, frowning slightly.

Lisa shook her head, refusing to give in to the temptation to look at him, to check and see whether, if she did, she would feel that heart-jolting surge of feminine awareness and arousal that she had just experienced in the car park for a second time.

'Stop thinking about him,' she heard Oliver say harshly to her as she turned away from him and stared out of the window. It took her several seconds to realise that he thought that Henry was the reason for her sudden silence. Perhaps it was just as well he did think that, she decided—for both their sakes.

Through the now drifting heavy snowflakes Lisa could see how quickly they had obscured the previously greeny-brown landscape, transforming it into a winter wonderland of breathtaking Christmas-card white.

Coming on top of the poignant simplicity of a church service which to Lisa, as an outsider, had somehow symbolised all she had always felt was missing from her own Christmases—a sense of community, of sharing…of involvement and belonging, of permanence going from one generation to the next—the sight of the falling snow brought an ache to her throat and the quick silvery shimmer of unexpected tears to her eyes.

Ashamed of her own emotionalism, she ducked her head, searching in her bag for a tissue, hoping to disguise her tears as a symptom of her cold. But Oliver was obviously too astute to be deceived by such a strategy and demanded brusquely, 'What is it? What's wrong?' adding curtly, 'You're wasting your tears on Henry; he isn't—'

'I'm not crying because of Henry,' Lisa denied. Did he really think that she was so lacking in self-esteem and self-preservation that she couldn't see for herself what a lucky escape she had had, if not from Henry then very definitely from Henry's mother?

'No? Then what are these?' Oliver demanded tauntingly, reaching out before she could stop him to rub the hard pad of his thumb beneath one eye and show her the dampness clinging to his skin. 'Scotch mist?'

'I didn't say I wasn't crying,' Lisa defended herself. 'Just that it wasn't because of… It's not because of Henry…'

'Then why?' Oliver challenged, obviously not believing her.

'Because of this,' Lisa told him simply, gesturing towards the scene outside the car window. 'And the church…'

She could see from the look he was giving her that he didn't really believe her, and because for some reason it had suddenly become very important that he did she took a deep breath and told him quickly, 'It's just so beautiful... The whole thing... the weather, the church service...'

As she felt him looking at her she turned her head to meet his eyes. She shook her head, not wanting to go on, feeling that she had perhaps said too much already, been too openly emotional. Men, in her experience, found it rather discomforting when women expressed their emotions. Henry certainly had.

If Oliver was discomforted by what she had said, though, he certainly wasn't showing it; in fact he wasn't showing any kind of reaction that she could identify at all. He had dropped his eyelids slightly over his eyes and turned his face away from her, ostensibly to concentrate on his driving, making it impossible for her to read his expression at all, his only comment, as he brought the car to a halt outside the house, a cautionary, 'Be careful you don't slip when you get out.'

'Be careful you don't slip...!' Just how old did he think she was? Lisa wondered wryly as she got out of the car, tilting up her face towards the still falling snowflakes and breathing in the clean, sharp air, a blissful expression on her face as she studied her surroundings, happiness bubbling up inside her.

'I still can't believe this...that it's actually snowing...on Christmas Day... Do you realise that this is my very first white Christmas?' As she whispered the words in awed delight she closed her eyes, took a deep breath of snow-scented air and promptly did what Oliver had warned her not to do and lost her footing.

Her startled cry was arrested almost before it had begun as Oliver reached out and caught hold of her, his strong hands gripping her waist, holding her tightly, safely...

Holding her closely, she recognised as her heart started

to pound with unfamiliar excitement and her breath caught in her throat. Not out of shock, Lisa acknowledged, her face flushing as she realised just what it was that was causing her heart and pulse-rate to go into overdrive, and she prayed that Oliver wouldn't be equally quick to recognise that her shallow breathing and sudden tension had nothing to do with the shock of her near fall and everything to do with his proximity.

Why was this happening to her? she wondered dizzily. She didn't even like the man and he certainly didn't like her—even if he *had* offered her a roof over her head for Christmas.

He was standing close enough for her to smell the clean man scent of his skin—or was it just that for some extraordinary reason she was acutely sensitive to the scent and heat of him?

Her legs started to tremble—in fact, her whole body was trembling.

'It's all right,' she heard Oliver saying calmly to her. 'I've got you...'

'Yes,' Lisa heard herself responding, her own voice unfamiliarly soft and husky, making the simple affirmation sound something much more sensual and inviting. Without having had the remotest intention of doing any such thing—it simply wasn't the kind of thing she did, ever—Lisa found that she was looking at Oliver's mouth, and that her gaze, having focused on it for far, far too long, was somehow drawn even more betrayingly to his eyes.

Her breath caught in her throat as she saw the way he was looking back at her, his head already lowering towards hers—as well it might do after the sensually open invitation that she had just given him.

But instead of avoiding what she knew was going to happen, instead of moving away from him, which she could quite easily have done, she simply stood there waiting, with her lips softly parted, her gaze fixed on the downward descent of his head and his mouth, her heart thudding frantically against her chest wall—not in case he kissed her, she acknowledged in semi-shock, but rather in case he didn't.

But of course he did. Slowly and deliberately at first, exploring the shape and feel of her mouth, shifting his weight slightly so that instead of that small but oh, so safe distance between them and the firm grip of his hands on her waist supporting her, it was the equally firm but oh, so much more sensual strength of his body that held her up as his arms closed round her, holding her in an embrace not as intimate as that of a lover but still intimate enough to make her powerfully aware of the fact that he was a man.

Lisa had forgotten that a man's kiss could be like this— slow, thorough and so sensually inventive and promising as he hinted at all the pleasures that there could be to come. And yet it wasn't a kiss of passion or demand—not yet—and Lisa was hazily aware that the slow stroke of his tongue against her lips was more sensually threatening to her self-control than to his, and that she was the one who was having to struggle to pull herself back from the verge of a far more dangerous kind of arousal when he finally lifted his mouth from hers.

'What was that for?' she asked stupidly as she tried to drag her gaze away from his eyes.

'No reason,' he told her in response. But as she started to turn her head away, expecting him to release her, he lifted one hand to her face, cupping the side of her jaw with warm, strong fingers, holding her captive as he told her softly, 'But this is.'

And he was kissing her again, but this time the passion that she had sensed was missing in his first kiss was clearly betrayed in the way his mouth hardened over hers, the way his body hardened against hers, his tongue probing the softness of her mouth as she totally abandoned her normal, cautious behaviour and responded to him with every single one of her aroused senses—every single one.

Her arms, without her knowing quite how it had happened, were wrapped tightly around him, holding him close, her fingertips absorbing the feel of his body, its warmth, its hardness, its sheer maleness; her eyes opened in dazed arousal as she looked up into his, her ears intensely attuned to the sound of his breathing and his heartbeat and their tell-tale quickened rate, the scent of him reaching her with every breath she took, and the taste of him. She closed her eyes and then opened them again as she heard him whispering against her mouth, 'Happy Christmas.'

'Happy Christmas'! Lisa came back to earth with a jolt. Of course. Hot colour flooded her face as she realised just how close she had been to making a complete fool of herself.

He hadn't kissed her because he had wanted her, because he had been overwhelmed by desire for her. He had kissed her because it was Christmas, and if that second kiss had been a good deal more intense than their extremely short-lived acquaintanceship really merited then that was probably her fault for... For what? For responding too intensely to him the first time?

'Happy Christmas!' she managed to respond as she hurriedly stepped back from him and turned towards the house.

As Oliver opened the door for her Lisa could smell the rich scent of the roasting turkey mingling with the fresh crispness of the tree.

'The turkey smells good,' she told him, shakily struggling to appear calm and unaffected by his kiss, sniffing the richly scented air. The kiss that they had so recently exchanged might never have been, judging from the way he was behaving towards her now, and she told herself firmly that it was probably best if she pretended that it hadn't too.

Oliver could never play a permanent role in her life, and this unfamiliar and dangerous intensity of physical desire that she had experienced was something she would be far better off without.

'Yes, I'd better go and check on it,' Oliver agreed.

'I'll come and give you a hand,' Lisa offered, adding as she glanced down at her clothes, 'I'd better go and get changed first, though.'

It didn't take her long to remove her coat and the dress she was wearing underneath it, but instead of re-dressing immediately she found that she was standing staring at her underwear-clad body in the mirror, trying to see it as a man might do... A man? Or Oliver?

Angry with herself, she reached into the wardrobe and pulled out the first thing that came to hand, only realising when she had started to put it on that it was the cream trouser suit which had caused so many problems already.

She paused, wondering whether or not to wear something else, and then heard Oliver rapping on the bedroom door and calling out, 'Lisa, are you all right...?'

'Yes, yes. I'm fine... I'm coming now,' she told him quickly, pulling on the jacket and fastening it. Hardly sensible apparel in which to help cook Christmas lunch, but with the sleeves of the jacket pushed back, she thought... And she could always remove the jacket if necessary. So what if the pretty little waistcoat that went underneath it was rather brief? Oliver was hardly likely to notice, was he?

He was waiting for her outside the bedroom door, and caught her off guard by catching hold of her arm and placing his hand on her forehead.

'Mmm...no temperature. Well, that's something, I suppose. Your pulse is very fast, though,' he observed as his hand circled her wrist and he measured her pulse-rate.

Quickly Lisa snatched her wrist away. 'I've just got a cold, that's all,' she told him huskily.

'Just a cold,' he reiterated. 'No broken heart...'

Lisa flashed him a doubtful look, half suspecting him of deliberately mocking her, but unable to make any response, knowing that she would be lying to him if she tried to pretend that she felt anything other than half-ashamed relief at breaking up with Henry.

'You might not want to accept it now, but you didn't really love him,' Oliver told her coolly. 'If you had—'

'You have no right to say that,' Lisa objected suddenly, angry with him—and, more tellingly, with herself, without wanting to analyse or really know why.

'What do you know about love?'

'I know enough about it to recognise it when I see it—and when I don't,' Oliver countered as she fell silent, but Lisa wasn't really listening; she was too caught up in the shock of realising that the pain spearing her, pinning her in helpless, emotional agony where she stood, was caused by the realisation that for all she knew there could have been, could still be a woman in Oliver's life whom he loved.

'Stop thinking about it,' she heard Oliver telling her grimly, her face flushing at the thought that he had so easily read her mind and guessed what she was feeling, until he added, 'You must have seen for yourself that it would never have worked. Henry's mother would never have allowed him to marry you.'

Relief made her expel her breath in a leaky sigh. It had been Henry whom he had warned her to stop thinking about and not him. He had not guessed what she had been thinking or feeling after all.

'I thought we'd agreed a truce,' she reminded him, adding softly, 'I still haven't thanked you properly for everything you've done. Helping—'

'Everything?'

For some reason the way he was looking at her made her feel closer to the shy teenager she had once been than the adult woman she now was.

'I meant…' she began, and then shook her head, knowing that she wouldn't be able to list all the reasons she had to thank him without at some point having to look at him, and knowing that once she did her gaze would be drawn irresistibly to his mouth, and once it was…

'I… That turkey smells wonderful.' She gave in cravenly. 'How long did you say it would be before we could eat?'

She could tell from the wry look he gave her as she glanced his way that he wasn't deceived, but to her relief he didn't push matters, leaving her to follow him instead as he turned back towards the stairs.

CHAPTER SIX

'I NEVER IMAGINED you'd be so domesticated.'

They were both in the large, well-equipped, comfortable kitchen, Lisa mixing the ingredients for the bread sauce whilst Oliver deftly prepared the vegetables, and she knew almost as soon as she had voiced her surprise that it had been the wrong thing to say. But it was too late to recall her impulsive comment because Oliver had stopped what he was doing to look frowningly across at her.

'I'm sorry,' she apologised ruefully. 'I didn't mean to—'

'To sound patronising,' Oliver supplied for her.

Lisa glanced warily at him and then defended herself robustly, telling him, 'Well, when we first met you just didn't seem the type to—'

'The "type".' Oliver pulled her up a second time. 'And what "type" would that be, exactly?'

Oh, dear. He had every right to sound annoyed, Lisa acknowledged.

'I didn't mean it the way it sounded,' she confessed. 'It's just that Henry—'

'Doesn't so much as know how to boil an egg,' Oliver supplied contemptuously for her. 'And that's something to be admired in a man, is it?'

Lisa's face gave her away even before she had protested truthfully, 'No, of course it isn't.'

'The reason Henry chooses to see even the most basically necessary domestic chores such as cooking for himself as beneath his male dignity is because that's the way his mother has brought him up and that's the way she intends him to stay. And woe betide any woman who doesn't spoonfeed her little boy the way she's taught him to expect.'

There was no mistaking the disgust in Oliver's voice as he underlined the weakness of Henry's character, and Lisa knew that there was no real argument that she could put forward in Henry's defence, even if she had wanted to do so.

'It might come as something of a surprise to you,' Oliver continued sardonically, obviously determined to drive home his point, 'but, quite frankly, the majority of the male sex—at least the more emotionally mature section of it—would not take too kindly at having Henry held up to them as a yardstick of what it means to be a man. And neither, for future reference, do most of us relish being classified as a "type".'

'I didn't mean it like that,' Lisa protested. 'It's just that when we first met you seemed so… I could never have imagined you…us…' She was floundering, and badly, she recognised, adding lamely, 'I wasn't comparing you to Henry at all.'

'No?' Oliver challenged her.

'No,' Lisa insisted, not entirely truthfully. She *had* been comparing them, of course, but not, as Oliver fortunately had incorrectly assumed, to his disadvantage. Far from it… She certainly didn't want to have to explain to him that there was something about *him* that was so very male that it made laughable the idea that he should in any way fail to measure up to Henry.

Measure up to him! When it came to exhibiting that certain quality that spelled quite essential maleness there was simply no contest between them. Oliver possessed it, and in abundance, or so it seemed to Lisa, and Henry did not have it at all. She was faintly shocked that she should so clearly recognise this—and not just recognise it, she admitted uneasily. She was quite definitely somehow or other very sensitively aware of it as a woman—too aware of it for her peace of mind.

'I happen to have an orderly mind,' Oliver was telling her, thankfully unaware of what she was thinking, 'and I loathe any unnecessary waste of time. To live in the midst of chaos and disorder seems to be totally counter-productive, and besides...' he gave a small shrug and drained the peeled and washed potatoes, turning away from her as he started to cut them, so that she could not see his expression '...after my mother died and my father and I were on our own, we both had to learn how to look after ourselves.'

Lisa discovered that there was a very large lump in her throat as she pictured the solemn, lonely little boy and his equally lonely father struggling together to master their chores as well as their loss.

'The behavioural habits one learns as a child have a tendency to become deeply ingrained, hence my advice to you that you are well rid of Henry. He will never cease being his mother's spoilt and emotionally immature little boy...' His tasks finished, he turned round and looked directly at her as he added drily, 'And I suspect that you will never cease thinking of Christmas as a specially magical time of year...'

'No, I don't expect I shall,' Lisa admitted, adding honestly, 'But then I don't really want to. I don't suppose I'll ever stop wanting, either, to put down roots, to marry and have children and to give them the stability and permanence I missed as a child,' she confessed, wanting to be as open and honest with him as he had been with her.

'I know a lot of my friends think that I'm rather odd for putting more emphasis on stability and the kind of relationship that focuses more on that than on the romantic and sexual aspects of love—'

'Does there have to be a choice?' Oliver asked her.

Lisa frowned. 'What do you mean?'

'Isn't it possible for there to be romance and good sex between a couple, as well as stability and permanence? I thought the modern woman was determined to have it all. Emotional love, orgasmic sex, a passionately loyal mate, children, career...'

'In theory, yes,' Lisa agreed ruefully. 'But I suppose if I'm honest...I'm perhaps not very highly sexed. So—'

'Who told you that? Henry?'

'No,' she said, stung by the mocking amusement that she could see in his eyes, aware that she had allowed herself to be drawn onto potentially very treacherous ground and that sex was the very last topic she should be discussing with this particular man—especially when her body was suddenly and very dangerously reinforcing the lack of wisdom in her laying claim to a low libido when it was strongly refuting that. Too strongly for her peace of mind. Much, much too strongly.

'I...I've always known it,' she told him hastily, more to convince herself, she suspected, than him.

'Always...?' The way the dark eyebrows rose reminded her of the way he had looked when he had come round to see her and demand the return of Emma's clothes, and that same frisson of danger that she had felt then returned, but this time for a very, very different reason.

'Well, from when I was old enough... When I knew... After...' she began, compelled by the look he was giving her to make some kind of response.

'You mean you convinced yourself that you had a low sex drive because, presumably, that was what your first lover told you,' Oliver challenged her, cutting through her unsuccessful attempts to appear breezily nonchalant about the whole thing.

'It wasn't just because of that,' Lisa defended herself quickly and, she realised uneasily, very betrayingly.

'No?' Oliver's eyebrows rose again. 'I'll take a bet that

there haven't been very many… Two, maybe three at the most, and that, of course, excludes Henry, who—'

'Three…?' Lisa was aghast. 'Certainly not,' she denied vehemently. 'I would never…' Too late she realised what she was doing…what she was saying.

It was one thing for her to feel that, despite the amusement of her peers, she had the sort of nature that would not allow her to feel comfortable about sharing the intimacy of her body with a variety of lovers and that her low sex drive made it feel right that there had only been that one not really too successful experience in her late teens, and it was one thing to feel that she could quite happily remain celibate and wait to re-explore her sexuality until she found a man she felt comfortable enough with to do so, but it was quite another to admit it to someone like Oliver, who, she was pretty sure, would think her views archaic and ridiculous.

'So, there has only been one.' He pounced, immediately and humiliatingly correct. 'Well, for your information, a man who tells a virgin that she's got a low sex drive tends to be doing so to protect his own inadequacy, not hers.'

Her inadequacy! Lisa drew in a sharp breath of panic at the fact that he should dare so accurately and acutely to put her deepest and most intimate secret fears into words, and promptly fought back.

'I'm twenty-four now, not eighteen, and I think I know myself well enough to be able to judge for myself what kind of sex drive I have…'

'You're certainly old enough and, I would suspect, strong-willed enough to tell yourself what kind of sex drive you think it safe to allow yourself to have,' Oliver agreed, staggering her with not just his forthrightness but his incisive astuteness as well.

Pride warred with caution as Lisa was torn between demanding to know exactly what he meant and, more cravenly, avoiding what she suspected could be a highly dangerous confrontation—highly dangerous to her, that was. Oliver, she thought, would thoroughly enjoy dissecting her emotional vulnerabilities and laying them out one by one in front of her.

In the end caution won and, keeping her back to him, she told him wildly, 'I think this bread sauce is just about ready... What else would you like me to do?'

She thought she heard him mutter under his breath, 'Don't tempt me,' before he said far more clearly, 'Since it's Christmas Day I suppose we should really eat in the dining room, although normally I prefer to eat in here. I'll show you where everything is, and if you could sort it all out—silver, crystal, china...'

'Yes...of course,' Lisa agreed hurriedly, finding a cloth to wipe her hands on as she followed him back into the hall.

The dining room was a well-proportioned, warm, panelled room at the rear of the house, comfortably large enough to take a table which, Oliver explained to her, could be extended to seat twelve people.

'It was a wedding present to my grandparents. In those days, of course, twelve was not a particularly large number. My grandmother was one of seven and my grandfather one of five.'

'Oh, it must be wonderful to be part of a large family,' Lisa could not help commenting enviously. 'My parents were both onlys and they only had me.'

'Being an only child does have its advantages,' Oliver told her firmly. 'I'm an only myself, and—'

'But you had the family—aunts, uncles, cousins...'

'Yes,' Oliver agreed.

But he had also lost his mother at a very vulnerable age, Lisa recognised, and to lose someone so close must inevitably have a far more traumatic effect on one's life than the mere absence of a non-existent extended family.

'I can guess what you're thinking,' she told him wryly. 'I just sound pathetically self-absorbed and self-pitying. I know how much both my parents need their work, their art, how important it is to them. It's just that…'

'There have been times when you needed to know that you came first,' Oliver guessed shrewdly. 'There are times when we all feel like that,' he told her. 'When we all need to know that we come first, that we are the most important person in someone else's life… What's wrong?' he asked when he saw the rueful acknowledgement of his perception in Lisa's eyes.

'Nothing,' she said. 'It's just that I can't…that you don't…' She shook her head. 'You seem so self-contained,' was the only thing she could say.

'Do I?' He gave her a wry look. 'Maybe I am now. It wasn't always that way, though. The reason for the breakup of my first teenage romance was that my girlfriend found me too emotionally demanding. She was right as well.'

'You must have loved her an awful lot,' was all she could find to say as she tried to absorb and conceal the unwanted and betraying searing surge of envy that hit her as she listened to him.

'I certainly thought I did,' Oliver agreed drily, 'but the reality was little more than a very intense teenage crush. Still, at least I learned something from the experience.'

What had she been like, the girl Oliver had loved as a teenager? Lisa wondered ten minutes later when he had returned to the kitchen and she was removing silverware and crystal from the cupboards he had shown her.

She found it hard to imagine anyone—*any* woman—rejecting a man like him.

Her hand trembled slightly as she placed one of the heavy crystal wineglasses on the table.

What was the matter with her? she scolded herself. Just because he had kissed her, that didn't mean... It didn't mean anything, and why should she want it to? If she was going to think about any member of the male sex right now she ought to be thinking about Henry. After all, less than twenty-four hours ago she had believed that she was going to marry him.

It unnerved her a little bit to realise how far she had travelled emotionally in such a short space of time. It was hard to imagine now how she could ever have thought that she and Henry were suited—in any way.

'I really don't think I should be drinking any more of this,' Lisa told Oliver solemnly as she raised the glass of rich red wine that he had just refilled to her lips.

They had finished eating fifteen minutes earlier, and at Oliver's insistence Lisa was now curled up cosily in one corner of the deep, comfortable sofa that he had drawn up close to the fire and where she had been ordered to remain whilst he stacked the dishwasher.

The meal had been as good as any Christmas dinner she could ever remember eating and better than most. It had amazed her how easily the conversation had flowed between them, and what had surprised her even more was to discover that he was a very witty raconteur who could make her laugh.

Henry had never made her laugh.

Hastily she took a quick gulp of her wine. It was warm and full-bodied and the perfect accompaniment for the meal they had just enjoyed.

When they had left the table to come and sit down in front of the fire to finish their wine, Oliver had closed the curtains, and now, possessed by a sudden urge to see if it was still snowing, Lisa abandoned her comfortable seat and walked rather unsteadily towards the curtained window.

The wine had been even stronger than she had believed, she admitted. She wasn't drunk—far from it—but she certainly felt rather light-headed and a little giddy.

As she tugged back the curtain she gave a small, soft sigh of delight as she stared through the window.

It was still snowing—thick, whirling-dervish-like, thick white flakes, like those in a child's glass snowstorm. As she looked up into the darkening sky she could see the early evening stars and the thin sickle shape of the moon.

It was her childhood dream of a white Christmas come true. And to think that if she had returned to London as she had originally planned to do she would have missed it! Emotion caught her by the throat.

She dropped the curtain, turning back into the room, stopping as she saw Oliver watching her. She hadn't heard him come back in and unaccountably she could feel herself starting to tremble slightly.

'What is it? What's wrong?' he asked her.

'Nothing,' she denied. 'It's just…' She gave a small shrug, closed her eyes and then opened them again as the darkness increased the heady effects of the wine. 'It's just that all of this…is so…so perfect,' she told him huskily, gesturing to the room and then towards the window and the view that lay beyond it. 'So…so magical… This house…the weather…the tree…church this morning…my stocking and…'

'And…?' Oliver prompted softly.

He was looking at her very intently—so intently, in fact, that she felt as though she could drown in the dark intensity of his eyes, as though she was being compelled to…

'And you,' she breathed, and as she said it she felt her heart slam fiercely against her chest wall, depriving her of breath, whilst the silence between them seemed to pulse and quicken and to take on a life of its own.

'I really shouldn't drink any more of this,' she heard herself whispering dizzily as she picked up her glass and took a nervous gulp, and then watched as Oliver walked softly towards her.

'No, you really shouldn't,' he agreed as he reached her and took the glass from her unresisting fingers, and then he took her equally unresisting body in his arms and her quiescent mouth into the warm captivity of his.

'We shouldn't be doing this,' she reproached him, mumbling the words against his mouth, her arms wrapped around him, her fingers burrowing into the thick darkness of his hair, her eyes luminous with the desire that was turning her whole body into molten liquid as she gazed up into his eyes.

'Oh, yes, we should,' was his sensuously whispered response. 'Oh, yes, we most definitely, assuredly should.' And then he was kissing her again. Not forcefully, but oh, so compellingly that it was impossible for her to resist him—impossible for her to want to resist him.

'You've already kissed me once for Christmas,' Lisa reminded him unsteadily as he slowly lifted his mouth from hers and looked down at her.

'This isn't for Christmas,' he whispered back as his hand slid under her hair, tilting her head back up towards him, sliding his other hand down her back, urging her closer to his own body.

Lisa could feel her heart hammering against her ribs as sensations that she had never experienced before—not with Henry and certainly not with the man who had been her first and only lover—flooded her body.

'Then what is it for?' she forced herself to ask him huskily.

'What do you think?' Oliver responded rawly. 'I wanted you the first time I saw you—did you know that?'

'How could you have done?' Lisa argued. 'You were so furious with me, and—'

'And even more furious with myself...with my body for the way it was reacting to you,' Oliver told her, adding rawly, 'The same way it's reacting to you right now.'

Uncertainly Lisa searched his face. Everything was happening so quickly that she couldn't fully take it all in. If she had felt dizzy before, with the combination of the rich wine and the warm fire, that was nothing to the headiness affecting her now, clouding her ability to reason logically, making her heart thump dangerously, heavily as her body reacted to what was happening to her—to them.

'I'll stop if you want me to,' she heard Oliver telling her hoarsely as he bent his head and gently nuzzled the soft, warm flesh of her throat. As she stifled the small, betraying sound she made when her body shuddered in shocked pleasure Lisa shook her head.

'No. No. I don't want you to stop,' she admitted huskily.

'Good,' Oliver told her thickly. 'Because I don't want to either. What I want is you, Lisa... God, how I want you.'

'I'm not used to this,' Lisa said shakily. 'I don't—'

'Do you think that I am...that I do?' he interrupted her almost roughly. 'For God's sake, Lisa, have you any idea how long it is since I was this intimate with a woman...since I wanted to be this intimate with a woman? I'm not a teenager,' he half growled at her when she shook her head. 'I don't normally... It's been a hell of a long time since anyone has affected me the way you do... One hell of a long time.'

Lisa was trembling as he took her back in his arms, but not because she was afraid. Oh, no, not because of anything like that.

At any other time the eagerness with which she met Oliver's

kiss would have shocked her, caused her to deny what she was experiencing, but now, for some reason, things were different—*he* was different. This was Christmas, after all—a special, magical time when special, magical things could happen.

As she felt the probing thrust of Oliver's tongue she reached out towards him, wrapping her arms around him, opening her mouth to him.

Somewhere outside this magical, firelit, pine-scented world where it seemed the most natural thing of all for her and Oliver to come together like this there existed another, different world. Lisa knew that, but right now...right now...

As she heard the rough deep sound of pleasure that Oliver made in his throat when he tasted the honeyed interior of her mouth Lisa gave up trying to think and behave logically. There was no point and, even more important, there was no need.

Instead, as she slid her fingers through the thick softness of Oliver's hair, she let her tongue meet his—slowly, hesitantly at first, such intimacy unfamiliar to her. The memories of her much younger, uncertain teenage explorations recalled sensations which bore no resemblance whatsoever to the sensations she was experiencing now as Oliver's tongue caressed hers, the weight of his body erotically masculine against the more slender femininity of her own as his hands caressed her back, her waist, before sliding down over her hips to cup the soft swell of her buttocks as he lifted her against him.

Lisa knew already that he was aroused, but until she felt the taut fullness of his erection against her own body she hadn't realised how physically and emotionally vulnerable and responsive she was to him. A sensation, a need that was totally outside her previous experience overtook her as she felt the liquid heat filling her own body, her hips lifting automatically, blindly seeking the sensual intimacy that her flesh craved.

'So much for your low sex drive,' she heard Oliver muttering thickly against her ear, before he added throatily, 'You're one hell of a sexy lady, Lisa. Do you know that? Do you know what you're doing to me...? How you're making me feel...? How you've made me feel since you stood there in your flat in that damned suit, with your breasts...?'

Lisa heard him groan as his hand reached upwards towards her breast, sliding beneath the fabric that covered it to cup its soft, eager weight, his thumb-tip caressing the hard peak of her nipple.

'Let me take this off,' he urged her, his hands removing her jacket, and then starting on the buttons of the waistcoat underneath it, his eyes dark with arousal as he looked deeply into hers. And then, without waiting for her to respond, his mouth curled in a small, sensual half-smile and he bent his head and kissed her briefly but very hard on her half-parted mouth. 'I want to see you, Lisa—all of you. I want to touch you, hold you, taste you, and I want you to want to do the same as me.'

Lisa knew that he must have felt the racking, sensual shudder that convulsed her body even if he hadn't heard her immediate response to the mental image that his words had aroused, in the low groan she was not quite able to suppress.

'You want that,' he pressed huskily. 'You want me to undress for you. You want to see me...to touch me...' He was kissing her again now—slow, lingering kisses all over her face and throat—whilst his hands moved deftly, freeing her from her clothes. But it wasn't the thought of her own nakedness beneath his hands that was causing her breath to quicken and her heart to lurch frantically against her ribs, but rather the thought of his nakedness beneath hers.

What was happening to her? she wondered dazedly. Her, to whom the thought of a man's naked body was something which she normally found rather discomforting and not in the least erotic. What was happening that she should now be so filled with desire that her whole body ached and pulsed with it at the mere thought of seeing Oliver's? The mere thought… Heaven knew what she would be like when that thought became a reality, when she was free to reach out and touch and taste him too.

Helplessly she closed her eyes, and then opened them again to find Oliver watching her.

'*Is* that what you want, Lisa?' he asked her softly whilst his thumb-tip drew a sensual line of pleasure around her sensitised mouth. 'Is that what you want—to see me…touch me…feel me…?'

Dry-mouthed, Lisa nodded. Her top was unfastened now, and she was vaguely aware of the half-exposed curves of her breasts gilded by the firelight, but her own semi-nudity seemed unimportant and irrelevant; her whole concentration was focused on Oliver, on the deft, steady movements of his hands as he unfastened the buttons on his shirt, his gaze never wavering from her as he started to remove it.

His chest was broad and sleekly muscled, tanned, with a dark arrowing of silky black hair down the centre, the sight of which made her muscles clench and her breath leak from her lungs in a rusty ache of sensory overload. His nipples, flat and dark, looked so different from her own.

As his hands reached for the fastening on his trousers, Lisa leaned forward, acting on impulse. The scent of him filled her nostrils, clouding her thought processes, drugging her…

As her lips closed around the small dark nub of flesh, she made a soft sound of feminine pleasure deep in her throat. Her tongue-tip circled his flesh, stroked it, explored the shape and texture of it before she finally returned to sucking gently on it.

'Lisa.'

The shock of being wrenched away from him was like having her whole body plunged in icy-cold water after it had been lapped in tropical warmth, the pain so great that it made her physically ache and cry out, her shocked gaze focusing in bewilderment on Oliver's, quick emotional tears filming her eyes as she wondered what it was she had done, why it was that he was being so cruelly brutal with her.

'It's too much, too soon,' she heard him telling her harshly. 'I can't… It's…'

Still half in shock she watched him as he shook his head.

'You're turning me on too much,' he told her more gently, 'and I can't…'

Lisa could feel the shock of it all the way through her body—the shock and an intensely feminine thrill that she could have such a powerful effect on him. As though he had guessed what she was feeling, she heard Oliver groan softly, and then he was reaching for her, holding her in his arms before she could evade them, kissing her now tightly closed eyelids, and then her mouth, and then he was telling her, 'Another few seconds of that and right now I'd be inside you and without—' He broke off and then added, 'That isn't how I want it to be for our first time together.'

Lisa moved instinctively against him, and then tensed as she felt the rough brush of his body hair against her naked breasts.

As she bent her head to look down at where her top had slid away from her Oliver's gaze followed hers, and then he bent his head, slowly easing her top completely away from her as he gradually kissed his way down her body, stopping only when he had reached the dark pink tautness of her nipple.

As he closed his mouth on it, repeating on her the caress she had given him, Lisa tensed in shock beneath the surge of pleasure that arced through her, arching her spine, locking her hands against his head, making her shudder as her body, beneath the weight of the flooding waves of pleasure that pulsed through her, was activated by the now urgent suckle of his mouth on her breast.

Was this how *he* had felt when she had caressed him in the same way? No, it couldn't have been, she denied. She could feel what he was doing to her, right deep down within her body, her womb. She could feel... With a small, shocked gasp she started to push him away.

'What is it?' she heard Oliver asking thickly as he released her nipple. He was breathing heavily and she could feel the warmth against her skin resensitising it, making her...

'I...' Nothing, she had been about to respond, but instead she heard herself saying helplessly in an unfamiliar and huskily sensual voice, 'I want you, Oliver... I want you.'

'Not one half as much as I want you,' he responded tautly as she quickly removed the remainder of her clothes and his own, and then, like a mystical, almost myth-like personification of all that was male inspired by some Greek legend, and filling her receptive senses with that maleness, he knelt over her, his dark head bowed as he gently eased her back against the soft fabric of the sofa and made love to her with a sensuality that took her breath away.

It didn't matter that no man had ever touched her, caressed her, kissed her so intimately before or that she had never imagined wanting one to do so. Somehow, when it was Oliver's hands, Oliver's mouth that caressed her...

So this was desire, need, physically wanting someone with an intensity that could scarcely be borne.

Lisa gasped, caught her breath, held out her arms, her body opening to him, wanting him, enfolding him as she felt the first powerful thrust of him within her and then felt it again and again until her whole world, her whole being was concentrated on the powerful, rhythmic surge of his body within her own and the sensation that lay beyond it—the ache, the urgency...the release...

Lisa heard herself cry out, felt the quickening thrust of Oliver's body, the hard, harsh sound of his breathing and his thudding heartbeat as she clung to him, moved with him, against him, aching, urging and finally losing herself completely, drowning in the liquid pulse of pleasure that flooded through her.

Later, still drowsy, sated, relaxed as she lay within the protective curve of Oliver's body, she told him sleepily, 'I think this is the best Christmas I have ever had.'

She could feel as well as hear him laughing.

'You do wonders for my ego, do you know that?' he told her as he tilted her face up to his own and kissed her lingeringly on the mouth.

'It's the truth,' Lisa insisted, her eyes clouding slightly as she added more self-consciously, 'I...I never realised before that it could be so... That I could feel...'

'It?' Oliver teased her.

'Sex,' Lisa told him with dignity.

'Sex?' She heard the question in his voice. She looked uncertainly up at him. He looked slightly withdrawn, his expression stern, forbidding...more like the Oliver she had first met than the man who had just held her in his arms and made such wonderful, cataclysmic, orgasmic love to her.

'What's wrong?' she asked him hesitantly, her heart starting to thump nervously. Wasn't this what all the books warned you about—the man's withdrawal and coldness after the act of sex had been completed, his desire to separate himself from his partner whilst she wanted to maintain their intimacy and to share with him her emotional awe at the physical pleasure their bodies had given one another?

'What we just shared may have been sex to you,' he told her quietly, 'but for me it was more than that. For me it was making love in the true sense of those words. Experimenting teenagers, shallow adults without maturity or sensitivity have sex, Lisa…'

'I don't understand,' she told him huskily, groping through the confusion of her thoughts and feelings to find the right words. 'I… You… We don't really know one another and…'

'And what?' Oliver challenged her. 'Because of that we can't have any feelings for one another?' He shook his head. 'I disagree.'

'But until today…until now…we didn't even like one another… We…'

'We what?' Oliver prompted her as she came to an uncertain stop. 'We were very physically aware of one another.'

Lisa opened her mouth to deny what he was saying and then closed it again.

'Not so very long ago you told me that you wanted me,' Oliver reminded her softly, 'and I certainly wanted you. I agree that the circumstances under which we met initially clouded our ability to judge one another clearly, but fate has given us an opportunity to start again…a second chance.'

'Twenty-four hours ago I was still planning to marry Henry,' Lisa protested helplessly.

'Twenty-four hours ago I still wanted to wring your pretty little neck,' Oliver offered with a smile.

'What's happening to us, Oliver?' she asked him uneasily. 'I don't understand.' She sat up and pushed the heavy weight of her hair off her face, her forehead creased in an anxious frown. 'I just don't do things like this. I've never… I thought it must be the wine at first… That…'

'That what? That the effect of three glasses of red wine was enough to make you want me?' He gave her a wry look. 'Well, I haven't even got that excuse. Not then, and certainly not now,' he added huskily as he reached towards her and took hold of her hand, guiding it towards his body whilst he bent his head and kissed her slowly.

To be aroused by him the first time might just possibly have been some kind of fluke, Lisa acknowledged, but there was no way she could blame her desire for him now on the wine. Not a second time, not now. And she did desire him, she acknowledged shakily as her fingers explored the hard strength of him. Oh, yes, she did want him.

It was gone midnight before they finally went upstairs, Lisa pausing to draw back the curtains and look out on the silent, snow-covered garden.

'It's still snowing,' she whispered to Oliver.

'Mmm...' he agreed, nuzzling the back of her neck. 'So it is... Lovely...'

But it wasn't the view through the window he was studying as he murmured his rich approval, and Lisa laughed softly as she saw the way he was studying her still naked breasts.

'No,' Oliver said to her, shaking his head as she paused outside the guest-bedroom door. 'Tonight I want you to sleep with me...in my bed...in my arms,' he told her, and as she listened to him Lisa felt her heart flood with emotion.

It was too soon yet to know just how she really felt about him, or so she told herself. And too dangerous, surely, when her body was still flooded with the pleasure he had given it? She was by nature cautious and careful; she always had been. It wasn't possible for her to fall in love over the space of a few hours with a man she barely knew.

But then less than twenty-four hours ago she would also have vehemently denied that it was possible for her to want that same man so much and with such a degree of intensity that, as he drew her towards his bed and held out his arms to her, her body was already starting to go liquid with pleasure and yearning for him.

CHAPTER SEVEN

'OUCH. THAT'S NOT FAIR. I was retying the snowman's scarf.'

Lisa laughed as Oliver removed from his collar the wet snow of the snowball she had just thrown at him, quickly darting out of the way as he bent down mock-threateningly to make a retaliatory snowball of his own.

She had been awoken two hours earlier by the soft thud of a snowball against the bedroom window, Oliver's half of the bed that they had shared all night being empty. Intrigued and amused, she had slid out of bed, wrapping the quilt around her naked body as she'd hurried across to the window. As she'd peered out she'd been able to see beneath the window Oliver standing in the garden next to a huge snowman, a pile of snowballs stacked at his feet.

'At last, sleepyhead, I thought you were never going to wake up,' he'd teased her as she had opened the window, laughing at her as she'd gasped a little at the cold shock of the frosty air.

'I'm not sleepy,' Lisa had corrected him indignantly. 'It's just that I'm…' she had begun, and then had stopped, flushing slightly as she'd acknowledged the real reason why her body was aching so deliciously, why her energy was so depleted.

As Oliver had looked silently back at her she had known that he too was remembering just why it was that she had fallen into such a deep sleep in the early hours of the morning.

She was remembering the night, the *hours* they had spent

together again now as she went to help him brush the snow from his collar, the scent of him, overlaid by the crisp, fresh smell of the snow, completely familiar to her now and yet at the same time still headily erotic.

When previously she had read of women being aroused by the body smell of their lover she had wrinkled her own nose just a little fastidiously, never imagining that there would ever come a time when she not only knew just how those women had felt but also actively wanted—no, *needed*, she corrected herself as her stomach muscles clenched on a weakening surge of emotion—to bury her face against her lover's body and breathe his scent, to trace the outline of his bones, his muscles, absorb the texture of his flesh and the whole living, breathing essence of him.

'It's too soon for this…for us…' she had whispered shakily last night in the aftermath of their second loving. 'We can't be…'

'Falling in love,' Oliver had supplied for her, and had challenged her softly between kisses. 'Why not? People do.

'What is it you're really afraid of, Lisa?' he had asked her later still, after his mouth had caressed every inch of her body, driven her to unimaginable heights of ecstasy and he had whispered to her that she was everything he had ever dreamed of finding in a woman…everything he'd begun to think he would never find, and she had tensed in his arms, suddenly afraid to let herself respond to him as her senses were urging her to do, to throw caution to the wind to tell him what she was feeling.

'I'm afraid of this,' she had whispered huskily back, 'of you…'

'Of me?' He held her slightly away from him, frowning at her in the darkness. 'Look, I know the circumstances surrounding our initial meeting weren't exactly auspicious, and yes, I agree, I did rather come the heavy, but to be confronted with Piers within thirty minutes of my plane landing from New York after a delay of over five hours and to discover what he'd done—'

'No, it's not that,' Lisa assured him quickly. She was fully aware now that the arrogance that she had believed she had seen in him was simply part of a protective mask behind which he hid his real personality. 'It's us…us together,' she told him, searching for the right words to express her feelings. 'I'm afraid that…everything's happening so fast. And it's not…I'm not…

'This isn't how I ever thought it would be for me,' she told him simply in the end. 'I never imagined I could feel so…that I could…' She paused, fumbling for the words and blushed a little as she tried to tell him how bemused, how shocked, almost, she still was by the intensity not just of his desire for her but of her own for him. It was so out of character for her, she told him, so unexpected…

'So unwanted,' he guessed shrewdly.

'It isn't how I thought my life was going to be,' she persisted. 'None of it seems quite real, and I'm afraid. I don't know if I can sustain this level of emotional intensity, Oliver… I feel like a child who has been handed a Christmas gift so far outside its expectations that it daren't believe it's actually got it. I'm afraid of letting myself believe because I'm afraid of the pain I'll suffer if…if it proves not to be real after all.'

'Don't you think I feel exactly the same way?' Oliver challenged her.

'You've been in love before,' she told him quietly. 'You've experienced this kind of sexual intimacy…sexual ecstasy before, but I—'

'No.' He shook his head decisively. 'Yes, I'm more sexually experienced than you are, but *this*… Take my word for it, Lisa—this is something different…something special.

'Look,' he added when she said nothing. 'With all this

snow, there's no way either of us can leave here now until it thaws; let's use the time to be together, to get to know one another, to give our feelings for one another a chance. Let's suspend reality, if you like, for a few days and just allow ourselves to feel instead of questioning, doubting...'

He had made it all sound so easy, and it was easy, Lisa acknowledged now as his arms closed around her. Too easy... That was the trouble.

Already after only a few short, fateful hours she was finding it hard to imagine how she had ever lived without him and even harder to imagine how she could ever live without him in the future. It would be so easy simply to close her eyes, close her mind to her thoughts and concentrate instead on her feelings. She could feel her heart starting to thump heavily with the intensity of her emotions.

'Stop worrying,' Oliver whispered against her mouth, correctly guessing what she was thinking. 'Everything's going to be fine. We're going to be fine.'

'This really is the best Christmas I have ever had,' she told him huskily ten minutes later as he lifted his mouth from hers.

'*You* are the best Christmas I have ever had,' Oliver responded. 'The best Christmas I ever will have.'

In the end they had four full days together, held for three of them in a captivity from which neither of them truly wanted to escape by the icy frost that kept the roads snowbound. And during those four days Lisa quickly discovered how wrong she had been in her original assessment of Oliver as being arrogantly uncaring.

He did care, and very deeply, about those who were closest to him but, as he freely admitted, the loss of his mother whilst he had still been so young had made him cautious about allowing others to get too close to him too quickly.

'But of course there are exceptions to every rule,' he had told her huskily, 'and *you* are my exception.'

She had given up protesting then that it was too soon for them to be in love. What was the point in denying what she knew she felt about him?

'I still can't believe that this...that we...that it's all really happening,' she whispered to Oliver on the fourth morning, when the thaw finally set in, her voice low and hushed, as though she was half-afraid of even putting her doubts into words.

'It *is* happening,' Oliver reassured her firmly, 'and it's going to go on happening for the rest of our lives.'

They were outside, Lisa watching as Oliver chopped logs to replace those they had used. Dressed in jeans and a black T-shirt, he had already discarded the checked woollen shirt that he had originally been wearing, the muscles and tendons on his upper arms revealed by the upward swing of the axe as he chopped the thick fir trunks into neatly quartered logs.

There was something about watching a man engaged in this kind of hard physical activity that created a feminine frisson of awareness of his masculinity, Lisa acknowledged as Oliver paused to wipe the sweat from his skin. She didn't want this special time that they were sharing to come to an end, she admitted. She was afraid of what might happen when it did. Everything had happened so fast—too fast?

'Nearly finished,' Oliver told her, mistaking the reason for her silence. 'I should be back from New York by the end of the week,' he added as Lisa bent down to retrieve the logs that he had already cut and carry them over to where the others were neatly stacked.

Lisa already knew that he was booked on a flight to New York to complete some protracted and difficult business talks he had begun before Christmas—the reason he had been so irritable and uncompromising the first time they had met, he had explained to her.

'I wish I didn't have to go,' he added, 'but at least we'll be able to spend New Year's Eve together and then… When are your parents due back from Japan?'

'Not until the end of February,' Lisa told him.

'That long.' He put down the axe and demanded hastily, 'Come here.'

Automatically Lisa walked towards him. The hand he extended to cup the side of her face and caress her skin smelled of freshly cut wood and felt slightly and very, very sensually abrasive, and the small shiver that ran through her body as he touched her had nothing to do with being cold.

'I could take some leave at the end of January and we could fly out to Japan together to see them then…'

Lisa knew what he was suggesting and her heart gave a fierce bound. So far they had not talked seriously about the future. Oliver had attempted to do so but on each occasion she had forestalled him, not wanting to do or say anything that might destroy the magic of what they were sharing, fearing that by allowing reality and practicality into their fragile, self-created world they might damage it. Their relationship, their love was so different from anything she had ever imagined experiencing or wanting to experience that part of her was still half-afraid to trust it…half of her?

And besides, she had already written to her parents to tell them that she and Henry would be getting engaged at Christmas and, whilst she suspected that they would never have been particularly keen on the idea of having Henry for a son-in-law, she felt acutely self-conscious about suddenly informing them that she had fallen head over heels in love with someone else.

It was so out of character for her, and the mere thought of having to confess her feelings for Oliver to anyone else made her feel defensive and vulnerable. She had always taken such a pride in being sensible and level-headed, in making carefully thought-out and structured decisions about her life. She wasn't sure how she herself really felt about this new aspect to her personality yet, never mind being ready to expose it to anyone else.

'What's wrong?' Oliver asked her as he felt her tensing against his touch. 'You don't seem very happy with the idea of me meeting your parents.'

'It's not that,' Lisa denied. There was, she had discovered, an unexpected corner of vulnerability in him which she suspected sprang from the loss of his mother—something that, if not exactly a fear of losing those close to him, certainly made him slightly more masculinely possessive than she would have expected in such an otherwise controlled and strongly emotionally grounded man. And it was, at least in part, because of this vulnerability that she had felt unable to tell him of her own fears and uncertainties.

'No? Then what exactly is it? Or is that yet another subject you don't want to discuss?' Oliver asked her sarcastically as he released her and picked up the axe, hefting it, raising it and then bringing it down on the log that he had just positioned with a force that betrayed his pent-up feelings.

Dismayed, Lisa watched him. What could she say? How could she explain without angering him still further? How could she explain to him what she felt when she truthfully didn't fully understand those feelings herself?

'It isn't that I don't want you to meet them,' she insisted. 'It's just…well, they don't even know yet that Henry and I aren't…' She knew immediately that she had said the wrong thing and winced as she witnessed the fury with which Oliver sliced into the unresisting wood, splitting it with one unbelievably powerful blow, the muscles in his arms cording and bunching as he tightened his grip on the axe.

'You're saying that they'd prefer you to be marrying Henry, is that it?' he suggested dangerously.

'No, of course they wouldn't,' Lisa denied impatiently. 'And besides, I'm old enough to be able to make up my own mind about who I want to commit myself to.'

'Now we're coming to it, aren't we?' Oliver told her, throwing down the axe and confronting her angrily, his hands on his hips, the faded fabric of his jeans stretching tautly against his thighs.

Just the sight of him made her body ache, Lisa acknowledged, but physical desire, sexual desire, could surely never be enough to build an enduring relationship on? And certainly it was not what she had envisaged building a lifetime's commitment on.

'It's not your parents who might reject me, is it, Lisa? It's you... Despite everything that has happened, all that we've shared.'

'No, that isn't true,' Lisa denied.

'Isn't it?' Oliver bit out grimly as he turned away from her to pick up another large chunk of wood.

Numbly Lisa watched him manhandling it onto the trestles that he was using to support the fir trunks whilst he chopped them into more easily manageable pieces. Above them the sky had started to cloud over, obliterating the bright promise of the morning's sunshine, making her feel shivery and inadequately protected from the nasty, raw little wind which had sprung up, even in the fine wool jacket she was wearing.

The weather, she recognised miserably, was very much only echoing what was happening to them—the bright promise of what they had shared was being threatened by the ominous thunderclouds furrowing Oliver's forehead and her own fear that what he had claimed he felt for her might prove too ephemeral to last.

After all, wasn't the classic advice always to treat falling in love too quickly and too passionately with caution and suspicion? Wasn't it an accepted rationale that good love—real love—needed time to grow and didn't just happen overnight?

As she watched Oliver silently releasing his anger on the wood, his jaw hardening a little bit more with each fierce blow of the axe, Lisa knew that she couldn't blame him for what he was feeling, but surely he could understand that it wasn't easy for her either? She was not programmed mentally for the kind of thing that had happened to her with him; she had not been prepared for it either, not...

'There's no need for you to stay.'

Lisa stared at Oliver as she heard the harsh words, the cutting edge to his voice reminding her more of the man she had first met than the lover she had become familiar with over the last few precious days.

'The wind's getting cold and you're shivering,' he added when she continued to stare mutely at him. 'You might as well go back inside; I've nearly finished anyway.'

He meant that there was no need for her to stay outside and wait for him, Lisa realised, and not that she might as well leave him and start her return journey home, as she had first imagined.

The relief that filled her was only temporary, though. Didn't the fact that she had so easily made such a mistake merely confirm what her sense of caution was already trying to make her understand—that she didn't really *know* Oliver, that no matter how compatible they might be in bed out of it there were still some very large and very important gaps in their knowledge of each other?

Quietly she turned away from him and started to walk back towards the house. Behind her she heard the sound of the axe hitting a fresh piece of wood. She had almost reached the house when she heard Oliver calling her name.

Stopping, she turned to watch him warily as he came running towards her.

As he reached her he took hold of her, wrapping her in his arms, telling her fiercely, 'God, Lisa, I'm such a... I'm sorry... the last thing I want us to do is fight, especially when we've got so little time left... Lisa?'

As she looked up at him he cupped her face in his hands, his thumbs caressing her skin, his hair tousled from the wind, his eyes dark with emotion.

Standing close to him like this, feeling the fierce beat of his heart and the heat of his body, breathing in the scent of him, unable to resist the temptation to lift her hand and rub away the streak of dried earth on his cheek, to feel already the beginning of the growth of his beard on his jaw which he had shaved only that morning, Lisa acknowledged that she might just as well have downed a double helping of some fatally irresistible aphrodisiac.

'Lisa...'

His voice was lower now, huskier, more questioning, and she knew that the shudder she could feel going through him had nothing to do with the after-effects of the punishing force he had used to cut up the logs.

She was the one who was responsible for that weakness, for that look in his eyes, that hardness in his body, and she knew that she was responding to it, as unable to deny him as he was her, her body nestling closer to his, her head lifting, her lips parting as he started to kiss her, tenderly at first and then with increasing passion.

'I can't bear the thought of losing you,' he whispered to her minutes later, his voice husky and raw with emotion. 'But you don't seem so concerned. What is it, Lisa...? Why won't—?'

'It's too soon, Oliver, too early,' Lisa protested, interrupting him, knowing that if she didn't stand her ground now, if she allowed her brain to be swayed not just by his emotions but by her own as well, it would be oh, so fatally easy, standing with him like this now, held in his arms, to believe that nothing but this mattered—it would be too late, and there would be no one but herself to blame if at some future date she discovered…

'I could make you commit yourself to me,' Oliver warned her, his mood changing as his earlier impatience returned. 'I could take you to bed now and show you…'

'Yes, you could,' Lisa agreed painfully. 'But can't you see, Oliver…? Please try to understand,' she begged him. 'It isn't that I don't love you or want you; it's just that…this…this… us…isn't how I envisaged it would be for me. You're just not the kind of man I—'

'You mean that I'm not Henry,' Oliver supplied harshly for her, his arms dropping back to his sides as he stepped back from her.

Lisa closed her eyes. Here we go again, she thought tiredly. She had meant one thing and Oliver had taken the words to mean something completely different—just as she had misunderstood him earlier when she had thought he was telling her to leave. And if they could misunderstand one another so easily what real chance did they have of developing the harmonious, placid relationship that she had always believed she needed? Some people enjoyed quarrels, fights, emotional highs and lows, but she just was not one of them.

'I don't want to fight with you, Oliver,' she told him quietly now. 'You must know that you have no possible reason to feel…to think that I want you to be Henry…'

'Haven't I?' he demanded bitterly. 'Why not? After all, you were prepared to marry him. Wanted to marry him… Wanted to so much in fact that you were prepared to let his mother browbeat and bully you and—'

'That's not true,' Lisa interrupted him swiftly. 'Look, Oliver, please,' she protested, spreading her hands in a gesture of emotive pleading for his temperance and understanding. 'Please... I can't talk. I don't want us to argue...not now, when everything has been so...perfect, so special and—'

'So perfect and special in fact that you don't want to continue it,' Oliver cut across her bitterly.

'You've given me the most wonderful Christmas I've ever had,' she whispered huskily, 'in so many different ways, in all the best of ways. Please don't spoil that for me...for us...now. I need time, though, Oliver; we *both* need time. It's just...'

'Just what?' he demanded, his eyes still ominously watchful and hard. 'Just that you're still not quite sure...that a part of you still thinks that perhaps Henry—?'

'No. Never,' Lisa insisted fiercely, adding more emotionally, 'That's a horrible thing to say. Do you really think that if I had any doubts about...about wanting you, that I would have—?'

'I didn't say that you don't prefer me in bed,' Oliver told her curtly, correctly guessing what she had been about to say, 'but the implication was there none the less—in the very words you used to describe what you wanted from marriage the first time we discussed it, the fact that you've been so reluctant to accept what's happening between us...the fact that you don't seem to want me to meet your parents.'

'You've got it all wrong,' she protested. 'My feelings...my doubts,' she amended when he snorted derisively over her use of the word 'feelings', 'they...they don't have anything to do with you. It isn't because I don't...because I don't care; in fact—'

'Oh, no,' Oliver told her cynically, not allowing her to finish what she was saying.

'It's me...not you,' Lisa told him. 'I've always been so cautious, so...so sensible... This...this falling in love with you— well, it's just so out of character for me and I'm afraid.'

'You're afraid of what?' he demanded.

The wind had picked up and was flattening his T-shirt against his body, but, unlike her, he seemed impervious to the cold and Lisa had to resist the temptation to creep closer to him and beg him to wrap his arms protectively around her to hold her and warm her.

'I don't know,' she answered, lifting her eyes to meet his as she added, 'I'm just afraid.'

How could she tell him without adding to his anger that a good part of what she feared was that he might fall out of love with her as quickly as he had fallen in love with her? He was quite obviously in no mood to understand her vulnerability and fear and she knew that he would take her comment as an indication that she did not fully trust him, an excuse or a refusal to commit herself to him completely.

'Please don't let's quarrel,' she repeated, reaching out her hand to touch his arm. His skin felt warm, the muscles taut beneath her touch, and the sensation of his flesh beneath her own even in this lightest of touches overwhelmed her with such an intense wave of desire that she had to bite down hard on her bottom lip to prevent herself crying out her need to him.

They were still standing outside, and through the windows she could see the tree that he had decorated for her, the magic he had created for her.

'Oh, Oliver,' she whispered shakily.

'Let's go inside,' he responded gruffly. 'You're getting cold and I'm... You're right,' he added rawly. 'We shouldn't be spoiling what little time we've got left.'

'It is still Christmas, isn't it?' Lisa asked him semi-pleadingly as he turned to open the door for her.

'Yes, it's still Christmas,' he agreed, but there was a look in his eyes that made her heart ache and warned her that Christmas could not be made to last for ever—like their love?

Was *that* why she doubted it—him? Because it seemed too perfect, too wonderful…too precious to be real?

They said their private goodbyes very early in the morning in the bedroom they had shared for the last four nights, and for Lisa the desolation which swept over her at the thought that for the next two nights to come she would not be sleeping within the protection of his arms, next to the warmth and intimacy of his body, only confirmed what in her heart of hearts she already knew.

It was already too late for her to protest that it was too soon for them to fall in love, too late to cling to the sensible guidelines that she had laid down for herself to live her life by: the sensible, cautious, pain-free guidelines which in reality had been submerged and obliterated days ago—from the first time that Oliver had kissed her, if she was honest—and there were tears in her eyes as she clung to him and kissed him.

What was she doing? she asked herself helplessly. What did guidelines, common sense, caution or even potential future heartache matter when they had this, when they had one another; when by simply opening her mouth and speaking honestly and from her heart she could tell Oliver what she was feeling and that she had changed her mind, that the last thing she wanted was to be apart from him?

'Oliver…' she began huskily.

But he shook his head and placed his fingertips over her mouth and told her softly, 'It's all right—I know. And I do understand. You're quite right—we do need time apart to think things through clearly. I've been guilty of trying to bully you, to coerce you into committing yourself to me too soon. Love—real love—doesn't disappear or vanish when two people aren't physically together; if anything, it strengthens and grows.

'I didn't mean to put pressure on you, Lisa, to rush you. We both have lives, commitments, career responsibilities to deal with. The weather has given us a special opportunity to be together, to discover one another, but the snow, like Christmas, can't last for ever.

'If I'd managed to get you to come to New York with me as I wanted, I probably wouldn't have got a stroke of work done,' he told her wryly. 'And a successful conclusion to these negotiations is vitally important for the future of the business—not just for me personally but for everyone else who is involved in it as well. Oh, and by the way, don't worry about not taking your car now; I'll make arrangements to have it picked up and returned to you later. I don't want you driving with the roads like this.'

Oliver had already told her about a large American corporation's desire to buy out part of his business, leaving him free to concentrate on the aspects of it he preferred and giving him the option to work from home.

'If Piers goes ahead and marries Emma, as he's planning, he's going to need the security of knowing he has a good financial future ahead of him. Naturally the Americans want to get the business as cheaply as they can.' He had started to frown slightly, and Lisa guessed that his thoughts were not so much on her and their relationship but on the heavy responsibility that lay ahead of him.

Her throat ached with pain; she desperately wanted to reach out to him and be taken in his arms, to tell him that she had made a mistake, that she didn't want to let him go even for a few short days. But how could she now after what he had said?

Suddenly, illuminatingly, she realised that what she had feared was not loving him but losing him. The space that she had told herself she needed—they both needed—had simply been a trick her brain had played on her, a coping mechanism to help her deal with the pain of being without his love.

Quietly she bowed her head. 'Thank you,' Lisa whispered to him as tears blurred her eyes.

'Are you sure there's nothing else you want...a book or...?'

Lisa shook her head. 'You've already bought me all these magazines,' she reminded Oliver huskily, indicating the pile of glossies that he had insisted on buying for her when they'd reached the station and which he was still carrying for her, together with her case, as he walked her along the platform to where the train was waiting.

She had tried to protest when he had insisted on buying her a first-class ticket but he had refused to listen, shaking his head and telling her, 'That damned independence of yours. Can't you at least let me do something for you, even if it's only to ensure that you travel home in some degree of comfort?'

She had, of course, given in then. How could she not have done so? How could she have refused not just his generosity but, she sensed, from the expression in his eyes at least, his desire to protect and cherish her as well?

'Make sure you have something to eat,' he urged her as they reached the train. 'It will be a long journey and...'

And she wouldn't be spending it eating, Lisa thought as he went on talking. Nor would she be doing anything more than flipping through the expensive magazines he had bought her. No, what she would be doing would be trying to hold back the tears and wishing that she were with him, thinking about him, reliving every single moment they had spent together...

A family—mother, father, three small children—paused to turn round and hug the grandparents; the smallest of them, a fair-haired little boy, clung to his grandmother, telling her, 'I don't want to go, Nana... Why can't you come home with us...?'

'I have to stay here and look after Grandpa,' his grandmother told him, but Lisa could hear the emotion in her voice and see the tears she was trying not to let him see.

Why did loving someone always seem to have to cause so much pain?

'Oh, to be his age and young enough to show what you're feeling,' Oliver murmured under his breath.

'It wouldn't make any difference if I did beg you to come home with me,' Lisa pointed out, trying to sound light-hearted but horribly aware that he must be able to hear the emotion in her voice. 'You'd still have to go to New York. We'd still have to be apart...'

'Yes, but I... At least I'd know that you want me.'

It was too much. What was the point in being sensible and listening to the voice of caution when all she really wanted to do was to be with him, to be held in his arms, to tell him that she loved and wanted him and that all she wanted—all she would ever want or need—was to be loved by him?

He was looking at her...watching...waiting almost.

'Oliver...' She wanted so desperately to tell him how she felt, to hear him tell her that he understood her vulnerability and that he understood all the things she hadn't been able to bring herself to say, but the guard was already starting to close the carriage doors, advancing towards them, asking her frowningly, 'Are you travelling, miss, because if so...?'

'Yes... Yes...'

'You'd better get on,' Oliver advised her.

She didn't want to go. She didn't want to leave him. Lisa could feel herself starting to panic, wanting to cling to him, wanting him to hold her...reassure her, but he was already starting to move away from her, lifting her case onto the train for her, bending his head to kiss her fiercely but far, far too briefly.

She had no alternative. She had to go.

Numbly Lisa stepped up into the train. The guard slammed

the door. She let down the window but the train was already starting to move.

'Oliver. Oliver, I love you...'

Had he heard her, or had the train already moved too far away? She could still see him...watching her...just.

Oliver waited until the train had completely disappeared before turning to leave, even though Lisa had long since gone from view. If only he didn't have these damned negotiations to conclude in New York. He wanted to be with Lisa, wanted to find a way to convince her.

Of what...? That she loved him?

Lisa pushed open the door of her flat and removed the pile of mail which had accumulated behind it. Despite the central heating, the flat felt cold and empty, but then that was perhaps because *she* felt cold and empty, Lisa recognised wryly—cold without Oliver's warmth beside her and empty without him... his love.

In her sitting room the invitation she had received from her friend Alison before Christmas to her annual New Year's Eve party was still propped up on the mantelpiece, reminding her that she would have to ring Alison and cancel her acceptance. The telephone started to ring, breaking into the silence. Her heart thumping, she picked up the receiver.

'You got home safely, then.'

'Oliver.'

Suddenly she was smiling. Suddenly the world was a warmer, brighter, happier place.

'Lisa, I've been thinking about what you said about us not rushing into things...about taking our time...'

Something about the sombreness in his voice checked the happiness bubbling up inside her, turning the warmth at hearing his voice to icy foreboding.

'Oliver...'

Lisa wanted to tell him how much she was missing him, how much she loved him, but suddenly she wasn't sure if that was what he wanted to hear.

'Look, Lisa, I've got to go. They've just made the last call for my flight...' The phone line went dead.

Silently she replaced the receiver. Had it really only been this morning that he had held her in his arms and told her how much he loved her? Suddenly, frighteningly, it was hard to believe that that was true. It seemed like another world, another lifetime, already in the past...over...as ephemeral as the fleeting magic of Christmas itself.

'No...it's not true,' she whispered painfully under her breath. 'He loves me; he said so.' But somehow her reassurance lacked conviction.

Even though she had been the one to insist that it was too soon for them to make a public commitment to one another, that they both needed time, she wished passionately now that Oliver had overruled her, that he had confirmed the power and strength of his love for her. How? By refusing to let her leave him?

What was the matter with her? Lisa asked herself impatiently. Could she really be so illogical, saying one thing, wanting another, torn between her emotions and her intelligence, unable to harmonise the two, keeping them in separate compartments in much the same way as Oliver had accused her of doing with sex and marriage?

Had she after all any real right to feel chagrined at the sense of urgency, almost of impatience in his voice as he had ended his brief call? She had, she admitted, during the last few days grown accustomed to being the sole focus of his attention, and now, when it was plain that he had something else on his mind...

She frowned, aware that instead of feeling relief when he

had told her that he agreed that they did need time to think things over she had actually felt—*still* felt—hurt and afraid, abandoned, vulnerably aware that he might be having second thoughts about his feelings for her.

How ironic if he had—especially since she had spent almost the entire journey home dwelling on the intensity of her own feelings and allowing herself to believe...

It would only be a few days before they were together again, she reminded herself firmly. Oliver had promised that he would be back for the New Year and that they would spend it together. There would be plenty of time for them to talk, for her to tell him how much she loved and missed him.

Even so... Sternly she made herself pick up her case and carry it through to her bedroom to unpack. A small, tender smile curled her mouth as she picked up the stocking that she had so carefully packed—the stocking that Oliver had left for her to find on Christmas morning.

There were other sentimental mementoes as well—a small box full of pine needles off the tree, still carrying its rich scent, the baubles that Oliver had removed from it and hung teasingly on her ears one night after dinner, a cracker that they had pulled together... She touched each and every one of them gently.

Through what he had done for her to make her Christmas so special Oliver had revealed a tender, compassionate, emotional side to his nature that made it impossible for her not to love him, not to respond to the love he had shown her. *Had* shown her?

Stop it, she warned herself. Stop creating problems that don't exist. Determinedly, she started to unpack the rest of her things.

CHAPTER EIGHT

IT WAS NEW YEAR'S EVE and almost three o'clock in the afternoon, and still Oliver hadn't rung. Lisa glared at the silent telephone, mentally willing it to ring. She had been awake since six o'clock in the morning and gradually, as the hours had ticked by, her elation and excitement had changed to edgy apprehension.

Where *was* Oliver? *Why* hadn't he been in touch? Was he just going to arrive at her door without any warning so that he could surprise her, instead of telephoning beforehand as she had anticipated?

Nervously she smoothed down the skirt of her dress and just managed to restrain herself from checking her reflection in the mirror for the umpteenth time.

She had spent most of her free time the previous day cleaning the flat and shopping for tonight. The lilies she had bought with such excitement and pleasure were now beginning to overpower her slightly with their scent. The champagne waiting in the fridge was surely chilled to perfection; the special meal she had cooked last night now only required reheating. Oliver might be planning to take her out somewhere for dinner, but the last thing she wanted was to have to share him with anyone else.

And even if she had dressed elegantly enough to dine at the most exclusive restaurant in town and her hair was immaculately shiny, her make-up subtly enhancing her features, it was not to win the approval of the public at large that she had taken such pains with her appearance, or donned the sheer, silky stockings, or bought that outrageously expensive and far too frothily impractical new silk underwear. Oh, no!

Where *was* Oliver? Why hadn't he been in touch? The small dining table which was all her flat could accommodate was lovingly polished and set with her small collection of good silver and crystal—unlike Oliver's grandparents she did not possess a matching set of a dozen of anything, and her parents, peripatetic gypsy souls that they were, would have laughed at the very idea of burdening themselves with such possessions.

However, through her work Lisa had developed a very good eye for a bargain, and the small pieces that she had lovingly collected over the years betrayed, she knew, the side of her nature that secretly would have enjoyed nothing better than using her dormant housewifely talents to garner a good old-fashioned bridal bottom drawer.

To help pass the time she tried to imagine Oliver's eventual arrival, her heartbeat starting to pick up and then race as she visualised herself opening the door to him and seeing him standing there, reaching out for her, holding her, telling her how much he had missed her and loved her.

Oliver, where are you? Where are you…?

Almost on cue the telephone started to ring—so much on cue in fact that for several seconds Lisa could only stand and listen to the shrill sound of it, before realising that she wasn't merely imagining it and that it had actually rung, was actually ringing.

A little to her own disgust she realised as she picked up the receiver that her hand was actually trembling slightly.

'Lisa…'

Her heart sank.

'Oliver…where are you? When will you—?'

'Bad news, I'm afraid.' Oliver cut her off abruptly.

'I'm not going to be able to make it after all; I'm stuck in New York and—'

'What?'

There was no way Lisa could conceal her feelings—shock, disappointment, almost disbelief, and even anger was sharpening her voice as she tried to take in what he was telling her. A horrid feeling of sick misery and despair was beginning to fill her but Lisa's pride wouldn't let her give in to it, although her hand was clenched so tightly on the receiver that her skin was sharp white over her knuckles.

'I'm still in New York,' she heard Oliver telling her, his voice curt and almost—so her sensitive ears told her—hostile as he added brusquely, 'I know it's not what I'd planned but there's simply nothing I can do...'

Nothing he could do or nothing he *wanted* to do?

All the doubts, the fears, the insecurities and the regrets that Lisa had been holding at bay ever since they had had to part suddenly began to multiply overwhelming and virtually obliterating all her self-confidence, her belief in Oliver's love. She had been right to be mistrustful of his assurances, his promises; she had been right to be wary of a love that had sprung into being so easily and now, it seemed, could just as easily disappear.

'Lisa?' Oliver said sharply.

'Yes, I'm still here.'

It was an effort to keep her voice level, not to give in to the temptation to beg and plead for some words of reassurance and love, but somehow she managed to stop herself from doing so, even though the effort made her jaw ache and her muscles lock in painful tension.

'You do understand, don't you?' he was asking her.

Oh, yes, she understood. How she understood.

'Yes,' she agreed indistinctly, her voice chilly and distant as she tried to focus on salvaging her pride instead of giving in to her pain. 'I understand perfectly.'

She wasn't going to weaken and let herself ask when he would be coming home, or why he had changed his mind... so obviously changed his mind.

Before he could say any more and before, more importantly, she could break down and reveal how hurt and let down she was feeling, Lisa fibbed tersely, 'I must go; there's someone at the door.' And without waiting to hear any more she replaced the receiver. She must not cry, she *would* not cry, she warned herself fiercely.

In the mirror she caught sight of her reflection; her face was paper-white, her eyes huge, revealing all too clearly what she was feeling, the contrast between her carefully made-up face and the misery in her eyes somehow almost pathetically grotesque.

Her flat, her clothes, her whole person, she decided angrily, made her feel like some modern-day Miss Havisham, decked out all ready for the embrace of a man who had deserted her. The thought was unbearable. She couldn't stay here, not now... not when everything around her reminded her of just how stupid she had been. Why, even now she was still emotionally trying to find excuses for Oliver, to convince herself that she had overreacted and that he felt as bad as she did and that he wasn't having second thoughts.

Alison's invitation was still on her mantelpiece. She reached for the telephone.

'Of course you can still come, you didn't need to ask,' Alison reproved her when she'd explained briefly that there had been a change in her plans and that she was now free for the evening. 'What happened? Has Henry—?'

'It's all off with Henry,' Lisa interrupted her.

There hadn't been time to explain to Alison just what had happened when she had telephoned her to ask her how her skiing holiday had gone and cancel her acceptance to her party and now Lisa was grateful for this omission, even though it did give her a small twinge of guilt when Alison immediately and staunchly, like the good friend she was, declared, 'He's let you down, has he? Well, you know my feelings about him, Lisa. I never thought he was the right man for you. Look, why don't you come over now? Quite a few people are coming early to help but we can always use another pair of hands.'

'Oh, Alison...'

Ridiculously, after the way she had managed to control herself when she'd been speaking to Oliver, she could feel her eyes starting to fill with tears at her friend's sturdy kindness.

'Forget him,' Alison advised her. 'He's not worth it...he never was. You may not believe me now, but, I promise you, you are better off without him, Lisa. Now go and put your glad rags on and get yourself over here... Are we going to party!'

As she replaced the telephone receiver Lisa told herself that Alison's words applied just as much to Oliver as they did to Henry, although for very different reasons.

Forget him. Yes, that was what she must do.

Tonight, with the old year ending and the new one beginning, she must find a way of beginning it without Oliver at her side. Without him in her life.

On impulse she went into the kitchen and removed the champagne from the fridge, pouring herself a glass and quickly drinking it. It was just as well that Alison's flat was within reasonably easy walking distance, she decided as the fizzy alcohol hit her empty, emotionally tensed stomach.

There was no need for her to get changed; the little black dress she was wearing—had put on for Oliver—was very suitable for a New Year's Eve celebration. All she had to do was redo her make-up to remove those tell-tale signs of her tears.

She poured herself a second glass of champagne, realising too late that instead of filling the original glass, which still had some liquid in the bottom, she had actually filled the empty one—Oliver's glass. Grimacing slightly, she picked them both up and carried them through to her bedroom with her, drinking from one before placing them both on the table beside her bed and then quickly repairing her make-up.

In New York Piers frowned as he walked into his cousin's hotel suite and saw Oliver seated in a chair, staring at the telephone.

'Is something wrong?' he asked him. His curiosity had been alerted earlier by the fact that Oliver had been extremely impatient to bring their discussions with the Americans to a conclusion, stating that he had to return to England without explaining why. Piers had happened to be looking at him when they had heard the news that the talks would have to continue. Oliver had been none too pleased.

'No,' Oliver responded shortly. Why had Lisa been so distant with him—so uninterested, so curt to the point of dismissal? She had every right to be angry and even upset about the fact that he had had to change their plans, but she had actually sounded as though she hadn't wanted to see him.

'Well, Jack Hywell is anxious to get on with the negotiations,' Piers told him. 'Apparently he's due to take his kids away the day after tomorrow, which is why he wants to take the discussion through the New Year period.

'Oh, by the way, Emma rang me this morning. She's been up to Yorkshire, and whilst she was up there she heard that Henry is getting married. Apparently, he's marrying someone he's known for a while. I must admit I'm surprised his mother finally sanctioned a marriage. Still, good luck to him, I say, and to her.

'What is it?' he asked Oliver. 'Hey, Oliver, watch it...'

he warned his cousin as he watched the latter's hand clench tightly on the glass he was holding. 'Look, I know how much pressure these negotiations are putting you under,' he commiserated, 'but with any luck they'll be over soon now, and... Oliver, where are you going?'

'Home,' Oliver told him brusquely.

'Home? But you *can't*,' Piers protested. 'The negotiations.'

Oliver snarled at him, telling him in no uncertain terms what should be done with the negotiations and leaving the room.

Piers stared open-mouthed at his departing back. Oliver hardly ever swore, and he certainly never used the kind of language that Piers had just heard him use. He was normally so laid back... Something was obviously wrong, but what?

'Ugh?'

Reluctantly Lisa opened her eyes. What *was* that noise? Was someone really banging a hammer inside her head or was someone at the door?

Someone was at the door. Flinging back the duvet, she reached for her robe, wincing at both the pain in her aching head and the state of her bedroom—clothes scattered everywhere in mute evidence of the decidedly unsober state in which she had returned to her flat in the early hours of the morning. She had never had a strong head for alcohol, she admitted to herself, and Alison's punch had been lethal. She would have to ring her later and thank her for the party, and for everything else as well.

'Don't even think about it,' Alison had advised Lisa drolly the previous evening after she had determinedly rescued her from the very earnest young man who had buttonholed her.

'He's even worse than Henry,' she had warned Lisa, rolling her eyes. 'He still lives with his parents and his hobby is collecting beetles or something equally repulsive. I only invited him because it was the only way I could escape from his mother. I know how much you like a lame dog, but really, Lisa, there are limits. Has he invited you round to look at his beetle collection yet?' she asked wickedly, making Lisa laugh in spite of herself.

'That's better,' she had approved, adding more seriously, 'I hadn't realised that Henry meant quite so much to you, but—'

'It isn't Henry,' Lisa had started to say, but someone had come up and dragged Alison away before she could explain properly and after that, rather than cause her friend any more concern, she had forced herself to be more enthusiastic and convivial, the result of which was her aching head this morning. No, this afternoon, she acknowledged as she saw in horror what time it was.

The doorbell was still ringing. Whoever it was was very determined. What if Oliver had changed his mind and come back after all? What if…?

Her fingers were trembling so much that she could hardly tie the belt of her robe. Quickly she hurried into the hallway, leaving her bedroom door open, and went to open the door, her heart beating so fast that she could hardly breathe.

Only it wasn't Oliver, it was Henry.

Henry!

Dumbly Lisa stood to one side as he walked self-importantly into her flat without bothering to close the door. Henry—what on earth was he doing here? What did he want? He was the last person Lisa wanted to see.

She pressed her fingers to her throbbing head. How could she have been stupid enough to think it might be Oliver? So much for all her promises to herself last night, as they'd all waited for midnight to come and the new year to start, that she would put him completely out of her mind and her heart.

'Henry, what is it? What are you doing here? What do you want?' she demanded shortly.

As she watched him breathe in then puff out his cheeks disapprovingly when he looked at her, she wondered how on earth she could ever have contemplated marrying him, how she had ever been so blind to the true reality of his character, his small-mindedness and fussiness, his lack of humour and generosity. Disapproval was written all over him as he looked at her.

'Surely you weren't still in bed?' he criticised her.

'No, I always dress like this. Of course I was still in bed,' Lisa snapped, losing her patience with him. She could hear him clearing his throat, the sound grating on her over-stretched nerves. If she had known it was only Henry at the door she would have stayed where she was.

'Mother thought I should come and see you,' he told her.

Lisa stared at him in angry disbelief.

'Your mother wanted you to come and see *me*... What on earth for? I would have thought I was the last person she would want you anywhere near. In fact, if I remember correctly, she said—'

'Er—yes, well...' Henry was flushing slightly as he cut her off. Why had she never noticed that slightly fishy bulge to his eyes when he was under pressure? Lisa wondered distastefully. Why had she never noticed, either, how very like his mother's his features were? She shuddered.

'The thing is, Lisa, that Mother thought I should make the situation absolutely clear to you, and—'

'What situation?' she demanded.

'Well...' Henry tugged at his collar. 'The thing is that I'm getting married to...to someone I've known for some time. She and I... Well, anyway, the wedding will be in June and we're having our official engagement party in February and...'

'And what?' Lisa pressed, irritated, wondering what on

earth Henry's engagement and intended marriage had to do
with her and why his mother should think she might want to
hear about them.

He coughed and told her. 'Well, Mother didn't want there
to be any misunderstandings…or embarrassment… She felt
that it was best that you knew what was happening just in case
you tried…'

Lisa couldn't believe what she was hearing.

'Just in case I tried what?' she demanded with ominous
calm. 'Just in case I tried to resuscitate our relationship—is
that what you're trying to say?' she asked him sharply. 'Is
that what your mother is afraid of?'

Did either of them really think…after what had been said,
after the accusations which had been made, that she wanted
anything…*anything* to do with Henry? Heavens, she wouldn't
so much as cross the street to say hello to him now, never mind
try to resuscitate a relationship which Oliver had been quite
right to tell her she was better off without, and she opened
her mouth to tell Henry as much and then closed it again.

There was no point in losing her temper with Henry; rather,
she ought to be pitying him.

'Who is the lucky bride-to-be?' she asked him with acid
sweetness instead. 'Or can I guess…? Your aunt's god-
daughter…?'

She saw from his expression that her guess had been right.
Poor girl—Lisa hoped she knew what she was taking on.

'It's all right, Henry,' she reassured him calmly. 'I *do* understand and you are quite safe. In fact I wish you and your
wife-to-be every happiness.'

And as she spoke she pulled open her front door and firmly
pushed Henry backwards towards it whilst at the same time
raising herself on her tiptoes to place her hands on his shoulders and deposit a dismissive and cold contemptuous kiss on
his cheek—just as Oliver crossed the foyer outside her flat

and to all intents and purposes saw her with her arms around Henry and kissing him.

There was a second's tense silence as Lisa saw Oliver over Henry's shoulder, his face set in a mask of furious anger, and then Henry was backing away from her and almost scurrying past Oliver as he headed for the stairs, whilst Oliver strode towards her, ignoring him.

'Oliver!' Lisa exclaimed weakly. 'What are *you* doing here? I wasn't expecting you. I thought you were in New York.'

'Very evidently,' Oliver agreed tautly as he slammed the front door behind him, enclosing them both in the suddenly far too small space of her hallway.

'It's just as well your fiancé has decided to leave. I want to have a few words with you... Not very brave of him, though. Some husband he's going to make... When I heard that your engagement was back on I couldn't believe it. I thought there must have been some mistake.'

'There has,' Lisa agreed. If only her head would stop aching, she thought.

'I tried to ring you from the airport,' she heard Oliver tell her.

'I was out at a party,' she responded.

'A party—to celebrate your engagement, no doubt,' he accused her grittily, adding savagely as he suddenly stiffened and looked past her and through her open bedroom door to where the clothes she had discarded the previous evening lay scattered all over the floor, 'Or did you save *that* until you were back here alone with him? My God, and to think I believed you when you told me that sexually he had never meant anything to you, that there had never been anything between you. What else did you lie to me about, Lisa? Not that it matters now...'

'I haven't lied to you,' Lisa protested, reminding him, 'And if anyone should be making any accusations surely it should be me? After all, I'm not the one who promised to be back for New Year's Eve and then broke that promise.'

Furious with herself, she closed her eyes. What on earth had prompted her to say that, to betray to him how much his broken promise had hurt her…how much *he* had hurt her?

'I had no choice,' she heard Oliver telling her angrily, 'but you did, Lisa, and you chose—'

'I chose nothing,' she interrupted him, as angry with him now as he patently was with her.

What right, after all, did he have to come back and make such ridiculous accusations—accusations he must surely know couldn't possibly be true? And how come he could manage to get back *now* when he hadn't been able to do so before?

'No?' Oliver strode past her and walked into her bedroom, demanding dangerously, 'No? Then would you mind explaining to me what the hell has been going on here?' He picked up the half-empty champagne glass that she had abandoned the previous evening and gestured to its now flat contents contemptuously as he snarled, 'Couldn't he even wait to let you finish this? *His* glass is empty I note…'

His glass?

Indignantly Lisa opened her mouth to put him right, but before she could say anything Oliver demanded savagely, 'It must have been quite some celebration the two of you had. What the hell did he do—tear the clothes off your back? You should have told me that that was what you liked,' he advised her, his voice suddenly dropping dangerously, his eyes glittering as his glance raked her from head to toe. 'I'd no idea your sexual tastes ran to such things. If I had—'

'Oliver, no…' she protested as he reached for her, catching hold of her arm and dragging her towards him as he ignored her angry denial.

'You don't understand,' she said, but he was beyond listening to reason or to any of her explanations, she realised, her heart lurching against her chest wall as she saw the way his gaze raked her, his look a mingling of loathing and desire.

'I think it's you who doesn't understand,' Oliver was correcting her softly, but there was nothing remotely soft about the way he was holding onto her or the way he was watching her. Her body trembled, her toes curling protestingly into the carpet. 'I thought we had something special, you and I... I thought I could believe in you, trust you... Like a fool I thought, when you told me you needed me, that you...

'What is it, what's wrong?' he asked her as he felt her body shiver and his apparent concern almost caught her off guard, until she saw the steely, almost cruel look in his eyes.

'Nothing's wrong,' Lisa denied. 'I just want you to let me go.'

'You're trembling,' Oliver pointed out, still in that same nerve-wrenchingly soft voice. 'And as for letting you go... I will let you go, Lisa, but not until I've reminded you of exactly why you shouldn't be marrying Henry...'

I'm not marrying Henry, Lisa wanted to say, but she only got as far as, 'I'm not—' before Oliver silenced her mouth, coming down hard on hers in a kiss of angry possession.

She tried to resist him and even physically to repel him, her own anger rising to meet his as she alternately tried to push him away and twist herself out of his grasp, but the more she fought to escape, the more her body came into contact with his, and as though something about her furious struggles only added extra fuel to the flames of his anger Oliver responded by propelling her back against the bedroom wall and holding her there with the hard strength of his body whilst he lifted her arms above her head and kept them pinioned there as he continued to brutalise her mouth with the savagery of his punishing kiss.

Lisa could feel his heart thudding heavily against her body, her own racing in frantic counterpoint, her breathing fast and uneven as her anger rose even higher. How dared he treat her like this? All thoughts of trying to explain and pacify him fled as she concentrated all her energy on trying to break free of him.

She could feel the heat coming off his body, the rough abrasion of the fabric of his clothes on her bare skin where her robe had come unfastened. Her mouth felt swollen and bruised from the savagery of his kisses, but there was no fear or panic in her; she recognised only an unfamiliar and fierce desire to match Oliver's fury with her own.

'You want me... Me...' she heard Oliver telling her thickly between plundering kisses.

'No,' she denied, but the sound was smothered by the soft moan that rose up in her throat as her body responded to its physical contact with his. Somehow, against all logic, against everything she herself had always thought she believed in, she was becoming aroused by him and by the furious force of their mutual anger, Lisa recognised. And so was he.

On a wave of shocked despair she closed her eyes, but that only made things worse; the feel of him, the scent of him, the weight of him against her—these were all so familiar to her aching, yearning body that they immediately fed her roaring, feral need, turning her furious attempt to wrench herself free from him into something that even to her came closer to a deliberately sensual indication of her body's need to be possessed by his than a genuine attempt to break free.

Her anger now wasn't just directed at him, it was directed at herself as well, but with it now she could feel a surge of sensual, languid weakness, a heat which seemed to spread irresistibly throughout her body, so that under the hard pressure of Oliver's searing kiss, instead of resisting him, her body turning cold and lifeless in rejection of him, she was actually moving, melting, yielding, moaning softly beneath her breath.

'Lisa, Lisa…' She could hear the responsive urgency in Oliver's voice, feel it in his hands as he released her pinioned arms to push aside her robe and caress her body.

Her anger was still there, Lisa saw as she watched him studying her semi-naked body, and so was his, but somehow it had been transmuted into a form of such intense physical desire that she could barely recognise either herself or him in the two human beings who had suddenly become possessed of such a rage of physical passion.

She had never dreamed that she could feel like this, want like this, react like this, she acknowledged dazedly several minutes later as she cried out beneath Oliver's savage suckling of her breast, clawing at his back in a response born not of anger or pain or fear but rather of a corresponding degree of intensity and compulsion.

And she made the shocking acknowledgement that there was something—some hitherto secret and sensually dark part of her—that actually found pleasure…that actually wanted savagery, a sensation that was only seconds away from actual pain, that a part of her needed this release of her pent-up emotions and desires, that this dark self-created floodtide of their mutual fury and arousal possessed a dangerously addictive alchemy that made her go back for more, made her cling dizzily to him as he wrenched off his clothes and lifted her, still semi-imprisoning her, against the wall.

He entered her with an urgency that could have been demeaning and unwanted and even painful but which was, in fact, so intensely craved and needed by her body that even she was caught off guard by the intensity of her almost instantaneous orgasm and by her inner knowledge that this was how she had wanted him, that part of her had needed that kind of appeasement, as Oliver allowed her to slide slowly down towards the floor.

Shocked, not just at what had happened but by Oliver's

behaviour and even more so by her own, Lisa discovered that she was trembling so much that she had to lean against the wall for support. Ignoring the hand that Oliver put out to steady her, she turned away from him. She couldn't bear to look at him, to see the triumph and the contempt she knew would be in his eyes.

'Lisa…'

Whatever it was he was going to say she couldn't bear to listen to it.

'Just go,' she told him woodenly. 'Now… I never want to see you again… Never…'

She could hear her voice starting to rise, feel herself starting to tremble as shock set in. Her face burned scarlet with mortification as she reached for her abandoned robe and pulled it around her body to shield her nakedness as Oliver got dressed in grim-faced silence. Now that it was over she felt sick with disbelief and shock, unable to comprehend how she could have behaved in the way that she had, how she could have been so…so…depraved, how she could have wanted…

'Lisa…'

Oliver was dressed now and standing by the door. A part of her could sense that he too had behaved in a way that was out of character but she didn't want to listen to him. What was the point? He had shown her with damning clarity just what he thought of her.

'No…don't touch me…'

For the first time panic hit her as she saw him turn and start to walk towards her. She couldn't bear him to touch her now, not after…

She could sense him, feel him willing her to look at him but she refused to do so, keeping her face averted from him.

'So that's it, then,' she heard him saying hoarsely. 'It's over…'

'Yes,' she agreed. 'It's over.'

It wasn't until well over an hour after he had gone, after she had cleaned the bedroom from top to bottom, changed the bed, polished every piece of furniture, thrown every item of discarded clothing into the washing machine and worked herself into a furore that she realised that she had never actually told Oliver that she and Henry were not getting married. She gave a small, fatalistic shrug. What did it matter? What did *anything* matter any more after the way the pair of them had destroyed and abused their love?

Their *love*… There had never been any love—at least not on Oliver's side. Only lust; that was all.

Lisa shuddered. How had it happened? How could anger—not just his but, even worse, her own—become so quickly and so fatally transmuted into such an intensity of arousal and desire? Even now she could hardly believe it had happened, that *she* had behaved like that, that she had felt like that.

Later she would mourn the loss of her love; right now all she wanted to do was to forget that the last few hours had ever happened.

CHAPTER NINE

LISA WOKE UP WITH A START, brought out of her deep, exhausted sleep, which she had fallen into just after the winter dawn had started to lighten the sky, by the shrill bleep of her alarm.

Tiredly she reached out to switch it off. She had spent most of the night lying in bed trying not to think about what had happened—and failing appallingly. Round and round her thoughts had gone until she'd been dizzy with the effort of trying to control them.

Shock, anger—against herself, against Oliver—grief, pain, despair and then anger again had followed in a relentless, going-nowhere circle, her final thought before she had eventually fallen asleep being that she must somehow stop dwelling on what was now past and get on with her life.

Her head ached and her throat felt sore—a sure sign, she suspected, that she was about to go down with a heavy cold. The faint ache in her muscles and her lethargy were due to another cause entirely, of course.

Quickly she averted her gaze from the space on the bedroom wall—the place where Oliver had held her as he…as they… The heat enveloping her body had nothing to do with her head cold, Lisa acknowledged grimly, and nor had the hot colour flooding her face.

It was bad enough that she had actually behaved in such an…an abandoned, yes, almost sexually aggressive way in the first place, but did her memory *have* to keep reminding her of what she had done, torturing her with it? she wondered wretchedly. She doubted that Oliver was tormented by any such feelings of shame and guilt, but then, of course, it was different for a man. A man was allowed to be sexually driven, to express anger and hurt.

But it hadn't been Oliver's behaviour—hurtful though it had been—that had kept her awake most of the night, she acknowledged; it had been her own, and she knew that she would never be able to feel comfortable about what she had done, about the intensity of her passion, her lack of control, her sexuality, unchecked as it had been by the softening gentleness of love and modesty.

Women like her did not behave like that—they did *not* scratch and bite and moan like wild animals, they did *not* urge and demand and incite...they did *not* take pleasure in meeting...in matching a man's sexual anger, they did *not*... Lisa gave a low moan and scrambled out of bed.

There was no point in going over and over what had happened. It wouldn't change anything; *she* couldn't change anything. How on earth *could* Oliver have possibly thought that she could want *any* other man, never mind a sorry specimen like Henry...? How could he have misinterpreted...accused her...?

Angrily she stepped into the shower and switched it on.

That was the difference between men and women, she decided bitterly. Whereas she as a woman had given herself totally, emotionally, physically, mentally to Oliver, committing herself to him and to her love in the act of love—an act which she naïvely had believed had been a special and a wonderful form of bonding between them—to Oliver, as a man, they had simply had sex.

Sex. She started to shudder, remembering. Stop thinking about it, she warned herself grimly.

As she dried her hair and stared into the mirror at her

heavy-eyed, pale-faced reflection she marvelled that such a short space of time could have brought so many changes to her life, set in motion events which had brought consequences that she would never be able to forget or escape.

Such a few short days, and yet they had changed her life for ever—changed *her* for ever. And the most ironic thing of all was that even if Henry or another man like him were to offer her marriage now she could not accept it. Thanks to Oliver she now knew that she could never be content with the kind of marriage and future which had seemed so perfect to her before.

Fergus her boss gave her an uneasy look as he heard her sneezing. He had a thing about germs and was a notorious hypochondriac.

'You don't sound very well,' he told Lisa accusingly as she started to open the mail which had accumulated over the Christmas break. 'You've probably caught this virus that's going round. There was something on last night's TV news about it. They're advising anyone who thinks they've got it to stay at home and keep warm...'

'Fergus, I've got a cold, that's all,' Lisa told him patiently. 'And besides, aren't we due to go down to Southampton on Thursday to start cataloguing the contents of Welton House?'

Welton House had been the property of one of Fergus's clients, and following her death her family had asked Fergus to catalogue its contents with a view to organising a sale. Normally it was the kind of job that Lisa loved, and she thought that it would do her good to get away from London.

'That's next week,' Fergus told her, his voice quickening with alarm as Lisa burst into another volley of sneezes. 'Look, my dear, you aren't well. I really think you should go home,' he said. 'In fact, I insist on it. I'll ring for a taxi for you...'

There was no point in continuing to protest, Lisa recognised wearily; Fergus had quite obviously got it into his head that she was dangerously infectious, and, if she was honest, she didn't feel very well. Nothing to do with her slight head cold, though. The pain that was exhausting her, draining every bit of her energy as she fought to keep it at bay had its source not in her head but in her emotions.

Her telephone was ringing as she unlocked her door; she stared at it for a few seconds, body stiffening. What if it was Oliver, ringing to apologise, to tell her that he had made a mistake, that he...?

Tensely she picked up the receiver, unsure of whether to be relieved or not when she heard her mother's voice on the other end of the line.

'Darling, I'm glad I caught you. I'm just ringing to wish you a Happy New Year. We tried to get through yesterday but we couldn't. How are you? Tell me all about your Christmas with Henry...'

Lisa couldn't help herself; to her own consternation and disbelief she burst into tears, managing to tell her mother between gulped sobs that she had not, after all, spent Christmas with Henry.

'What on earth has happened?' she heard her mother enquiring solicitously. 'I thought you and Henry—'

'It's not Henry,' Lisa gulped. 'He's getting married to someone else anyway. It's Oliver...'

'Oliver. Who's Oliver?' her mother asked anxiously, but the mere effort of saying Oliver's name had caused her so much pain that Lisa couldn't answer her questions.

'I've got to go, Mum,' Lisa fibbed, unable to bear any more. 'Thanks for ringing.'

'Lisa,' she could hear her mother protesting, but she was already replacing the receiver.

There was nothing she wanted to do more than fling herself on her bed and cry until there were no more tears left, until she had cried all her pain away, but what was the point of such emotional self-indulgence?

What she needed, she acknowledged firmly, was something to keep her thoughts away from Oliver not focused on him. It was a pity that the panacea that work would have provided had been taken away from her, she fretted as she stared round her sitting room, the small space no longer a warm, safe haven but a trap imprisoning her with her thoughts, her memories of Oliver.

Impulsively she pulled on her coat. She needed to get away, go somewhere, anywhere, just so long as it was somewhere that wasn't tainted with any memories of Oliver.

Oliver was in a foul mood. He had flown straight back to New York after his confrontation with Lisa, ostensibly to conclude the negotiations he had left hanging fire in his furious determination to find out what was going on. Well, he had found out all right. He doubted if he would ever forget that stomach-sickening, heart-destroying, split second of time when he had seen Lisa—*his* Lisa—in Henry's arms.

And as for what had happened... His mouth hardened firmly as he fought to suppress the memory of how easily—how very and humiliatingly easily—with Lisa in his arms he had been on the point of begging her to change her mind, of pleading with her at least to give him a chance to show her how good it could be for them.

He had known, of course, how reluctant, how wary she had been about committing herself fully to him, how afraid she had been of her own suppressed, deeply passionate nature. Then it had seemed a vulnerability in her which had only added to his love for her. Then he had not realised... How could he have been so blind—he of all people? How could

she have been so blind? Couldn't she see what they had had…
what they *could* have had?

The American negotiations were concluded now and he
and Piers were on their way back north. They had flown back
into London four hours ago to cold grey skies and thin rain.

'Oliver, is something wrong?'

He frowned, concentrating on the steely-grey ribbon of the
motorway as he pulled out to overtake a large lorry.

'No, why should there be?' he denied, without looking at
his cousin.

'No reason. Only you never explained why you had to fly
back home like that and since you flew back to the States…
well, it's obvious that something is bothering you. You're not
having second thoughts about selling off part of the business,
are you?' Piers asked him.

Oliver relaxed slightly, and without taking his eyes off the
road responded, 'No, it was the right decision, but the timing
could, perhaps, have been better. When is Emma due back?'
he asked, changing the subject.

His cousin's girlfriend had been away visiting her family,
and to his relief Piers, not realising that he was being deliberately sidetracked, started to talk enthusiastically about the
reunion with her.

'It's official, by the way,' he informed Oliver. 'We're definitely going to get married this summer. In Harrowby if
that's OK with you. We thought…well, I thought with Emma's
family being so scattered… We…we're not sure how many
of them will want to come up for the wedding yet, but the
house is big enough to house twenty or so and…' He paused
and gave Oliver a sidelong glance.

'I…I'd like you to be my best man, Oliver. Funny things,
women,' he added ruminatively. 'Up until we actually started
talking properly about it Emma had always insisted she didn't
want a traditional wedding, that they were out of date and

unnecessary, and yet now…she wants the whole works—bridesmaids, page-boys… She says it's to please her mother but I know different.

'That will mean two big weddings for Harrowby this summer. I still can't get over old Henry getting married—or rather his mother allowing him to… Hell, Oliver… watch out!' he protested sharply as his cousin suddenly had to brake quickly to avoid getting too close to the car in front.

'You're sure you're OK?' he asked in concern. 'Perhaps we should have stayed in London overnight instead of driving north straight from the flight. If you're tired, I can take over for a while…'

Oliver made no reply but his mouth had compressed into a hard line and there was a bleak, cold look in his eyes that reminded Piers very much of a younger Oliver just after he'd lost his mother. Something was bothering his cousin, but Piers knew him well enough to know that Oliver wasn't likely to tell him or anyone else exactly what it was.

'What the hell is that still doing here?'

Piers frowned as Oliver glared at the Christmas tree in the hallway. There was nothing about it so far as he could see to merit that tone of icy, almost bitter hatred in his cousin's voice. In fact, he decided judiciously, it was a rather nice tree—wilting now slightly, but still…

'It's not Twelfth Night until tomorrow,' he pointed out to Oliver. 'I'll give you a hand dismantling it then, if you like, and—'

'No,' Oliver told him curtly. 'I'll give Mrs Green a ring and ask her to arrange for Tom to come in and do it. We're going to be too busy catching up with everything that's been going on whilst we've been in New York.'

Thoughtfully Piers followed Oliver into the kitchen. It wasn't like his cousin to be so snappy and edgy, and, in point of fact, he had planned to drive across to York to see his parents whilst they were in the north, but now it seemed as though Oliver had other plans for him.

'Well, if we're going to work I'd better go and unpack and have a shower, freshen up a bit,' he told Oliver.

Upstairs he pushed open the door of the room which traditionally was his whenever he visited. The bed was neatly made up with crisp, clean bedlinen, the room spotless apart from...

Piers' eyes widened slightly as he saw the small, intimate item of women's clothing which Mrs Green had obviously laundered and left neatly folded on the bed, no doubt thinking that the small pair of white briefs belonged to Emma.

Only Piers was pretty sure that they didn't. So who did they belong to and where was their owner now?

Piers knew enough about his cousin to be quite sure that Oliver would not indulge in any kind of brief, meaningless sexual fling. Piers had endured enough lectures from his elder cousin on that subject himself to know that much.

So what exactly was going on? Oliver had made no mention to him of having any visitors recently, either male or female. He could always, of course, show him the briefs and ask him who they belonged to, but, judging from his current mood, such an enquiry was not likely to be very well received.

Another thought occurred to Piers. Was there any connection between the owner of the briefs and his cousin's present uncharacteristic bad mood?

When Piers returned downstairs Oliver was in his study opening the mail that had accumulated in his absence.

'Mmm...isn't it amazing how much junk gets sent through the post?' Piers commented as he started to help him. 'Oh, this one looks interesting, Oliver—an invite to Henry's betrothal party. Well, they certainly are doing things the traditional way, aren't they?'

'Give that to me,' Oliver instructed, his tone of voice so curt that Piers started to frown. He knew that Oliver had never particularly liked either Henry or his parents, especially his mother, but, so far as he knew, the anger he was exhibiting now was completely different from his normal attitude of relaxed indifference towards them.

Silently Piers handed him the invitation and saw the way Oliver's hands trembled slightly as he started to tear the invitation in two, and then he abruptly stopped, his concentration fixed on the black script which he had previously merely been glancing at furiously, his whole body so still and tense that Piers automatically moved round the desk to stand beside him, wondering what on earth it was that was written on the invitation that was causing such a reaction.

It had seemed unremarkable enough to him.

'"The betrothal is announced of Miss Louise Saunders, daughter of Colonel and Lady Anne Saunders, to—" Henry is marrying Louise Saunders,' Oliver intoned in a flat and totally unfamiliar voice.

'That's what it says,' Piers agreed, watching him in concern. 'It makes sense. They've known one another for ever and, of course, there's money in the family. Louise stands to inherit quite a considerable sum from her grandparents.

'Oliver, what is it, what's wrong?' he demanded as he saw the colour draining out of his cousin's face, leaving it grey and haggard, the skin stretched tightly over his facial bones as he lifted his head and stared unseeingly across the room.

'Nothing,' he told Piers tonelessly. 'Nothing.' And then he added in a sharper more incisive voice, 'Piers, there's something I have to do. I need to get back to London. I'll leave you here…'

'London…? You can't drive back there now,' Piers protested. 'It's too late. You haven't had any sleep in the last twenty-four hours that I know of, and not much in the three days before that. Oliver, what's going on? I—'

'Nothing's going on,' Oliver denied harshly.

'Look, if you must go back to London, at least wait until the morning when you've had some sleep,' said Piers. 'Surely whatever it is can wait that long?'

'Maybe it can,' Oliver agreed savagely, 'but *I* can't.'

In London Lisa's cold had turned into the full-blown virus, just as Fergus had predicted. Common sense told her that she ought to see a doctor but she felt too full of self-pity, too weak, too weighed down with misery to care how ill she was. And so instead she remained in her flat curled up in her bed, alternately sweating and shivering and being sick, wishing that she could just close her eyes and never have to open them again.

At first when she heard the sound of someone knocking urgently on her door after ten o'clock at night she thought she was imagining things, and then when the knocking continued and she realised that it was, in fact, real her heart started to bang so fiercely against her chest wall that it made her feel even more physically weak.

It was Oliver! It had to be. But it didn't matter what he had to say because she wasn't going to listen. She had always known that sooner or later he would discover his mistake. But nothing—no amount of apologising on his part—could take away the pain he had caused her.

If he had really loved her he would never have doubted her in the first place. *If* he had really loved her he would never...

The knocking had stopped, and Lisa discovered that she was almost running in her sudden urgency to open the door.

When she did so, flinging it wide, Oliver's name already on her lips, it wasn't Oliver who was standing there at all...

It was...

She blinked and then blinked again, and then to her own consternation she burst into tears and flung herself into the arms that had opened to hold her, weepingly demanding, 'Mother, what are you doing here?'

'You sounded so unhappy when I rang that I was worried about you,' her mother told her.

'You came all the way home from Japan because you were worried about me?'

Lisa stared at her mother in disbelief, remembering all the times when, as a child, she had refused to give in to her need to plead for her parents to return from whatever far-flung part of the world they were working in, telling herself stoically that she didn't mind that they weren't there, that she didn't mind that they didn't love her enough to be with her all the time.

'Don't sound so surprised,' her mother chided her gently. 'You may be an adult, Lisa, but to us, your father and me, you are still our child... Your father wanted to come with me, but unfortunately...' She spread her hands.

'Now,' she instructed as she smoothed Lisa's damp hair back from her forehead and studied her face with maternal intuition, 'tell me what's really wrong... All of it... Starting with this Oliver...'

'Oliver...'

Lisa shook her head, her mouth compressing against her emotions.

'I can't,' she whispered, and then added, 'Oh, Mum, I've been such a fool. I thought he loved me... I thought...'

'Oh, my poor darling girl. Come on, let me put the kettle on and make us both a drink and something to eat. You need it, by the looks of you. You're so thin... Oh, Lisa, what have you been doing to yourself?'

Half an hour later, having been bullied into having a hot bath by her mother, Lisa was ensconced on her small sofa, wrapped in her quilt, dutifully eating the deliciously creamy scrambled eggs that her mother had cooked for her whilst the latter sat on a chair opposite, waiting for her to finish eating before exclaiming as she removed the empty plate, 'Right, now! First things first—*who* is this Oliver?'

'He's... He's...' Lisa shook her head. 'I hate him,' she told her mother emotionally, 'and it hurts so much. He said he loved me but he couldn't have done—not and said what he did...'

Slowly, under her mother's patient and gentle questioning, the whole story came out. Although Lisa would not have said that she was particularly close to her parents, she had always felt able to talk to them. But, even so, she was slightly shocked to discover how easy it was to confide in her mother and how much she wanted to talk to her. Of course, there were bits she missed out—things so personal that she could not have discussed them with anyone. But she sensed from her mother's expression that she guessed when Lisa was withholding things from her and why.

Only when it came to outlining what had happened the night that Oliver had discovered her kissing Henry did her voice falter slightly.

'It must have been a shock for him to find Henry here,' her mother suggested when Lisa had fallen silent.

'He seemed to think that I was going to marry Henry. I...'

'And you told him, of course, that you weren't?' her mother offered.

Lisa shook her head. 'I tried to but...' She bit her lip, turning away, her face flushing slightly. 'He was so...

'I had been honest with him right from the start, told him why I was marrying Henry, told him that I hadn't...that I didn't think that sex...' She bit her lip again and stopped.

'After what had happened between us I don't understand

how he could possibly have thought that I'd go back to Henry and to use what we had…all that we'd shared, to abuse it and destroy… To make me feel… How could he do that?' she whispered, more to herself than her mother.

'Perhaps because he's a man and because he felt jealous and insecure, because a part of him feared that what he had to offer you wasn't enough…that *he* wasn't enough.'

'But how could he possibly think that?' Lisa demanded, looking at her mother, her eyes dark and shadowed with pain. 'He knew how I felt about him, how I… He knew…'

'When you were in bed together, yes,' her mother agreed, softening the directness of her words with a small smile. 'But it isn't only our sex who fear that the emotions aroused when two people are sexually intimate may not be there once that intimacy is over.

'Your Oliver obviously knew he could arouse you, make you want him physically, but you had already told him that he was not what you wanted, what you had planned for. He already knew that a part of you feared the intensity of the emotions he had for you and aroused in you. You said yourself that he was anxious for you to make a commitment to him.'

'Initially, yes. But later…when I tried to tell him how I felt just before he left for New York, he didn't seem to want to listen.'

'Perhaps because he was afraid of what you might say,' her mother suggested gently, adding, 'He had no way of knowing you were going to tell him that you had changed your mind, that you were ready to make the commitment you had previously told him he must wait for. For all he knew, you might have wanted to say something very different—to tell him in fact that you had changed your mind and didn't want him at all.'

'But he couldn't possibly have thought that,' Lisa gasped,

'could he? It isn't important now anyway,' she said tiredly. 'I can never forgive him for—'

'Is it really *Oliver* you can't forgive, or yourself?' her mother interposed quietly, watching as Lisa stared at her and then frowned.

'You said that he was angry…that he made love to you,' she reminded Lisa. 'That he used your feelings to punish and humiliate you. But you never said that you didn't want him, or that he hurt or abused you. Anger against the person we love when he is our lover can result in some very passionate sex.

'For a woman, the first time she discovers that fact, it can be very traumatic and painful because it goes against everything that society has told us we should want from sexual intimacy. It can seem very frightening, very alien, very wrong to admit that we found pleasure in expressing our sexuality and desire in anger and, of course, that it was the only way we could express it…'

'He was so angry with me,' Lisa told her mother, not making any response to what she had said but mentally digesting it, acknowledging that her mother had a point, allowing herself for the first time since it had happened to see her own uninhibited and passionate response to Oliver as a natural expression of her own emotions.

'Oliver was probably as shocked and caught off guard by what happened as you were,' her mother told her wryly.

'You're not the only one something like this has happened to, you know,' she added comfortingly. 'I can still remember the first time your father and I had a major row… I was working on a piece for a gallery showing and I'd forgotten that your father was picking me up to take me out to dinner… He came storming into my work room demanding to know what was more important to me—my work or him… I had just finished working on the final piece for the exhibition. He picked it up and threw it against the wall.'

Lisa stared at her mother in shock.

'Dad did that? But he always seems so laid back…so…'

'Well, most of the time he is, but this particular incident was the culmination of a series of small misunderstandings. He didn't take second place to my work at all, of course, but…'

'Go on—what happened, after he had broken the piece?' Lisa demanded, intrigued.

'Well, I'm ashamed to say that I was so angry that I actually tried to hit him. He caught hold of me, we struggled for a while and then…'

As her mother flushed and laughed, Lisa guessed what the outcome of their fight had been.

'Afterwards your father stormed off and left me there on my own… I vowed I wasn't going to have anything more to do with him, but then—well, I started to miss him and to realise that what had happened hadn't been entirely his fault.'

'So what did you do?' Lisa asked.

Her mother laughed. 'Well, I made a small ceramic heart which I then deliberately broke in two and I sent him one half of it.'

'What did he do?' Lisa demanded breathlessly.

'Well, not what I had expected,' her mother admitted. 'When I sent him the heart I had been trying to tell him that my heart was broken. I kept the other half hoping he would come for it and that we could mend the break, but when several days went by and he didn't I began to think that he had changed his mind and that he didn't want me any more.

'I was in despair,' she told Lisa quietly. 'Exactly the same kind of despair you are facing now, but then, just when I had given up hope, your father turned up one night.'

'With the broken heart,' Lisa guessed.

'With the mended heart,' her mother told her, smiling. 'The reason he had delayed so long before coming to see me had been because he had been having a matching piece to the broken one I had sent him made, and where the two pieces were bonded together he had used a special bond to, as he put it, "make the mended heart stronger than it had been before and unbreakable".'

'I never dreamed Dad could be so romantic!' Lisa exclaimed.

'Oh, he can,' her mother told her. 'You should have seen him the night you were born. He had desperately wanted you to be a little girl. He was overjoyed when you were born—we both were—and he swore that no matter where our work might take us, as long as it was physically possible, we would take you with us...'

Lisa could feel fresh tears starting to sting her eyes. All these years and she had misunderstood the motivation behind her parents' constant uprooting of her, had never known how much she was actually loved.

As they looked at one another her mother reached out and took Lisa's hand, telling her firmly, 'When Oliver comes to see you—and he will—listen to what he has to say, Lisa—'

'When,' Lisa interrupted her. 'Don't you mean if...?'

'No, I mean when.'

'But how could he believe I could go behind his back and return to Henry?'

'He's a man and he's vulnerable, as I've already told you, and sometimes, when we feel vulnerable and afraid, we do things which are out of character. You said yourself that losing his mother when he did made him feel wary of loving someone in case he lost them too. Such emotions, even when they're only felt subconsciously, can have a very dramatic effect on our actions.'

'He won't come back,' Lisa protested dully. 'I told him I never wanted to see him again. We both agreed it was over.'

'Well, in that case, why don't you come back to Japan with me?' her mother suggested prosaically.

'I can't… My job… Fergus—'

'Fergus would give you some extended leave if you asked him,' her mother told her. 'He adores you, you know that…'

'Not when he thinks I'm full of germs,' Lisa told her ruefully. 'I'd like to come back with you,' she added hesitantly, 'but…'

'But not yet,' her mother finished for her, getting up to kiss her gently on the forehead and tell her, 'Well, I'm going to be here for a few days so you've got time to change your mind. But right now you're going to bed and I'm going to ring your father. I promised him I would. He'll be worrying himself to death wondering if you're all right. Now, bed…'

'Yes, Mum.' Lisa yawned obediently.

It felt so good to have her mother here with her, to know that she was cared for and loved, but no amount of parental love, no matter how valued, could erase the pain of losing Oliver.

He'll be back, her mother had promised her. But would he? Had they perhaps between them destroyed the tender, vulnerable plant of their love?

CHAPTER TEN

PIERS HAD BEEN RIGHT to caution him against driving back to London tonight, Oliver admitted as his concentration wavered and he found himself having to blink away the grittiness of his aching eyes as he tried to focus on the road. With all that adrenalin and anxiety pumping through his veins it should have been impossible to start drifting off to sleep, but the compulsion to yawn and close his eyes kept on returning.

Up ahead of him he could see the lights of a motorway service station. Perhaps it would be wiser for him to stop, even if it was only for a hot, reviving cup of coffee. He knew there was no point in his trying to sleep; how could he when all he could think of was Lisa and the injustice he had done her?

The motorway services were closer than he had thought; he had started to pull into the lane taking him off the motorway, when the metal barrier at the edge of the road loomed up in front of him. The shrill squeal of brakes was followed by the harsh sound of metal against metal and his head jolted forward, pain exploding all around him.

'If it's that bad why don't you go out for a walk? It will be cheaper than wearing the carpet out.'

Lisa frowned as she looked at her mother.

'You've been pacing up and down the sitting room for the last half-hour,' her mother pointed out. 'And besides, it will do you good to get some fresh air.'

'Yes, perhaps you're right,' Lisa agreed. 'A walk might do me good.'

'Put your jacket on and some gloves,' her mother instructed her as Lisa headed for the hallway. 'I know the sun is out but we had frost last night.'

'Yes, Mother,' Lisa agreed dutifully, amusement briefly lightening her eyes and touching her mouth.

It had been three days since her mother's unexpected arrival now; in another two she would be returning to Japan. She was still pressing Lisa to return with her, and Lisa knew that she had spoken the truth when she had said that Fergus would give her the extra leave. There had been plenty of occasions in the past when she had put in extra hours at work, given up weekends and been cheerfully flexible about how long she worked. No, it wasn't the thought of Fergus that was stopping her.

'Why don't you come with me?' she suggested to her mother as she pulled on her jacket and found her gloves. The virus she had picked up had been thankfully short-lived, but Fergus had insisted that she did not return to work for at least a full week, and although she was enjoying her mother's company there were times when she was filled with restless energy that nothing seem to dissipate—a sense of urgency and anxiety.

Both of them knew what was causing it, of course, but since the night she had confided in her mother neither of them had ever referred to Oliver—Lisa because she couldn't bear to, couldn't trust herself to so much as think, never mind say his name, without losing control and being swamped by her emotions, and her mother, she suspected, because despite her initial conviction that Oliver would discover the truth and want to make amends she too was now beginning to share Lisa's belief that it was over between them.

'I won't be too long,' she told her mother as she opened the front door.

'No...there's an exhibition on at the Tate that I thought we might go to this afternoon, and then I thought we might have dinner at that Italian place in Covent Garden that your father likes so much.'

Her mother was doing her best to keep her occupied and busy, Lisa knew, and she was doing all she could to respond, but both of them also knew that she was losing weight and that she didn't sleep very well at night, and that sometimes when she did she woke up crying Oliver's name.

Her head down against the sharp January wind, she set off in the direction of the park.

Once she had gone Lisa's mother picked up the receiver and dialled her husband's number in Japan.

'I still haven't managed to persuade Lisa to come back with me,' she told him after they had exchanged hellos. 'I'm worried about her, David. She looks so pale and thin... I wish there was some way we could get in touch with this Oliver. No, I know we mustn't interfere,' she agreed, 'but if you could see her. She looks so... I must go,' she told him. 'There's someone at the door.' Quickly she replaced the receiver and went to open the front door.

The tall, dark-haired man wearing one arm in a sling with a huge, purpling bruise on his cheekbone and a black eye and a nasty-looking cut on his forehead was completely unfamiliar to her and yet she knew who he was immediately.

'You must be Oliver,' she told him simply, extending her hand to shake his. 'I'm so glad you're here. I'd just about begun to give up on you. Silly of me really, especially when... You look rather the worse for wear; have you been in an accident...? I'm Lisa's mother, by the way; she's out at the moment but she'll be back soon. Do come in...'

'I had a bump in my car a few days ago,' Oliver told her as

he followed her into the flat. 'Fortunately nothing too serious. I say fortunately because it was my own fault; I virtually fell asleep at the wheel...' He caught the frowning look that Lisa's mother gave him and explained tersely, 'I was on my way back to London to see Lisa. Where did you say she was...?'

'She's gone out for a walk; she shouldn't be too long. She's been ill and I thought some fresh—'

'How ill?' Oliver pounced sharply.

Hiding her small, satisfied smile, Lisa's mother responded airily, 'Well, as a matter of fact, the doctor seemed quite concerned, but I'm a great believer in the efficacy of plenty of fresh air myself. She did say she felt a bit weak but—'

'A bit weak... Should she be out on her own?'

Poor man, he really had got it badly, Lisa's mother decided. As she witnessed his obvious concern Lisa's mother relented a little; this was no uncaring sexual predator, this was quite definitely a man very, very deeply in love.

'She's a lot better than she was,' she told him more gently.

Her half-hour in the park might have brought a pink flush to her skin and made her fingertips and toes tingle, Lisa acknowledged, but it had done nothing to alleviate the pain of loving Oliver. Only one person could do that, and with every day that passed her common sense told her that there was less and less chance of Oliver doing what her mother had claimed he was bound to do and coming in search of her, to tell her that he had discovered his mistake and to beg her to forgive him.

Grimly, Lisa retraced her steps towards her flat. Part of her wished desperately that she had never met Oliver, that she had never been exposed to the agony of loving him and then losing him, and yet another part of her clung passionately to the memory of their brief time together.

As her mother opened the door to her knock she told

Lisa, 'I'm just going out. Oh, and by the way, you've got a visitor.'

'Oliver?'

Hope, disbelief, the desire to push open the door and run to him and the equally strong desire to turn on her heels and run from him were all there in Lisa's eyes.

'Treat him gently,' her mother advised her as she took hold of her and gave her a supportive hug.

'Treat him gently', after what he had done to her? In a daze Lisa walked past her mother and into the flat, closing the door behind her. Oliver was actually here…here. The angry relief that flooded her was that same emotion so familiar to parents when a child had emerged unscathed from a forbidden risk—relief at its safety and anger that it should have taken such a risk with itself, with something so precious and irreplaceable.

In fact she was so angry that she was actually shaking as she pushed open the sitting-room door, Lisa discovered, her mouth compressing, and without even waiting to look directly at Oliver, without daring to take the risk of allowing her hungry heart, her starved senses to feast on the reality of him, she demanded tersely, 'What are you doing here?'

He was standing with his back to her, facing the window, apparently absorbed in the view outside. He must have seen her walking back to the flat, Lisa recognised, her heart giving a small, shaky bound. He turned round and every single thought, every single word she had been about to voice vanished as Lisa saw his cut and bruised face, his arm in a sling.

'Oliver…' Her voice cracked suddenly, becoming thready and weak, her eyes mirroring her shock and anxiety as she whispered, 'What's happened? Why…?'

'It's nothing…just a minor bump in my car,' Oliver assured her quickly. 'In fact I got off far more easily than I deserved.'

'You've been in an accident. But how?' she demanded, ignoring his attempts to make light of his injuries and instinctively hurrying towards him, realising only when it was too late and she was standing within easy distance of the free arm he stretched forward to her just how physically close to him she actually was.

Immediately she raised her hand in an automatic gesture of rejection, but Oliver had already stepped forward and the hand she had lifted in the body-language sign that meant 'No, keep away from me' was somehow resting against his shirt-covered chest with a very different meaning indeed.

'Oliver,' she protested weakly, but it wasn't any use; it wasn't just her legs and her body that were trembling now, her mouth was trembling as well, tears spilling over from her eyes as she said his name, causing Oliver to groan and reach for her, cradling her against his body with his good arm as he said, 'Lisa, darling, please don't…please don't cry. I can't bear to see you unhappy. I'll never forgive myself for what I've done—*never*. My only excuse is that I was half-crazed with jealousy over Henry.'

'Jealous?' Lisa questioned. 'You actually believed…? You were jealous of Henry?' She couldn't quite keep the disbelief out of her voice.

'Yes,' Oliver admitted ruefully. 'It all seemed to slot so neatly into place—your reluctance to commit yourself to me, the news that Henry was marrying an old flame, the sight of the two of you together. I know I overreacted. I was jealous, vulnerable,' he told her simply. 'You'd already made it plain that I wasn't the kind of man you wanted for a husband. I knew how reluctant you'd been to commit yourself to me, to our love.

'I knew, as well, how much I was rushing you, pressurising you, using the intensity of what we both felt for one another to win you over. I suppose a part of me will always be the child who felt that in dying my mother deliberately abandoned me. Logically I know that isn't what happened, but there's always that small worm of fear there—fear of losing the one you love—and the more you love someone, the greater the fear is. And I love you more than I can possibly tell you. I'm not trying to look for excuses for myself, Lisa; there aren't really any. What I did was…' He paused and shook his head as she touched his hand gently with understanding for what he was trying to say. 'At the time it seemed logical that you should have changed your mind, decided you preferred the safe life you had already mapped out for yourself.'

'Oh, Oliver.' Lisa shook her head.

'I was wrong, I know, and what I did was…unforgivable…'

The bleakness in his eyes and voice made Lisa want to reach out and hold him, but she restrained herself. She was already in his arms, and once she touched him…

'I…I didn't know that loving someone could be like that,' she told him in a husky voice. 'That anger could… That physically… I felt so ashamed after you had gone,' she admitted shakily.

'To have wanted you the way I did, to have responded to you, said the things I did, when I knew that you weren't touching me out of love. I felt so…' She shook her head, unable to find the words to express her own sense of horror at what, at the time, had seemed to her to be her own totally unacceptable and almost abnormal behaviour.

'Being angry with someone doesn't stop you loving them,' Oliver told her quietly. 'I was angry, bitter—furiously, destructively so; I can't deny that. I wanted to hurt you in the same way that I felt you had hurt me, but those feelings, strong as they were, destructive as they were, did not stop me loving you. In fact…'

He paused and looked down into her upturned face,

searching her eyes before telling her roughly, 'I tried to tell myself that I was punishing you...that I *wanted* to punish you...but almost from the moment I held you in my arms...' He stopped and shook his head. 'No matter what I might have *said*, my *body* was loving you, Lisa—loving you and wanting you and hating me for what I was trying to do.'

'What made you think I was marrying Henry in the first place?' Lisa questioned him.

'My cousin,' he informed her briefly. 'Emma had phoned from Yorkshire and she'd heard that Henry was getting married to someone he had already known for some time.'

'And you assumed it was me...'

'I assumed it was you,' Oliver agreed.

A little uncertainly Lisa looked up at him. The sadness she could see in his eyes made her heart jolt against her ribs.

'Have I completely ruined everything between us?' he asked her huskily. 'Tell me I haven't, Lisa. I can't... Being without you these last few days has been hell, but if you...'

He paused and Lisa told him shakily, 'I've missed you as well...'

Missed him!

'I should have rung you from New York and talked to you instead of flying back like that, but it looked like those damned negotiations were going to go on for ever and I'd already missed being with you on New Year's Eve. And then when I reached your flat and saw you there with Henry...'

'He came to tell me that he was getting married. His mother had sent him,' Lisa explained drily. 'She was concerned that I might get in touch with him and try to patch up our differences... I had just finished telling Henry that there was absolutely no chance whatsoever of that happening when you appeared. I thought when you didn't make New Year's Eve that you were having second thoughts...about us,' she confessed.

'*Me* having second thoughts… There's no way I could ever have second thoughts about the way I feel about you…about what I want with you…'

Lisa took a deep breath. There was something she had to tell him now, whilst they were both being so open and honest with one another.

'I did,' she confessed. '*I* had second thoughts…the day we parted…' She looked anxiously up at him; his face was unreadable, grave, craven almost, as he watched her in silence.

'I tried to tell you then,' she hurried on. 'I tried to say that I had changed my mind, but you didn't seem to want to listen and I thought that perhaps you had changed yours and that—'

'Changed your mind about what?' Oliver demanded hoarsely, cutting across her.

'About…about wanting to make a commitment,' Lisa admitted, stammering slightly as she searched his face anxiously, looking for some indication as to how he felt about what she was saying, but she could see none. Her heart started to hammer nervously against her ribs. Had she said too much? Had she…? Determinedly she pushed her uncertainty away.

'I knew then that it was just fear that had stopped me from telling you what I already knew… That I *did* love you and that I did want to be with you… I was even going to suggest that I went to New York with you.' She paused, laughing shakily. 'When it came to it I just couldn't bear the thought of not being with you, but you seemed so preoccupied and distant that I thought—'

'You were going to tell me that…?' Oliver interrupted her. 'Oh, my God, Lisa… Lisa…'

Any response she might have made was muffled by the hard pressure of his mouth against hers as, ignoring her protests that he might hurt his injured arm, he gathered her up, held her against his body and kissed her with all the hungry passion she had dreamed of in the time they had been apart.

'Lisa, Lisa, *why* didn't you say something to me?' Oliver groaned when he had finally finished kissing her. 'Why...?'

'Because I didn't think you wanted to hear,' Lisa told him simply. 'You were so distant and—'

'I was trying to stop myself from pleading with you to change your mind and come with me,' Oliver told her grimly. '*That* was why I was quiet.'

'Oh, Oliver...'

'Oh, Lisa,' he mimicked. 'How long do you suppose your mother will be gone?' he asked her as he bent his head to kiss her a second time.

'I don't know, but she did say something about going to see an exhibition at the Tate,' Lisa mumbled through his kiss.

'Mmm...' He was looking, Lisa noticed, towards the half-open bedroom door, and her own body started to react to the message she could read in his eyes as she followed his gaze.

'We can't,' she protested without conviction. 'What about your arm? And you still haven't told me about the accident,' she reminded him.

'I will,' he promised her, and added wickedly, 'They said at the hospital that I should get plenty of rest and that I shouldn't stand up for too long. They said that the best cure for me would be...' And he bent his head and whispered in Lisa's ear exactly what he had in mind for the two of them for the rest of the afternoon.

'Tell me about the accident first,' Lisa insisted, blushing a little as she saw the look he gave her when he caught that betraying 'first'.

'Very well,' he agreed, adding ruefully, 'Although, it doesn't make very good hearing.

'I didn't find out until we were back in Yorkshire that you weren't marrying Henry, but once I did and I realised what I'd done I broke all the rules and drove straight back here despite the fact that I hadn't had any sleep for going on three days and that I was jet-lagged into the bargain. Hardly a sensible or safety-conscious decision but...' He gave a small, self-deprecatory grimace. 'I was hardly feeling either sensible or safety-conscious; after all, what else had I got left to lose? I'd already destroyed the most precious thing I had in my life.

'Anyway...I must have started to doze off at the wheel; fortunately I'd already decided to stop at a motorway service station and I'd slowed down and pulled onto the approach road, and even more fortunately there was no other vehicle, no other person around to be involved in my self-imposed accident. The authorities told me that I was lucky my car was fitted with so many safety features...otherwise...'

'No, don't,' Lisa begged him, shuddering as her imagination painted an all too vivid picture of just how differently things could have turned out.

'Lisa, I know there is nothing I can say or do that can take away the memory of what I did; all I can do is promise you that it will never happen again and ask if you can forgive me.'

'It did hurt that you could think such a thing of me,' Lisa admitted quietly, 'and that you could...could treat me in such a way, but I *do* understand. In a way both of us were responsible for what happened; both of us should have trusted the other and our love more. If we had had more mutual trust, more mutual faith in our love then... Oh, Oliver,' she finished, torn between laughter and tears as she clung onto him. 'How could you possibly think I could even contemplate the idea of marrying anyone else, never mind Henry, after you...after the way you and I...?'

'Even when mentally I was trying to hate you I was still loving you physically and emotionally,' Oliver told her huskily. 'The moment I touched you... I never intended things to go so far; I'd just meant to kiss you one last time, that was all, but once I had...'

'Once you had what?' Lisa encouraged him, raising herself up on tiptoe to feather her lips teasingly against his.

'Once I had...this,' Oliver responded, smothering a groan deep in his throat as he pulled her against him with his good arm and held her there, letting her feel the immediate and passionate response of his body to her as he kissed her.

'We really ought to get up,' Lisa murmured sleepily, her words belying her actions as she snuggled closer to Oliver's side. 'The day's almost gone and...'

'Soon it will be bedtime. I know,' Oliver finished mock-wickedly for her. 'It was very thoughtful of your mother to telephone and say that she'd decided to go and visit some friends this evening and to stay overnight with them...'

'Mmm...very,' Lisa agreed, sighing leisurely as Oliver's hand cupped her breast.

'Mmm...that feels nice,' she told him.

'It certainly does,' Oliver agreed, and asked her softly, 'And does this?' as he bent his head and started to kiss the soft curve of her throat.

'I'm not sure... Perhaps if you did it for a bit longer,' Lisa suggested helpfully. 'A lot longer,' she amended more huskily as his mouth started to drift with delicious intent towards her breast... 'A lot, *lot* longer.'

EPILOGUE

'HOW DOES THAT LOOK?'

Lisa put her head to one side judiciously as she studied the huge Christmas tree that Oliver had just finished erecting in the hallway.

'I think it needs moving a little to the left; it's leaning slightly,' she told him, and then laughed as she saw his pained expression.

'No, darling, it's perfect,' she added with a happy sigh. They had been married for eight months, their wedding having preceded both Henry's and Piers'. Lisa's parents had both flown home for the wedding and Lisa and Oliver had flown out to Japan to spend three weeks with them in October.

Fergus had been disappointed when Lisa had handed in her notice, but she and Oliver were talking about the possibility of her setting up her own business in the north in partnership with Fergus. It seemed almost impossible to Lisa that it was almost twelve months since that fateful night when Oliver had found her stranded on the road and brought her home with him. Her smile deepened as she glanced down at the Armani suit she was wearing—a surprise gift from Oliver to mark the anniversary of the day they had initially met.

'Happy?' Oliver asked her, bending his head to kiss her.

'Mmm...how could I not be?' Lisa answered, snuggling closer to him. 'Oh, Oliver, last Christmas was wonderful, special, something I'll never forget, but this Christmas is going to be special too; I'm so glad that everyone's been able to come—your family and my parents.'

'We're certainly going to have a houseful,' Oliver agreed, laughing.

He had raised his eyebrows slightly at first when Lisa had suggested to him that they invite all his own relatives and her parents to spend their Christmas with them, but Lisa's enthusiasm for the idea had soon won him over.

'You really do love all this, don't you?' he commented now, indicating the large hallway festooned now for Christmas with the garlands and decorations that Lisa had spent hours making.

'Yes, I do,' Lisa agreed, 'but not anything like as much as I love you. Oh, Oliver,' she told him, her voice suddenly husky with emotion, 'you've made me so happy. It's hard to imagine that twelve months ago we barely knew one another and that—I love you so much.'

'Not half as much as I love you,' Oliver whispered back, his mouth feathering against hers and then hardening as he felt her happy response.

'We still haven't put the star on the tree,' Lisa reminded Oliver through their kiss.

'*You* are my star,' he told her tenderly, 'and without you I'd be lost in the darkness of unhappiness. You light up my life, Lisa, and I never, ever want to be without you.'

'You never, ever will,' Lisa promised him.

'Hey, come on, you two, break it up,' Piers demanded, coming into the hallway carrying a basket of logs for the fire. 'You're married now—remember?'

'Yes, we're married,' Oliver agreed, giving Lisa a look that made her laugh and blush slightly at the same time, as he picked up the star waiting to be placed at the top of the tree—the final touch to a Christmas that would be all the things that Christmas should be, that Christmas and every day *would* be for her from now on.

Oliver *was* her Christmas, all her special times, her life, her love.

* * * * *

THE WINTER BRIDE

USA TODAY Bestselling Author
Lynne Graham

CHAPTER ONE

'A RISE...YOU'RE ACTUALLY *asking* us for a *rise*?' Claudia looked at the younger woman with shocked and incredulous eyes, much as if the girl had asked for a half-share in the house. 'I think we're more than generous as it is. You have your salary as well as free board and lodging, and do please remember that we're keeping *two* of you!'

Although Angie was severely embarrassed by that response, she forced herself to continue. 'I often work six days a week and I baby-sit several nights as well...'

Her persistence fired angry colour in the elegant brunette's cheeks. 'I can't believe that we're even having this conversation. You do some housework and you mind the children. Why shouldn't you baby-sit? You have to sit in every night to look after Jake...surely you're not expecting us to pay extra for what you'd be doing anyway? I don't know how you can be so ungrateful after all we've done for you—'

'I'm just finding it very hard to make ends meet,' Angie slotted in tightly, a deep sense of humiliation creeping over her.

'Well, I'm sure I don't know what you're doing with your salary when you have all your bills paid for you,' her employer retorted very drily. 'What I do know is that my husband, George, will be extremely shocked when I tell him about this demand of yours.'

'It wasn't a demand,' Angie countered tensely. 'It was a request.'

'Request refused, then,' Claudia told her sharply as she stalked to the kitchen door. 'I'm very annoyed about this and *very* disappointed in you, Angie. You have a really cushy job here. Gosh, I wish someone would pay *me* to stay home and fill the dishwasher! We treat you and Jake like part of our family. We kept you on when you were pregnant...and let me assure you that not one of our friends would even have *considered* retaining a pregnant and unmarried au pair in their home!'

Angie said nothing. There was nothing more to say unless she was prepared to risk Claudia's explosive temper and the threat of dismissal. No au pair worked the hours Angie did. But then she wasn't an au pair even though Claudia persisted in calling her one. She might have come to the Dickson family in that guise, accepting the equivalent of pocket money in place of a salary, but slowly and surely her hours had crept up until she was doing the full-time job of a housekeeper and childminder. At the time she had been so grateful to still have a roof over her head that she had made no objection.

But then she had been very naive when she was pregnant. She had seen the Dicksons as a temporary staging post, had fondly imagined that once she had her baby she would be able to move on to better-paid employment and build up her life again. But piece by piece that confidence had faded once she appreciated the cost of child care and the even greater cost of renting accommodation in a city as expensive as London. Ultimately it had come down to a choice between continuing to work for the Dicksons and moving out to live on welfare.

'We'll say no more about this,' Claudia murmured graciously from the doorway, well aware that silence meant that she had won. 'Do you think you could start putting the children in the bath now? It is half past six, and they're so dreadfully noisy when they get over-tired.'

By the time Angie had got the children to bed it was well

after eight, and George and Claudia had long since gone out
to dine. Six-year-old Sophia and the four-year-old twins, Bene-
dict and Oscar, were lovely children—very rich in material
possessions but pretty much starved of parental attention.
Their father was a circuit judge, regularly away from home,
and their mother a high-powered businesswoman, who only
rarely left her office before seven in the evening.

They had a spacious, beautifully furnished home and a
Porsche and a Range Rover, but Claudia was so mean with
money that she had had a pay meter installed on the gas fire
in Angie's room over the attached garage. Since the room had
no central heating, and had originally been cheaply converted
only for the purpose of storage space, it was freezing cold in
winter.

The doorbell shrilled while Angie was ensuring that the
only part of her son exposed to that chilly air was the crown
of his dark, curly head. She tucked the duvet round Jake in
a rush and hurtled through the door that connected with the
bedroom corridor to race downstairs before the bell could go
again and wake Sophia, who was a very light sleeper.

Thrusting back the wild tangle of platinum pale hair that
had flown round her anxious face, she pressed the intercom.
'Who is it?' she asked breathlessly.

'Angie…?'

In severe shock, Angie fell back from the intercom. Like
sand on silk, and splinteringly, shatteringly sexy, the voice had
a husky Greek accent that roughened every vowel sound. It
had been over two years since she had heard that masculine
drawl and recognition filled her with sheer, blind panic.

The doorbell went again in a short, impatient burst.

'Please don't do that…you'll wake the children!' Angie
gasped into the intercom.

'Angie…open the door,' Leo drawled flatly.

'I—I *can't*…I'm not allowed to open it when I'm alone in

the house at night,' Angie muttered with feverish relief in telling the truth. 'I don't know what you want or how you found me, and I don't care. Just go away!'

In answer, Leo hit the doorbell again.

With a groan of frustration, Angie flew out into the porch, wrenched back the curtains, undid the bolts and the chain and dragged open the front door.

'Thank you,' Leo responded with icy precision.

Poleaxed by his very presence, Angie gaped at him, her pulse thudding wildly at the foot of her throat. 'You still can't come in...'

A winged ebony brow lifted with hauteur. 'Don't be ridiculous.'

Involuntarily, Angie gazed up into eyes the colour of a wild and stormy night, and a shiver of shaken reaction ran through her. Leo Demetrios in the flesh. He was standing close enough to touch on the Dicksons' doorstep, six feet three inches of daunting sophistication and devastating masculinity. Broad shoulders filled out his superbly cut dinner jacket, perfectly tailored black trousers accentuating lean hips and long, long legs. The overhead security light delineated every carved angle of his savagely handsome features and glinted over his thick blue-black hair, but she still couldn't believe that he was really, genuinely there in front of her.

'You can't come in,' she said again, running damp palms down over her faded jeans.

'Angie...I wanna drink...I'm thirsty,' Sophia mumbled sleepily from the stairs.

Angie jumped and spun round to rush back into the dimly lit hall. 'Go back to bed and I'll bring you one up...'

Leo stepped into the porch and quietly closed the door. Angie turned again, giving him a dismayed and pleading look, but she didn't want to speak to him and alert the sleepy Sophia to the presence of a forbidden visitor. Biting her lip in frantic frustration, she left him there and sped into the kitchen to pour a glass of water and took it upstairs. Claudia and George had only gone out for a quick meal and they might be on their way back even now. They would be absolutely outraged if they found her entertaining a strange man in their home.

Her thoughts in complete turmoil as she struggled to understand why Leo should have sought her out, she settled Sophia and started hurriedly down the stairs again. Mercifully, Leo was still standing in the hall. She wouldn't have been surprised to find him installed on one of the leather sofas in the drawing room. People ran out red carpets when Leo condescended to visit; they didn't keep him on the doorstep or leave him to hover in the hall. His hugely successful global electronics empire generated immense wealth, and he wielded formidable power and influence in the business world.

Belatedly encountering Leo's raking and uninhibited scrutiny of her slender but shapely figure, Angie faltered on the last step of the stairs. His spectacular dark, deep-set eyes smouldered as they skimmed up from the surprisingly full thrust of her breasts to strike her own eyes in direct collision. She ran out of breath and mobility simultaneously, throat closing over, heart pounding so suffocatingly fast behind her ribcage that she felt dizzy.

'I won't keep you long,' Leo informed her with a sardonic smile.

'What are you doing here?' Angie practically whispered, struggling to surmount that momentary loss of concentration and finding it almost impossible until a stark current of foreboding assailed her and her bright blue eyes widened in sudden dismay. 'Are you here because of my father? Is he ill or something?'

Leo frowned. 'To my knowledge, Brown is in good health.'

Angie flushed brick-red, utterly mortified by the spurt of

fear that had prompted her foolish enquiry. She perfectly understood Leo's brief look of disconcertion. No doubt it would be a cold day in hell before Leo Demetrios stooped to act as a messenger boy for one of his grandfather's servants!

In an awkward invitation and sudden revolt against Claudia's rigid rules, she pressed open the door of the little TV room. 'We can talk in here,' she said stiffly, striving desperately for an air of normality.

But oh, dear heaven, that was an impossible challenge with Jake enjoying the sleep of the innocent upstairs and Leo behaving like a coldly polite stranger. Maybe he was afraid that if he was friendly she might throw herself at him again, Angie thought in sudden, cringing horror. Her colour fluctuating wildly, she dropped her head, but cruelly humiliating memories still bombarded her like guided missiles finding an easy target.

She had been foolishly obsessed with Leo for more years than she now cared to recall. And she had not been the sort of dreaming teenager who sat around simply hoping for a miracle to occur. At nineteen, she had plotted and planned like crazy to get her chance with Leo. She had broken every rule in the book to catch him. She had forgotten who he was and who she was in the chase. And, at the end of the day, she had got very much what she had asked for—Leo had dumped her so hard and fast, her head had spun.

The silence pounded and pulsed.

Nervously, Angie glanced up to find Leo watching her again. Involuntarily, she was entrapped, pulses quickening, skin dampening. Colour drenched her complexion. She ran a nervous hand through the long hair falling round her face, and moved her head to toss it back out of her way. Leo's gaze followed the rippling motion of that cascade of pale, shining strands, increasing her self-consciousness. Then dense black lashes veiled his burnished dark eyes, and his beautifully shaped, sensual mouth hardened again.

'How did you find out where I lived?' Angie asked in a jerky rush, because the silence was unbearable. She did not have his nerves of steel and self-discipline.

'My grandfather asked me to trace you—'

Her fine brows pleated. '*Wallace?*' she broke in incredulously, referring to his English grandfather whose daughter had married Leo's father, a Greek shipping magnate.

'I'm here only to pass on an invitation,' Leo imparted smoothly. 'Wallace would like you to spend Christmas with him.'

'Christmas?' Angie parroted weakly.

'He wants to become acquainted with his great-grandson.'

That final, shattering announcement left Angie gaping at him in even deeper shock. Her knees threatening to give way, she groped her passage down into an armchair. Leo *knew* she had been pregnant? Leo *knew* that she now had a child? She had never dreamt that Wallace Neville might share that secret with his grandson.

And now Wallace actually wanted to *meet* Jake? Yet Wallace had forcefully urged her to terminate her pregnancy over two years ago. The news that the butler's daughter had been impregnated by one of his grandsons had so appalled him, he had been apoplectic with rage. An unapologetic snob with a horror of scandal, he had been eager to facilitate Angie's departure from Deveraux Court that very same day.

'Old men feel their mortality.' Leo's dark eyes rested unreadably on her stunningly beautiful face. 'And, frankly, curiosity seems to be killing him. Obviously it will be in your best interests to grovel gratefully in the face of his generosity.'

'Grovel?' Angie echoed in complete bewilderment.

Leo's appraisal became grim, his mouth twisting. 'I know

about the deal you made with Wallace, Angie. I know the *whole* story.'

Angie stiffened in disbelief, lashes dropping low on fiercely anxious eyes. 'I haven't a clue what you're talking about.'

'You know very well what I'm talking about,' Leo countered steadily.

Her slim fingers closed together and clenched. She studied the carpet until it blurred, her stomach churning with sick apprehension.

'The thefts, Angie,' Leo supplied without remorse. 'Wallace caught you in the act and you confessed.'

Her head flew up, anguish and resentment mingling in her stricken face. 'He promised that he would never tell anyone!'

She wanted to die right there and then. Wallace had promised, Wallace had promised faithfully—and by 'anyone' Angie had meant specifically *Leo*. She could not bear the knowledge that Leo thought she had been the thief, responsible for stealing several small but valuable *objets d'art* from Deveraux Court where her father and stepmother both worked and lived.

'Angie, nothing disappeared after your departure. That fact rather spoke for itself. Wallace had little hope of keeping the identity of the culprit under wraps.'

'So my father must know as well,' she mumbled, mortified pain clogging up her vocal cords as she made that final leap in understanding.

'I've never discussed the matter with him,' Leo retorted crisply.

In all her life, Angie knew she had never tasted greater humiliation. Her shaken eyes stung fiercely. She studied Leo's hand-stitched Italian leather shoes and hated him for believing and accepting that she had been the thief. And, even more cruelly, throwing that conviction in her face. Was this why he had referred to Jake as if her child were nothing whatsoever to do with him?

Was her supposed dishonesty so offensive that Leo could not bring himself to acknowledge that she was the mother of his child? she asked herself in growing bewilderment. What had Leo said? *Wallace* wanted to become acquainted with his great-grandson. Had that been Leo's way of telling her that he himself had no intention of taking the smallest interest in Jake? She found that she couldn't think straight because nothing Leo had yet said had made any kind of sense to her.

'I want you to leave,' Angie confided shakily. 'I didn't ask you to come looking for me.'

'That's an irrational response and you'll think better of it within a very short space of time,' Leo asserted crushingly. 'Wallace would have called the police if you hadn't told him that you were pregnant. You were fortunate to escape a prison sentence. Those thefts took place over a long period. They were neither opportunistic nor the result of someone succumbing to sudden temptation.'

Briefly, Angie closed her aching eyes in a spasm of bitter regret. When in the heat of the moment she had confessed to something she hadn't done, she had been bolstered by the belief that she was protecting someone she loved and that, in any case, she herself had nothing more to lose. After all, she had already lost Leo, had already accepted that she would have to leave Deveraux Court before her condition became obvious. She had been too proud and too devastated by Leo's rejection to confront him with the consequences of their stolen weekend of passion.

'Wallace is prepared to overlook the past for the sake of your child,' Leo continued levelly.

'My child has a name…and his name is Jake,' Angie told him thinly.

If possible, Leo's rawly handsome features set even harder

as he ignored that unasked-for piece of information. 'In your position it would be very foolish to ignore the offer of an olive branch. I believe that Wallace may now be willing to give you financial assistance.'

'I want nothing from any of you.' Hotly flushed and deeply chagrined by the assurance, Angie leapt upright again. 'But I would like to know why Wallace should feel it's *his* responsibility to offer me money!'

Diamond-hard dark eyes assailed hers in icy collision. 'Obviously because his grandson Drew has failed to observe his duty to support you both.'

In stark confusion, Angie froze. How was it Drew's duty to support her and Jake? And then finally, and most belatedly, comprehension gripped her, only to leave her drowning in bemusement again. Evidently, Leo was under the impression that his cousin, Drew, had fathered her child. How on earth could he think that? How on earth could *anyone* think that?

Outrage swelled inside Angie until she thought the top of her head might come flying off. In that instant it didn't matter how such a ludicrous misapprehension had come about. Angie was too infuriated by Leo's evident opinion of her morals to concern herself with anything else. So, Leo saw her as a thief *and* a tart. After all, only a fairly promiscuous young woman would have become intimate with *both* of Wallace's grandsons within the space of three months. But Leo was clearly quite happy to believe that she had slept with his cousin after sleeping with him, and no doubt was even more content to believe that responsibility for her illegitimate child could be laid at Drew's door rather than his own.

'Angie, I didn't come here to argue with you or to become involved in personal matters which are frankly nothing to do with me,' Leo drawled in a tone of cool reproof. 'I've issued the invitation on Wallace's behalf, and I haven't got the time to wrangle with you—I have a date, and I'm already running very late.'

For a split second, Angie felt as though he had plunged a knife into her ribs and stabbed her to the heart. *A date?* So the grieving widower was finally back in social circulation... Wow, bully for him! And, naturally, Angie's sordid personal problems were beneath his notice and wholly devoid of interest to him. Indeed, knowing Leo as she did—brutally candid, highly intelligent and uncontrolled only in bed, she enumerated painfully—he had probably been congratulating himself on a narrow escape from severe embarrassment ever since she'd been exposed as the household thief.

'Angie...?' Leo prompted.

She turned round, her perfect features pale and set. As the bitterness rose inside her, it was the most unbearable moment of temptation she had ever experienced. She had a sudden fierce urge to smash Leo's self-possession, punish him for his deliberate distancing of himself from her predicament and hurt him, as he was hurting her with the humiliating pretence that they had never been anything to each other but casual acquaintances.

His hard, dark features were impatient. 'Wallace is expecting you to arrive on Thursday. I assume I can give him the assurance that you will be accepting his invitation?'

In the unstable hold of a tidal wave of conflicting emotion, Angie tore her pained eyes from the dark, savage splendour of Leo as he stood there, so effortlessly detached from her. The anger went out of her at that same moment.

'You've just got to be kidding,' she breathed with a forced and brittle smile. 'I have no desire to spend Christmas with your grandfather, and I should think he would have even less desire to spend it with me.'

'I thought you might, at the very least, be tempted by the possibility of a reconciliation with your own family.'

A humourless laugh was dredged from Angie. Reconciliation? He didn't know what he was talking about. She had never had anything but an uneasy and difficult relationship with her father. Now an unwed mother, and labelled a thief into the bargain, what possible welcome did Leo fondly imagine she would receive?

'When I walked out of Deveraux Court...' her throat thickened, making her voice gruff '...I knew I would never be walking back. I wasn't sorry to leave and I don't want to return even for a visit. That whole phase of my life is behind me now.'

Bold dark eyes scanned her strained profile in exasperation. 'I suppose it was less than tactful of me to mention the thefts.'

Angie grimaced, willing back tears, determined not to break down in front of him. 'I would never expect tact or consideration from you,' she told him helplessly. 'But I really do object to being patronised. You're out of your mind if you think I would be willing to go cap in hand to your grandfather like some pathetic charity case! I've managed fine on my own.'

The very faintest darkening of colour emphasised the hard slant of Leo's high cheekbones. 'You are working as a servant...you always swore that you would never do that.'

Angie flinched, fingernails biting painfully into her palms. Servant. Not for Leo, surrounded from birth by the faceless breed, with the more egalitarian label of 'domestic staff'. As hot pink scored her complexion, she whirled away from him before she was tempted to slap him for that most undiplomatic reminder.

'*Theos*... Only the most stupid and selfish pride could make you refuse so magnanimous an invitation! Wallace could do a great deal for your son. Think of the child. Why should he suffer for your mistakes?' Leo demanded abrasively. 'It is your duty as a mother to consider his future.'

A raw ripple of pain and fury sizzled through Angie as she spun back, blue eyes gleaming like sapphires. 'And what about his father's duty?'

His wide, sensual mouth twisted. 'When you got into bed with someone as self-centred and irresponsible as Drew, you must've known that you'd be on your own if anything went wrong.'

Leo was angry, Angie registered in surprise. Tension splintered from the fierce cast of his strong features and icy condemnation glittered in his narrowed gaze. Recognising that look for what it was, Angie realised that Leo was not quite as indifferent as he would like to pretend when it came to his conviction that she had leapt into his cousin's bed so soon after she had succumbed to him. Bitter amusement filled her at the awareness. *He* hadn't wanted her but it seemed he hadn't wanted any other man to want her either.

'Believe it or not, at the time I thought Jake's father was as steady as a rock,' Angie heard herself admit, tongue-in-cheek. 'I was very much in love with him. In fact I believed he was the very last man likely to leave me in the lurch.'

'You were only nineteen...what did you know then of men or their motivations?' Leo's response was harsh, dismissive, as he glanced with sudden, unconcealed impatience at the thin gold watch on his wrist and strode towards the door. 'I'm afraid I really do have to leave.'

The abruptness of his exit took Angie by surprise. She sped out after him and by then he was already in the porch. As she opened the door, he stared broodingly down at her and, without warning, time slid dangerously back for Angie and served up a disturbingly intimate memory. Leo...responding with shockingly primal dominance to her flirtation, pinning her down in the meadow grass by the lake and crushing her lips beneath his with an explosive, driving hunger that had just blown her away. Embarrassed heat coiled like a burning, aching taunt low in Angie's stomach.

A feverish darkness now overlaid the oblique slant of Leo's cheekbones, but sardonic amusement glittered in his brilliant eyes. He raised a hand and let a long brown forefinger trail gently along the tremulous line of her soft, full mouth, leaving a stunning chain of prickling sensitivity in his wake and sentencing her to shaken stillness. 'You really are wasted in a domestic role, Angie.'

And then, before she could catch her arrested breath, he swung away, striding out into the night air. 'Think over what I have said,' he urged almost carelessly. 'Wallace is keen to meet the child... I'll call tomorrow for your answer.'

'No, don't. There's no point. I've made up my mind and I don't need a night's sleep to consider it,' Angie told him tightly. 'In any case, I couldn't get the time off. The Dicksons have a very busy social calendar over the next ten days, and the house is always full of visitors over Christmas.'

'Can you really have changed so much?' Leo murmured lazily. 'I believed you would walk out of this house like you walked out of my grandfather's without a backward glance.'

Angie flushed furiously. Naturally Leo had assumed that the prospect of money would make her eagerly snatch at his grandfather's invitation, but he had miscalculated. Had *she*? She hadn't told him that Jake was his—had almost done so in anger, but had ultimately remained silent. Why? At the back of her mind lurked the shameful and mortifying recollection that she had told Leo that it was safe to make love to her that weekend...and she had lied, with both purpose and full knowledge of what she was doing.

From the doorway, she watched numbly as Leo strode towards the sleek black Ferrari parked at a careless angle across the paved frontage of the house. Dimly, she registered that she was trembling; reaction was setting in after the terrible tension, sudden coldness biting into her bones.

Headlights suddenly lit up the front garden. Dredged from her introspection, Angie uttered a soundless groan as George's Range Rover raked to a halt.

Claudia virtually leapt from the car. 'What on earth is going on here?' she demanded, casting Leo, who stood in the shadows, a haughty, questioning look, but aiming her ire at Angie as she stalked towards her.

'I called with a message for Angie,' Leo drawled coolly.

'You let a strange man into the house with my children sleeping upstairs?' Claudia ranted in furious attack.

'Darling…' her less volatile husband said rather loudly. 'I don't believe that Mr Demetrios quite qualifies as a strange man.'

'My father works for Leo,' Angie said for the sake of brevity. 'I've known him for years.'

Claudia had come to a halt, glancing uncertainly at her husband for guidance. Her tall, thin spouse was calmly shaking hands with Leo. Angrily conscious that she might have made a fool of herself, Claudia gave Angie a filthy look. 'We'll discuss this matter in private.'

'If you don't mind, I'm going to bed now,' Angie replied with quiet dignity. 'Leo kept on ringing the bell. I had to let him in.'

She climbed the stairs, conscious that she had no hope of ultimately escaping one of Claudia's bossy lectures, but too weary and shaken by Leo's visit to care. Considering the length of Angie's employment with her, Claudia ought to be able to trust her by now not to invite an armed robber or child molester into the house. She was almost twenty-two, not a feckless teenage baby-sitter.

Yet Leo had made her feel very much like a teenager again, she conceded grudgingly—hot, bothered, awkward, over-sensitive to atmosphere. It had been embarrassment, she told herself—the embarrassment of memories that no woman with any pride would want to recall. And that was *all*.

Determined to be satisfied with that explanation, she climbed into the bed across the room from Jake's, having fought a very heavy battle against a feverish longing to snatch him out of bed and hug him tight to comfort herself. That would be selfish, and she was *not* a selfish mother...was she? No, of course she wasn't.

She put up with an employer who would have taxed the temper of a saint just so that Jake could eat well, live in a comfortable house and play in a spacious garden with lots of toys. So he had virtually nothing to call his own, and his clothes were all the twins' hand-me-downs, but he was still too little to appreciate those facts. This year she had wanted to give him a proper Christmas, though. That was why she had dared to risk Claudia's wrath to ask for more money, but the recollection of the earlier part of the evening could no longer hold her concentration...

It was almost impossible for her to believe that Wallace Neville was willing to entertain the butler's daughter at his vast ancestral home. Would he have invited her to stay in the main house, or would he have expected her to squash herself back into her father and stepmother's disgracefully damp and desolate little basement flat? And if Leo's grandfather *had* offered her financial help, would she have been weak enough to accept it?

Uneasy with the thought, Angie tossed and turned sleeplessly. It was out of the question anyway. Claudia would blow a gasket if Angie demanded time off over Christmas, and until Jake was old enough to start nursery school at least the Dicksons were their security.

Even so, she still lay awake, staring into the darkness, helplessly remembering the first time she had seen Leo when she was thirteen. Every Christmas and every summer he had come to stay with his grandfather, and although his English was perfect he had remained quintessentially Greek. Exotic, fascinating and extravagantly handsome, he had become the natural focus of Angie's first crush. Of course, eight years her senior, he had barely noticed that she was alive in those days.

During the summer when she was fourteen, Leo had brought a girlfriend with him. She had had a very irritating giggle. With intense amusement, Angie had watched Leo wince. But the following year laughter had been thin on the ground. Petrina Phillipides had come to visit—a porcelain-perfect and dainty little Greek heiress with a cloud of silky black hair and an elderly maiden aunt in tow as a chaperon. Angie had ground her teeth in disbelief while she had watched Leo fall in love. Couldn't he see that Petrina was too spoilt, too conceited, too empty-headed, with her silly clothes and even sillier hairstyles, to provide lasting appeal for an intelligent man?

No, Leo had been blind, and the summer after that Petrina had had even better reason to look smug. She had been wearing Leo's engagement ring. Angie had been aghast, but even then she hadn't given up all hope. After all, many an engagement was broken before the altar was reached, she had reasoned, snatching at straws.

However, when Wallace had finally flown out to Leo's wedding and no last-minute miracle had prevented the dreadful deed from being done, Angie had been inconsolable. But by then she had been seventeen, and thoroughly fed up with herself for ever having wasted time languishing over a male who had always been out of reach and who was now another woman's husband. So she had started dating herself and, boy, had she dated! Her five-foot-ten-inch model-slim body, sym-

metrical features and waist-length mane of pale blonde hair
had ensured that she was never short of eager admirers.

Petrina had been sullenly pregnant that Christmas, and the
unimpressed mother of a beautiful baby girl a few months
later. Leo had adored his daughter. Angie's heart had ached
when she'd seen him lavish unashamed love and warmth on
little Jenny, who had been named after his late mother. Petrina
had been an indifferent and petulant parent, thrusting her
baby back at the nanny as soon as she decently could, visibly
resenting the fact that her daughter and not herself was now
the centre of attention. And Angie had thought, Oh, Leo,
Leo…why didn't you wait for me to grow up?

But that very same year tragedy had intervened to destroy
Leo's family. Christmas hadn't been celebrated at Deveraux
Court. Wallace hadn't had the heart for it, and Leo had remained in Greece. His wife and his baby daughter had been
killed in a car crash. That next summer, however, Leo had
come back, alone and brooding, and he had taken up residence
in the Folly by the lake, shunning all company.

And Angie, in her complete and utter stupidity, had decided
that she was finally to have her chance with Leo, and that it
had to be then or never, before he flew back to Greece and
fell madly in love with some other unsuitable woman…

'Now that I know *who* Leo Demetrios is,' Claudia droned on
in her most gracious mood the following afternoon, 'I realise
that you could scarcely keep a man of his importance outside
the house. But he has to be the single exception to the rule,
Angie. Don't open that door again when we're out.'

Money fairly talked, Angie conceded grimly. Claudia had
already been on the phone to all her friends, saying things in
her carrying voice like, 'You'll never guess who we had in our
house last night…the most *utterly* charming man… Must be
worth *billions*… Yes, employs our au pair's father… Can you

believe, she didn't even offer him a cup of coffee? Probably quite overpowered by him just turning up like that... I don't think Greeks can be as class-conscious as we are...'

Oh, don't you believe it, Angie reflected with gritted teeth as she slammed shut the door on the washing machine and switched it on to drown out Claudia's verbal ecstasy. When Leo had sobered up to a dawn that woke him to the unlovely reality that he was actually sharing a bed with the butler's daughter, he had vacated that bed so fast, Angie had been cut to the bone. But even then she had been poorly prepared for the blunt and wounding force of the rejection which had so swiftly concluded their brief intimacy and left her bereft of any hope...or pride.

The doorbell went. Angie padded through to the hall and then stopped dead in the porch. Through the side window, she could see the long, impressive bonnet of a chauffeur-driven limousine. Suddenly breathless with an undeniable sense of anticipation, she pulled open the door. Leo, a breathtakingly elegant vision in a dove-grey suit, white silk shirt and pale blue tie, gazed down at her. He looked drop-dead gorgeous.

And Angie's treacherous heartbeat hit a dizzy peak, as if she were riding a big dipper. The most intense and shattering surge of physical awareness paralysed her to the spot.

'I wasn't expecting you to come back,' Angie whispered.

Leo dealt her the most fleeting glance before flashing a brilliant smile at something or someone over her shoulder. 'Mrs Dickson?'

'Claudia, *please*...' the brunette carolled.

Leo strode past Angie as if she were the invisible woman and grasped Claudia's eagerly extended hand.

'Leo...?' Angie muttered in confusion.

'I'm here to speak to your employer, Angie, if you would excuse us?'

'Come into the drawing room.' Claudia gave Leo a delighted smile. 'Make some coffee, Angie.'

Fizzing with incredulous annoyance at the dismissal, Angie went to put on the kettle then returned to the hall.

'*So* dreadfully sorry, but I'm afraid we couldn't possibly spare her at present. We'll have visitors staying over Christmas,' Claudia was saying apologetically.

Angie pressed the door wider and stood on the threshold, furious that she had been deliberately excluded from a discussion that related to her. How dared Leo do this? How dared he go over her head as if she were a child who could not speak up for herself?

'When *did* Angie last have a holiday?' Leo drawled softly from his stance by the marble fireplace.

Caught unprepared by the question, Claudia frowned. 'Well, er...'

'In fact, Angie doesn't receive holidays in this household, does she, Mrs Dickson?' Raw contempt glittered in Leo's steady gaze.

'Where on earth did you get that idea?' Claudia asked rather shrilly.

'Leo—' Angie began weakly.

'Angie's working conditions are the talk of the neighbourhood,' Leo countered with biting censure, his strong, hard-boned features grim. 'Indeed, sweatshop labour would be a generous description of her terms of employment within your home.'

'I...I beg your pardon?' Her face mottling with ugly colour, Claudia was openly shocked by the sudden attack.

'*Leo*, for heaven's sake!' Angie intervened in horror.

But Leo didn't even glance in her direction. 'You took advantage of a pregnant teenager. For more than two years you have worked her round the clock and paid her peanuts for the privilege. One has a duty of care towards one's staff, but you have disregarded that fact. As you are neither poor nor unintelligent, there is no extenuating circumstance which might excuse such unscrupulous behaviour.'

'How *dare* you speak to me like that? Get out of my house!' Claudia was now brick-red with disbelieving fury.

'Go and pack, Angie,' Leo murmured without batting a magnificent eyelash; indeed, the curious beginnings of a smile were already tugging at the corners of his sensual mouth. 'I will wait in the car.'

'I'm not going anywhere...' Angie began unevenly.

'The *talk* of the neighbourhood, am I?' Claudia sent the younger woman a look of outraged accusation. 'When I think of what we've done for you—'

'You've done nothing but use her for your own selfish purposes,' Leo interposed with sardonic cool.

'You're sacked... I want you and that child of yours out of this house—*right now*!' Claudia screeched at Angie, full blast.

CHAPTER TWO

WHITE-FACED, ANGIE LUGGED a battered suitcase out through the front door with Claudia still shouting recriminations in her wake. A sturdy older man in a chauffeur's uniform was waiting in silent readiness to take her case. The front door slammed thunderously shut behind her.

Lifting an unsteady hand to press it to her pounding, perspiring brow, Angie hurried round the side of the house to the fenced-in back garden where Jake had mercifully remained throughout the agonising minutes it had taken for her to strip their room of their possessions. And with Claudia standing over her, bent on retribution, their possessions, such as they were, had shrunk alarmingly. The brunette had angrily refused to allow Angie to pack any of Jake's clothes, saying that the twins' cast-offs had only been given to her on loan and not to keep. She had maintained the same line when it came to Jake's toys, which the Dickson children had long since outgrown.

A frightening vision of her former employer forcibly stripping Jake to the buff in the teeth of the winter wind impelling her, Angie raced across the back garden to the sandpit and literally snatched Jake's sturdy little body into her arms. He looked up at her with a startled frown, huge dark eyes wide. 'Oh, Jake,' she almost sobbed as she cuddled her son close and buried her face momentarily in his sweet-smelling, springy black curls. 'I will kill Leo for doing this to you...I swear it!'

The chauffeur whipped open the passenger door of the

limousine. Seeing that Claudia had now emerged from the house, Angie leapt in before Jake could be wrenched out of his shabby duffel coat and dungarees, not to mention his wellington boots.

As the chauffeur closed the door and walked round the bonnet at a stately pace which seemed to challenge Claudia's aggressive stance, the silence in the spacious, leather-upholstered back seat seemed to thunder. Struggling for breath, her breasts still heaving from her frantic rush to protect Jake from a direct collision with Claudia's malice, Angie glanced up. A stark frown drawing his winged black brows together, Leo was staring fixedly at the child on her lap.

'He is very…dark,' Leo selected after some hesitation.

Angie cloaked startled eyes and bent her head as she swung Jake off her knees onto the seat and began to fiddle with the belt to strap him safely in.

'I thought the child would be blond…' Leo added half under his breath, still staring as Jake swivelled to look up at him with lustrous dark brown eyes fringed with curling black lashes, the natural olive tone of his skin obvious against the white polo neck rolled under his dimpled chin.

In panic, Angie thought fast. 'He takes after my mother… she was as dark as a Celt. It happens that way sometimes—genes, you know, throwback genes,' Angie muttered rather wildly, and then, reddening, she compressed her lips.

'I never met your mother.'

Angie had been very much hoping that he hadn't for her late mother had been as blonde as her daughter. But her mother had only lived at Deveraux Court for a few months before she had walked out on her marriage, pregnant but preferring to go it alone rather than stay with a husband whom she had swiftly learned to despise for his lack of ambition.

Angie breathed in slowly and deeply. It didn't help to steady her leaping nerves or to subdue the dangerous surge of anger ready to explode from her lips. She focused on Jake's down-bent dark head and faithfully promised herself that she would not raise her voice and risk upsetting her son.

'Do you realise what you've done?' Her low-pitched enquiry shook with the effort it took to control her temper.

'*Theos*... It is beginning to sink in,' Leo confessed with outrageous calm. 'I cannot take you to Deveraux Court until Thursday at the earliest. Wallace has guests. It would be inappropriate for you to arrive while they remain.'

Angie trembled and threw her head up, eyes shimmering like piercing blue arrows of accusation. 'You have deprived my son of the only home and security he has ever known...'

'You should be thanking me.' Bold black eyes instantly challenged her.

'Th-thanking you?' Angie stammered in disbelief.

'How could you remain in that house enslaved by that harpy? Where is your spirit and sense, that you should've accepted such terms for so long?'

As raw rage splintered explosively through Angie's slender frame, she sucked in oxygen like a drowning swimmer in an effort to contain it. 'I stayed for my son's benefit,' she bit out tautly. 'I was able to be with him all day...and he's enjoyed many advantages there that I could never have given him.'

'I made a polite approach and a most modest request. That woman was not reasonable,' Leo asserted, smoothly disclaiming all responsibility.

'You interfered in something which was none of your business, and you gave Claudia precisely two minutes to snap to attention and do your bidding before you went on the offensive. I told you there was no way that I could leave the Dicksons over Christmas... I *told* you that nothing on earth would persuade me to go back to Deveraux Court,' Angie reminded him in a steadily rising crescendo. 'But you wouldn't listen, and now we're homeless and I'm out of a job!'

Leo cast her a gleaming look of reproof. 'Drop the dramatics, Angie. Naturally, I will assume responsibility for you both until such time as Wallace relieves me of the necessity.'

Angie was so close to exploding, she couldn't trust herself to speak.

'Thursday, you go to Deveraux Court and eat humble pie. I don't care if it chokes you. It is the price of reacceptance, and you will pay it,' Leo informed her with daunting conviction. 'Today I did you a favour.'

Angie gulped. 'A favour? As of this moment, my son has only the clothes he is wearing and not one single toy to his name—'

'Waff.' Jake spoke up for the first time, with an air of expectancy. 'Want Waff...'

Angie froze in dismay. 'Waff's at home, darling,' she muttered weakly. 'He couldn't come.'

Jake scowled, looking so shockingly like a miniature version of his father that for an instant Angie could not believe that Leo had not guessed the truth the minute he'd seen him. 'Want Waff...Waff like cars too.'

Angie swallowed the great lump threatening her throat and shot Leo a look of accusing censure. 'Perhaps you would like to explain that the T-O-Y,' she spelt out, 'which he has slept with every night of his life, no longer belongs to him.'

'What are you talking about? Ah...you mean you were careless enough to forget it in your rushed departure.'

'N-no, that's not what I meant,' Angie managed unevenly. 'All his clothes and almost all his playthings originally belonged to Claudia's children and she refused to let me remove any of them from the house—not very surprising, after the way you insulted her. She couldn't get back at you, so she took her temper out on my child instead!'

His lean, dark features stiffened with incredulous comprehension. 'His clothes...his *toys*?'

Angie nodded jerkily.

'Toy,' Jake said doggedly. 'Waff toy.'

'So we buy some more—particularly this Waff thing,' Leo gritted with stark impatience. 'I wouldn't have believed that any woman could exercise such petty spite!'

'A W-A-F-F cannot be bought at any price,' Angie informed him in a voice thick with condemnation and a deep inner dread of Jake's bedtime. 'It was made by Claudia's grandmother for Sophia. It's a pink giraffe.'

Leo spread unimpressed and autocratic lean brown hands. 'I will buy a proper giraffe.'

'It won't fool him, Leo.' Slowly, numbly, Angie shook her aching head, wondering why she was focusing on a humble but much loved soft toy when she didn't even know where they would be sleeping tonight. 'Where are you planning to take us?'

'My town house—where else?'

'I'm not going home with you!' Angie exclaimed in shock.

'Home,' Jake said more cheerfully. 'Waff...'

'He's obsessed,' Leo remarked disapprovingly.

'He's still only a baby,' Angie said defensively. 'How could you do this to us?'

'With the greatest of ease. I did what was right—'

'Right?'

'For better or for worse your child is a Neville. He is a part of my family circle,' Leo ground out in grudging concession. 'He should not suffer for the faults of his parents.'

Angie slung him a scorching glance. 'I am not at fault as a parent in any way.'

'I would suggest that we save this conversation until we are alone.'

'I don't want to go to your house,' Angie told him between clenched teeth.

'I'm not checking you into a hotel. You might be stupid enough to disappear again, and I have wasted enough time tracking you down—'

'I thought it was Wallace who—'

'My grandfather is in his eighties,' Leo reminded her drily. 'I employed the investigation agency and dealt with them, and you were far from easily found.'

'I didn't want to be found,' Angie whispered in sudden, dragging weariness, her taut shoulders slumping in defeat.

Silence fell. For a minute or two, she stared blindly out at the passing traffic but then slowly she turned until she was watching Leo instead. The relaxation of his impressive lean length had an indolent quality which mocked her own explosive tension, yet was, in its own way, highly deceptive for there was nothing indolent about Leo. A white-hot core of raw energy drove him, not to mention his fierce Greek pride. And even without that spectacular bone structure and build Leo would have commanded attention in any company for he had a presence equalled by few men, and women were mesmerised by the high-voltage charge of his intense sexuality.

His hard, classic profile turned, brilliant dark eyes catching her out, lingering unashamedly as she coloured, his lush lashes dropping low to study her intently with nothing of her own inhibition. A curl of heat clenched her stomach and tensed every muscle in her slender body.

'I was afraid that you might have ended up on the streets.' Leo broke the silence with that devastatingly candid admission.

Her jaw dropping, Angie's eyes widened in outrage.

'It was a natural fear,' Leo stated quietly. 'What money you had wouldn't have lasted long in a city like this. I believed that you might be forced to rely on your looks to survive.'

'No. I wasn't quite that desperate.' Angie's hands closed

fiercely together on her lap, her voice shaky but acidic. 'I got by—*without* relying on my looks.'

'And I can only hope that the experience taught you a lesson. Drew was dazzled by you, but he always planned to marry money. Only a wealthy woman could afford to keep my cousin in the style he believes to be his due,' Leo delivered with supreme scorn.

'I don't want to talk about Drew.' Hatred was burning like a bright, blinding light inside Angie's battered heart at that moment. 'Right now, I'm just trying to come to terms with what you have done to our lives.'

Leo smiled slightly, very much as a lion might have smiled at a puny and not very bright prey. 'Soon you will be grateful for my interference.'

'Never. You can't play with people's lives like this!' But even as Angie told him that she felt as if she was spouting hot air.

Penniless, homeless, jobless. Leo had destroyed everything they had. And Leo had done the unforgivable—he had put her in the degrading position of having to accept that they were now dependent on *his* generosity. That devastated her pride and stuck in her throat like an indigestible concrete block, but, with a small child's needs to consider, she couldn't just walk away in a temper...for where would she walk *to*?

The car drew up outside a large, impressive town house in a quiet, elegant square. Angie climbed out and reached for Jake, but he scrambled out on his own, deliberately evading her hand, displaying the wilful and stubborn independent streak which she was seeing more and more as he left babyhood behind. An older woman had the front door open even before they reached the top step. She bent her greying head, her attention locking onto Jake and staying there.

'My housekeeper, Epifania. She will see to the child,' Leo informed Angie.

'The child'. Angie swore that she would scream if Leo used that phrase just one more time within her hearing. '*I* will see to him.'

'Epifania was once my nursemaid,' Leo revealed drily. 'I can assure you that she is more than capable of managing one small boy.'

Epifania dragged her attention from Jake, glanced fleetingly at Angie and then swiftly away again to attend to her employer's instructions.

Leo's nursemaid. This definitely wasn't her day, Angie conceded, turning pink with discomfiture. The Greek woman might well notice the resemblance, particularly if she had looked after Leo when he'd been the same age. But how likely was it that the housekeeper would risk causing offence by making any comment? Angie told herself that her secret was safe.

After all, she had no intention of telling Leo that he was the father of her son. Why? It would mean exposing her own lie and taking advantage of Leo in a way that even now she could not bear to do. It wouldn't be fair because she had quite deliberately run the risk of becoming pregnant. Indeed, hard as it was to recall without a shamed feeling of self-loathing, Angie had actually *wanted* to conceive that weekend.

More than anything else, she had longed to give Leo a child to replace the one he had lost. And she simply hadn't thought beyond that crazy, spur-of-the-moment decision...or had she? At the back of her mind, hadn't she also believed that Leo might find it almost impossible to walk away from the mother of his child? Inwardly, Angie shrank from the depth of calculation which Leo would read into her past behaviour if she admitted that Jake was his son.

She had been stupid and reckless, had known the instant that Leo rejected her just *how* stupid. She had been hopelessly in love with him and very immature. But Leo would neither

understand nor forgive what she had done. He would assume
that she had lied to ensnare him because he was a very rich
man. With a confession of theft hanging over her head, what
else could he possibly think? He would scarcely attribute any
purer motive to her planned pregnancy.

Concluding his conversation with Epifania, who already
had Jake in her arms, Leo cast open a door. 'We can talk now,
Angie,' he murmured, yet the soft assurance somehow fell on
her ears with all the weight of a threat.

Scolding herself for that fancy, she preceded him into a
wonderfully furnished library and, glimpsing her own reflection in the gilded mirror on the wall opposite, she winced.
Her hair was in a wild, wind-blown tangle, her face bare of
make-up because cosmetics were among the many things she
had quickly learned weren't a necessity. She was wearing a
black sweater, jeans and a fleece jacket, all of which had been
bought second-hand from charity shops.

She looked poor and shabby, and she was standing in a
room decorated with a truly awesome disregard for expense,
with its discreetly gleaming antique furniture, ornate floor-
length curtains, fresh flowers and glowing Persian rugs.
Digging her hands into her pockets, she glanced uneasily at
Leo.

Lounging back against the edge of a mahogany desk in a
stray patch of sunlight, he was watching her, brilliant, beautiful eyes now boldly and ruthlessly appraising. Caught unprepared, Angie felt that appraisal like a physical touch. Her
slender figure tensed, colour staining her taut cheekbones as
she found herself inexorably meeting that look. And just as
suddenly she was running out of breath, mouth drying, heartbeat racing as she connected with the electrifying shimmer
of those dark golden eyes. Heat like an insidious spark that
built terrifyingly fast into a forest fire blazed deep in the pit
of her stomach.

Slowly Leo uncoiled himself, straightened and strolled, sure-footed and silent as a prowling predator, towards her. Her throat closed over convulsively, her lips parting as she strove with every atom of her being to break away from the compelling stare. He halted two feet away from her and the silence between them stretched tighter and tighter until it clawed at her nerves.

'Alone at last,' Leo purred with intense satisfaction.

Angie blinked in bemusement. Her heart was pounding so frighteningly fast, she was convinced it might burst.

'Tell me,' Leo continued in that same mesmeric undertone that sent a shiver of the most appalling sexual awareness down her rigid spinal cord.

'Tell you what?' Something like pure panic beginning to assail her as she registered how she was reacting to his proximity, Angie stepped back from him.

Leo merely closed the distance again, virtually cornering her against the bookshelves. 'I ask only for an honest answer to one very simple question. It is a question which I have had to wait a very long time to ask. Did you use me like man bait to make Drew jealous? *Or…*did you end up in bed with him on the rebound from me?'

As Leo calmly resurrected the past—or *his* version of the past—sheer shock immobilised Angie. The tip of her tongue flicked out nervously to moisten her full lower lip. Leo's gaze narrowed and dropped to follow the tiny movement, his entire attention nailed to the generous pink curve of her mouth.

Momentarily released from his forceful scrutiny, Angie sucked in an audible, sharp, swift breath of relief and gasped, 'Neither!'

'Oh, it has to be one of them—unless you have the morals of a whore, and I would be most reluctant to assume that of a girl of nineteen,' Leo informed her with ruthless cynicism.

'I'm giving you the benefit of the doubt in conceding that perhaps you felt something for *one* of us!'

Angie flinched and turned scarlet simultaneously, anger flaring in her bright blue eyes. 'You have no right to ask.'

'Two men...and one very, very beautiful girl,' Leo spelt out slowly. 'A recipe for disaster when the very beautiful girl was also impulsive, passionate and rebellious.'

'I don't know why you're talking to me like this. I don't like it.'

Unmoved dark eyes rested on her. 'That won't make me stop asking because I need to know. Drew always wanted you...but he never wanted you more than when he thought you were mine.'

Angie jerked her blonde head away, her stomach muscles clenching in dismay at his persistence and his insight. He wasn't telling her anything she hadn't known but, ironically, she had never been attracted to Drew. Compared to Leo, he had been like gilt beside gold, always overshadowed and diminished. But, for all that, Drew's attention had been balm to her savaged ego after Leo had ditched her.

And for a while she had gone around with Drew and his friends, nightclubbing and partying, deaf to her father's outraged disapproval. Was that how the belief that her child was Drew's had come about? she wondered abstractedly. Or had she been so incoherent in her distress the day that Wallace found her with the miniature portrait that she had left the old man suffering from a genuine misapprehension?

Lean brown fingers reached out and tugged a long strand of silvery pale hair. 'Angie...?'

Her eyes flew back to Leo, and he was so close that her nostrils flared on the warm and achingly familiar scent of him. A long shiver racked her and her eyes collided unwarily with his darkly intent gaze. A hint of cruel amusement gleamed in his eyes.

'Stop it,' she whispered jerkily.

'Stop what? Playing games?' An unrepentant winged ebony brow climbed. 'Why? You played plenty with me that summer.'

The colour drained from Angie's cheeks, leaving her pale.

'*Theos*...of course, I knew,' Leo drawled very drily. 'Like Artemis, goddess of the chase and the forest, you hunted me down. It would've taken a stronger male than I to withstand the temptation you offered.'

Angie wanted to sink through the floor. Unable to execute that feat, she sidled along the shelving instead, desperate to escape. 'I'd better go and check on Jake.'

Long tanned fingers closed round her wrist and tugged her inexorably back within reach. 'Not so fast,' Leo murmured with deceptive gentleness. 'You haven't answered my question yet.'

Angie had the demeaning suspicion that she was playing mouse to Leo's cat. Abruptly, her chin came up, denying that image. 'There's one possibility that doesn't seem to have occurred to you...'

'And what is that?'

'Maybe, at the end of the day, I couldn't tell the difference between you and Drew,' Angie clarified with a studied desire to insult.

In reward, a dark rush of blood fired over Leo's blunt cheekbones, his savagely handsome features suddenly wiped clean of every ounce of mockery. His lean face hardening, he leant forward without warning and planted two spread hands on the shelves on either side of her head, effectively imprisoning her with the solid breadth and strength of his supremely powerful physique.

'*Ohi*...no?' Leo questioned with a shockingly intimidating blaze of anger in his glittering stare.

Angie's spine grated into bruising collision with the shelving as she instinctively attempted to back away from that dangerous fire. 'Leo…'

Long fingers whipped across to curve on her cheekbones and hold her still. 'Let me teach you the difference,' Leo gritted darkly.

'No—'

But as her anxious gaze melded with the drowning darkness of his, explosive anticipation tore through her like a storm warning, tightening every muscle and firing every nerve-ending with tortured expectancy. With a guttural sound somewhere between a harsh laugh and a groan, Leo dropped his strong hands to the swell of her hips and took her mouth hotly and hungrily with his own.

He crushed her to him, and the very blood in her veins sang with the heat of her excitement. Under the onslaught of his demanding lips and the carnal thrust of his tongue, Angie burned. He ravaged her mouth with the fierce heat of an innately sexual male, hell-bent on possession, and she fell victim to a hot and disorientating tide of intimate memory that tore down every remaining barrier and reduced her to submissive rubble.

As suddenly as he had reached for her, Leo dragged his mouth from hers again. Glittering dark eyes cloaked, he thrust himself back from her and strode over to the window.

For a split second, Angie thought she might slide down to the rug because her knees were ready to fold beneath her. For a split second, Angie didn't even recall where she was. But her body ached and pulsed in a way she had almost forgotten, sensually alive and hurting in a way she did not want to acknowledge. She felt the swollen tenderness of her breasts, the painful sense of tormenting emptiness between her thighs, and shivered in disbelieving horror that Leo could still have that devastating an effect on her body.

She studied his back view with stricken eyes, reading the savage tension in his broad shoulders and the rigid bracing of his long, powerful thighs. And just as swiftly she suspected that that sudden flare of physical hunger and even more physical connection might have been no more welcome to him.

'The difference between my cousin and I,' Leo framed rawly as he swung back to face her, burnished, censorious dark eyes like flaring arrows of gold, 'is that I was ashamed of what happened between us two and a half years ago!'

'Ashamed?' Angie repeated sickly.

'*Cristos*…what else?' Leo demanded in a wrathful growl of rebuke. 'What did you expect? My wife had been dead only seven months…and you were nineteen and naive as they come, for all your wiles! Did you think I could be proud of making such a conquest? The teenage daughter of one of my grandfather's most loyal and trusted dependants? And, even worse, a virgin?'

CHAPTER THREE

ANGIE HAD TURNED TO STONE, the pallor of her perfect features pronounced but rigidly uninformative—for one necessary skill she had learned working for Claudia was the ability to keep her face devoid of expression. But, inside herself, she was cringing. 'Conquest'...'dependant'...'virgin'... Not one single term welcome to her ears—indeed each and every one of them emphasising the humiliating inequality which had always divided her from Leo.

In bitter mortification, she flew out of the room and down the hall, not even knowing where she was going in an unfamiliar house. Espying a cloakroom, she hurriedly and gratefully took refuge there. No, she had never had the advantage of a level playing field with Leo, she conceded wretchedly. Everything had separated them—age, background and experience. But, worst of all, she had met Leo in the time-warp world of Deveraux Court, leaving herself forever fixed in his mind as the butler's daughter and never, it seemed, to be anything else.

Why on earth had he kissed her? The ultimate put-down? Her insult had drawn an overwhelmingly primitive masculine response. But then, in the grip of strong emotion, Leo was no English gentleman of restraint, and he was very highly sexed. A dangerous little quiver of remembrance ran through Angie and her face burned with shame. She had no excuse to offer for her own behaviour. Leo still attracted her in much the same way that a magnet attracted iron filings. But it was just a physical thing now, she told herself with driven defensive-ness—all down to body chemistry and hormones, and nothing whatsoever to do with her emotions.

A knock sounded on the door. Angie ignored it.

'Angie, you have a count of five to show yourself...'

Leo's warning sent Angie flying for a towel to dry her face with, which she had splashed thoroughly with cold water in the forlorn hope of cooling herself down.

She unlocked the door. 'Where's Jake?' she questioned stiffly, focusing on Leo's pale blue silk tie.

'Upstairs with Epifania. Listen,' Leo advised impa-tiently.

And she heard Jake's delighted chortles of glee filtering down from the floor above. Her son sounded as if he was having a whale of a time.

'I don't want to talk about the past!' Angie stated fiercely.

'It's unfinished business. I want it dealt with,' Leo coun-tered without apology.

Angie flung her head high, blue eyes darkened by stress. 'There was nothing unfinished about it. You made yourself perfectly plain at the time—sorry, Angie, I needed a woman and I was drunk!' she interpreted with a raw bitterness she could not conceal.

Leo's even white teeth gritted. 'That *wasn't* what I said—'

'That's what it came down to!' In too much pain from her memories to find such proximity to Leo bearable, Angie wrapped her arms around herself in a starkly protective move-ment. 'Don't you ever touch me again. Once bitten, forever shy!'

Leo sent her a flashfire glance of involuntary amusement. 'That rejection routine of yours needs some extensive work and application.'

A deep flush of mortification lit Angie's cheeks as he reminded her of her eager response in his arms. Her skin felt super-thin, as if the tiniest dent might wound her to the death. And it was Leo who was doing that to her, and that appalled her because she had honestly believed that Leo could not have the power to hurt her any more. She had buried that foolish teenager deep and fancied herself mature beyond imagining. Now she was discovering her error.

Leo curved a hand over her tense shoulder and she flinched away. He vented a soft, soothing sound that was terrifyingly sexy. 'You're trembling...'

'I'll never forgive you for bringing me here! Where the heck are we supposed to go now? I'm not crawling back to Deveraux Court to grovel—or eat humble pie—so where does that leave us?'

Leo surveyed her mutinous face with reflective cool. 'Enjoying my hospitality,' he supplied smoothly, and swung on his heel.

'But I don't want to accept your hospitality, Leo.'

Leo stilled, and responded without turning his arrogant dark head. 'In five days' time, you will have seen sense and you will be heading to the Court. If you haven't the wit to grovel, you will undoubtedly feel the rough edge of Wallace's tongue—but then that's your business, *not* mine.'

As he left her standing there, Angie felt horribly alone and scared for the first time in a long while. The feeling of insecurity gripping her now was intense. The very last place she wanted to go was Deveraux Court, and the very last place she wanted to stay was in Leo's house.

She finally headed upstairs, where the housekeeper showed her into a large bedroom which connected with the even more spacious room where the older woman had been keeping Jake occupied. An evening meal was suggested, and her son's likes and dislikes were discussed in almost embarrassing detail.

But not by word, look or gesture did Epifania even hint that Jake might be anything more than the child of a guest. Angie scolded herself for the guilty conscience which had made her far too imaginative earlier. Of course Epifania hadn't spotted any instant resemblance which linked Jake to her employer! Clearly the housekeeper was just extremely fond of children.

Forty minutes later, Angie and her son were summoned down to eat. One solitary place was set at the massive polished table in the imposing gold and blue dining room, and, to the left of it, a high chair for Jake. Evidently Leo was not to join them. But then undoubtedly Leo did not dine at so early an hour. When Angie took Jake back upstairs, a positive feast of plush soft toys and a small mound of packages awaited them in his bedroom. A giant furry giraffe was prominent in the spread.

As Jake whooped in delight and rushed to investigate, Angie stilled in surprise and dismay on the threshold.

'You see? A young child is easily distracted with new toys,' Leo drawled with cool superiority from behind her.

Sharply disconcerted because she hadn't heard his approach, Angie whipped round. 'Where did all these things come from?'

'A friend made the selection for me and had them sent over. There should be some clothes as well.'

Angie reddened with discomfiture. 'And how much did this generous gesture of yours cost?'

Leo shifted a relaxed shoulder in a dismissive shrug. 'That's irrelevant.'

'Is it?' Angie queried with embarrassed heat. 'Surely you can appreciate that I can't accept this stuff?'

'It was nothing…forget it,' Leo responded drily.

'But I can't let you just pay for it all!'

His beautifully expressive mouth curled. 'Don't make me drag up that past you're so very reluctant to recall.'

'And what's that supposed to mean?'

'When it comes to moral principles, we both know you are not Pollyanna.'

Understanding came too late to protect Angie from that humiliating reminder. She turned white as if Leo had struck her. He was referring to the thefts.

Leo made an impatient movement with one brown hand. 'Try just to be yourself around me, Angie. I loathe hypocrisy...and all this fuss about a few necessities for a child? Who do you think you are impressing with this charade of objections?'

Angie backed unsteadily into the bedroom and closed the door. She wanted to race back out again and grab Leo by his arrogant, judgemental throat and scream, I am not a thief! She wanted to proclaim her innocence with the very strongest force. But she had surrendered that right of her own volition over two years ago. Only by naming the true culprit could she clear her own name, and, if she did that, she would *still* cause unthinkable damage...

Leo would not allow even a reformed and deeply repentant thief to remain in his grandfather's home. He would bring in the police and press charges without hesitation. Leo had no liberal convictions where crime and punishment were concerned.

Lost in increasingly distressing introspection, Angie undressed Jake and bathed him in the *en suite*. Leo despised her for her apparent greed and dishonesty. Why hadn't she faced up to that harsh fact sooner? Just minutes ago, his distaste and anger had rung out as clear as a bell. And she had drawn his censure by daring to behave as if she wasn't the greedy, grasping profiteer and eager free-loader he undoubtedly saw her as. Leo believed she had got off too lightly for her sins.

And no doubt he also thought that returning to Deveraux Court to grovel to Wallace and cringe at the knowledge that everyone knew her to be a thief was a long-overdue slice of her just desserts.

The packages revealed a sensible skeleton wardrobe for Jake. Underwear and pyjamas, a duo of sweaters, shirts and trousers, all bearing the brand name of a reasonably priced chain store—unlike the array of blatantly expensive toys. Sighing, Angie tucked Jake into the comfortable single bed. Over-tired now, her son flipped fussily between the soft toys which had earlier enthralled him, and then he said that fatal word which Angie had been hoping not to hear.

'Waff...where Waff?'

'Waff's not here. I'm sorry,' Angie groaned as Jake's bottom lip began to wobble alarmingly, big dark eyes suddenly flooding with tears.

'Want Waff!' Jake sobbed.

Fifteen minutes of lamentations later, the housekeeper had joined Angie in her efforts to console and distract Jake, but the whole house continued to echo with the boy's noisy, convulsive sobs.

Without warning, Leo strode in. In an off-white dinner jacket and black silk bow-tie, he was clearly on his way out for the evening. He cast a grim glance down at Jake, an abandoned slump of utter misery on the bed. 'Your son knows how to get what he wants.'

'That's not fair, Leo,' Angie muttered in reproach.

Releasing his breath in a slow, driven hiss, Leo crouched fluidly down beside the bed and gently shook Jake's shoulder to gain his attention. 'Jake...I'm going to get Waff.'

'Don't make promises you can't keep,' Angie hissed, but it was too late. Her son's damp, tousled head had come off the pillow and a look of pathetic hope was already blossoming in his tear-drenched eyes.

'If George Dickson wants to be sued through the courts for a pink giraffe, I'll do it,' Leo swore, vaulting upright again.

'Don't be daft…that would take forever.'

'Give me an hour… George struck me as a very level-headed and rational man.'

Stunned, Angie watched him stride back out again. Leo was planning to drive over to the Dicksons' to demand custody of a pink giraffe? Jake sat up, rubbing at his eyes. 'Waff…?' he mumbled with a hint of a wobbly smile.

'Wait and see…maybe,' Angie said carefully.

Leo was back, however, within the hour. He came through the door with Waff extended like a small but tremendously important peace offering. Jake shot out of bed like a jet-propelled missile, hurled himself ecstatically at Leo's knees and accepted Waff back, tucking the battered toy possessively under his arm. 'Night, night,' he said happily, accepting Angie's help to climb back into bed.

'How did you do it?' Angie whispered as Leo moved back to the door again.

'Dickson was so embarrassed, he couldn't hand Waff over fast enough. He sends his apologies for what he termed "an unfortunate misunderstanding",' Leo informed Angie very drily over his shoulder.

'Really?' Angie followed Leo out into the corridor. 'What else did he say?'

'I'm afraid I don't have the time to tell you.'

Belatedly, Angie reread the significance of the dinner jacket he wore and flushed uncomfortably. 'You're running late again.'

His dark eyes gleamed as he studied her. 'And tomorrow morning I'm flying over to Brussels for a few days. You'll have the house to yourself until Thursday.'

He went on down the stairs, and Angie listened to the distant thud of the front door and glanced in at Jake again.

Leo's son had gone out like a light, Waff a barely visible pink splodge tucked under his chin. For some reason she found that she couldn't stop wondering who the lady in Leo's life was… Did *she* play games? Probably not. Games were the province of the young and brash and insecure, she reminded herself heavily. And quite the reverse of appealing when recognised for what they were by the quarry.

In the early hours, Angie lay awake. Leo hadn't come home, Leo obviously wasn't *coming* home—and why had she been unconsciously straining to hear his return? she asked herself with angry self-loathing. Take the average single male on a Saturday night—he did not sit in toasting his feet by the fire. When that same male was also gorgeous, rich, oversexed and spoilt for female choice, he was undoubtedly involved in an intimate relationship, and extremely unlikely to come racing home like Cinderella, struggling to beat the clock at midnight.

Switching on the light, she peered at her alarm clock. Almost two. The house was silent as the grave. Desperate for something to read to pass the time, she slid out of bed, automatically reached for her towelling dressing gown and then realised that, in her eagerness to escape Claudia, she hadn't retrieved it, *or* several other garments which she could ill afford to lose, from the wash. More things to replace, and she had barely five pounds to her name, she reflected dully. Furthermore Christmas was hurtling towards them at break-neck speed and she had next to nothing bought for Jake.

She crept downstairs and into the library. Surprise, surprise… Leo's shelves were packed with books written in Greek. As she began flipping irritably through a pile of business magazines in search of something lighter, the door suddenly opened. In fright, Angie almost jumped a foot in the air.

Bold dark eyes whipped over her paralysed figure. 'What are you doing in here?'

Recovering, Angie pushed an awkward hand through her tumbled hair. 'I was looking for something to read—'

'On my desk?' Leo prompted drily, possibly because she was standing only a foot from it with the air of being caught in mid-flight.

'I haven't been anywhere near your desk,' Angie muttered defensively, backing away from it as Leo moved slowly forward. 'I was glancing through the magazines on that chair.'

'Since when were you interested in electronics?'

Angie stared at him. His black hair was tousled. His bow-tie was missing and his shirt partially unbuttoned, revealing a disturbing triangle of brown skin and the start of the riot of dark, curling hair that she knew covered his pectoral muscles. Embarrassed by that knowledge and the memory, Angie momentarily shut her eyes. But still she saw Leo standing there, strong jawline blue-shadowed with the same early-morning stubble which had once felt so interestingly, arousingly rough against her softer, smoother skin.

Inside her own head, she shrieked at her treacherous subconscious to leave her alone and stop throwing up things she didn't want to remember—most particularly when it was obvious that Leo had recently vacated some other woman's bed. As that conviction assailed her, a searing spasm of hot jealousy and resentment shot through Angie, leaving her deeply shaken.

'Were you looking for money?'

Her dazed and troubled eyes flew wide. 'M-money?' she stammered blankly.

Leo gave her a grim smile. 'Somehow I don't think you have graduated to safe-cracking yet.'

As Angie grasped his meaning, pain and anger combined in the bitter look she threw at him. 'Damn you to hell, Leo. I wouldn't *steal* from you!' she flung at him, and turned strick-enly away, devastated by the extent of his distrust.

'You don't need to,' Leo breathed harshly. 'I'll give you money if you want it.'

Angie covered her anguished face with spread hands. 'You swine! I was only looking for something to read because I couldn't sleep!'

'I wish you had been a kleptomaniac,' Leo drawled softly. 'Intellectually, I could have dealt with kleptomania. But sadly the victims of that particular illness hoard what they take—they don't sell it on for profit…as you did.'

Snatching in a shuddering breath, Angie whirled back to him with clenched fists. 'I don't want to talk about it—'

'I'm afraid it left rather a bitter taste in my mouth when I worked out that, if you were the thief, you stole from my grandfather the very day before you shared my bed,' Leo admitted, his relentless dark eyes scanning her taut face.

'I *said* that I didn't want to talk about it!' Angie launched at him furiously.

'And you must have been remarkably nifty in that particular operation. As I recall you spent most of that morning riding so that you could accidentally on purpose keep on bumping into me on the estate. You then brought me lunch, which you had definitely made with your own fair hands because it was infinitely superior to anything Wallace's geriatric cook could possibly have prepared,' Leo continued with a disturbing glimmer of raw amusement breaking through the forbidding cast of his features.

'Leo…' Angie gritted.

'After lunch, you spent the afternoon haunting the woods round the lake and gathering flowers in a basket…most pic-turesque. My evening meal you also supplied and that same night you walked Wallace's dog until it almost dropped dead with exhaustion. In fact, your pursuit of me was very much a f-full-time occupation...'

As Leo's increasingly unsteady voice broke down altogether, his hard dark face suddenly slashed into a breathtakingly charismatic smile, and he threw his arrogant head back and laughed with uninhibited appreciation. '*Cristos*... Angie, when I watched you struggling to carry that fat old dog home, I was doubled up!'

Angie had stood there listening to that recitation of her past behaviour with an initially defiant and unmoved stare, but, as Leo had persisted in enumerating the lengths her desperate desire to be noticed by him had driven her to, boiling mortification had engulfed her in waves of regret. 'I'm so glad I entertained you!' she snapped, and tried to sidestep him.

Leo reached out and stilled her in her tracks with strong hands, laughter dying out of his strikingly handsome features to leave only a flaring, drugging intensity in his bold black eyes. 'You made me laugh...and, at the time, I was very grateful.'

'Let go of me—'

'I was intending to ask where you found the time that day to flex light fingers, but right now I don't really care,' Leo confided, his rich, dark drawl thickening and deepening on that startling admission. 'Not when I have you in my arms half-naked...'

Angie's eyes widened, and dropped in belated awareness to the green nightshirt she wore. There was nothing remotely provocative about its crew neckline or the hem that came to her knees. Even deeper colour staining her cheeks, she gazed up at him in angry reproach. 'I am *not* half-naked.'

Leo was not listening. 'The average Greek male does not require even this much encouragement when he is presented with a beautiful blonde, *pethi mou*,' he informed her in an earthy amused undertone as he banded his arms slowly round her.

'What are you d-doing?' Angie gasped, heart hammering in shock as he determinedly brought her into contact with his tautly muscular length and the heat of his big, powerful body penetrated the fine cotton she wore, suddenly making her feel as if she was indeed only semi-clothed. 'Leo...'

Burning dark eyes gazed down into hers. 'You quiver when I touch you...and you can scarcely be impervious to the effect you're having on me.'

Angie was trembling, face flushing hot pink as Leo shamelessly clamped his hands to the curve of her hips and hauled her into collision with the unmistakable thrust of his hard male arousal. Her legs went hollow, her nipples pinching into agonisingly erect peaks as a wave of the most terrifying and shameless yearning swept over her, and she fought it with all her might. 'Don't be disgusting.'

Leo dropped his head lower, his breath softly fanning her temples, shimmering dark golden eyes holding her in shivering stasis. 'If I can surrender to my desire, so can you...'

'No!'

'I see that same hunger in you, *feel* it,' Leo delivered with husky satisfaction. 'I saw it last night, swore I would play hard to get for at least a few days... But what a waste of time and opportunity that would be. Let's go to bed.'

That word, 'bed,' beckoned like a sensual invitation to paradise, and Angie hated herself so much for her own weakness of both body and will-power that that self-loathing gave her the strength to tear herself free of Leo's powerfully seductive spell.

'If I went to bed with you again, I'd deserve to be hung, drawn and quartered!' Angie slung at him wildly as she pulled back from him. 'And I can't imagine why you think I still want you like that...because I don't; I really don't!'

'*Cristos*… Of course you do!' Leo shot back at her with a look of impatience. 'Why do you think I ensured you would be with me by tonight?'

Barely able to assemble her thoughts, Angie nonetheless caught the truly shattering drift of that blunt admission. 'Ensured?' she queried. 'How could you possibly have *ensured* that I would be here?'

Leo's mouth twisted. 'Your former employer leapt at the provocation I offered and reacted exactly as I had foreseen.'

Angie was so taken aback by that confession, she just gaped at him.

'Angie, I had no intention of leaving that house without you. Why do you think I brought the limo?' he asked drily. 'Only a complete idiot would try to transport a woman, a child and all their worldly possessions in a Ferrari!'

'You got me thrown out of that house *deliberately*…' Angie was horrified by his complete lack of scruples and the even greater arrogance which had prompted him to freely admit it. She studied him with appalled blue eyes. 'Dear heaven… how could you be so selfish and destructive?'

'I acted in your best interests,' Leo countered.

Abruptly, Angie backed away from him, utterly chilled by that dispassionate response. 'It was an absolutely unforgivable thing to do to us—you don't even *understand* that, do you?' she condemned shakily. 'But then how could someone like you understand what it feels like to be broke, unemployed and without a roof over your head when you have a child's needs to consider?'

Leo dealt her a smouldering look. 'Whatever happens with Wallace, I will personally ensure that your circumstances will be vastly improved from what they were in that house. That is a promise.'

Her teeth clenched, eyes wild with censure. 'Oh, that's so big of you, Leo! But your help would come at a cost, wouldn't it? Something for nothing not being a goal you're famed for following!'

'What the hell is that supposed to mean?' Leo growled.

'And you were *so* patronising and superior just a few short hours ago!' Angie recalled with fierce mortification. 'What was that about me needing to learn the lesson that I couldn't rely on my looks to survive? And exactly what are *you* offering me, Leo?'

Slow-building anger now glittered in Leo's shimmering dark eyes. 'I am only offering you what we both know you want.'

Angie flinched. 'A sleazy roll in the hay with an oversexed louse who has just climbed out of some other woman's bed?' she bit out painfully, scorning him as much as she scorned herself, for she had been all too willing to forget that probability when Leo had come too close.

He vented a harsh laugh and raked his fingers through his luxuriant black hair. Tousled, those thick, sleek strands demonstrated a strong tendency to curl. So like Jake's hair that, momentarily, she ached just looking at him.

'"A sleazy roll in the hay",' he repeated with a darkly reflective look. 'Yet it is so very appealing a prospect when I am with you... Furthermore, I have not been in another woman's bed!'

Angie folded her arms in a jerky movement, devastated by how very personal things were getting at such mind-blowing speed. Meaning to walk out of the room but somehow finding herself glued to the carpet, she said, 'I don't believe you.'

'Would that I had had either the desire or the common sense to fulfil your expectation!' Leo ground out with wrathful emphasis. 'But from the minute I laid eyes on you last night I wanted you again, and I haven't yet sunk so low that I would try to dull that desire in any other bed—most especially not with a woman who deserves only my respect!'

Angie unravelled and absorbed that speech. She saw that she had already been allotted the blame for the reawakening of that sexual hunger. The eternal Eve, tempting and luring—but Leo was no innocent and trusting Adam likely to be drawn blindly to destruction! And she could've done without the silent confirmation that she was not worthy of the same respect as the unknown woman he had spent so many hours with, in bed or otherwise. 'I hate you, Leo.'

'No, you don't. A little hatred would be a big help to us both right now,' Leo breathed with savage candour as he strode restively away from her, chiselled classic profile hard as iron. 'I didn't seek this attraction, but it is still there between us...'

'Is that your excuse for coming on to me like a bull in a china shop?' Angie whispered unsteadily.

Leo wheeled round, outraged black eyes glittering over her in a stormy arc. He hissed something in Greek.

Unimpressed, Angie gave him a look blistering with all the hatred he had so recently denied she could be feeling, but inside she still felt about an inch tall and sick to the stomach with humiliation. 'Because you thought I'd be easy; you thought all you had to do was take one look and stretch out a hand and say, "Let's go to bed," and I would naturally fall over myself to please. After all, you are *so* rich and *so* good-looking and *so* tremendous in bed that some lesser being like me who does other people's washing and cleaning wouldn't require any more taxing or charming approach from you!'

A blaze of dark colour fired over Leo's bold cheekbones. He spread both hands wide in front of him in a violent movement that sought to silence her. 'You are making me furious... and I can barely believe that you should dare to insult me like this!'

'That stupid teenager who thought she was calling all the shots got rings run round her two and a half years ago— and that is the lesson I learned best, Leo,' Angie informed him bitterly. 'I was nothing to you; I was just a body you used—'

He strode forward and settled two powerful hands on her slim shoulders. He was so enraged that she let out a startled yelp of fear, and his hands flew off her again as he gritted a sharp expletive and drew back from her. 'You twist the past so much, I don't recognise it on your lips…and don't you *dare* jump like that as if I'm about to hit you!' he roared down at her in angry reproach.

'Is it my fault you don't like the plain speaking you're so good at yourself?' Angie swiftly recovered the ground she had lost with that craven cry of fright.

'I know what is wrong with you now. You can't handle the fact that I should admit that I didn't want this attraction to be reborn,' Leo sliced back at her crushingly.

'From where I'm standing there *is* no attraction!'

'No?' Leo gave her a very dangerous look, redolent of a male well aware of his own powers of seduction.

'Just you stay away from me, Leo.'

'Is not the proof of the pudding in the eating?' Leo enquired thickly.

'You're furious with me right now,' Angie reminded him, because he appeared to be in need of that reminder.

'No man could stay angry with a woman who looks like you…'

'The king of the cliché too.'

Leo snaked out a long arm and closed it round her waist so fast that he gave a great shout of laughter when he saw her disconcerted face. 'Come to Brussels with me in the morning. Give me something to look forward to in the evenings—and I will look after you in every way you can think of…and in many that you probably can't,' he promised in a savouring tone of such intense desire that she shivered violently, exhaustion suddenly engulfing her as she struggled to react to his lightning-fast and disorientating change of mood.

'Dream on,' Angie advised raggedly, but even her weary pulses leapt as she met those brilliant dark eyes.

'Why fight me? Why pretend?' Leo demanded in equally sudden exasperation as he freed her again to stare down at her in brooding challenge. 'I am not suggesting a couple of stolen nights on the tiles... Stay with me until this burns out for both of us!'

And Angie recalled that day in the meadow by the lake when Leo had become bored with her girlish brand of teasing flirtation and had impatiently dragged her down into a passion which had far exceeded her naive expectations, swiftly, surely and ruthlessly overstepping the boundaries she had foolishly believed she could retain. When Leo wanted something, he wanted it yesterday. And, just below that sophisticated and cool cosmopolitan surface, Leo was as shockingly domineering and unashamedly primal in his appetites as a sixteenth-century pirate marauding the seven seas.

'No—and I won't say thank you for asking,' Angie muttered, but she was striving not to reel visibly from a proposition which had shaken her to her very depths.

'*Theos*, Angie,' Leo breathed grimly, his eloquent mouth curling. 'What more could you expect me to offer you now?'

Angie's paralysis gave and a sharp laugh empty of humour was dragged from her. She loathed Leo so much in that moment, she frankly marvelled that she did not succumb to physically attacking him. Neanderthal hypocrite, with his double standards, and proud of it! He thought she was a tart and a thief, didn't even trust her near his big fancy desk, so he wouldn't treat her as he might have treated any other woman.

'If I'd been interested, which I'm *not*,' she stressed with

cloaked and embittered eyes, 'you might have just begun the
way guys usually begin—you might just have asked me for a
date—'

'A *date*?' Leo ejaculated with savage incredulity.

'Who knows? If you'd given me roses and poured enough
champagne down my throat, and chatted me up with all that
hypocrisy you consider beneath your exalted status, you might
even have got lucky,' Angie framed with a suffocating, choking sense of injustice and wounded pride. 'As it is you just
burnt out at supersonic speed, Leo. Congratulations!'

And with that last word Angie walked out of the library
before the angry, scorching tears stinging her eyes overcame
her in front of him.

Leo had certainly told her what he wanted from her—just
sex, and the opportunity to rid himself of a lust for her body
that was no more welcome to him now than it had been in the
past. Gosh, that weekend must have been something special
in his memory too! She had had nobody to compare him to
then and nobody even now, and suddenly that reality infuriated her. All these wretched, mixed-up emotions tumbling
around inside her, the terrible pain lurking ready to pounce
at the very heart of that turmoil. Leo... Leo...Leo. Yet she
knew she wanted him every bit as much as she hated him for
not offering her more—so where did that leave her?

A determined hand shook her awake. Like a zombie, Angie
fought to focus on the dark and forceful male features swimming above hers. 'Go away,' she groaned, closing her heavy
eyes again.

The warm duvet was rolled back and Leo scooped her up
into his arms before she could even register what was happening to her.

'What the heck are you doing?' she squawked.

'Bringing you down for breakfast.'

'Is there no food in the house?'

After a pause, the broad, muscular chest against which Leo had her firmly cradled rumbled with appreciative amusement. 'Funny…'

'What time is it?'

'Six—'

'*Six?*' Angie yelped as he carried her down the stairs with complete cool. 'That means I've only been in bed for a couple of hours!'

'I'm leaving for the airport at seven.'

'Go ahead; just put me back in bed before you go…and for heaven's sake put me down before you drop me!'

Leo lowered her down to the cold, tiled floor of the hall with a controlled strength that was deeply impressive, and finger-combed her tumbled hair back from her sleep-flushed face with an easy familiarity that shocked her back out of being impressed. But then plunging her into shock, she conceded dazedly, was what Leo had always excelled at.

Only during that stolen weekend had she learnt that Leo was a male of volatile temperament and intense passion. That cool, controlled front he wore to the world had been no more indicative of his true character than a one dimensional image. And that revelation, that shocking but joyous discovery of a fire that burned even hotter than her own, had sent Angie flying from the height of what had probably been infatuation down into the infinitely more dangerous and vulnerable depths of deep and very real love. From that point on, loving Leo had been a one-way ticket ever downward to hell, she acknowledged painfully.

'Why are you doing this to me?' she whispered tightly.

'I wanted to speak to you before I left.'

'Speak…'

In answer, Leo threw wide the dining-room door. 'We'll breakfast first.'

'I don't eat before I wash.'

'Unwashed, you look tousled and pink and sexy... I love it.'

Unnerved by that blatant admission and the scorchingly sensual smile that went with it, Angie raced back upstairs again and slammed the door on his laughter. Leo was advancing on her like an invading army on all fronts. Strange, wasn't it? When she had chased him up hill and down dale he had been most frustratingly elusive. But when she now attempted to do the sensible thing and run the other way Leo went into hot pursuit mode. But then no doubt it was Leo's natural drive to be the hunter rather than the quarry...and it certainly hadn't taken him long to turn the tables on her that weekend.

It took Angie precisely five minutes to wash her face and brush her teeth and dive into jeans and a sweatshirt. Jake was still soundly asleep. She stalked into the dining room and took a seat opposite Leo. As Epifania poured coffee into fine porcelain cups, Leo lounged back indolently in his carved dining chair, a vision of continental elegance in an exquisitely tailored navy suit and burgundy silk tie. He had all the dark and brooding magnificence of a Renaissance prince. Her pulse fluttered at the base of her throat like a trapped butterfly.

Awesomely aware of his level scrutiny, Angie refused the housekeeper's offer of a cooked breakfast and helped herself with a not quite steady hand to toast. The silence lingered until the door closed.

'I want your promise that you'll still be here when I return,' Leo said quietly then.

'To serve myself up on a platter to Wallace like the Christmas turkey? You have just got to be joking!'

Leo surveyed her steadily, and somehow that dark, piercing gaze made her squirm. 'He's a very old man who grew up in a radically different world and, whether or not you like to face it, you wronged him. You should have respect for his wish to meet his only great-grandchild. I confess that I myself was surprised that he should be prepared to express that wish.'

Angie was very tense. 'I'm sorry, but I'm not going.'

'I'm afraid I can't even offer Drew as bait,' Leo murmured with a curled lip.

Angie gave him an abstracted frown. 'Sorry?'

'My cousin won't be featuring in the seasonal festivities. Shortly after your departure, Wallace and Drew had an almighty row about his debts and a bitter parting of the ways,' Leo revealed wryly. 'Since then, Drew has been living in New York.'

Angie nodded, not really that surprised by the news. Drew Neville had lost his parents when he was ten, and Wallace had raised him to adulthood, fondly fulfilling his grandson's every desire, only to become outraged by the end result of that indulgence. He had expected Drew to take over the management of the estate, but Drew had demonstrated the strongest possible aversion to working for a living.

Indeed, battles over his extravagance and his laziness had been frequent and explosive. In Angie's time, however, Drew had still been coasting along fairly happily on an extremely generous allowance and the comfortable conviction that, as he had had the good fortune to be born in the direct male line, and not to a mere, insignificant daughter like Leo, he would one day inherit the Court and all it contained.

'No comment?'

Her brow furrowing, Angie met intent dark eyes and finally registered *why* Leo was treating her to that frowning scrutiny. Naturally, he had been expecting rather more of a reaction to his announcement that the supposed father of her child now lived way across the Atlantic!

Angie lowered her head and stared into her coffee cup. She could've kicked herself for not working out sooner that Drew *had* to be estranged from his family. How else could the belief that he was her son's father ever have arisen? After all, had Drew been on the spot to defend himself, he would soon have scotched any belief that there was the remotest chance that he could have had anything to do with Angie's pregnancy! And, all of a sudden, Angie felt quite weak with relief that Drew was thousands of miles away and out of touch. Had it been otherwise, she would not have been able to conserve her pride and save face by taking advantage of Leo's staunch conviction that Jake was his cousin's child.

'Frankly, after all this time, I couldn't care less where Drew lives. And certainly his absence, or indeed even his presence,' Angie went on daringly, 'wouldn't make the slightest difference to my determination not to go back to Deveraux Court.'

'But nonetheless you will go,' Leo told her very quietly.

There was something about that tone which sent a little ripple of apprehension down Angie's already taut spinal cord but irritably denying the impression, she forced a mocking smile. 'How? Are you planning to tie me up and stuff me in the boot of your car?'

Leo released his breath in an almost languorous sigh, spiky black lashes low on hooded dark eyes. 'Don't make me use pressure on you, Angie. I'm not in the habit of taking a sledgehammer to a nut but, if you push me, I'll shatter you into so many pieces you will find it a great challenge to put yourself together again.'

The blood slowly drained from Angie's shattered face. That silken, soft tone of threat had been infinitely more effective than an angry shout would have been. And the chilling scrutiny which went with it churned up her stomach. 'You can't intimidate me.'

'I believe I just did…and it shouldn't have been necessary,' Leo drawled. 'You *owe* Wallace at least one visit.'

'And where does that fit in with the pass you made at me last night?' Angie prompted in helpless confusion.

'It doesn't. You and I are one thing, and my grandfather and I another,' Leo informed her very drily. 'And at his age I think he's got to come first, don't you?'

CHAPTER FOUR

THE MORNING LEO WAS DUE BACK, Epifania bustled round the town house humming under her breath, so Angie sat in the beautifully landscaped back garden, glumly watching Jake gather gravel off the paths into tiny piles and transfer each stone individually into a bucket with the happy concentration of a little boy knowing he was getting thoroughly dirty.

She curled her chilled hands up inside her sleeves. Her one presentable outfit—a loose dark blue cotton jacket and matching short skirt—was more summer-weight than winter-weight. Her head was sore and her throat raw with the onset of a cold and, even in the sunlight and the shelter of the walls, she was freezing. And all she had to look forward to was a return to Deveraux Court, she reflected with an appalled shiver.

Wallace would get to meet his great-grandchild simply because she had less than five pounds to her name and was too much of a coward to face up to Leo's nebulous threat of retribution. Although really there hadn't been anything *remotely* nebulous about that threat, she reminded herself grimly. She had labelled herself a thief and she was aware that she could still be prosecuted. Naturally Leo would crack that whip of reality over her head. He hadn't had to spell out his meaning any more clearly.

And she had duly cringed and shuddered, not so much from the intimidation itself but from a stupid sense of savage shock and pain that Leo could turn those hard, dark, ice-cold eyes on her as he had and frighten the living daylights out of her without remorse.

He had phoned twice over the past few days. Angie had refused to speak to him. Epifania had been aghast at such a rude response. Leo was her idol, and idols deserved fulsome worship and appreciation. The housekeeper had been very chatty until she'd finally appreciated that Angie didn't want to hear generously offered little titbits about Leo from the age of nought to thirty.

In fact the less Angie heard about Leo's wonderfully idyllic childhood, genius-level brilliance and meteoric rise to success and power in contrast to the deep and abiding tragedies of his private life—death of his mother, his father, his wife, his child—well, the safer she would be. Don't feed an obsession, starve it to death, Angie had urged herself staunchly. She had stopped loving him years ago. Yet somehow Leo *still* had the power to reach down inside her and hurt her so deeply that he terrified her.

Leo paused to watch her where she perched on the ornate bench, her mane of hair blowing back from her perfect profile, slim shoulders taut, long, shapely legs crossed. His strong, dark face instantly lightened and relaxed. Jake saw him first, surging upright and hurtling across the gravel to throw himself at Leo's knees. 'Waff man!' he cried excitedly.

It was hard to say which of them was most taken aback by that unexpected welcome. Angie froze, but Leo froze even more, his big, powerful body rigid. She saw into him then. A male who genuinely loved children but who didn't want anything to do with *her* child. Mean, nasty, she thought painfully, and then Leo suddenly bent down to lift Jake up and Jake, unable to distinguish strained pretence from sincerity, flung his little arms round Leo and hugged him tight.

'Put him down...' Just as suddenly, Angie could not bear

the knowledge and weight of her own pretence. Seeing father and son so close, and yet so far from each other in their mutual ignorance of their true relationship, pierced her like a guilty knife. Mean and nasty, she repeated afresh to herself. Well, the lie that had made Jake's conception possible had been pretty mean and nasty too, she conceded heavily.

'Every time I look at him I think of you with Drew,' Leo admitted grimly as he settled the restive toddler in his arms gently back down onto solid earth. 'But that's not your son's fault, is it? And I hope I am man enough to recognise my own failings.'

'That old dog-in-the-manger feeling?' Angie questioned tartly, but a tiny betraying catch in her voice interfered with her delivery. 'I'm glad you recognise it as a failing...for you certainly didn't want me—'

'I didn't let you go to stand back and watch you make a bloody fool of yourself over my cousin!' Leo responded with biting censure.

'You didn't, *let me go*, Leo. You binned me like yesterday's newspaper.'

His even white teeth gritted. 'For a woman, you can be very blunt.'

'You taught me that.'

Drew again, Angie reflected bitterly. Leo was so certain that his cousin was Jake's father. He hadn't the slightest doubt— and suddenly she marvelled at that *absolute* certainty of his. Mightn't the average male have at least wondered whether there was a small possibility that her child might be his? No form of contraception was foolproof.

She cleared her throat, no longer able to deny her own dangerous curiosity to know how and in what manner Leo had first learnt of her pregnancy. 'When did Wallace tell you that I was pregnant?' she asked stiffly.

A winged black brow lifted. 'He didn't tell me…at least, not until I opened the subject with him.'

Angie frowned in confusion. 'Then *how*…?'

Leo dealt her an almost pitying look. 'It was Drew who couldn't wait to tell me. In fact, he boasted about his virility—'

'Drew b-boasted…?' Angie heard herself stammering in stunned disbelief.

Leo absorbed the beetroot-red flush of chagrin washing over her face but misunderstood its source. 'Presumably he felt it was safe to own up. By then you had been gone several weeks…and I believe he gave you the money for an abortion. No doubt he believed that that would be the end of the episode.'

Angie was very still, and then her tremulous mouth compressed rock-hard and she dropped her head. She marvelled that she didn't explode with sheer outrage, for no longer did she need to wonder at Leo's unquestioning acceptance that Jake was another man's child. His cousin's confession, his cousin's crude, cruel *lies*, evidently couched in the most offensive male terms, had ensured Leo's conviction. For if Drew had accepted responsibility and even pretended that he had offered her the money for a termination as a send-off, what normal, rational male would then doubt the paternity of the unborn child involved?

'If it's any consolation, I hit him,' Leo informed her lazily.

'You hit him…?' Angie framed weakly, still numb with fury at the betrayal of someone she had considered a friend, and unable at that moment to even begin to understand why Drew should have done such a crazy thing. She snatched in a deep, shuddering breath. 'If he's still alive, you didn't hit him hard enough!'

The silence thundered and then Leo flung back his arrogant dark head and laughed with earthy appreciation.

Startled by that disorientating response, Angie glanced up. She saw Leo as she had so often seen him that long-ago weekend—shorn of all cool reserve and distance, and utterly irresistible. The breathtakingly charismatic smile slashing his hard, dark features stopped her heart dead in its tracks. Her breathing quickening, Angie simply stared, helpless as a bird caught in the hunter's net.

Then Leo glanced down at his watch, faint impatience drawing his black brows together as he registered the time. 'We'll leave for the Court as soon as you're ready.'

Dragged back down to reality and ashamed of every leaping sense that sought to betray her, Angie stood up. 'I'll never forgive you for forcing me to go back there.'

'Occasionally one has to be cruel to be kind,' Leo said drily. 'If you had been foolish enough to do a disappearing act while I was away, I might not have been able to find you again.'

Angie wasn't listening; she was already picturing the horrors of humiliation awaiting her. Return of the prodigal, but not to a feast of celebration. Wallace would meet his great-grandson, even if the paternity of that great-grandson was not quite what he apparently imagined it to be. And her father was either in for a heck of a nasty shock or presently praying nightly that his scarlet woman of a daughter would not dare to show her face again and embarrass him. Jake's illegitimacy would be as big a badge of public shame in Samuel Brown's eyes as it would be in his elderly employer's.

However, her exposure as the household thief would've been an even greater sin to a man whose unswerving devotion to the Neville family, their every minute interest and their ancestral home was so extreme, he would probably have handed his daughter over to the police personally had he found her with that miniature portrait in her possession.

'Angie...?'

Angie swallowed hard on the thickness in her throat. 'I think you owe me one favour, Leo. I want you to promise me that as soon as this wretched visit is over you'll fix me up with a job somewhere.'

'You won't need a job. Your future is already assured. Either I will keep you or Wallace will keep you.'

'Nobody needs to keep me, Leo.'

'My offer is open any time you want to take it up.'

She spun away, jumpy as a cat on hot bricks. 'You're astonishingly persistent.'

Leo laced long, lean fingers into several strands of her pale hair and tugged her head gently back to him. Raw desire blazed in his bold dark eyes. 'Hungry...very, very hungry,' he corrected her without shame.

That close to him, Angie trembled, her nostrils flaring on the clean, warm male scent, so distinctively his and as addictive as a drug to her. That same hunger thundered through every fibre of her being without conscience. She could no more have denied his power over her than she could have denied her need to breathe, but when her awareness shrank to the lustrous brilliance of those spectacular eyes she knew that her own physical weakness would tear her apart at the seams if she wasn't careful.

Leo looked nothing short of spectacular in a superb double-breasted navy pinstripe suit which outlined every honed angle of his magnificent physique. Just four and a half days he had been away, but it had felt like a lifetime to Angie. The urge to accept that wretched phone just to hear that deep, dark, rich drawl had tormented her, *shamed* her. Her nails carved sharp crescents into her moist palms as she balled her hands into defensive fists because she wanted so badly to touch him.

Leo inclined his dark head, lean fingers rising to tilt her chin so that he could look at her. 'You look so bloody haunted and miserable...anybody would think I have insulted you!' he condemned with suppressed savagery. 'I am expressing a need openly, honestly, but I won't promise you anything I won't deliver, and at the end of it I will leave you and your son secure. You want the roses and the champagne, I'll give them to you—but all I want from you is *you*.'

Angie twisted her pounding head away. 'Back off, Leo.'

'I don't know how... I have hardly slept since I left London... I was *angry* with you! We could have been together in Brussels—'

'Yes... A few days is about the limit of your attention span as I recall—'

With a stifled expletive, Leo gathered her into his arms and brought his mouth down on hers, all explosive fire and frustration. Her head spun and her lower limbs shook, and the heat of her own treacherous craving stormed through her chilled flesh, leaving her weak and pliable and yet oh, so hot, oh, so sensitive that her skin felt as if it was burning up. Moaning deep in her throat beneath the erotically invasive thrust of his tongue, she clung to him with the same desperation with which she might have clung to the edge of a cliff.

And then a little hand tugged at her nylon-covered thigh, demanding attention, and Jake said insistently, 'Mummy?' and the effect was as good as a bucket of icy water thrown over her racing pulses and madly accelerated heartbeat.

In one charged motion, Leo released her and stepped back, a dull flush across his high cheekbones. Jake gazed up at his mother in frank curiosity, and then he gazed up at the tall, dark Greek towering over him. Angie gave her son a shaky smile and, satisfied, he finally toddled off again back to his bucket and his gravel.

'I forgot that we were not alone,' Leo murmured in a distant tone, and his accent was very thick.

'Please don't touch me like that again.' Angie didn't even trust herself enough to look at him, not when her body still screamed and pulsed with guilty, wicked, unsated excitement. 'I want you to stay away from me.'

'Impossible. I'm driven by a very powerful need to possess you again.'

'But I won't be possessed ever again by you!' Angie blazed up at him with explosive abruptness.

'You can fight me...but can you keep on fighting yourself as well?' Leo enquired with lethal effect.

Paling in fear of the merciless insight behind that question, Angie spun away, snatched up her son—who vented a startled chorus of complaint—and stalked back into the house.

After washing Jake's hands and dusting him down, she closed her suitcase and hauled it off the bed. She searched her face in the mirror, dwelling accusingly on her swollen mouth and the vulnerable brightness in her eyes. You fall by the wayside again, you deserve everything you suffered before and *worse*, she warned her reflection. Yet in some secretive, shameful way the raw strength of Leo's desire excited her and encouraged her thoughts to fly off in dangerous directions. Was it possible that Leo might actually have regretted that rejection two and a half years ago? Six weeks after that weekend they had spent together, Leo had returned to the Court for a flying visit...

He had climbed out of his glossy limousine in the rear courtyard, watching her pick her way across the cobbles in spindly heels and a tiny satin slip dress. The hand she had been resting on Drew's arm to balance herself had then chosen to cling in a possessive display, and she had tossed her hair back and smiled brilliantly.

'Hi, Leo!' she had called, all brave and bright and uncon-cerned, walking past as if he were just anyone, instead of the man who had torn her heart in two and left her more dead than alive.

And when she had come home in the early hours of the following morning, still dying that murderously slow death of deprivation inside herself, the party-girl façade abandoned for lack of an audience, Leo had strolled out through the French windows in the south wing and blocked her path.

'You're messing up your life, Angie.'

He had sounded horribly like her father, and she had treated him to an appropriately bored smile of indifference. 'If I am, I'm having a lot of fun, Leo.'

'What an incredible thrill it must be to play nightly chauf-feur to a drunk.'

'Drew's not a drunk…he just likes to have a good time, that's all,' she had protested, defending the young man she had come to rely on as her only real friend. 'He takes me to parties and clubs, and I'm meeting a lot of people. In fact I'm having the most wonderful time I've ever had in my life! So what's that to you? What do you want from me?'

Given that foolish invitation to be frank, Leo's dark eyes had glittered like black ice in the moonlight. 'Nothing. Abso-lutely and finally nothing,' he had drawled with brutal convic-tion. 'What could I possibly want that I haven't already had? Sorry, but I don't go for the new look, Angie. That is a very trashy dress.'

And she had stood there for a very long time after he had gone, mascara-smeared round eyes emptied of tears, lipstick smudged, provocative dress lurching off one bowed shoulder, brave and bright no longer, doused like an already spent and flickering candle flame by his contemptuous distaste. She had known then that she would not tell Leo she was carrying his baby. She had known then that no matter how scared she was, no matter how desperate, she would never again allow Leo the opportunity to look down at her as if she were something that had just crawled up out of the gutter at his feet.

'You'll get over him,' Drew had said bracingly on one of the rare occasions when he was sober enough to make rational conversation. 'You had a crush and he just broke out of months of enforced celibacy. Don't build it into something it wasn't. I did try to warn you, didn't I? Leo's been chased the length and the breadth of two countries since he was a teenager. He's had besotted secretaries spread themselves across his desk, pornographic invitations from complete strangers and gorgeous lookers risking life and limb to attract his attention everywhere he goes… Angie, you're lovely, but, sadly, there's a whole host of even lovelier women out there. You never had a hope of holding Leo.'

Drew had been so honest with her then. He had just told it as it was. Fact of life. Like to like. Leo would inevitably love and marry another rich, spoilt woman who would spend half the day complaining about a broken nail, the suspicion of a draught or the damp English climate which made her hair flop. In short, Leo would wed another Petrina, a self-obsessed, whinging moan…

'Shall I take your case down now, Miss Brown?'

Angie whipped round, scarlet with discomfiture, as if that last thought might be written in block capitals across her face. Leo's chauffeur was hovering expectantly outside the bedroom door. As she nodded and turned away to lift her son, she thought about Drew again and finally conceded that she had been foolish to trust him as a friend and confidant.

Drew had grown up the apple of his grandfather's eye,

only to then find himself subjected to constant unflattering comparisons with Leo. As a result, Drew had learned to loathe Leo. And Drew must have sensed Leo's vein of lingering sexual possessiveness where the butler's daughter was concerned. The younger man could only have claimed an intimate relationship with Angie out of some hateful male competitive need to get a rise out of his cousin.

But she was still appalled that Drew, whom she had trusted with the secret of her pregnancy, could have sunk so low the minute she was out of sight and hearing. As for him giving her money towards an abortion…complete rubbish! Angie had never at any stage considered that possibility because Jake's conception had not been an accident. She could not have lived with that truth and gone on to contemplate a termination.

And perhaps she shouldn't have been so shocked by Leo's revelations, she acknowledged ruefully. She should have remembered that although there had never been anything but platonic friendship between her and Drew, although she had never been less than honest about her feelings for Leo, Drew had still stormed off in a furious sulk when she'd made the mistake of telling him that she was carrying Leo's baby.

Leo frowned at Angie's appearance as she descended the stairs, Jake anchored on her hip. '*Cristos*…it's the middle of winter out there!' he exclaimed. 'You'll freeze in that outfit. I assumed that you were changing into something more appropriate.'

Angie reddened with considerable embarrassment. 'It's either this or my jeans, and I happen to think I look smarter dressed like this.'

'We'll stop and buy you a coat on the way,' Leo said drily, as if he were talking to a very small and silly child.

'No. We will not stop anywhere and buy me *anything*,'

Angie stressed, bright blue eyes spitting angry, defiant pride. 'I hope I know enough to be very, very wary of Greeks bearing gifts!'

Stunned by that acid retaliation, Leo froze. His aggressive jawline squared, anger flaring in his gleaming dark eyes. 'You insult me—'

'Isn't it strange how sensitive you can be when you're so very *in*sensitive about my feelings?' Angie slotted in between furiously clenched teeth.

Nostrils flaring, all volatile Greek in that instant, Leo flung wide the front door. Untouched by the wariness most individuals employed around Leo when he was in the wrong mood, Angie stalked down the steps, head held high, and climbed into the limousine. There she settled Jake into the brand-new child's car seat anchored opposite. It had obviously been purchased purely for her son's use...

However, new clothes for herself were one thing, her child's comfort and safety quite another. As Leo folded himself in beside her like a prowling sabre-toothed tiger, Angie said precisely nothing about the car seat. Indeed she turned her head rigidly away from him and stared blindly into space.

Angie woke up groggily, her cheek pillowed on a hard male thigh, her fingers loosely resting on another. Registering that she was virtually in Leo's lap, and that the warm, heavy weight round her shoulders was his arm, she turned scarlet, and in her haste to detach herself from him she very nearly catapulted herself onto the floor of the limousine.

Steadying herself perilously on the very edge of the seat, she pushed her tumbled hair back off her brow and thrust herself back into her former position in the opposite corner to do up the belt which Leo must have undone. Jake was asleep, baby-sized, breathy little snores emerging from him.

'He was marvellous company until about twenty minutes ago,' Leo remarked, grimly amused dark eyes absorbing her tousled discomfiture. 'You wouldn't believe how many cows, sheep and horses there are to exclaim over in the space of a hundred and fifty miles—'

'For heaven's sake, what time is it?' Angie looked at her watch in horror, registering that she had been asleep for almost two hours. It was late afternoon. Electric tension filled her as she appreciated that they would very shortly be reaching their destination.

'We saw a train too; that was a major highlight of our journey,' Leo continued silkily. 'But the memory I will cherish most was Jake's request for an urgent pit stop at the precise moment we *passed* the motorway services. The next fifteen miles went by in a blur of edge-of-the-seat excitement—'

'You had to take him to the toilet…why on earth didn't you wake me up?' Angie gasped in stricken embarrassment.

'You were dead to the world, and I was feeling generous.'

The back of Angie's nose tickled unbearably and she started sneezing. She fumbled for a tissue even though she knew she didn't have one. A pristine folded linen handkerchief was tossed on her lap.

'Thanks,' she mumbled round the fifth sneeze, and then she held her breath, hoping that it worked for sneezes the way it worked for hiccups. It didn't. Choking and spluttering, she began coughing instead. 'S-sorry…I seem to have caught a cold.'

'You can go straight to bed as soon as we arrive.'

'Do you think I could stay there until the New Year?' Angie asked facetiously because her heart was sinking like a stone with every mile that brought them closer to Deveraux Court.

'Take me with you and you'll be lucky to see daylight before the spring.'

Angie swallowed the next cough and shot him a startled glance.

Leo gazed back at her, his sensual mouth curving into a sudden slashing smile of vibrant amusement. Her drowsy eyes widened and, powerless to drag her attention from him again, she stared. Whoosh... That smile, full of such utterly mesmeric charm, dug talons into her heart. She had seen so much of that smile that long ago weekend...

It isn't just sex on his side, she had told herself then, buoyant with relief and optimism. He likes me, he understands my jokes, he looks so happy just to be with me. Angie stiffened at the recollection, the dreamy look in her eyes hardening into bitter self-reproach. She had really *believed* that Leo was feeling the same intense emotional sense of recognition that she was feeling. In between frantic bouts of sex, of course, she affixed painfully. She whipped her head round so abruptly to look out of the window that she hurt her neck.

And as she recognised the road her heart started beating suffocatingly fast behind her ribcage. Minutes later, the limousine drove beneath the turreted gates of Deveraux Court and up the thickly wooded, winding drive. Angie sat forward, taut as a piece of elastic drawn too tight and ready to break, imagery as sharp as needles stabbing at her and tearing at the breath in her throat.

'Relax, Angie,' Leo advised lazily. 'You're coming home.'

Home? Yes; painful and ironic as it was to remember, she had once loved this place more than any other on earth. She watched the vista of the parkland opening up, the rolling acres of the estate adorned by mature and stately trees, beautiful even without the softening veil of spring leaves. Then the drive rounded the last bend and the house itself unfolded, an architectural triumph of elaborate but wonderfully time-mellowed Elizabethan brick.

The limo crunched across the gravel frontage and rolled to a halt. Angie only had eyes now for the imposing front door.

Sleepily stretching, Jake woke up and crowed in delight as Leo unclasped the belt on the car seat and lifted him into his arms.

Angie didn't even notice. For once she was blind and deaf to her child as she slid out of the car and began walking slowly towards the door. She saw her father waiting, a slight, dapper man in his early sixties, clad in an old-fashioned dark suit. He looked so stiff, so unyielding, she thought in sudden familiar pain, as if someone had sown in a poker where his backbone should have been.

'Dad...?' she began unevenly.

'Good afternoon, madam...sir,' Samuel Brown murmured without any expression at all and the slight bow of the head that he always practised around those people he saw as his social superiors. 'I hope you had a good journey down from town. A pleasant, fresh afternoon, isn't it?'

Angie was frozen to the spot. At that greeting, even Leo stilled for a split second. Then he freed a hand from the child clinging to his shoulder and rested it against Angie's tense back. 'Brown—?'

'Mr Neville is awaiting your arrival, sir,' her father continued with wooden precision. 'Do you wish me to show your guests upstairs first?'

'When the time comes, I shall conduct my guests upstairs, Brown,' Leo drawled with ice-cold clarity, long, lean fingers eloquent of his incredulity flexing against Angie's quivering spine. 'We will see my grandfather immediately but there is no need for you to announce us.'

'As you wish, sir,' the butler said punctiliously, and then he turned away to allow them through the door.

CHAPTER FIVE

As SAMUEL BROWN TROD, rigid-backed, back across the echoing Great Hall and vanished beyond the green baize door below the magnificent Jacobean staircase, Angie gazed after her father, utterly savaged by his behaviour.

Leo lowered Jake to the floor. 'Wallace will be in the drawing room.'

'Don't you dare try to pretend that what just happened *didn't* happen!' Tears of distress lashed Angie's eyes. 'Did either you or Wallace even consider how my father might react to this situation?'

'I feel desperately sorry for a man who feels he has to go to such ridiculous lengths to demonstrate his disapproval,' Leo drawled with sardonic bite. 'But that little scene was pure, outrageous farce!'

'Dad doesn't think I belong here in this part of the house… In fact he obviously doesn't want me anywhere under this roof, and whose fault is that?'

'Drew's,' Leo slotted in grimly. 'And to a very large extent your own. Your relationship with your father was strained even before you left.'

'It's always been strained,' Angie muttered with driven honesty. 'Just you try inheriting a father who is a total stranger at the age of thirteen and see how you get on!'

'Brown will come round…he has no other choice,' Leo asserted with chilling conviction, his strong jawline hardening.

'Don't you dare say anything to him…don't you dare humiliate him like that!' Angie warned him fiercely, her anxiety on her parent's behalf palpable. 'I don't care if he treats me like the invisible woman; I can live with that. But don't you *dare* interfere, Leo. He has a private life and a family, and neither are any of your business!'

In fascination, Leo scanned her passionately defensive face. '*Theos*…you are deeply attached to your father.'

Having wearied of yanking at Leo's trouser leg for attention, the forgotten toddler hovering at their feet threw his little arms extravagantly wide and howled mournfully, 'Cuddle, Leo!'

Dredged from her self-preoccupation, Angie stared down at her child with a dropped jaw.

'Want cuddle,' Jake said less stridently, sidling up against Leo's knees and looking up at him pleadingly. 'Want carried.'

Angie tugged her son towards her, but he resisted every step of the way. 'Want Leo,' he told her stubbornly, stunning his mother with that bluntly stated preference.

'He's just not used to men,' she said in a rush. 'George Dickson was barely home long enough to notice his own kids, never mind one extra. I'm sorry.'

'Why should you apologise? Jake and I got to know each other while you were asleep.'

'I just didn't want him bothering you,' Angie muttered half under her breath.

'I like children…and I'm not proud of my initial response to your son. Do try not to keep on ramming it down my throat,' Leo urged with immense irritation.

But all over again Angie was seeing her son throw his arms wide in emphasis, spreading his little hands demonstratively in a direct and strikingly apt imitation of Leo's expressive body language. The sight had sent Angie's nervous tension

rocketing sky-high. Guilt and a powerful current of dismay
had seized her. Wallace Neville was a very shrewd old man.
Suppose he saw that resemblance and exposed the charade
she had allowed to continue? But wasn't it even more probable
that he might simply take one astonished look at Jake's dark
colouring and angrily proclaim his disbelief that his blond,
blue-eyed grandson could possibly have fathered a child who
looked so little like him?

Leo thrust open the door of the drawing room. Taut with
apprehension, Angie preceded him, clutching her son's hand.
Leo's grandfather stood in front of the fire, one frail hand
braced on a walking stick, but his upright carriage, the proud
set of his white head and the eagle-eyed sharpness of his gaze
defied his eighty-odd years.

Angie hovered. Leo prodded her forward and closed the
door. As Wallace Neville studied the little boy dragging his
hand free of his mother's to run across to the huge wolfhound
rising drowsily from the hearth, the most electrifying silence
held. Then, as Angie began to move forward in dismay at
Jake's headlong charge at the animal the old man raised an
abrupt hand to stay her.

'Boris loves children, and the boy is fearless. You should
be proud of him.'

As the wolfhound dropped obligingly back down on the rug
so that it could rub its great head against Jake's chest, Angie
stilled. 'I am,' she said rather defensively.

Wallace surveyed child and dog for several tense moments,
and then he murmured with apparent satisfaction, 'He's a
fetching little fellow with a strong look of the family about
him. What do you think, Leo?'

Angie gulped and stopped breathing.

'He's an attractive child,' Leo conceded without voicing
an opinion.

'I know a Neville nose when I see one,' his grandfather

asserted as he pulled the bell rope by the massive fireplace. 'Precious little escapes these eyes of mine.'

Angie stiffened. But Wallace Neville turned back to her with a bland smile. 'You've done well to raise him this long alone, Angie. It couldn't have been easy.'

Angie swallowed uneasily, wondering if it was madness to imagine that that smile had a curious shark-like quality when she was being greeted with infinitely greater courtesy than she had ever expected to receive. 'It wasn't.'

'Well, that's over with now. Your life is about to change,' Wallace informed her.

'I'm not sure I want my—'

'I'm really looking forward to having a young child in the house over Christmas,' Wallace continued heartily as if he hadn't heard her. 'The festive season just isn't the same once the family all grow up.'

Angie was briefly sidetracked by that unexpected burst of sentiment. Christmas at Deveraux Court…how drab the season had seemed spent anywhere else, she conceded ruefully. Mistletoe and holly strung up round the Great Hall, the giant tree felled on the estate itself, the party for the staff…

'You'll wish to freshen up before dinner,' Wallace told her, springing her back out of her memories and making her tense up again. 'I hope you'll be very comfortable here, Angie. You ought to be…we've brought in a nanny to help out.'

'A nanny?' Angie exclaimed incredulously.

'Harriet Davis used to work for one of our neighbours and comes with excellent references.' Wallace nodded approvingly to himself. 'She's fairly panting with eagerness to get her hands on this little chap.'

As Angie parted her lips to voice her objections to such an arrangement being made without recourse to her, the door opened and the rotund and decidedly determined-looking shape of Nanny Davis swam into view. She gave Angie a wide, excited smile, but her attention swung almost immediately to the child kneeling beside the wolfhound.

'Oh, what a little pet,' she carolled with warm appreciation. 'What a portrait that would make, sir!'

'Nanny's going to keep an eye on us both while Jake and I become acquainted,' Wallace announced, exercising the same prerogative as royalty in concluding the interview the instant it had served his purpose.

Leo curved a lean hand round Angie's elbow and pressed her out of the room. 'Jake won't come to any harm,' he said as he absorbed her angry disconcertion. 'And you can't be tied night and day to a toddler's demands while you're here. I'll show you to your room.'

'Now that you have divested me of my child...mission accomplished, is that it?' Angie accused as she followed him up the stairs.

'If my mission had been accomplished...' Leo paused on the minstrel's gallery to wait for her, densely lashed dark eyes scanning her beautiful face and flaring to hot gold. '...I wouldn't still be seething with lust.'

Angie's heartbeat hit the Richter scale as her eyes clashed with that smouldering, explicit look. A frisson of treacherous heat slivered through her tensing limbs, and she trembled. 'Leo—'

'On the other hand, satisfaction didn't lead to satiation the last time,' Leo conceded in a throaty purr of intimate recollection. 'I couldn't get enough of you. And you couldn't get enough of me. No man could possibly forget a reception like that.'

Angie went scarlet with shame at the reminder, but her breasts still stirred and swelled inside her cotton bra, her nipples peaking into taut, achingly sensitive buds.

'And if I want to experience that all over again who could blame me?' Leo murmured softly. 'You would be a liar if you pretended to be any less eager. And why *should* you lie? There's no disgrace in acknowledging sexual hunger…or in satisfying it.'

Angie snatched in a tremulous breath and looked away, a hot pink flush delineating her cheekbones. Leo made it sound so easy, so simple. Sex as a mere bodily appetite, a hunger to assuage. He foresaw no complications. But then why should he? The very ease with which she had once surrendered her body had strongly influenced Leo's opinion of her. But Leo was a dangerously unpredictable mix of two very different cultures. He could sound so liberal, but he was fundamentally Greek and he hadn't loved or married a woman with permissive values. Drew had been very snide about the lack of intimacy between Leo and Petrina before their wedding…

'It tells you so much about the *real* Leo,' Drew had sneered. 'He's no more British in his attitudes than an alien! He had a load of hot affairs, but when it came to settling down he went back home and chose a prissy little Greek girl with a padlock on her virtue!'

The recollection made Angie flush uncomfortably. Belatedly registering that she had been dawdling and that Leo was subjecting her to a questioning appraisal while he waited for her to catch up, she parted her lips and asked jerkily, 'Where am I sleeping…the attics?'

In answer, Leo strolled forward and cast the door wide on the magnificent Chinese bedroom suite. Drawing level with him, Angie stilled on the threshold, stealing a shocked and intimidated glance over the exquisite hand-blocked wallpaper and the delicate antique satinwood suite of furniture, which complemented the ornate four-poster bed with its superbly embroidered drapes and gilded and domed canopy lined with pleated scarlet silk. Then, straightening her back, she stepped over the invisible line of unease which had briefly gripped her.

'Go to bed for a while before dinner,' Leo urged almost gently.

The instant she was alone, Angie inched forward almost guiltily onto the rich expanse of the oriental rug. Through the connecting door lay a grand Edwardian bathroom and dressing room. This was the south wing, which housed the principal guest rooms. Built in the late eighteenth century, a tribute to classical elegance, the south wing provided a radical contrast to the dark, oak-panelled rooms of the original Tudor house.

Her father and stepmother lived in the basement of the north wing, which was only about a hundred and fifty years old, but ironically that final Victorian addition to the Court had proved to be the least resistant to the cruel ravages of time...

'A dark, dank little hole of a place,' Angie's mother, Grace, had called it with a shudder of contemptuous distaste. 'I couldn't believe that your father expected me to live in a dump like that!'

The break between her parents had been bitter and final. Her mother had gone for a divorce and she had never looked back. A qualified caterer, she had started up her own restaurant and Angie had been attending an exclusive boarding-school by the age of seven. Only then had Grace told her daughter that the father she had never met was a butler, but that it had to be a big secret because her schoolfriends would laugh at her if they ever found out.

In short, Angie had been brought up to be ashamed of both her father and his means of making a living. But when Angie was thirteen her mother had died very suddenly of a heart attack and, simultaneously, Samuel Brown had become an unavoidable element of his teenage daughter's life.

The restaurant and the apartment above it had been mort-gaged to the hilt. Grace had lived well and died at forty-two,

and she hadn't prepared for that possibility. Angie had had
to leave her expensive fee-paying school. In the space of one
shattering month, she had been forced to relinquish everything
familiar and secure, and she had moved to Devon to attend a
local school and live at Deveraux Court.

Like a too brightly coloured and strident parrot, she had
swooped into her father and stepmother's bland lives, her
habits, her expectations, her very outlook and image of herself
utterly foreign and threatening to theirs. Their damp little flat
had appalled her and, like her mother before her, she had had
little respect for her father's unswerving loyalty to an old man
who paid him so little that even his best suit was patched.

The discovery that her father had recently remarried *had*
initially been a shock, but timid, rather colourless little Emily
had been no wicked stepmother. The middle-aged daughter
of a retired estate worker, and as indoctrinated with the tradition of serving the Nevilles as her butler husband, Emily had
seemed the perfect wife, tailor-made for a man of Samuel's
old-fashioned ilk...

Chewing uncomfortably at her lower lip, Angie hunched
her shoulders beneath her jacket, thinking uneasily about her
stepmother, a woman she had never really got to know until it
was too late. She stared out of the window towards the distant
boundaries of the ancient woodland which she had once loved
with a passion only equalled by the love she had learnt to feel
for the house itself. The Court was like an ever expanding time
capsule, crammed full of wonderful, personal reminders of
all the people who had ever lived within its walls right down
through the ages.

But about four years ago some of those wonderful and
irreplaceable items had begun to go missing, Angie recalled
painfully. First a small brass carriage clock and, shortly afterwards, a little silver manicure set, both taken from rarely
used bedrooms. Then the thefts had entered a new phase,

the articles clearly picked for their infinitely greater value. A Dresden shepherdess, a pair of exquisite matching salt-cellars, a Georgian tea caddy in the shape of a pear...

'It has to be someone with easy access to the house,' the police had told Wallace.

All the staff had been grilled repeatedly. Angie herself had been interviewed twice over. As her father had discovered and announced each fresh disappearance, the entire household had gone into uproar. Suspicion had divided everybody into uneasy camps. For weeks, Samuel Brown had prowled about at night, hoping to catch the culprit. He had responded to those thefts as if he had personally failed in his duty towards his employer. And nobody, not a single one of them, had once, to Angie's knowledge, even begun to suspect the person whom Angie had ultimately found in possession of that miniature...

Angie had been shattered, too, but desperately keen to mount a cover-up. She had rushed to replace the miniature before its absence could be noted. But Wallace had surprised her with the tiny portrait still clasped in her hand, and had naturally assumed that she'd been stealing it. Angie had appreciated too late the risk she had run.

Downstairs today, Wallace had betrayed not an ounce of recollection of that previous humiliating encounter. But Angie would never forget that instant of being caught, the old man's shock and outrage and the terror which had made her proclaim her pregnancy. She shook her head to clear it of the unpleasant memory, and focused then on the three figures walking slowly towards the stable block in the fading light. Wallace and her son, Nanny Davis bringing up the rear.

With a sigh, Angie sank down on the edge of the bed, feeling her own superfluity. But since she couldn't imagine Leo's grandfather dining in the messy presence of a toddler—and that same toddler would by that hour be ready only for bed, yet still in need of careful supervision in so large and unfamiliar a house—perhaps Leo had been right about her needing some help. More right certainly, it seemed, than he had been about Wallace requiring her to grovel…

Her head was heavy. Deciding that she might as well lie down for a while, Angie undressed down to her bra and pants. She studied the fire burning in the marble fireplace. Such luxury for the butler's daughter—but then she was really stealing a ride on her son's bandwagon, she reminded herself ruefully. After carefully rolling back the opulent bedspread, she slid between the crisp, laundered sheets.

Wallace had outlived his own children, become estranged from one grandson and endured the death of his first great-grandchild, Leo's baby daughter. Now he was prepared to welcome Jake into his home in spite of the manner of his birth. Why was it that she wasn't wholly convinced by Wallace's change of heart? Her son was the old man's flesh and blood, and the passage of time could work miracles…

Only not when it came to her response to Leo, Angie affixed in stark shame. No, nothing had changed there. Leo looked at her and she still burned. She pressed her hot face into the cool of the pillow, but it couldn't ease her growing apprehension. One moment of weakness and she would put both herself and her son in an intolerable—indeed, unthinkable—position.

A small sound woke Angie up, sending her eyes flying wide. A lamp by the bed had been lit, the curtains pulled. Leo was poised by the fire, a brooding frown on his strong, dark face. It was there, and then it was gone the instant he met her startled eyes, his vibrantly handsome features smoothing back into impassivity.

'What are you doing in here?' Angie whispered shakily.

'I came to see how you were and stayed to replenish the fire.'

'I'm feeling OK,' Angie lied tautly, having been brought

up to believe that it was bad manners to admit to not feeling well in the company of others.

'You don't look it. I suggest you give dinner a miss and remain in bed.'

Abruptly, Angie sat up. 'Oh, that would make a great impression on your grandfather, wouldn't it? The guest who arrived and took straight to her bed like a dying swan!'

'Jake is a major hit. I don't think you need to worry about the impression you might be making.'

'I wasn't worrying.' Her voice was tart because she hated it when Leo saw her weaknesses and insecurities.

'You've been jumping at your own shadow ever since you arrived,' Leo traded, unimpressed. 'Peace and quiet might soothe your nerves—'

'I don't have nerves!'

'You have them all over every inch of that exquisitely responsive body, and in some of the most truly entrancing and unexpected places,' Leo countered with indolent cool, glittering dark eyes anchored without remorse to the colour rising in her cheeks as he strolled round to the side of the bed.

'Stay away from me!' Angie warned half an octave higher as she scrambled across the mattress in the other direction.

Leo stilled to look reflectively down at her. 'Is this another game, *pethi mou*?'

'I don't know what you're talking about.'

'All the virginal screeching and evasive manoeuvres.'

Angie's unsteady hands clenched hard. 'I just don't want to get involved with you again.'

Leo loosened his jacket and sank fluidly down onto the edge of the bed. 'Did I hurt you so much?' he enquired softly, casually, making it intimidatingly obvious that he was in complete control. 'You bit off rather more than you could chew with me, Angie. Isn't that the truth? Two and a half years ago you wanted to tease and play, and I yanked the rug from beneath your feet and took more than I believe you ever intended to give.'

'Shut up, Leo!' Angie flopped back down against the pillows, her eyes over-bright, her soft mouth tremulous with pain.

'I ask you now…what did you expect from a man who had buried both his wife and his child only months earlier and who was still haunted by his memories and his conscience?' Leo continued levelly. 'I wanted to be alone and you crowded me. You forced me to notice you and, in some ways, I hated you for that. But even then I couldn't deny that I wanted you too.'

'All I want now is for you to leave me alone!'

Leo ran a caressing forefinger down over the taut, slim fingers clutching the sheet, and she snatched her hand out of reach as if the warm touch of his skin had scorched her. 'You've learnt to be wary…you're scared this time—'

'I'm not scared!'

'No?' Leo gazed down at her steadily, and her world shrank to the drowning darkness of his spectacular eyes. 'Then why do you behave like a frightened child every time I come close?'

'That's rubbish…'

Leo laced long brown fingers slowly into a hank of pale blonde hair and, with his other hand, drew her inexorably up to him. Her heart was banging like clashing cymbals against her taut ribcage. She could hardly get breath into her lungs for she knew that if he touched her she was lost, and yet she could not summon up the strength to break away from him.

'You're all woman, Angie…you melt in my arms,' he breathed caressingly. 'That is how it should be…'

Alarm bells rang in Angie's head. 'Like heck it is…it's blasted dangerous!'

'Safe things can be very boring,' Leo told her thickly as he lowered his dark, arrogant head and pressed his mouth with raw, driving hunger to hers.

She fell into that kiss like a starving woman at a banquet. Anguished desire stormed through her, and suddenly her arms were opening and reaching up, finding his broad shoulders, rejoicing in the hard muscles and the heat she could feel through his jacket. Pulses racing, heartbeat thundering in her eardrums, her own need rose up inside her and overflowed with devastating effect.

Leo gave a growl of satisfaction and rolled over, hauling the sheet out of his path to pull her fully into his arms, one powerful hand curving round a slender hip to press her into contact with the forceful thrust of his erection. Angie trembled as he sealed her to him, and shut her eyes tightly as a wild tide of longing quivered along her weakened length. Her body remembered the hard, sleek heat of his possession and ached intolerably for what it had once known so briefly.

His tongue played an erotic, teasing game with the sensitive interior of her mouth, and she jerked and squirmed against him as if she were being tortured, tiny little pleading cries breaking low in her throat as she clutched at every part of him she could reach, hands sliding beneath his jacket to feel the warmth of his skin through the silk shirt beneath.

Leo lifted his head, dark golden eyes ablaze with primal satisfaction. 'You need this as much as I do...'

With an expert hand he reached beneath her and unclasped her bra, staring intently down at her as he smoothed the straps down her extended arms and tossed the garment out of his way. His smouldering and appreciative gaze swept down, like a kiss of fire, over the full, pouting mounds of breasts crowned by hard rosy nipples, and Angie made a sudden instinctive move to cover herself from that all-encompassing scrutiny. With a ragged laugh, Leo closed both hands over hers and prevented her.

'I ache...I want to ravish every bit of you at once,' Leo confided hungrily. 'But at the same time I want to make you beg because it's better that way—a slow, steady torment all the way to paradise.'

His intense sensuality sent treacherous excitement sweeping over her. She couldn't look away from his eyes any more than she could stop the burning deep down inside her. And, when he bowed his sleek dark head over her bared breasts and allowed the tip of his tongue to flick one taut pink crest, Angie's spine arched up and she gasped and tore her hands free to plunge them into his hair and force him down to her. He curved knowing fingers round the sensitive flesh straining up for his attention, and gently toyed with the aching tips until she thought she might pass out from sheer frustration.

She heard someone moaning, didn't realise it was herself. She couldn't stay still, and she gave a cry of satisfaction as Leo suddenly drove his hands beneath her hips and crushed her beneath him, the carnal force of his mouth devouring hers as he settled himself hungrily between her eagerly spread thighs. The weight and the feel of him against the most sensitive spot in her entire body drove her wild. Unbearable heat pulsed at the very heart of her...until Leo rolled back from her with a low-pitched but splintering curse.

Only then did Angie hear the knocking on the door. Raking smoothing fingers through his black hair, Leo sprang off the bed. Forced back to reality by his desertion, Angie initially froze, and then every nerve switched channel from screaming frustration to appalled shock at her own abandoned behaviour.

'Don't you dare answer that door!' she whispered fiercely in horror as she flew off the bed and intercepted him. 'I don't want anyone to know you've been in here!'

Tugging the door open a couple of inches, keeping her partially clothed body well out of view, Angie popped her head into the gap to say breathlessly, 'Sorry; I was in the bath.'

'Miss Davis asked me to tell you that she would be putting your little boy to bed soon,' an unfamiliar maid in a uniform informed her.

'Thanks. I'll be with her in ten minutes,' Angie promised, assailed by a rollicking tide of maternal guilt as she closed the door again.

Leo strode forward with flaring dark eyes. 'I said that you weren't to be disturbed—'

'What a pity you didn't observe that same courtesy yourself!' Her face was scorched with mortified colour as she looked down at the wanton bareness of her swollen breasts and hurriedly turned a defensive back on him. 'Now, will you please leave? I want nothing more to do with you—'

'Until the next time...and the next time after that,' Leo incised with supreme self-assurance, making her rigid spine notch even tighter with tension. 'Some hungers you can't fight and this is one of them. You're mine now, and you might as well get used to the idea. After all, I can offer you so much.'

That cynicism sliced jagged pain through Angie. 'You're so romantic, Leo.'

'You'd be surprised how romantic I once was.' A soft, derisive laugh punctuated the admission as he opened the door. 'But I grew out of that particular habit. What we have now is basic, honest and much more to my taste.'

'Damn you, we have nothing! Don't you listen to anything I say?' Angie flung almost wildly over her shoulder.

'I'll listen when you start talking sense.' His shrewd gaze scanned her flushed and defensive face. 'I also suggest that after you see Jake you go back to bed and dine off a tray. To be frank, you look lousy.'

Her head was still heavy, her throat raw, but she wasn't prepared to use a common cold as an excuse to avoid the dinner table. Indeed, as she slid in haste into the scoop-necked black body and long turquoise cotton skirt which were the only remotely suitable garments she had to grace such an occasion, she marvelled at Leo's unusually poor advice.

Wallace Neville despised cowardice, and if she failed to put in an appearance he would assume that she had shrunk from the challenge of behaving like a normal guest. Refusing to let herself think of what had almost happened with Leo, Angie dragged a brush through her tangled hair and hurried down the corridor to the nursery suite.

Harriet Davis was reading Jake a story. He was tucked into a bed with a safety rail attached, drowsy dark eyes already halfway to closing. He livened up briefly at his mother's appearance, and chattered at an incoherent rate of knots about the horses he had seen. Winding down again, he accepted a hug and was asleep within minutes.

'Sorry you were left to hold the fort,' Angie said uncomfortably.

'But that's what I'm here for, Miss Brown,' the older woman responded in some surprise. 'Jake's a joy to look after, too, not a bit shy or strange. You won't need to worry about him while you're downstairs either. I'll be just through there—' she indicated the connecting bedroom '—with the door wide open in case he should wake up.'

Angie tensed as the big Edwardian gong that announced pre-dinner drinks sounded in the distance. 'Jake usually only wakes up if he has a nightmare.'

She started back down the corridor, moving very much more slowly this time. Leo, she thought in sudden tearing pain, without conscience employing her own physical weakness against her like a weapon of destruction. He had no doubt that she would surrender. He had had no doubt two and a half years ago either, and in the space of forty-eight hours he had satisfied his curiosity and his lust and walked away from her again. He had taught her a hard lesson, but she might have handled that rejection better had he been less brutally candid...

'*This*...' Leo had drawled with ice-cold clarity, 'has been a serious error of judgement on my part. Sober and in a more stable state of mind, I would never have taken you to my bed.'

'You wanted me.' Angie had been devastated by the speed with which he had changed towards her. She had slept the night through with a lover and woken up to a stranger.

'*Cristos*...I have had nothing but my own company for months on end! I wanted a woman...I *needed* a woman,' Leo had spelt out with harsh emphasis. 'And you were in the wrong place at the wrong time.'

Just like an accident waiting to happen, Angie reflected now in growing anguish. What had been true then was no less true now. Unlike Leo, she didn't make serious errors of judgement where matters of the heart were concerned. Nothing so logical had betrayed her...because she wasn't logical about Leo Demetrios. Never had been. Not from the day he had married Petrina and Angie had been physically sick with distress—and certainly not when he had lounged back in the meadow grass two years later in tight, faded jeans and an open-necked shirt, a bottle of Metaxa brandy in one hand and the look of the devil about to reel in a poor lost soul in his smouldering dark eyes...

She had fallen so hard and so heavy, she hadn't known what had hit her, had sunk without trace the minute he'd switched the heat on. Overpowered, overwhelmed, *obsessed*, she conceded fearfully, recoiling. Pale and trembling, she finally reached the ground floor, torn in two already, wanting, *needing* to see Leo again with that part of her she couldn't control, but what brain power she retained frantically urging her to keep her distance and protect herself. She hesitated and then her chin came up and she walked, head held high, into the drawing room.

Leo swung round and she saw only him, the severe tailoring of his dinner jacket accentuating his magnificent physique and spectacular dark good looks. Angie's heart gave a gigantic thud much as if she had just fallen down a ravine. She stilled, wild rose-pink suffusing her cheeks as she met his intensely dark eyes. With a far from steady hand she accepted a glass of sherry from the tray extended by a maid, and Leo curved an arm round Angie's waist, welding her up against a lean hip with an intimacy that was completely unexpected.

'Angie…?' a familiar male voice questioned dubiously.

Her startled gaze only then took in the rest of the room, skimming to the slimly built blond man lodged beside Wallace. And there her attention stayed. She went white. It was Drew, his handsome face revealing his astonishment at her sudden appearance in the family drawing room.

Shock set in hard and fast on Angie. Instantly she registered the danger she was in. While she struggled to conceal her horror, her mind reeled off in fearful, frantic circles. What price Drew's supposed fathering of Jake now? When Drew had made that malicious claim he had undoubtedly assumed that Angie would choose to have an abortion. Drew would have had no thought of his own lies coming back to haunt him. Was he now aware that she had given birth, and that that child was at this very moment sleeping upstairs, acknowledged by both Wallace and Leo as *his* son?

'Someone might have told me that Angie was back.' Drew was rather flushed and stiff, but he managed to laugh.

'Christmas is a time of reconciliation,' Wallace remarked smoothly.

'Dining with us too,' Drew continued tightly. 'Has something changed around here that I should know about?'

'Doubtless Leo has Angie in an arm-lock for some good

reason best known to himself.' His grandfather angled a surprisingly amused look of enquiry in their direction.

Angie reddened, and jerked away from Leo as if she had been surprised in an indecent act. Outside the door, the dinner gong sounded again.

Drew was frowning at Angie. 'You're here with Leo?'

Angie uttered a strangled laugh. 'Good heavens, are you kidding? Leo and *me*?' she appealed in an emphatic but distinctly high-pitched denial.

A split second later, she stole an involuntary glance at Leo and then wished she hadn't. Leo gave her a hard-edged smile that chilled her to the marrow and turned her already queasy stomach over sickly.

'Dinner, before the staff get in a fuss,' Wallace decreed, seemingly oblivious to the strong discordant undertones in the atmosphere.

Drew shot forward and planted himself beside Angie as she moved out of the room. 'What the hell's going on here?' he whispered confidentially out of the side of his mouth.

Angie ignored him, distaste and bitterness suddenly filling her. Drew, who had maligned her to Leo. He might at least have left her with her reputation. As for Leo, why hadn't he at least warned her that Drew was here? And did his cousin's arrival lie behind his firmly delivered suggestion that she remain upstairs for the evening?

Her stomach churned. How soon would the balloon go up on her charade? Unless she was very much mistaken, Drew was the only person present not yet aware of Jake's existence and the lie she had allowed to stand unchallenged.

Dinner was served in the sombre oak-panelled dining room. A manservant pulled out her chair and shook out her napkin. Even in her abstracted state, Angie was disconcerted by the sheer number of new staff in the house, each of them as unfamiliar to her as the maid who had earlier come to her bedroom door. When she'd been here two and a half years ago, her father had served the meals with the aid of the cook's helper. Now he was stationed at the head of the room, frowning loftily in this direction, angling his head in another, silently orchestrating the whole show like some grand master of ceremonies.

While Angie ignored the first course and sank two glasses of wine as she waited for the axe of retribution to fall, Drew dealt her frequent curious glances, but concentrated on talking at length about his career as an advertising executive in New York. He referred on three separate occasions to an award he had won, and energetically pushed the image of himself as a thrusting success story.

Apparently enthralled, Leo asked several encouraging questions which seemed perfectly polite, yet inexplicably Drew's replies continually made the younger man sound boastful, vain and smug. Wallace merely responded to the flood of information with an occasional distant nod of acknowledgement.

'Of course, I'm presently considering a transfer to London,' Drew informed them all with an expansive smile during the main course. 'I can't tell you how good it feels to be home again, Gramps. I can see there's been a few improvements around here too...'

'Possibly rather more than you can imagine,' his grandfather remarked.

'The old place did need some work. If you like, you can take me round after dinner and show me what you've been doing,' Drew told the old man with the selfless air of one bestowing a generous favour he didn't expect to enjoy.

'I should think you would be very bored,' Leo murmured drily, his strong, dark face hard as iron.

Drew's smile held, but with the suggestion of gritted teeth. 'If there's one thing that living abroad has taught me, it's the importance of valuing my home.'

'I'm afraid it's rather too late for that, Drew,' Wallace said flatly. 'Two years ago, I sold the Court, lock, stock and barrel, to Leo.'

Her eyes dilating in sheer shock, Angie's hand jerked and she almost knocked her wineglass over. Drew gaped at his grandfather in rampant disbelief. A grim smile of satisfaction set Wallace's mouth and it was, Angie sensed, the first genuine emotion the old man had so far revealed. Only Leo was left untouched by the byplay.

CHAPTER SIX

WALLACE NEVILLE CLEARED his throat with precision, his attention now squarely centred on Drew's shattered face. 'Thanks to your mismanagement, the estate was running at a loss and your debts almost ruined me. The Court needed extensive repairs and I was in no position to finance them. I always believed that I only held this estate in trust for future generations. It will be safe in Leo's hands as it would not have been safe in yours.'

Drew's face went from shocked pallor to furiously flushed during that speech. Angie didn't know where to look and wasn't sure how much more her nerves could take. She too was devastated by the news that Leo now owned Deveraux Court, but she was also feeling grossly uncomfortable sitting in on a discussion of confidential family matters.

'Why didn't you tell me two years ago?' Drew demanded with stark, angry resentment. 'Didn't you think I had the right to know?'

'No,' Wallace said simply. 'When you left me alone to sink or swim with your debts, you lost any right you might have had to have a say in what I did with the Court. But don't worry, Drew...Leo paid a most handsome price, and my personal coffers are full again.'

As Drew recoiled from that unvarnished insult, Angie rose abruptly from her seat. 'I think you'd all be much more comfortable having this conversation in private—'

'Nonsense, girl!' Wallace told her with sharp impatience.

'Sit down and keep quiet. There's more, and it concerns you as well.'

'*Me?*' Angie questioned as she sank reluctantly back down into her chair.

'How can it possibly concern her? And would someone please tell me what she's doing here in the middle of all this?' Drew grated in furious frustration.

'You have a short memory,' Leo breathed very softly.

'*She* is the cat's mother,' Wallace responded with sardonic amusement as he surveyed his bewildered and furious grandson. 'Angie is the mother of your child, Drew. Now isn't that an unexpected Christmas present?'

Angie's facial muscles froze. She was aghast by the announcement.

'The mother of my *what*...?' Drew repeated explosively.

'Angie didn't have that convenient abortion,' Leo supplied very drily. 'She has a son.'

'If she has, he's—' His mouth suddenly snapping shut again like a trap as he evidently recalled his own claim to be the father of her child, Drew shot Angie an incredulous, nakedly accusing glance. 'Bloody hell, what is this?' he demanded rawly as he shot upright and glowered down at his grandfather. 'Some sort of ceremonial witch hunt? Why did you invite me home for Christmas?'

'As long as I'm alive, you'll always be welcome here,' Wallace informed him smoothly. 'But I thought I ought to inform you that you now stand in great danger of being disinherited in favour of your son.'

'*Disinherited...?*' Drew ejaculated wrathfully.

Leo had stiffened. Beneath Angie's shattered gaze, a stark frown drew his black brows together as he studied his grandfather. It was obvious to Angie even in her shaken state that that particular announcement had come as a complete surprise to Leo as well.

Without a word or a further look in anyone's direction, Angie thrust her chair noisily back, rose unsteadily and walked quickly out of the room.

She was so devastated by what had taken place in the dining room that she was trembling, her head pounding, beads of perspiration dampening her brow as she took instant flight deep into the bowels of the house. She had been right to be suspicious of Wallace's change of heart, she thought strickenly. Outraged by his grandson's desertion, Wallace Neville had set them all up. The old man was trying to use her son as a weapon with which to punish Drew.

And she couldn't let Wallace do that; she couldn't possibly…indeed she ought to be walking back in there right now and telling the lot of them that Jake was Leo's son, not Drew's. But no doubt Drew was already loudly performing that particular task for her, she could not credit that he would remain silent in the face of that final, outrageous threat.

She found herself in the Orangery in the north wing—in its time a favourite schoolgirl haunt of hers because it had never been used by the family. But that vast and once extremely shabby forerunner of the modern day conservatory was barely recognisable to her astonished gaze. The worn mosaic-tiled floor had been restored to perfection. Water now played softly in the bronze lion fountain, and the lush foliage of towering, healthy plants was accentuated by concealed and undoubtedly very expensive lighting. A choked laugh escaped Angie then.

Oh, dear heaven, where had her eyes been since they'd arrived? The unusually pristine order of the grounds, the huge increase in staff, the absence of the smallest speck of dust, the exquisitely presented food and elaborate menu at the dinner table… So many changes, and all of them speaking of infinitely greater wealth than Wallace had ever possessed.

'Angie…?'

Her bowed shoulders jerked up straight again, but she just couldn't make herself turn round and face Leo. But at least she knew that he didn't know he was a father yet, she conceded dully... *How* did she know? That deep, dark drawl had been too quiet and too controlled.

Predictably, Leo strode right into her view path to challenge her evasion. His heartbreakingly handsome features had a hard, forbidding cast that instantly disturbed her and she tore her eyes swiftly from him again.

'I wasn't aware that Wallace had invited Drew. He didn't tell me,' Leo admitted harshly. 'Nor had I any idea what his plans were. I would not have knowingly brought you into a situation like this.'

'My father works for you now,' Angie whispered shakily.

Light and shadow played across the sculpted angles of Leo's strong face, his lean, hard body poised in predatory masculine stillness. He allowed the silence to gather and lie.

Angie shivered, skin clammy, head beginning to swim. She spun violently away. 'Damn you, Leo,' she said chokily. 'You should've told me!'

'It wasn't relevant—'

'Not relevant?' she echoed unevenly, thinking that only a male as immensely wealthy as Leo could dismiss the purchase of an ancestral home, an estate which ran to several thousand acres and a whole village full of tenants with such careless cool.

'Wallace now occupies a suite of rooms on the ground floor, but only because he was finding the stairs a challenge. To all intents and purposes, he is as much master here as he ever was, and I would not have it any other way,' Leo told her curtly. 'Drew almost bankrupted him. I bought because I had to buy, *not* out of any desire to deprive Drew of what he always fondly believed would be his.'

Angie was finding it very hard to concentrate. 'He would've

sold it anyway,' she muttered, speaking the thought out loud without meaning to.

The silence came back, thunderous as a storm warning.

'It's been an educational evening,' Leo finally murmured darkly, striking off on a conversational tangent just as she had minutes earlier, and in so doing revealing that on some deep, atavistic level below that surface composure Leo was infinitely more tense than he appeared.

Angie curved her arms round her trembling body, aching just at the sound of his voice. 'Terrifying,' she whispered in stark truth.

'Look at me...' Leo urged harshly.

'I *can't*...' How was she ever going to meet his eyes while she told him? Told him that her son was also his son? He would hit the roof. He would hate her. He wouldn't turn his back and walk away from Jake. No, he would accept the burden of responsibility, but despise her utterly for putting him in that position.

'*Cristos!*' Leo grated with explosive abruptness as he settled a powerful hand on her shoulder and flipped her round to face him. 'I said, look at me!'

Shivering and unsteady on her feet, she staggered slightly until he steadied her. She stared up at him, mouth dry, heart hammering like a wild thing in terror inside her breast. He searched her huge, shadowed eyes, the feverish flush demarcating her taut cheekbones, and just as suddenly set her back from him in a move of open, outright repulsion, his bold, dark features clenching with fierce derision.

Without warning, Leo attacked. 'You little bitch...you couldn't take your eyes off him!'

The onslaught of that black, murderous fury shook Angie inside out with shock. 'No—I—'

Leo spread his arms in an all-encompassing and violent gesture of disgust and dropped them again, glittering dark eyes raking over her quailing figure. 'He bedded you, he knocked you up and then he dumped you. *Theos*…not content with that, he bragged about his so-macho behaviour! And yet tonight he walked in after over two years and all of a sudden there was nobody else in that room for you *but* him!'

Angie was feeling horribly dizzy. 'It w-wasn't like that—'

'Perhaps you didn't note his reaction to the news that you had had the baby,' Leo derided with blistering effect. 'He'd forgotten that there was ever a problem, and he was appalled. If he hadn't remembered just in time that he had boasted about his virility, he would've denied all responsibility!'

Angie pressed a weak hand to her throbbing brow. 'Leo…I have something to tell you—'

'No, you have nothing to tell me and nothing I could want to hear,' Leo interrupted with ruthless finality as he scanned her distraught face. 'What I wanted to know I learnt at first hand tonight. You're still besotted with Drew.'

'I'm not besot—'

'You're pathetic, Angie!' Leo gritted half under his breath as he slung her one last hard, punishing glance then strode away.

'Leo!' she gasped strickenly, moving after him, and then freezing into mortified paralysis as Drew appeared in the doorway.

'She's all yours!' Leo drawled with crushing clarity as he brushed past his cousin.

Feeling as weak as a half-drowned kitten, Angie made it over to one of the capacious basketwork armchairs and fell down into it before her wobbling legs folded beneath her.

'What's got into him?' Drew enquired irritably as he came to a halt several feet away.

'Your filthy lies,' Angie informed him with a convulsive swallow.

Drew stiffened. 'So Leo told you…'

'Yes.'

'Well, we all get a little foolish when we've had a few drinks too many,' Drew said in insultingly casual acknowledgement and dismissal of what he had done. 'But that still doesn't explain why everyone is running round with the idea that your brat is mine! Why didn't *you* tell Wallace and Leo the truth?'

Angie buried her aching head in her hands. 'I'm not feeling well enough for this.'

'Too bad…you've made a real hash of my homecoming!' he condemned.

'You did a hateful thing, Drew…don't try to put all the blame for this situation on me,' Angie warned him heavily.

Silence stretched for several taut seconds.

'It's very easily sorted,' Drew told her with studied casualness then. 'You just tell Leo that when you first became pregnant you assumed that the baby was mine, and then later realised your mistake.'

A hoarse laugh was dredged from Angie. Same old Drew, she noted dully. Drew had always been enormously, ridiculously conscious of his image where Leo was concerned. He didn't want to be branded a boastful liar. He didn't want it known even now that they had *never* been lovers! Disgusted by his selfishness, Angie forced her hands down on the chair arms and raised herself up again.

'Where are you going?'

'Bed… I'll tell Leo the truth when you tell him the truth,' Angie asserted unsteadily, but the look in her feverish blue eyes was one of fierce, immovable conviction.

Drew looked angrily incredulous at the challenge. 'He wouldn't believe me!'

'Then you'll have to work at being convincing…because

I will not pretend that I was a promiscuous slut to promote your Mr Cool image!'

'My God...what do you have to lose? *Leo?* You never could catch him to keep, but that kid of yours could be your meal ticket for life! So why hold off on breaking the glad tidings?'

Appalled by a viciousness that Drew had never aimed at her before, Angie stared back at him with pained incomprehension.

'OK...so Leo isn't likely to greet a little bastard with joy,' Drew conceded with a twist of his lips. 'Particularly not when he's already got Marisa Laurence lined up as Mrs Demetrios number two. But I should think he'll make it well worth your while to keep a low profile, and you'll certainly never have to hire yourself out as an au pair again.'

Angie had turned bone-white. A trickle of perspiration ran down between her heaving breasts as she dragged in a tremulously short and inadequate breath to sustain herself. 'Marisa...Laurence?'

Drew elevated a knowing brow, cruel amusement in his gaze as he scanned her stricken pallor. 'He's known her practically all his life,' he reminded her unnecessarily. 'Whatever recent spoke you contrived to put in the wheel of their relationship would seem to me to have snapped tonight...and Marisa is a very determined lady. If I were you, I'd settle for what I could get off Leo fast!'

Briefly, Angie closed her aching eyes, and then she began to walk away, afraid she would collapse where she stood if she didn't stay on the move. Marisa Laurence...daughter of the only other major landowner in the area and, even in Angie's time, a regular visitor to the Court. An elegant, dainty blonde, who had always made Angie feel like a great, hulking amazon. An ocean of pain filled her to overflowing and it was almost more than she could bear. So *that* was who Leo had been with the night before he flew to Brussels!

'Tell me one thing…' she whispered tautly without turning her head again. 'What changed you from a friend I trusted into an enemy?'

Drew gave her a sullen look. 'You've finally noticed, have you? Haven't you worked it out yet?' he prompted thinly. 'Two and a half years ago, I was in love with you!'

Stunned, Angie jerked as if he had struck her. 'No…'

'Oh, yes,' Drew countered, with a bitter edge to the assurance that was horribly persuasive. 'I wasn't too proud to take on my lofty cousin's left-overs but, unfortunately, Leo didn't leave much of you intact, did he? You were like a walking, talking shell with nobody home inside. You just used me to save face with Leo!'

Angie felt sick to her stomach with shame. It was true. In a sense, she had. She had been every bit as obsessed with her own agony as he accused her of being, wholly blind, it seemed, to what was happening right under her own nose.

'I'm sorry, Drew…I really am,' she managed through the thickness of tears clogging her throat as she forced herself back round to look at him.

'Forget it. If you hadn't been pregnant by him, I might have persuaded you to marry me.' Drew grimaced as he drew level with her. 'And what a huge mistake that would have been! No, don't bother to apologise…if you'd married me, I would've had to lock you up and throw away the key every time Leo came to visit. You've been his so long I don't think you could ever learn to be anyone else's.'

'It's not like that any more!' she protested instantaneously.

'Isn't it?' Drew studied her ashen colour and bruised eyes with a superior smile that savaged her already battered ego. 'All you've got left now is your pride, Angie. That's the real

eason why you don't want to tell Leo that he's the father
of your son. And even I have sympathy for what you've got
ahead of you. Scratch an inch beneath Leo's tough hide and
you'll uncover the rigid moral values of a far from swinging
dinosaur. An illegitimate son will hit his ego where it really
hurts, and he is one of the most unforgiving bastards I've ever
come across!'

As Drew strode off down the corridor, Angie steadied herself on the door handle and then pressed her burning brow
against the cold glass pane.

A careful arm drew her back. 'You should be in bed...
you're running one of those crazy temperatures you always
run when you catch a cold.'

Woozily, Angie focused on her father's concerned face.
Dad?' she said, frowning with disconcertion.

'I like to keep my personal life private,' Samuel Brown
admitted stiffly as he supported her uncertain steps down the
dimly lit corridor. 'It's been over two years, Angie. I didn't
want to greet my daughter and meet my grandson for the first
time in front of my employer. It wasn't the time or the place.
But you're still my daughter, and nothing can change that.'

Tears drenched her already strained eyes. 'I thought you
were so a-angry with me...'

'We all make mistakes, Angie. Me...you,' he responded
stiltedly. 'Perhaps if you'd talked to me before you ran away
I could have helped.'

Briefly, she angled her head down awkwardly on his shoulder. It was difficult. He was so much smaller than she was,
but it was the closest she dared come to giving him a grateful
hug. He was not a demonstrative man and emotional displays
embarrassed him. Possibly that more than anything else had
served to keep them in their separate corners when she'd first
arrived in his life as a grieving and undeniably resentful teenager. Yet now she sensed the alteration in him, the softening

of his rigid outlook and values, and absently wondered what on earth could have brought about such a change at his time in life.

'I'll send Emily up, shall I?' he offered as they reached the top of the service staircase he had used as a short cut. 'She could help you into bed.'

Angie stiffened and drew away from her father into the bedroom corridor. 'No...don't bother Em; I'll be fine now. Goodnight, Dad...and thanks,' she completed, almost as stilted in her careful restraint as he was.

Her head was spinning round and round. She felt nauseous and cold and horribly dizzy. She trailed a hand along the wall as a guide, and then that hand became a necessary brace to keep herself upright as she stopped, dimly registered the sound of hurrying footsteps, and turned her swimming head.

Leo seemed to be striding towards her in slow motion. She swayed and then a pair of hands caught her as she began to slide inexorably down. But it was Leo who snatched her up into his arms, Leo whom she saw last before the blackness folded in, and Leo whom she heard say grimly, 'All right, Brown...I'll deal with this.'

'Angie wouldn't thank you for calling a doctor, sir,' Samuel Brown was saying in his most distant voice when Angie surfaced in what felt like a delirious dream. 'She hates a fuss being made, and she'll probably be right as rain by the morning—'

'*Probably?*' Leo interrupted, sounding exasperated. 'She could have pneumonia—'

'I don't think so, sir. The first time she ran a temperature like that, she gave us quite a fright too, but it's just the way she is. Please don't concern yourself. Emily's got her into bed now, and she'll stay with her tonight—'

'I said I would…do I need a chaperon?' Leo enquired grittily.

'Mr Wallace once said that my daughter needed a full-time bodyguard in this household. In my capacity as a parent, I agreed with the concern he expressed, sir.'

In the electric silence which followed, Angie focused hazily on Leo. His hard, classic profile had all the yielding qualities of granite. She sensed his outrage, and marvelled at her father's comeback.

'I was concerned about her,' Leo breathed tautly.

'Most kind of you, sir…but there's really no need for you to disturb yourself.'

No, no need at all for him to disturb himself, Angie thought wretchedly. If Drew was right, Leo already had another far more suitable woman in his life. Angie drifted away again into an uneasy slumber.

The next time her eyes opened, her head no longer swam and she felt infinitely more normal, but she was desperately thirsty. Daylight was filtering through a gap in the curtains, outlining the dark shapes of the furniture and framing the male poised by the tall window. Leo, immaculate in a fabulous silver-grey suit worn with a pale shirt and dark tie. As she began to sit up, he swung fluidly round and looked right at her.

Her heart slammed against her breastbone so hard, she couldn't breathe. Those brilliant dark eyes of his, full of such festive energy and such fierce strength of will. Those eyes pierced her like a hot knife sinking into honey, made her burn and ache and crave…made her so very, very weak. And she knew then—could no longer lie to herself—that she still loved Leo. Drew's sharp tongue had penetrated her defences and forced her to accept that truth. No cure, just endure, she reflected painfully.

'I found your stepmother asleep in the chair in the early hours. I sent her to bed.'

Angie had a dim recollection of Emily fussing round her at some stage of the night, silently offering her a refreshing drink and then retreating as fast as she possibly could back into the shadows. Both of them felt uncomfortable with each other now. That was hardly surprising after what had happened, but Angie knew that she would need to seal that breach with her stepmother if she didn't want her father to notice that there was something wrong.

'I'm heading back to London for a couple of days tomorrow,' Leo continued without any expression at all.

Heart and hope hit the floor with a resounding crash and she hated herself, snatching at the glass of water by the bed with a clumsy hand, cupping the cold tumbler between spread fingers and sipping with all the finesse of a toddler at a plastic cup.

'Drew's girlfriend, Tally, will be arriving soon…'

Tell him he's Jake's father; get it over with, common sense urged. Why bother? Why cause all that trouble? a little voice enquired more seductively. Tell Wallace, let the old man do what he will with that news and then leave while Leo is away. Her father would loan her some money to get by on…

'So I suggest that you return to London with me,' Leo completed quietly.

'No!' Her tortured eyes flew back to him in reproach.

Leo vented a soft, chilling laugh. 'Not to share my bed, or even to share the same roof. I did assume that I'd been sufficiently frank last night, but apparently not. I've withdrawn from the fray, Angie… But I *was* responsible for bringing you here and I don't think it's a very good idea for you to remain.'

A tide of unbearable pain engulfed Angie. 'So I'm being thrown out.'

'Rescued, saved from yourself,' Leo contradicted her drily. 'Do I really need to spell it out? You, Jake, Drew and his girlfriend round the same table… Currently, Wallace appears to be remarkably indifferent to everything but his own over-weening desire to make Drew sweat blood. At heart, however, he's still fond of my cousin, and, while he may well make provision for Jake in his will, I seriously doubt that Drew will lose much by it.'

Those thefts, those wretched, ghastly thefts, she reflected in anguished resentment. Naturally, Leo believed that she would hang around like the spectre at the feast if there was any prospect of eventual profit. And the truth would never come out now; how could it? Emily would take her guilty secret to the grave with her and, for her father's sake, Angie had urged that secrecy on her terrified stepmother.

She turned very pale. 'You think that money really matters to me, don't you?'

Leo studied her with glittering dark eyes, his high cheek-bones and his faintly blue-shadowed jaw taut and hard as steel. 'I think you're dangerous, and that as my mistress you would be even more dangerous and quite capable of tearing this family apart.'

'I won't *be* your mistress…there was never any chance of that!' Angie swore on the back of an angry sob.

A black brow rose in arrogant disagreement. 'Wasn't there? But that's immaterial now. I still refuse to stand back on the sidelines and watch you with Drew.'

A phone buzzed, preternaturally loud in the oppressive silence. Leo dug a portable out of his pocket, frowned and strode to the door. 'I'll see you later,' he told her flatly.

'*Leo…!*' Angie called after him in frustration.

But the door closed and, just as suddenly, Angie had had enough of her charade. As soon as she was dressed, she would face Leo and get it over with. With that decision made, she scrambled out of bed, ran herself a bath, decided that her hair simply had to be washed and finally emerged to pull on a straight denim skirt and her favourite black sweater. Only while she was drying her hair did she realise that she had slept in and that it was already almost ten in the morning.

The nursery was empty, both Jake and his nanny absent. Angie descended the stairs and, espying her father in the hall below, leant over to ask, 'Where's Jake?'

'Out on a walk with Harriet and the dog.'

'Leo...?'

'Business. He's gone for the day, I should think.'

Angie groaned. She should have thought of that, shouldn't have baulked at racing down the corridor after him in her nightie and bare feet. 'Do you have the number of his mobile phone?' she asked abruptly.

Her father went poker-faced as if he had been asked for the crown jewels.

'Dad, don't be silly.'

In possession of the number, Angie went into the study to use the extension there.

'Demetrios,' Leo answered impatiently, and she could hear male voices talking somewhere in the background.

'It's Angie...' She sucked in a deep, audible breath. 'I've been thinking and...I really do need to talk to you.'

'This is not the most convenient moment,' Leo responded coolly. 'What is it?'

'Leo, this isn't something I could discuss on the phone... it's something very...well, very—'

'Very, very *what*?'

'Private, personal...' Angie almost whispered, twisting the phone cord round and round her restive fingers. 'It concerns you and...er...me.'

The silence on the line thundered.

'Really...?' Leo breathed very low, his deep, dark

drawl roughening to send a curious buzz down her tense spinal cord.

'I just wanted to be sure of seeing you alone as soon as you get back. I thought we could meet in the Orangery.'

'Make it my private suite. The Orangery struck me as distinctly over-populated last night.'

'When?' Angie muttered tautly.

'I'll use the helicopter...expect me within the hour,' Leo murmured huskily, and then she heard him say quite distinctly, 'Gentlemen, this meeting is dismissed,' before he cut the connection.

Within the hour? That *was* a surprise, but a very welcome one. She would feel much better once this confrontation with Leo was over, she told herself staunchly. She was incredibly grateful that he had evidently recognised her anxiety and grasped that she had something very important to tell him.

As Wallace rarely made a public appearance before noon and Drew had never been an early riser, Angie breakfasted alone in the cosy morning room where she flipped nervously through the newspapers and drank coffee like a caffeine addict. She wondered about Marisa Laurence and resisted the temptation to try and pump her father for information. That sort of request would put him in an awkward position and he would resent it. And, very probably, Drew had only named Marisa out of pure malice. Leo could not be heavily involved with the other woman, she decided.

When Jake came surging in to see her, Angie swept him up in a fierce hug. Twenty minutes later, her father put his head round the door to ask if he could take Jake downstairs to meet the staff.

Both surprised and touched by the request, Angie watched her father and her son walk off hand in hand, and marvelled that her parent had not yet asked her a single awkward question. But then perhaps he judged it wisest not to probe too soon. And he would not be labouring under any misapprehension regarding his grandson's paternity. Angie's cheeks warmed. There had been the most almighty, earth-shattering row when her father had discovered that she'd spent two nights down at the Folly with Leo while he'd been in London with Wallace, staying at the Neville apartment.

Leo's stated hour was almost up. She went upstairs, heading for the Long Gallery where Leo had had his own suite for years. Vibrant Minton majolica ware was displayed in the ornate plaster alcoves. Regency gilt and ebony sofas covered in lemon moire sat at regular intervals below the endless stretch of the mullioned windows. The walls opposite were closely hung with huge family portraits, below which marched an imposing line of marble busts on plinths.

When Angie heard the distant whine of a helicopter, she quickened her steps and in a nerve-racked surge hurried through the main door off the gallery into a part of the house which had until now been forbidden to her. Her father had always held that the family's private rooms were sacrosanct, and she had never dared to take a peek without permission.

She found herself in a very spacious and rather grand sitting room, full of breathtaking early oak furniture and wonderfully comfortable-looking settees and armchairs. According to her father, through the door on the left lay a bedroom, dressing room and bathroom, and through the door on the right lay a room Leo used as an office. She wanted to steal a look beyond both doors, but was terrified of being caught in the act like a nosy schoolgirl.

In fact, terror pretty much encapsulated her entire frame of mind, Angie acknowledged, shamefaced. Leo was so logical, so brutally candid. To ask Leo to understand why she had allowed such a misapprehension to stand…well, it was the equivalent of asking Leo to comprehend madness when he himself was sane.

There was no forewarning of his arrival. The walls were too solid for that. Angie was fiddling with her hair and smoothing down her skirt with moist palms for about the forty-eighth time when the door jerked open. She flinched. Leo thrust it shut behind him with a lean hip while giving Angie the most dazzling smile of raw amusement. That was all she saw—that fantastic smile flashing across his darkly handsome features like blinding sunshine on a wintry day. It transfixed her to the spot, every pulse in her body going crazy in tune to her racing heartbeat.

But then Leo broke the spell of his own enchantment by suddenly tossing the most enormous bouquet of red roses into her startled arms. Wide-eyed and wildly taken aback by that unforeseen development, Angie only just managed to catch them, and only then noticed the silver ice bucket he had had tucked under one arm and which he was now setting down. While Angie watched in sheer, wordless paralysis, Leo withdrew two glasses from a cabinet, popped the cork on the champagne with a noise as loud as a pistol crack and sent the contents foaming expertly down into the waiting glasses.

'Do you know I've never bought flowers for a woman before? I guess you might have worked that out for yourself when I threw them at you,' he murmured with wry self-mockery. 'My father always said that the giving of flowers was irredeemably wet, the sole exception to the rule being illness or burial.'

Angie's throat closed over as if a giant hand had squeezed all the life from her vocal cords.

'We'll dine out tonight,' Leo promised, smouldering dark eyes raking over her slender figure in an explicit look of possession. 'This was the best I could do at such short notice, and I have to confess that I'm beginning to feel like a randy teenager trying to slyly seduce a daughter under her father's roof. I will feel much more relaxed about this relationship in London…'

Roses and champagne, Angie reflected, struck dumb by astonishment, her concentration utterly shot by Leo's blazing good humour and the sinking, sick awareness that somewhere along the line—most probably on the phone line—one of them had got their wires very, very badly crossed…

CHAPTER SEVEN

ANGIE clasped the glass Leo extended, took a deep swig of champagne to moisten her bone-dry mouth and in excruciating discomfiture muttered, 'The roses are just beautiful, *really* they are...but I'm afraid you don't understand why—'

'I understand perfectly.' Helpfully, Leo removed the bouquet she was clutching awkwardly beneath one arm, unbuttoned his well-cut jacket and shrugged indolently free of it. 'You've made the logical choice.' He sipped his champagne, loosened his tie and discarded it one-handed beneath her arrested gaze. 'There's no room for you now in Drew's life. At worst, you'd be an embarrassment, at best a temptation he can ill afford. Tally Richardson is his boss's daughter and he's in deep—'

'That's not what I m-meant, Leo,' Angie interposed in a voice that wobbled in spite of her desperate efforts to keep it steady.

A lean brown hand smoothly detached the glass from her convulsive grip, set it aside with his own. 'Don't be embarrassed, Angie. We won't ever need to discuss Drew again because I won't bring you to the Court when he's visiting Wallace.'

The tip of her tongue snaked out to lick along her lower lip in a frantic, flickering motion, every inch of her whip-taut with tension. 'But you've got the wrong idea... When I phoned you, I wasn't—'

'You're talking too much, *pethi mou*...' His slumbrous gaze appeared to be welded to the soft pink fullness of her mouth and she ran out of breath completely, her breasts tingling in awareness, a shaft of heat feathering between her trembling thighs. In one slow, powerful movement, Leo reached out and tugged her into his arms. 'And I am not in the mood to talk right now...what I want is to lay you down on my bed and take you over and over again. Then I will know that there will be *no* going back,' he completed with ragged emphasis.

His hungry mouth plunged down onto hers in a devouringly passionate kiss that almost brought Angie to her knees. As he let his tongue slide deep between her lips in electrifying mimicry of the possession he fully intended to take place, and she felt the hard, restive probe of his arousal pressing against her stomach, Angie was clutched by such a driving, desperate longing to let him do exactly what he liked with her quivering and all too willing body that she gave a muffled moan of agonised self-loathing.

With an unashamed growl of hunger, Leo bent and swept her right off her feet. As he shouldered his sure passage into the bedroom beyond, Angie was seeing whirling lights and beckoning paradise. Her fingers speared caressingly into his thick black hair, palm resting lovingly against one hard cheekbone. She pressed her reddened lips helplessly onto the smooth brown skin below his shirt collar and slowly inhaled the hot, musky scent of him, and then, with an aching shudder of regret, she gasped, 'Leo...put me down...*please*!'

He settled her down onto the oak four-poster bed. Whipping her legs below her and sitting up on her knees, Angie steadied herself on one of the heavily carved, bulbous posts, guilty blue eyes flying to him as she pushed her tumbled hair off her brow with a shaking hand. 'You misunderstood me on the phone...'

In the act of moving towards her, Leo stopped dead. Ebony brows drawing together, he scanned the pale, tense triangle of her face. 'What could I possibly have misunderstood? Something very private and personal concerning you and me; what else is there but *this*?'

Angie gulped. 'It's my fault. How could you know what else there was before I told you?'

'What the hell are you talking about?'

'You'll be very angry—'

'I'm already angry,' Leo countered without a second of hesitation. 'You switch on, you switch off—'

'This isn't about sex. It's about something much more important—'

'At this moment *nothing* could be more important!' Leo delivered with an unashamed snarl of all-male frustration, glittering dark eyes communicating his outrage.

'Leo... Oh, hell, there is just no way to work up to this,' Angie confessed in desperation as she forced herself to meet that fulminating stare. 'Jake is not Drew's son...Jake is yours.'

The silence held...and held long beyond her expectations. She snatched in a shivering breath. Leo was so still, she might not have spoken. And then his bold, dark features clenched in fierce condemnation. 'What kind of a sick joke is that?'

Angie flinched. Tears of stress were building up to burn behind her eyes. 'Ask Drew if you don't believe me,' she advised hoarsely. 'Before I left, I *told* Drew that I was expecting your baby, and, however much of the truth he might choose to give you, he will at least admit that!'

'This is outrageous...' Leo glowered at her in disbelief. 'Drew told me—'

Without warning, temper sparked out of control inside Angie. 'I don't give a hoot what Drew blasted well told you!' she flung at him in a surge of angry humiliation. 'I don't have to make excuses or try to explain away your cousin's stupid, crude lies about me because I had nothing to do with any of that…I wasn't even here!'

Leo had turned very pale beneath his naturally dark skin tone. 'You are lying…you *have* to be—'

'Why must I be lying?' Angie broke in, her voice rising even more steeply in pitch. 'Because you don't like what you're hearing? Well, that's fine by me, Leo…just you go ahead and tell yourself I'm lying and ignore this whole conversation if—'

'*Keep quiet!*' Leo thundered back at her.

Angie jerked, lashes fluttering in shock.

'Why are you raving at me like a hysteric?' Leo shot at her in wrathful reproof. '*Theos*…you think any man would just swallow a story like this when you throw it at him out of the blue? I slept with you two and a half years ago. If you were pregnant, you had ample opportunity to tell me then.'

'I didn't want to.'

'And what sort of sense does that make?' His scorching dark eyes were still raw with incredulity. 'Will you listen to yourself?'

Angie lowered her head, intense mortification engulfing her. 'I'm sorry that he is yours, I really am but it's not something I can change. Leo,' she muttered in a driven, unsteady plea, 'what do you see when you look at Jake? He has dark brown eyes, black hair and olive skin—'

'You said that he'd inherited your mother's colouring.'

'I lied. My mother was as fair as I am,' Angie mumbled wretchedly.

'You ran around with Drew and his far from clean-living crowd for many weeks, and half the time he was too drunk to know *what* you were doing!' Leo spelt out with grim emphasis. 'You think I'm fool enough to be impressed by a child's black hair and brown eyes? Who knows who else you might have slept with during that period?'

Angie's stomach clenched. 'I think you've said enough.' She unfolded her legs and slid down off the bed, her lower limbs feeling horribly uncoordinated and clumsy. 'I don't have to take that sort of abuse from anybody.'

Leo closed a lean hand round her forearm before she could sidestep him. 'I'm not about to apologise for saying out loud what any man might think. That's the way I'm made,' he bit out.

Angie was shaking like a leaf in his hold, but her tear-filled eyes blazed with bitter censure. 'You were the first man I ever slept with...on what grounds do you base your suspicion that I turned into a tart within weeks of being with you?'

A dark rise of blood fired over the hard slant of Leo's cheekbones.

'Jake was born eight months and three weeks after that weekend. I have a birth certificate to prove it. He couldn't possibly be anyone else's child.'

'But we didn't have unprotected sex.'

'How do you know?' Angie muttered in reluctant challenge of that point, tension suddenly rocketing sky-high within her again.

Leo stared down at her, spiky black lashes low on his piercing dark eyes. 'You *said* you were on the contraceptive pill. Are you saying that it failed?'

Angie dragged in a slow, shivering breath. 'No...'

'Then what are you saying?' Leo enquired intently.

'I was never on the pill,' Angie said shakily, but she was determined to tell the entire truth. 'I lied about that too.'

'You lied...?' Leo echoed not quite steadily as his hand dropped away from her arm.

Angie tore her shamed gaze from his, face scarlet with guilt, heartbeat banging somewhere in the region of her aching throat, and finally nodded in acknowledgement.

'*Why?*' Leo pressed.

Immense weariness flooded Angie. 'I wanted to get pregnant.'

'You *wanted* to get pregnant?' Leo repeated in an accented drawl thick with incredulity. He prowled restively away from her like a panther pacing a too small cage, only to swing back again within seconds. 'You are openly admitting that to me?'

'Not much point in lying about it now. So you see it's OK to hate me,' Angie conceded chokily.

But Leo wasn't looking at her any more, and a flood of guttural Greek suddenly erupted from him. Before Angie could even catch her breath, Leo strode out of the bedroom at speed, crossed the sitting room beyond and hauled the door onto the Long Gallery open with such raw, physical force that it went slamming back against the wall with a thunderous crash.

'Leo!' Angie cried, chasing after him. 'Where are you going?'

Pure rage blazed from Leo's aggressively set features as he spread both incredibly expressive hands in a violent arc. 'Where do you think?' he slung at her from between clenched white teeth. 'I'm going to rip Drew apart...I want to slam him up against the nearest wall and beat him into a pulp for lying to me!'

In panic, Angie grabbed his arm. 'Leo, *no!*'

Leo shook her off his sleeve and powered on down the gallery with long, purposeful strides. 'I don't care what you did to him...I don't care how infatuated he was...I don't even care that you may well have tried to pass off my child as his to hang onto him!' he vented in a soaring, savage crescendo as he stopped dead to stare back at her where she stood several feet away.

He moved his eloquent hands in raw rebuttal. 'None of that matters. None of that matters a damn,' he framed hoarsely. 'But nothing could ever excuse his lies when my child was at risk… He let you leave this house alone, penniless, and he knew…that sick, selfish, destructive little bastard *knew* that you were carrying my baby, and not only did he not tell me, but he did everything he could to make *sure* that I would have no reason to follow you!'

'Leo…I did not try to pass off my baby as Drew's when I found out I was pregnant,' Angie protested painfully. 'Even if I'd been that kind of woman, I couldn't have because Drew and I were never—'

'*Cristos*…if you hadn't shared yourself between two men in the same family, none of this would ever have happened!' Leo condemned in an onslaught of scorching derision that cut through her like a whip. 'You played us off one against the other and this is the end result!'

'That's not fair,' Angie gasped strickenly. 'I never slept with Drew!'

'I tell you what is not fair,' Leo responded wrathfully, seeming to ignore that claim, and if possible his dark eyes blistered over her distraught face with even greater contempt and condemnation. 'What is not fair is what *you* have done to my son…of all of us the only innocent victim involved!'

Every remaining scrap of colour drained from Angie's cheeks and she fell back from him. Like a juggernaut on automatic pilot, Leo powered on towards the main staircase. But Angie was no longer so keen to race after him and save Drew from certain death. She hadn't played Drew and Leo off one against the other…that was an appalling thing to accuse her of! She had been in too much distress over losing Leo and then discovering that she was pregnant to suspect that Drew cherished far from platonic feelings for her.

An angry shout rudely penetrated her fierce preoccupation, and, with a stifled moan, Angie raced for the stairs, got halfway down them and then froze. Down below in the Great Hall Drew had clearly emerged in all innocence from the morning room, but now he was in definite and hasty retreat. Leo was striding towards him, his dark features set in a mask of savage threat.

'Do I have to chase you to get you to fight?' Leo flung at him with sizzling scorn.

'So Angie finally told you… What's the matter with you?' Drew demanded weakly. 'I did you a favour with that story of mine…and if you'd left well enough alone she'd never have shown her face here again!'

Leo hit Drew with such speed and force that all Angie saw was a blur of motion and then Drew struggling to pick himself up from the floor. Pale as milk and trembling, Angie braced herself on the bannister, her stomach churning.

'Why are you trying to blame me for the fact that you've landed your embarrassing little mistake back on your own doorstep?' Drew spat resentfully.

Just as Leo raked back at him in Greek, the green baize door at the back of the hall swung noisily open and catapulted Jake into the proceedings. With a squeal of pleasure, Jake hurtled across the floor and flung himself in high excitement at Leo's legs. Drew took swift advantage of that unexpected stay of execution and headed fast towards the front door.

'I'm off to the airport to pick up Tally…we'll use the town apartment for a night or two,' Drew flung rather nasally over his shoulder.

Leo said nothing. He didn't even look in his cousin's direction. He was staring fixedly down at Jake, his chiselled profile taut and drawn with strain. Impervious to the atmosphere, the toddler continued to bounce impatiently round his feet, holding his arms up high to be lifted. 'Carry, Leo…carry!' he urged pleadingly.

As Angie's eyes flooded with moisture, man and child swam out of focus. She twisted her head away, fighting to get a grip on her emotions. When she looked again, Leo was

crouched down at Jake's level, talking to him. She could see
the electric tension in his broad shoulders but she couldn't
see his face. As she reached the foot of the stairs, Leo leant
forward, scooped his chattering son up into his arms and
sprang up again.

He moved with fluid grace in a slow circle as he held Jake
high and studied him with fierce, unashamed emotional intensity. A revealing glitter made his lustrous dark eyes seem
more brilliant than ever. Angie's throat closed over. And then
he saw her over his son's shoulder and he went rigid, shooting
her a look of such volatile and angry condemnation that her
stomach muscles contracted as if he had thrown her a punch
as well.

'I'm sorry...' she said thickly, overwhelmed by guilt.

'You couldn't ever be sorry enough to satisfy me,' Leo
swore with a bitter curve to his eloquent mouth.

Angie made no attempt to follow him as he carried Jake upstairs. In the mood Leo was in, she knew she couldn't handle
him, knew that, while she was completely drained, Leo might
well warm up for another attack if she put herself in his path
again. And he had the right to some time alone with Jake.

'He'll cool off...eventually,' Wallace commented from
behind her, making her jump. 'I should give him a very wide
berth, though, until he does.'

Angie spun round. Leo's grandfather was already returning
to the drawing room. 'It's cold out here. Close the door behind
you.'

After a second's pause, Angie recognised the unspoken
invitation and followed him. 'You *knew*...?'

'I suspected it long before you even arrived,' the old man
confirmed. 'But I knew beyond all reasonable doubt the instant I laid eyes on the little chap.'

'But you...you told Drew...*here* only last night that I was
the mother of his child!'

Wallace lowered himself carefully down into an armchair. 'He deserved a good fright. When he lied to Leo, he behaved despicably.' His faded blue eyes rested on Angie's bemused face. 'And if you hadn't told Leo the truth I would've told him for you. If he's like an angry bear now, you have only yourself to thank. You should've known what that little boy would mean to him.'

That rebuke inflamed Angie. 'Not so long ago, you didn't even want me to *have* that child!'

'No, I didn't,' Wallace agreed grimly. 'Not when I was suffering from the mistaken belief that Drew had fathered him. Drew never could measure up to Leo, and the last thing he needed was a wife who had only turned to him because she couldn't have his cousin!'

Angie reddened fiercely. 'I only ever looked on Drew as a friend.'

'And, at the time, I hadn't the foggiest idea that you and Leo had been up to no good down at the Folly,' Wallace admitted with blatant disapproval. 'You'd been keeping company with Drew for weeks. Naturally I assumed that he was responsible for your condition, but I didn't face him with it.'

Angie shifted uncomfortably from one foot to the other, defiance squashed by Wallace's mortifying frankness. She waited in an agony of tension for him to refer to the thefts. Naturally his conviction that she was the household thief had heavily influenced his attitude towards her then as well.

'Then Leo let drop that Drew was bragging about having sent you off for an abortion,' Wallace continued with strong distaste. 'That didn't make sense to me. Drew was infatuated with you and he should've been eager to marry you. The most obvious explanation was that your child was *not* his…and I didn't have to look far to see that Leo was not behaving like a disinterested bystander.'

'How *did* he behave?' Angie was lured into asking.

Wallace cast knowing eyes over her unwittingly expressive face. 'Still Leo's most devoted admirer, aren't you?' he said with galling amusement. 'I'll say one thing for you, Angie—you're not flighty. You've got staying power, and I admire that in a woman.'

The door opened and her father came in with the day's post.

Wallace gave him a tired but surprisingly warm smile of appreciation. 'Brown, you crafty old codger…letting loose Jake was a master-stroke of ingenuity!'

'Thank you, sir.'

Angie absorbed that exchange with shaken eyes. Her son's timely appearance in the hall had evidently not been the lucky chance she had assumed it to be.

'It certainly lessened the damage,' Wallace said approvingly.

'Quite so, sir…and after some time spent in the soothing company of his American lady Mr Drew will find it quite possible to pretend it never happened.'

'You think he'll be back for Christmas?' Wallace smothered a yawn with a frail hand, and he looked anxious.

'Oh, yes, sir. I shouldn't worry about that.' A surprisingly cynical twist briefly slanted her father's mouth as he picked up a mohair rug and almost tenderly spread it over Wallace's lap.

'I do so wish I could be proud of the boy,' the old man confided heavily. 'Leo's as straight as a die, nothing of the bad egg about him… One out of two; shouldn't complain, should I?'

In an undeniable daze, well aware that she had been quite forgotten about, Angie crept back to the door. Yet she knew that she would never forget that glimpse of Wallace and her father comfortably engaged in the candid dialogue of two older men who had known each other all their lives. For the first time, she had seen that the formal distance they maintained in public was a very poor indicator of the nature of their relationship, and that behind her father's loyalty lay a very real affection.

Afraid to go upstairs in case she ran into Leo and the tension between them exploded in Jake's presence, Angie headed through the green baize door for the first time since her arrival and slammed straight into her stepmother, a small, thin woman in her late fifties with greying hair and rather protuberant eyes.

'Angie...oh!' Emily gasped, looking hunted and dismayed.

'Thank you for sitting up with me last night—'

'Do you know where Mr Leo is?' Emily interrupted shrilly.

'He's with Jake upstairs...I think. If you've got a message for him, I should give it to Dad...' Her voice trailed away in surprise as the older woman simply scurried on past her with what could have been a stifled sob.

Angie hesitated, wondering if she ought to go after her stepmother, but she was in no mood after so traumatic a morning to deal with anyone. She would see Emily later. She hurried on past the kitchens, which were noisy with the busy feet and chatter of lunchtime activity. At the end of the long, flagstoned corridor, she dived into the butler's room to borrow her father's overcoat off the back of the door.

It was a new coat, she noted in some surprise, the cloth heavy and expensive. Maybe it had been a misfit for Wallace. She dug her arms into the sleeves while she scanned the contents of the key cupboard. A minute later she had located the key she sought, and she headed for the old servants' tunnel. It was as dark and dank as it had ever been, created over a century earlier to enable the servants and estate workers to enter the house without intruding into the gardens above, and thus offending the eyes of the family and their guests. Now the tunnel provided a very useful and concealed short cut into the grounds.

She dug her hands into her pockets. Beyond the old ice house she slanted off on the path to the lake. One of Drew's least successful ideas had been the transformation of the Folly into self-catering tourist accommodation. Blithely ignoring his grandfather's love of privacy, Drew had spent a small fortune on the conversion.

'Honeymooners will love it!' he had forecast, putting in a Jacuzzi with gold taps and a bed the size of a small football pitch.

But nobody had ever got the chance to stay there. Apart from Leo. She walked by the lake, no longer seeing the wind-blown grass and the bare trees but remembering instead the lushness of that early summer two and a half years earlier, the glory of the wild flowers, the drugging heat of midday... and Leo miraculously waiting for her...

'Join me,' he had suggested casually, indicating the elaborate picnic hamper resting on the rug. 'Today, I start life anew.'

Leo had been far from sober and dangerously volatile but, in her excitement, she hadn't seen that, had only registered that he was finally paying attention to her and expressing a desire for her company. With her father safely distant in London, Angie had spent the entirety of the preceding week throwing herself in Leo's path with increasing desperation, waking up every day in terror of hearing that he was returning to Greece.

But once ensconced on that cashmere rug, headily conscious of Leo's smouldering appraisal and vainly aware that most men considered her beautiful, Angie had been on a triumphant high, and ripe for a rude awakening to the harsher realities of life. And Leo had been right on one count—nothing that had happened that weekend had been on Angie's agenda.

'You remind me of a little cat lapping cream,' Leo had confided, reaching for her with indolently amused confidence and kissing her breathless.

She had had no control over the incredibly powerful physical feelings he'd aroused in her. Leo had not been remotely like the admiring, unsophisticated young men whom she had easily held at a distance. Sooner than she cared to recall, Leo had carried her into the Folly and made love to her with a wild, passionate impatience that had taken her by shock and storm.

Remembering how she had behaved still made Angie feel quite sick and shaky. She must have seemed so shameless, so pathetically obsessed. In her lowest moments, she sometimes wondered if Leo had gone to bed with her just to get rid of her.

Withdrawing the key, she stuck it into the door of the Folly and walked inside. Dismay stilled her in her tracks. All the evidence of Drew's conversion had gone. The building had been returned to its former purpose—a viewpoint on the hill above the lake, a comfortable place to sit even on a cold day. She mounted the stone staircase in the corner and surveyed the empty room above. Then, suddenly, she was flying downstairs and back out into the cold fresh air, scalding tears of regret running down her face and an agony of pain mushrooming up inside her.

She had been so happy that weekend, and so stupid that she had believed he was happy too!

'I like a woman who knows what she wants...as long as it's what I want too...and it was, it *was*,' Leo had confided with tender satisfaction as he'd gazed intently down at her, seemingly revelling in the tidal wave of affection and warmth she had been engulfing him in. 'And I like it even more when you look at me as if I'm the very centre of your universe…'

Dear God, how could he *ever* have asked her if she had used him as bait to make Drew jealous? She hadn't been able to hide her feelings that weekend, had been so helplessly, deliriously content—like a lost puppy finally finding its way home, she reflected, hating herself and just about the whole world at that instant, and scrubbing at her wet cheeks with feverishly unsteady hands.

How could she go on loving Leo when he had never, ever wanted her in the first place? And now he hated her like poison…of course he did! What male would welcome the fruit of a casual sexual encounter with a woman who meant nothing to him? But Leo, famed in the family for his sense of honour, would love and accept his son because Jake was an innocent victim of his mother's irresponsible behaviour.

The crack of a snapping twig broke through Angie's brooding, miserable thoughts and she whirled round. Leo fell still under the cover of the trees, his hooded dark gaze disturbingly level as he studied her. Angie snatched one appalled look at him and whipped her reddened eyes away again. He must have seen her from the house and, doubtless, had followed her up here to stage a showdown where nobody would be likely to hear them. She braced herself for the onslaught of bitter recriminations.

'Jake fell asleep in the middle of his lunch. I over-tired him,' Leo said prosaically.

Angie blinked, hands stuffed deep into her pockets, shoulders rigid with strain.

'It would be complete hypocrisy for me to bemoan his existence,' Leo mused, almost as if he were talking out loud to himself. 'He is a part of me, he is my son and, now that the shock has faded a little, I have to confess that I am delighted with him. I could be very angry that I missed out on the first years of his life, but what would be the point?'

Totally bemused by what she was hearing, Angie found herself gaping at him.

'It would've been much easier for you to have an abortion.' A grim smile of acknowledgement curved Leo's wide, sensual mouth. 'But you didn't. I have to be grateful for that.'

'Grateful…?' Angie parroted, so deeply shaken by the concept that she could barely frame the word.

'I was equally grateful for your candour earlier.' Leo continued to watch her with disturbing intensity, spiky black lashes low on his penetrating dark eyes. 'Few women would admit that they cold-bloodedly set out to try and entrap a rich husband.'

Angie jolted back into life and flushed to the roots of her hair. 'I…I…' she began, but she got no further because disabusing him of the conviction that she had been a committed, calculating little gold-digger would entail admitting that she had been madly in love with him—and, even worse, actually dumb enough to believe that she could miraculously replace the baby daughter he had lost, and thereafter bask in his warm and devoted appreciation.

In the electric silence, Leo regarded her expectantly, a black brow slightly raised as he waited for a further response.

'Yes, well,' Angie finally mumbled with a jerky shrug. 'Now you know.'

'So why didn't you ever make a bid to collect on your fertility?'

Angie tensed in dismay, not having been prepared for that very obvious question.

'You see, I'm having something of a problem understanding that aspect,' Leo confided softly. 'Wallace might in the heat of temper have forged that ridiculous deal with you, but all you had to do was contact me. Obviously there would've been no question of a prosecution. Your pregnancy gave you a fistful of aces, yet for some peculiar reason you made no attempt to play them.'

Angie squirmed. Leo had started out by allaying her worst fears, and had then cruelly pounced when she was a sitting duck. She didn't feel equal to the challenge of searching questions for clarification of what had motivated her at the time.

The silence lingered and grew until it clawed at her nerves.

'I just couldn't face telling you that I was pregnant…OK?' she shot back in the sudden desperation that swiftly translated into temper. 'In fact, after the way you treated me, I would've sooner drunk cyanide!'

'That seems reasonably comprehensive,' Leo responded with considerable irony, glittering dark eyes resting coolly on her hectically flushed and defiant face. 'I dented your ego and nothing, not even greed or ambition, could somehow persuade you to put my son's needs ahead of your own wounded pride.'

Angie winced and spun her head away. 'I wondered how long it would take you to start talking like that.'

'You're quite right,' Leo slotted in in unsettling agreement. 'Talk of that nature is most unproductive. And this *is*, after all, that very special moment when all that keen plotting and planning of two and a half years ago, all that assiduous tracking, hunting and tempting, leads to what now seems its almost inevitable conclusion…'

Every silky word hitting its shrinking target, Angie's strained blue eyes skimmed back to him in growing bewilderment.

Leo's brilliant dark gaze held hers fast. 'I can only legitimise my son's birth by marrying you.' A glimmer of a hard smile slanted his lips as he took in her utter stupefaction at his making that point. 'And I intend to carry through on that absolute necessity. Nobody will get the chance to call my son an "embarrassing little mistake" ever again!'

CHAPTER EIGHT

'YOU'RE asking me to m-marry you?' Angie stammered in frank astonishment.

'Not asking—*telling* you.' In emphasis of that not so subtle distinction, Leo closed the distance between them and stilled mere inches from her, his hard, dark features set with relentless determination. 'We are getting married.'

Angie swallowed with difficulty and simply gaped at him. Here, at least, was confirmation that there could be no other woman in Leo's life.

'*Before* the tabloids dream up crashingly crude and comic headlines about the butler's daughter, the Demetrios love-child and droit du seigneur in the steamy depths of Devon,' Leo clarified with a slashing twist of his sardonic mouth. 'Before Jake or anyone else starts asking awkward questions. And, last but not least, so that I can have full access to and rights over my own child!'

Slowly, Angie brought her lower lip up into contact with the upper again. It took considerable courage even to do that with Leo standing over her in the most intimidating fashion, bold dark eyes waiting to pounce on the smallest sign of opposition.

'But—'

'But *nothing*!' Leo blazed down at her with explosive menace. 'You owe it to your son and you owe it to me!'

Angie tried to retreat a step, but Leo was ready for that too. His hands shot out and entrapped hers, imprisoning her to the spot. Volatile dark eyes struck hers like a shower of lightning sparks. 'And let us not pretend that sharing a marital bed is likely to be a huge sacrifice for either of us. While you console yourself with my wealth, I will console myself with your beautiful body…I think it sounds like a match made in heaven, *pethi mou*.'

He backed her up against one of the pillars supporting the Folly's porticoed entrance, freed her hands and settled his own on the feminine swell of her hips. Angie shivered violently, legs weak as water, brain power in stunned suspension, the glorious heat and feel of Leo's lean, muscular body against her yielding softness provoking the most shattering surge of raw excitement inside her.

'Leo…' she whispered almost pleadingly.

Eyes burning pure gold, he pushed back the coat and skimmed long, lean fingers slowly up the straining length of her trembling thighs. She shuddered, leant back, throat extending. He took the invitation she offered with a wild, hot hunger that electrified her, crushing her mouth under his, and then, with a ragged groan, he jerked back from her. Angie's eyes opened again, defenceless in their confusion. It was like recovering consciousness after a stunning blow to the head.

Leo expelled his breath in a pent-up hiss. '*Theos*…we're in full view of the house!'

Angie flushed with mortified colour and looked away, fighting to regain control of her quivering body.

'I can't keep my hands off you,' Leo gritted half under his breath. 'But I shouldn't start things I can't finish and, to satisfy Wallace, we have a Christmas tree to choose.'

'A Ch-Christmas tree…?' Angie mumbled, wide-eyed.

'Tradition, Angie,' Leo imparted in stern reproof as he eased her off the pillar, smoothed down her skirt and rearranged her father's coat since it was perfectly obvious she was in no state to do it herself. He urged her back down the path. 'My grandfather is a stickler for tradition. As the future mistress of the Court, you get to pick the tree and watch me chop it down.'

'I haven't said I'll marry you.'

'I can't think of a single reason why you should refuse.'

You don't love me. Her warm colour bled away on that stark truth. Leo, her hero from adolescence, her one and only lover and the father of her child. He had been her most destructive weakness from the age of thirteen. But to be Leo's wife, to possess him in body and legality, if not in soul…to turn over in bed at night and find him…to have the right to lift the phone and hear his voice whenever she felt like it… A rush of intoxicating emotion gripped Angie.

'All right…I'll marry you.' Shamefaced, she addressed the ground at her feet, horribly conscious of that overpowering surge of love and its lack of pride or conscience.

'Of course you will…I rather took agreement for granted when you leant back against that pillar and offered yourself to me in broad daylight.'

Crimson-cheeked, Angie flung up her head and met spectacular dark eyes ablaze with sharply disconcerting amusement. That shook her. But then nothing Leo had said or done over the past minutes had even come close to matching her expectations, she conceded dazedly as he walked her across the bridge over the lake.

It was as if there was a core of joyous vibrancy now lit deep inside him and it was a major effort for him to keep it concealed. It was Jake, of course. Her son had walked right into Leo's heart and immediately found a place there as she herself had never managed to do. Her shoulders drooped, the high-wire tension that had kept her on edge for hours draining away.

'I'll make arrangements for a special licence,' Leo announced as they crunched across the gravel at the front of the Court. 'We'll get the ceremony out of the way before Christmas—'

'*Before* Christmas?' Angie gasped.

'Christmas Eve, if the rector's agreeable. A quiet family ceremony. You'll need a ring, not to mention a new wardrobe,' Leo mused reflectively. 'Then there's the matter of Jake's Christmas presents. I know it's far from cool, but I can hardly wait to sack the toy shops. We'll fly up to London tomorrow.'

'Yes,' Angie muttered rather weakly, conscious of her growing exhaustion as they entered the house.

Her father was waiting in the Great Hall, Emily beside him, her face pinched and pale, her eyes evasive. 'Could we have a word with you, sir?' he asked stiffly.

Belatedly recalling that her stepmother had been looking for Leo earlier, Angie tensed. A frown line of surprise and unease divided her brows but, with a faint smile, Leo settled a hand on her taut spine and swept her with him into the study.

The door hadn't even closed before Emily broke into speech.

'It wasn't Angie who stole those things... I let her take the b-blame,' her stepmother stammered in a tearful rush, 'but I was the one who took them and sold them. Angie was trying to put the miniature back when Mr Wallace found her with it!'

Angie's stunned gaze leapt from her father's impenetrable gravity to her stepmother's open terror and then to Leo's stasis in the centre of the room.

'Mr Neville has known the truth for a long time,' Samuel Brown admitted tautly.

Angie stiffened in shock, finally understanding why Wallace had found it possible to welcome her so warmly back into his home.

His magnificent bone structure rigid, Leo studied his butler incredulously. 'My grandfather *knew*?'

'My wife didn't confide in me until she was in hospital, and by—'

'When was Emily in hospital?' Angie broke in anxiously.

'A few months after you left, I had a nervous breakdown,' her stepmother confided tightly.

'Why wasn't I told about all this?' Leo demanded rawly.

'By the time I was able to tell Mr Wallace what Emily had done, the Court had already been sold to you, sir,' Samuel explained. 'Mr Wallace advised us to keep quiet.'

'To keep quiet,' Leo echoed half under his breath, a perceptible shudder racking him. 'My grandfather advised you not to tell me?'

'Mr Wallace believed that you would sack me, and it would've been no more than we deserved... But at the time, with my wife ill and no savings to fall back on...' the older man framed with growing difficulty.

'Simon Legree or Judge Jeffreys...take your pick,' Leo filled in grimly. 'What a salutary experience it is to see myself through the eyes of others!'

Angie crossed the room to wrap her arms round her petrified stepmother and give her a soothing hug. 'It's all right, Em,' she said gently while shooting Leo a positively pleading look. 'Leo understands. He isn't angry. It's all over and done with now.'

Her father was poker-straight, but sickly pale. 'Obviously I'm tendering my resignation, sir.'

'I'm marrying your daughter, Samuel. I'm afraid you're stuck with this family for the rest of your days.'

'Marrying my daughter?' The older man was visibly shaken by the announcement.

'Yes...we're getting married,' Angie confirmed.

A slow smile blossomed on her father's strained face. 'That's wonderful news.' He hesitated then, discomfiture with this new situation clearly overtaking him almost as quickly. 'I'll take Emily downstairs now, if I may? Facing up to this has taken a lot out of her, sir.'

Silence fell as they left the room. Angie's gaze connected apprehensively with Leo's now blatant stare of outraged condemnation. 'I would've told you once we were married!' she asserted.

'Thank you for that slender vote of confidence!' Leo grated with a curled lip. 'Why the hell didn't you just tell me last week?'

'Well, for a start, I didn't know that Emily had even owned up to my father,' Angie groaned, her head beginning to ache. 'And it wasn't my story to tell. It wasn't me who was going to suffer if you reacted badly and decided to prosecute and threw the two of them out of the house.'

'So instead you let me call you a thief.' His mouth hard as iron, Leo thrust raking, not quite steady fingers through his glossy black hair.

Angie hastened to explain why her stepmother had gone so wildly off the rails. Emily had got into secret debt with a credit card. Too ashamed to confide in her husband, and conscious that their tiny budget would never stretch to meet the payments being demanded, desperation had driven her to stealing. She had sold everything for next to nothing to an unscrupulous trader in a local market. By pure chance, Angie had found the miniature portrait hidden in the flat. After dragging the whole sorry story out of the terrified older woman, Angie had made the last payment on the card, using her savings from a part-time job she had had.

'Your father's salary was static for almost fifteen years,' Leo volunteered flatly. 'He didn't complain, and it wasn't noticed until my staff took over and examined the household accounts. I imagine that goes some way to explaining why your stepmother got herself into a mess.'

He understood. He genuinely understood. Angie felt quite sick with relief and, simultaneously, her legs began shaking beneath her. Those thefts had hung round her neck like an albatross for *so* long. She had never dared to hope that Emily would work up the courage to confess the truth to anyone, had even feared that Leo might not believe her if she did choose to speak up.

'I never doubted your guilt,' Leo bit out roughly, his lean, strong features fiercely taut as he made that grudging but honest admission. 'When I saw the disgusting state of your father's flat two years ago, I was appalled. Wallace hadn't been down there in twenty years, and wouldn't even have thought to check up. I understood your resentment on your family's behalf, and for that reason I accepted that you were the thief.'

Angie now had a thumping tension headache, and her weary shoulders sagged. 'I'm sorry I couldn't risk telling you the truth—'

'And now I know everything, do I?' Leo prompted with a sudden soft and disturbing quietness, brilliant eyes resting on her pale, drawn profile. 'The butler's daughter chose not to steal but instead set her sights squarely and very sensibly on marrying the richest prospect in the family?'

'I'm not feeling very well, Leo,' she mumbled, pushing her hair off her damp brow as a wave of dismaying dizziness ran over her.

'Because you haven't the wit of a flea when it comes to looking after yourself.' Striding forward, Leo swept her swaying figure up into his powerful arms. 'You were ill last night… so what do you do? You skip lunch, stand around in temperatures below freezing for hours and, for good measure, neglect to button up that wretched coat. There is this huge horrific

gap inside you where other people have common sense…
and the extraordinary thing is that at this moment *I'm* feeling
tremendous!'

'Because of Jake,' she mumbled miserably.

'Don't whine, *pethi mou*…you've caught yourself a
billionaire.'

'I wasn't whining.'

'It sounded remarkably like a whine to me. Relax; we'll
reschedule the historic choosing of the tree until tomorrow.
Even Wallace will understand that I don't want a bride on the
brink of collapse. Right now, you will eat and then sleep.'

Angie was too utterly exhausted to argue. It had been the
most emotionally draining day of her life, and now that the ar-
tificial stimulant of stress had been removed she could barely
keep her heavy eyes open.

Angie breakfasted in bed the next morning, feeling deliciously
pampered and incredibly insouciant. She had slept the clock
round. She was seeing the whole world through rose-coloured
glasses. She was going to marry the man she loved… Leo was
right—whining would be most inappropriate.

As soon as she was dressed, she took Jake down to the
basement where her father and stepmother lived in their self-
contained flat.

'You're in for a surprise,' her father warned as he opened
the smart new front door.

She certainly was. The damp and cramped accommodation
she recalled had been extended and transformed into a light,
bright and comfortably furnished home.

'Mr Leo had it all done up just for us,' Samuel Brown
explained. 'He increased my salary too…he's been a very
generous employer.'

The previous day's distress overcome, Emily smiled uncertainly at Angie. 'I feel so much better now it's all come out,' she admitted.

'It *had* to be sorted out once you came back,' her father pointed out awkwardly to Angie. 'I would never have allowed you to take the blame for those thefts, but by the time I found out that you had you were gone and Mr Leo owned the Court. I didn't feel right about keeping quiet—'

'It's all right, Dad. With Em ill, you had enough to worry about,' Angie reassured him hurriedly.

'Like the police, everyone else thinks that the thief was never caught, but most of the stolen items *were* recovered,' her father stressed.

'How do you feel about me marrying Leo?' Angie asked baldly.

'I'm happy for you, of course I am…but it'll take some getting used to,' Samuel Brown admitted with a rueful smile.

Angie went back upstairs to get Jake's coat, brimming happiness adding a bounce to her step. When she came down again on the same wave of euphoria, Leo was waiting in the Great Hall for her. Tall, dark, spectacular, she thought giddily. He extended an unfamiliar coat to her in much the same way as a matador might have flourished his cape at a bull.

'Where did you borrow this?' Having put on the coat, Angie twisted round to look at herself in the nearest mirror, loving the fact that the coat was very long and black and dramatic, and, lifting the luxurious furry collar up round her face, feeling like Anna Karenina.

'It was an impulse buy.'

Angie stroked the soft cashmere with covetous hands and twirled again, eyes starry. 'It's just breathtaking,' she told him chokily, because she couldn't remember when she had last had anything to wear that she really liked, never mind loved.

'Changed your attitude to Greeks bearing gifts?'

'Depends what you want in return,' she teased daringly as they walked out to the Range Rover outside.

'You…tonight,' Leo said succinctly.

Angie's face flamed and she sent him a speaking glance of shaken reproach.

'My wealth in exchange for your body,' Leo reminded her without a flicker of remorse, stunningly dark eyes gleaming over her. 'It's really not a sensitive or deeply meaningful exchange, Angie…but I'm certainly not complaining. What male in his right mind would? After all, if you were in love with me, great feats of romantic effort would be expected from me.'

'I think you'd find yourself facing an impossible challenge,' Angie responded thinly, mouth flat, eyes stony but suspiciously bright.

CHAPTER NINE

'YOU'VE got completely the wrong idea about why I'm marrying you,' Angie told Leo tremulously, pacing up and down on the flattened grass. 'Oh, do stop hacking at that wretched tree for a minute!'

Leo straightened, whipcord muscles rippling beneath the thin, damp silk of his shirt. Angie became so busy running absorbed and helplessly appreciative eyes over his magnificent physique, she very nearly tripped over a log. He looked hot and sweaty and unbelievably sexy. She felt like a Stone Age woman surveying the king of the gene pool, and shivered deliciously while she imagined Leo carrying her back to some wintry, prehistoric cave and ravishing her to within an inch of her life. Colour fluctuating wildly, eyes glowing like sapphires, Angie emerged from that vision, shocked rigid by it, and was appalled to find Leo studying her with an enquiringly raised brow.

'I'm listening,' he encouraged silkily. 'You said I had the wrong idea about—'

'Oh, yes,' Angie recalled jerkily, and commenced pacing in a tortured circle again while Jake jumped on and off the log. 'As I was saying...I'm marrying you for some very good reasons—'

'Name them.' Leo struck the twenty-foot-tall tree another resounding blow with the axe.

'One, Jake needs a father...two, I want him to have absolutely the very best of everything...three...' Angie trailed off, sidetracked by a complete inability to drag her eyes from the powerful muscles flexing in Leo's long, denim-clad thighs, and becoming increasingly breathless and disjointed in her delivery.

'Three?' Leo prompted, not even breathing hard.

'You're so fit...I mean...' Throwing him a flustered look, Angie started frantically pacing again. 'I mean, you're healthy—that's a plus too! Obviously I wouldn't want to marry someone who was likely to peg out on me.'

'Don't worry...I won't peg out on you tonight, and I do see that that would be a matter of concern to you when tonight is just about all you can think about.' Leo gave the shuddering, leaning trunk a sudden forceful thrust, and the Scots pine went crashing down in thunderous emphasis.

Jake leapt up and down in awed appreciation of the sight, and then went careening round the fallen tree with excited whoops. Angie dug trembling hands into her pockets and affected not to have heard that last awesomely shrewd assurance. She could feel her face burning with chagrined colour, and Leo, watching her, was no doubt highly amused by her lack of sophistication and her inability to hide her response to him.

'I just didn't want you thinking that...' she began awkwardly again.

'It's not a problem, Angie. Petrina married me for my money too, but she was considerably less honest about it.'

Sheer astonishment paralysed Angie to the spot.

Having delivered that revelation in the most offhand manner, Leo vented a sudden, startled expletive and roared, 'Jake...*no!*' as he moved with the speed of light to prevent the toddler from getting his eager hands on the axe lying on the ground.

Shocked by that roar, Jake went off into frightened howls. Leo lifted him up and hugged him in consolation.

'You should've been watching him,' he said quite unnecessarily because Angie was already feeling all the guilt of a mother whose attention had strayed.

'You shouldn't have left the axe where he could get hold of it!' Angie was not to be outdone.

The tree would be delivered to the house and set up in the Great Hall to be dressed. A mutually dissatisfied silence reigned as they climbed back into the Range Rover, but Angie could think of nothing but that staggering statement that Petrina had married him for his wealth.

'I thought Petrina was an heiress,' she said abruptly as they drew up in front of the house.

'I neglected to run a credit check on my in-laws. Her father's companies were in serious trouble. The day after the wedding—which Petrina had pushed forward on his behalf—I was informed that it was my duty to solve his problems. The experience left me with few illusions.' Leo sprang out of the car.

'When are we leaving?'

'I need a shower.' Reflective dark eyes rested on her, amusement slanting his mouth. 'You can take your coat off for a while. I doubt if it will run away.'

After an early lunch, enlivened by Wallace's good humour, they flew up to London in the helicopter with Leo at the controls. Jake was ecstatic, but Angie spent most of the trip calming Harriet Davis, who was a nervous flyer. At the airport, they split up. Jake and his nanny were going to the town house while Leo took Angie to Cartier.

Half an hour later, they were outside on the pavement again. A pair of matching wedding rings had been bought. But Angie was also the stunned owner of an opulent sapphire and diamond engagement ring, not to mention the exquisite gold watch and the two pairs of earrings which had somehow happened to attract Leo's attention. Angie, who had never seen anyone buy so much at such speed, was in shock.

'I really wasn't expecting an engagement ring,' she confided breathlessly as she scrambled back into the limousine, turning her hand this way and that to catch the light in the precious gems, quite unable to hide the sheen of dreamy pleasure in her eyes.

'Naturally I will make every effort to ensure that this relationship appears normal to other people,' Leo drawled almost gently.

The sparkle went right out of Angie's engagement ring even as she looked at it. Her buoyancy vanished as if he had plunged a hat pin into the balloon of happiness swelling inside her heart.

'I've also instructed my lawyers to draw up a pre-nuptial agreement,' Leo continued, his lustrous dark gaze intent on her startled face. 'It will tie you up so tight that if I should ever think of divorcing you you will be down on your knees begging me to change my mind!'

'Excuse me?' A deep flush had burned Angie's cheekbones to carmine.

Leo elevated an ebony brow. 'It would be very foolish of me not to restrict your boundaries. In a marriage where the bonds are strictly of a convenient nature, I have to consider the possibility that your attention might stray—'

'We haven't even got married yet!' Angie blistered back at him in disbelief. 'And you're talking about my attention straying?'

'I like to consider every conceivable angle. I'm a businessman,' Leo pointed out with a fluid shrug.

Angie was cut to the bone, but she was also furious with him. He was still convinced she was after his wretched money! But then perhaps she needed that reminder to bring her back down to solid earth again, she reflected with shrinking selfbathing. From the moment Leo had asked her to marry him, the larger part of her brain had been wheeling and dipping in some heavenly never-never land. Why? Marrying Leo had always been her dream. Only now she had to face the fact that, while she had always loved him, he had never loved her, and that his preparations for the wedding had nothing to do with either romance or celebration.

He insisted on taking her shopping for clothes. Angie's temper steadily rose. She was starting to feel like a possession to be paraded, an inanimate object to be suitably dressed and presented for public consumption. In an exclusive salon, while Leo sat in a gilded chair, nursing a glass of mulled wine, Angie tried on one fabulously expensive outfit after another.

She stalked in and out of the changing room, quite magnificent in her growing rage, and sashayed, twirled and flounced in three-inch heels, striving to make him feel uncomfortable. But, impervious to her feelings, Leo lounged back, indolently relaxed, and watched her with deeply appreciative night-dark eyes, lush black lashes sinking lower and lower to give him a deceptively sleepy look.

'Keep that on,' he murmured when she emerged in a scarlet suit with black facings that made a superb frame for the long, lithe shape of her figure. 'What about lingerie?'

Angie cast him a murderous look since it was perfectly obvious to her that Leo was living out the worst kind of male fantasy. 'I'll see to that when I'm on my own.'

'I'm enjoying myself,' Leo confided without shame.

'I want a wedding dress,' Angie told him from between clenched teeth. 'I want a wedding dress with yards and yards of train, and a veil and flowers and loads of lace—'

'Good idea,' Leo slotted in approvingly. 'Wallace will revel in all the traditional bridal trimmings, but we don't have time today.'

'I should wear black with little pound signs printed all over it!' Angie hissed furiously under her breath. 'That's what you deserve.'

Leo cast her a vibrantly amused look. 'Oh, I think I know exactly what I deserve, and I can hardly contain my ardour, *pethi mou*.'

Face flaming with hot colour and every pulse in her taut body humming, Angie was the one to break that sizzlingly sensual visual connection first. She returned to the spacious cubicle to run back carefully through the various outfits she had decided to take, and agonise over one or two borderline choices. It took her some time, and, after that, it gave her the most truly enormous thrill to stroll through to the shoe and handbag department and just point at what she liked.

'You can have anything you want,' Leo had stressed. '*Anything*...and don't you dare look at the prices!'

All the Christmas lights were on when they emerged back onto the street. Multicoloured, bright and beautiful, lighting up the darkening sky and the bustling shoppers crowding the pavements, they stopped Angie in her tracks. 'Gorgeous, aren't they?' she said wistfully.

'Yes.' Leo wasn't looking at the lights, he was looking at her, but she was sublimely unaware of the fact.

'I've always been a bit childish about Christmas,' she muttered, suddenly embarrassed.

'That's not without its charm.' With a slow smile, Leo urged her back into the waiting limousine. 'We have a date to keep with Jake in his bath.'

Forty minutes later, Angie stood back, watching Leo happily dive-bombing plastic boats with a toy aeroplane while Jake squealed with delight and splashed water everywhere in his excitement. She could have dropped dead without Leo noticing, she thought miserably, ashamed and annoyed with herself for experiencing such strong pangs of envy.

He was going to be a wonderful father. Few men had the ability to get down and play at a toddler's level with honest enjoyment. But it was the tenderness, the caring that she could already see in that dark gaze trained on their son that wrenched most at her aching heart. Leo would never look at her like that. She would always be on the outside of the charmed circle of Leo's love—an adjunct, never a necessity.

They were going to be dining out, and she wanted to change. As soon as Jake was settled for the night, Angie went through to the adjoining bedroom and then stilled at the sight of Harriet's overnight bag on the bed. In silence, Leo strolled up behind her, closed his hand over hers and walked her back out again, down the corridor and into the master bedroom.

'In three days' time, we'll be married,' Leo delivered gently. 'I have no plans to tiptoe over creaking floorboards in my own home.'

Angie blushed fierily and hurried into the dressing room, opening doors until she found what she sought. A midnight blue shift dress of wonderful simplicity and elegance. As she emerged from the wardrobe, Leo pulled open three drawers in succession to reveal the soft jewel colours of silk and lace lingerie sets.

'I made my own selections while you were otherwise engaged,' he explained.

Head bent, Angie skated an uncertain finger over the nearest item, heat surging inside her at the knowledge that he had personally chosen such intimate apparel.

'You can be incredibly shy.' Leo laughed huskily, trailing a mocking forefinger across the tremulous fullness of her lower lip to awaken a tingling, intense awareness of his dominant masculinity. 'But it is still a challenge to believe that, in all the time you were with Drew, you didn't once say yes.'

Taken aback by that disturbingly soft and unsettling statement, Angie glanced up unwarily and clashed directly with searching dark golden eyes. Her breath feathered in her throat. 'Drew never *asked*.'

Derision glittered in Leo's steady perusal. 'Don't treat me like an idiot.'

Angie tilted her chin. 'We were friends. That's all I offered, and Drew accepted that.'

Leo looked supremely unimpressed by the explanation.

Angie spun angrily away. He couldn't believe that she had never slept with Drew. But, when she thought about it, she understood his reasoning. Leo didn't have the one missing piece that would have made sense of the puzzle: her love for him and his cousin's full awareness of it had kept Drew at arm's length.

'I've already given you my answer, and now I want to get dressed,' Angie said tautly.

Leo held her anxious gaze for several taut seconds and then, with a smile she didn't like at all, he inclined his arrogant dark head.

As he swung on his heel, Angie cleared her throat. 'And I don't ever want to be put through a second round of this conversation, Leo!'

'An honest response will forever close the subject.'

'You're jealous of Drew...I can't believe it!' Angie exclaimed helplessly. 'A man I don't even like any more...'

Leo flashed her a look of outraged censure over one broad shoulder. 'I...jealous of Drew?' he slung back at her grittily. 'Are you out of your mind?'

'I'm really glad that you're not the jealous type,' Angie managed, and averted her eyes lest they betray her extreme lack of honesty.

In three days' time, she would become the wife of a ferociously jealous and possessive male. The darker passions seethed below that cool, sophisticated surface of his. Angie had the most extraordinary desire to wrap her arms round

im and tell him that she adored him, but as she recalled that
re-nuptial agreement he had mentioned and the engagement
ng that she had only received for the edification of the gen-
al public the desire to give generously of her love withered
tterly on the vine.

She got dressed in the *en suite* bathroom and emerged to
nd that Leo had already gone downstairs. As she descended
he staircase, she saw him waiting in the hall. Tall, dark,
evastating. Her susceptible heart leapt. There he was, finally
earing a dinner jacket for *her*, and, for an appalled moment,
he was honestly afraid that the upsurge of emotion inside her
might make her cry.

'You look breathtaking,' Leo murmured huskily.

'Yeah, well…you bought the dress.' Angie grimaced to hold
he tears back, and surreptitiously sniffed. And demanded the
ght to take me out of it again, she couldn't help thinking,
heeks warming as she struggled not to mentally anticipate
he evening's closing agenda.

Leo burst out laughing.

'What's so funny?'

He wrapped her into her cashmere coat. 'It wouldn't trans-
te very well.'

He took her to an extremely smart restaurant. Heads turned
nd eyes lingered on their entrance. They made a striking
ouple. A dozen people murmured greetings to Leo, their
uriosity about his beautiful blonde companion unconcealed.
eo smiled and nodded in recognition, but he didn't once
ause.

'I gather this is part and parcel of the making-the-
elationship-look-normal-and-introducing-me-to-the-public-
ye bit,' Angie condemned tightly. 'Some first date, Leo!'

'Our first date took place a long time ago. It was a picnic
y the lake,' Leo responded silkily. 'We may not actually have
aten anything out of that hamper until late in the evening,

but it's the one and only date that I've ever had that lasted an entire weekend.'

Face heating at that mortifying reminder, Angie hid behind her menu until a tiny, delicate woven basket of wild flowers was delivered to their table. She blinked in bemusement at the attached card bearing Leo's signature. Where the heck had he got wild flowers in the middle of winter? She found she *had* to ask.

'I had them flown in from a warmer climate.'

'Oh…' There had been wild flowers that day by the lake, the scent of the crushed blooms sweet and heady in the hot, still air as she'd lain in his arms… Surely nothing so specific as tender memory could have prompted his gesture?

During the first course, Leo rested bold dark eyes resolutely on her. 'I planned the whole exercise. I ordered the hamper and then I lay in wait for you, secure in the knowledge that *you* would find *me*.'

Angie very nearly choked on a luscious cube of melon.

Leo poured her a glass of iced water. 'I have to confess that I didn't have a single decent intention in my head.'

Coughing and spluttering into her napkin, Angie pushed back her plate and snatched at the glass to sip the water and soothe her convulsing throat muscles.

'And I had to punish you for infiltrating my every sexual fantasy. I was also feeling very guilty. I was seven months out of a marriage which had been a disaster in the bedroom,' Leo continued with devastating candour. 'And there you were, brazenly ignoring all my keep-off signals, and targeting me with a single-minded tenacity of purpose that was so blatant—'

'Please don't say any more, Leo,' Angie whispered, verbally on her knees and pleading as she drank down great gulps of iced water, cheeks hot enough to fry eggs on.

'So unashamed and so *honest*, it was a very powerful draw for me.'

Her brow furrowed as she ran back over that last sentence.

Leo vented a grim laugh of amusement. '*Ohi*...no, you didn't realise that, did you? That all the time I was freezing you out on another level I was reluctantly impressed and attracted by your persistence?'

'It didn't show.' Angie's gaze was riveted to the dark splendour of his, her heartbeat speeding up.

'I didn't even acknowledge it to myself then,' Leo conceded, his dark, deep drawl husky. 'But Petrina never wanted me like that. She wasn't capable of that kind of passion. You were, and you seemed to be offering me exactly what I wanted and needed.'

Heated colour blossomed afresh in her cheeks yet she was held fast by the brooding, magnetic intensity of his stare.

An odd little silence fell, thick and heavy. Angie licked nervously at her dry lower lip. Watching her, Leo flinched.

'Let's get out of here,' he breathed abruptly, a ragged, fevered edge to his voice. 'It was a cardinal error to start talking about *that* weekend in public!'

In astonishment, she tensed, but Leo was already rising, dark eyes blazing with a sexual hunger he made no attempt to conceal.

The *maître d'* surged towards their table. Angie stood up jerkily, her shaken gaze welded to Leo. He snaked a possessive arm around her trembling body and dismissed the older man's concern with an easy, wry reference to an overlooked appointment.

Dimly aware of the rush of curious comment as Leo swept her back outside, Angie's face burned, but she could no more have resisted Leo in that particular mood than she could have resisted the need to draw life-giving air into her lungs.

He signalled to his chauffeur across the street. 'My flowers, Leo...my flowers!' Angie cried in dismay. 'I forgot—'

She fell silent as a grinning waiter emerged from the restaurant with the precious little basket. Leo vented an incredulous laugh. 'But they're useless...they'll be dead in another couple of hours!'

Angie clutched the basket to her as if she was afraid it might be thrust in the nearest waste-paper bin. With a look of rueful amusement and a stifled, husky sound of impatience, Leo pulled her to him without warning and brought his mouth down in hot demand on hers. She went down into that wildly passionate kiss with buckling knees, and stumbled into the car after it in a welter of shell-shocked excitement.

'Don't come near me,' Leo advised hoarsely as the limo moved off again, street lights glancing over his spectacular bone structure, accentuating the harsh, taut slant of his cheekbones and the golden burn of his smouldering gaze. 'Not unless you want to be dragged down and ravished right here and now...plundered and pillaged by a male close to the edge.'

Angie shivered convulsively, her body boneless and utterly pliant as she shifted infinitesimally, the pounding pulse beat of desire sending helpless little tremors through her.

Leo gritted something raw in Greek. 'Don't look at me like that...it doesn't help!'

Dry-mouthed, Angie stared back at him, absorbing the splintering, ferocious tension he emanated.

'I'd do it... I'm not an English gentleman like my cousin. And I have this feeling that you are going to learn to make love in some very unusual places because sometimes, when I look at you, I think I *can't* wait...not another day, not another hour, not another *second*!' he groaned, and flung his arrogant dark head back, closing his eyes, dense black lashes almost hitting his cheekbones. 'And knowing that you feel the same way adds a whole new dimension to my agony!'

'You think I'm wanton, don't you?' Angie prompted chokily.

'Wanton works wonderfully well for me, Angie,' Leo confided raggedly. 'In fact, when you fix those huge blue eyes on me, my testosterone count probably hits danger levels. Going from a famine to a feast two and a half years ago was the most unnerving part of the whole experience!'

Unseen by him, Angie was cringing. She was learning a lot, but nothing that made comfortable listening. So the intimate side of his first marriage had been less than satisfactory. If she had ever been able to bring herself to consider that issue, she would have suspected that reality for herself. Leo was a very physical male, tactile, hot-blooded, spontaneous. Petrina had been cool and essentially narcissistic. But it hurt Angie a great deal to accept that all that had ever drawn Leo to her was his sexual frustration, his recognition of her as a willing bed partner likely to satisfy his needs with the minimum of fuss and demands.

'You were just a silly kid,' Leo breathed with startling abruptness as he lifted his head to look directly at her again, brilliant dark eyes innately shrewd and his accented drawl disturbingly rough. 'On the outside a woman, but inside one very reckless little girl. But I didn't see that...I didn't even realise you were still a teenager until it was too late.'

Angie had tensed. 'Didn't you?'

'I remembered you romping about in the background over the years...but, if you hadn't been so good on a horse, I'd never have noticed you at all,' he admitted bluntly. 'You were very, very careful not to tell me that you'd just finished school that summer. You talked about the job you were starting in August, but you never admitted that it would be your *first*.'

Angie studied her tightly linked hands, too guilty to meet his gaze. 'I was a full year older than everyone else in sixth year...I more or less lost the year that my mother died because

I got behind with my work and I had to repeat a year. I wasn't *really* trying to hide my age from you.'

'Excuse me...you *were*,' Leo countered.

'I just w-wanted to seem more mature,' Angie protested.

'Oh, you managed that all right.' His expressive mouth quirked as the chauffeur opened the door beside her, letting in a flood of cool night air.

Angie scrambled out with intense relief. Leo unlocked the front door, thrust it wide. 'In fact you managed that right up until the magic moment when I realised that I was in bed with a virgin.'

Angie shed her coat and headed for the stairs at speed, escape from the extremely embarrassing nature of the conversation her only ambition.

'I never would have dreamt that a virgin could be such a polished little temptress,' Leo whispered in her shrinking ear from behind, curving restraining hands round her slim hips when she attempted to take flight. 'Naturally I'd assumed that you were experienced.'

Temper stirring, Angie broke free of his hold and raced up to the landing. 'You certainly didn't complain when you found out I wasn't!'

Leo drew level with her, an aggressive strength and poise in his stance, long legs set slightly apart as he gazed down at her. 'A certain primitive streak in me rejoiced in the knowledge that I was your first lover...but when sanity returned I felt like a complete bastard.'

'Only you were careful not to feel bad until *after* you'd had what you wanted!' Bitter and accusing chagrin laced her every word.

'*Theos*...you get one idea in your head and then you stick to it like superglue! There are times when I could quite happily strangle you,' Leo confessed with raw impatience as he reached for her with hands that brooked no refusal and swept her up into his arms. 'But that is nothing to what I wanted to do to you when I saw you with Drew! And you smirked at me as if you were a cheap, malicious little—'

Biting off the rest of that wrathful sentence, he swore in Greek at a memory that still evidently whipped him on the raw. His arms tightening round her, he treated her to a grim look of condemnation for that past offence as he strode into his bedroom.

'I did not smirk...I *didn't*!' Angie gasped furiously. 'Put me down!'

'With pleasure...' Leo dropped her down on the well-sprung divan in an inelegant heap of splayed limbs, her hair flying everywhere. 'It's past time that we had a little plain speaking between us. Not something you excel at, *pethi mou*...but something you will learn to be really, really good at around me!'

'You think so?' Angie sliced back, clawing her wildly disordered hair off her outraged face.

'I *know* so. You accused me of ditching you like yesterday's newspaper. You talk and behave as if I took deliberate advantage of your innocence,' Leo launched down at her in an intimidating growl of censure. 'But we both know that you played a starring role in your own downfall. When a woman throws herself at a man, he sees a sexual invitation, not the opening chapter of a serious affair!'

'How *dare* you?' Angie was so mad at him, she was shaking.

'And perhaps you'd care to tell me how I could have continued that affair when everything that had already happened between us was utterly indefensible!' Leo bit out savagely. 'You were far too young. I was twenty-seven, you were nineteen.'

Angie flung her head back, eyes bright blue chips of fiery scorn. 'And I was the butler's daughter...let's not forget that!'

Leo shot her a menacing look that would have ground a lesser woman into the dust. 'Two generations back my family in Greece were fishermen, but I was raised to be proud of my roots. Open your eyes…these days social mobility is everywhere, and highly regarded!'

'But some of us prefer not to sleep our way to that regard!' Angie told him with a proud toss of her head as she swung her legs towards the edge of the bed.

'You stay where you are,' Leo told her with a warning flare in his intimidating gaze as he peeled off his dinner jacket in an impatient movement. 'We will have this out if it takes all night! We both betrayed our respective families' trust that weekend, but at least I acknowledge that I was in the wrong— *when* will you?'

Shaken by that pointed demand, Angie gulped, 'I did…I do, but—'

Leo sent his jacket sailing across the room onto a chair as if she had given ground on a long-awaited concession. 'And when you appreciate that you have made a wrong step, do you then say to yourself, "This feels good, so even though it's wrong I'll keep on doing it"?'

Angie got even more flustered. 'No…but—'

'There is no *but*,' Leo slotted in fiercely. 'I did what I believed was right at that moment in time. Since I was not prepared to make a proper commitment to you, I ended it!'

'You crushed me…' Angie mumbled tightly.

Leo released his breath in a dark, driven hiss. 'It wouldn't have been fair to leave you with the impression that I might come back to you.'

A humourless laugh was squeezed from her thickened throat. 'You should be proud of yourself; you were very successful!'

'I *know*…' Leo gave that low-pitched agreement a strange, weighted significance, his lean, strong face shadowed and taut.

'I'm very thorough in most things that I set out to do. It was a crazy, wonderful weekend, but it became too intense too soon. I had to draw back to take stock for both our sakes.'

Suddenly, Angie couldn't bring herself to look at him. Tears sprang to her eyes. This was the real truth she was hearing now, she thought in agony. 'Too intense.' She had shown her feelings too openly, and no doubt he had registered what an embarrassment she could become. So 'wonderful' a weekend, but not one he had had any desire to repeat...not so wonderful after all.

The mattress gave slightly with his weight. With surprising gentleness, Leo looped the veil of her pale hair off her strained profile and let his knuckles brush softly across one taut cheekbone. 'You're such a baby sometimes...you just won't look before you leap. I'm not an impulsive man, but that weekend I seized the moment and I didn't see the consequences until it was too late. There was a price to be paid. I didn't *want* to hurt you—'

'But you did...you couldn't get away from me quickly enough!'

Leo closed a powerful arm round her rigid shoulders and forced her close. 'I didn't trust myself anywhere near you...'

Struggling for breath, terrified she might lose control and howl all over him, Angie thrust her damp face into his broad shoulder, dimly wondering how on earth she had ended up welded to his long, hard frame like a second skin, but receiving too much vicarious security from the embrace to have the will-power to move away.

'And I still don't,' Leo muttered in unexpected continuance, burying his mouth with a muffled groan in the scented hollow of her collarbone, and ensuring that every pulse in her body leapt into sudden, startled and treacherous life.

Leo lifted his head again. Angie pressed helpless fingers

to the tiny pulse flickering like mad at the base of her throat.
She was trembling without even being aware of it.

In the rushing silence, Leo reached behind her to pull down
the zip on her dress. He eased it down over her arms, exposing
the firm swell of her breasts, cupped in a blue lace bra and
shifting with every jerky breath she snatched in. Slowly he
pushed her back against the pillows.

Shimmering dark golden eyes roamed over her with intense
male appreciation. He peeled the dress expertly down over her
hips, drew it off and cast it aside. Then he slid fluidly off the
bed and began to undress, ripping open the press studs on his
shirt, revealing sun-bronzed skin and the rough pelt of black
curls hazing his powerful pectoral muscles. He shrugged out
of the garment, sleek brown shoulders emerging, a taut, flat
stomach. Her attention locked onto him, mouth running dry,
pulses starting to race.

'You make me feel like an exhibitionist,' Leo murmured
with vibrant amusement.

Angie lowered her lashes, cheeks on fire. 'You've never
been shy,' she breathed unevenly.

Leo laughed softly and shed the rest of his clothing. He was
hugely aroused, supremely unconcerned by the fact. Angie
tensed, suddenly desperately shy of him and aware of his virile
masculinity with every skin-cell in her taut body.

'Come here...' He eased her to him, sliding a long, lean,
darkly haired thigh between hers as he leant over her, all
male in his dominance, and circled her lips teasingly with his.
Angie stopped breathing. He nibbled at her full lower lip and
she gave a little jump, the coil of wicked anticipation within
her twisting ever tighter. He shifted sinuously over her and let
the tip of his tongue dip erotically between her lips, making
her shudder.

'Leo...'

'Patience, *pethi mou*... I've waited a very long time for

this, and I intend to savour every moment,' Leo breathed huskily.

And then he crushed her soft mouth under his until every sense swam and she closed her arms round him in a sudden, convulsive movement.

Leo raised his head. 'That's better,' he told her, angling back from her to flick loose the front-fastening bra, baring her full breasts for his perusal.

He ran a caressing fingertip over one achingly erect rosy nipple, and a choked little sound broke in the back of Angie's throat. Leo surveyed her with immense satisfaction and dropped his dark head to torment that sensitive peak with his mouth. Frantic heat sprang up low in her stomach. Heartbeat hammering, Angie twisted beneath him, her fingers biting into his smooth brown back and then sweeping up to lace tightly into his thick, glossy hair instead.

'You're so beautiful,' Leo murmured intently, shaping her pouting breasts with reverent hands, letting his tongue flick sensually over the shamelessly engorged tips. Clenching her teeth, Angie squirmed in tortured excitement. She gasped and struggled for every breath as waves of sensation thrummed through her. Then he let his teeth graze her swollen, straining flesh, and her hips rose and she moaned out loud in pure torment.

Leo stared down at her, golden eyes blazing, a fevered line of colour over his hard cheekbones. 'When you're out of control,' he confessed raggedly, 'it drives me wild.'

'I want you...' she gasped. 'I want you *so* much it hurts!'

Leo expelled his breath in a shaken hiss and, arching over her, almost crushed her beneath his full weight, his tongue plunging with explicit, driving need into the moist interior of her mouth over and over again.

'Am I being too rough?' he asked thickly.

'Oh, no...' Angie mumbled when she could catch her

breath, reaching up an unsteady hand to touch his beautiful mouth, rubbing her fingers along that anxiously tensed line, a desperate tide of love overwhelming her.

Knotting a possessive hand into her tumbled hair, he smiled wolfishly down at her and smoothly disposed of the fragile barrier of silk and lace still encircling her hips. 'You're my woman…and I need to possess you so badly, I *ache*.'

Sending a sure hand skimming through the damp cluster of pale curls at the apex of her trembling thighs, he delicately traced the swollen, moist centre of her. Angie jerked, a moan of anguished need betraying her. Leo watched her with hungry appreciation, skilful fingers finding the most sensitive place of all and playing there until she was frantic with mindless, whimpering pleasure.

'Leo…*please*,' she begged, her whole body straining up to him.

He came over her in one strong movement and entered her yielding softness with a shuddering groan of raw satisfaction. The sensation surpassed her every expectation. He had only begun and her heart was banging wildly against her ribcage, making her weak with sheer over-excitement. Every screaming nerve was centred on his slow, powerful invasion, her passion-glazed eyes welded to the fierce control etched in his taut features.

'Leo…' she cried achingly. *'Leo!'*

And then he moved, thrusting deep into the heart of her. The power of speech was wrenched from her by the most shattering surge of physical pleasure. He felt so incredibly good, and she felt so deliciously possessed, she surrendered herself utterly. He drove into her with hard, rhythmic force. She cried out in strangled ecstasy and clung while the fierce ache of hunger surged higher and higher until, uncontrolled and out of her mind with excitement, she hit an electrifying starburst of sensation and fell over the edge into heaven.

She didn't float back to earth again either. Leo was holding her so close when she opened her dazed eyes, a breath of fresh air couldn't have got between their damp, hot bodies, and that felt like heaven too.

'May I continue?' Leo enquired raggedly.

Her lashes fluttered and then she registered that he was *still*…

'Oh…' she said guiltily, face burning as he lifted himself up to gaze down at her.

Glittering dark eyes vibrantly amused, Leo murmured forgivingly, 'You lasted a whole three minutes…that has to be some kind of record.'

In the middle of the night, Angie put on the light and watched Leo sleep for a good half-hour. All she wanted to do was feast her eyes on him. He was sprawled on his stomach, black hair tousled, lashes down like ebony silk fans, jawline blue-shadowed, a lot of rather embarrassing scratches scoring his once flawless back and one long, lean thigh partially exposed by the tangled sheet. Even sleeping, he was so gorgeous, it was the most appalling struggle for Angie not to seek actual physical contact.

Feeling incredibly possessive, she covered him up as gently and carefully as she covered up Jake, and then she slid restively out of bed to tiptoe round, picking up their discarded clothes. She was so ecstatically happy, she couldn't sleep. Only one tiny cloud marred her horizon. It had taken until after midnight to exhaust him, but that wasn't the cloud. Indeed Angie couldn't think of anything more wonderful than Leo's insatiable need to subject her to endless pleasure.

He had been so passionate, so tender, everything she recalled from before…only this time around she was absolutely terrified of him guessing that she was still madly in love with him. 'Too intense'. That was precisely what had driven him

away from her two and a half years ago. Leo might have talked
a lot of impressive sounding twaddle about her having been
too young, but Angie remained unconvinced.

In two days *she* would be Leo's wife. He didn't love her but,
if Leo had it in him to love, he would love her by the time she
was finished with him. She would sign that stupid pre-nuptial
agreement thing he had mentioned and surely then he would
appreciate that she wasn't a gold-digger? Aside from that, a
little coolness, a little distance, indeed a little mystery ought
to make her all the more desirable a wife in his eyes... Abstractedly she breathed in the scent of him from his discarded
shirt, eyes starry as she plotted and planned.

Angie woke up in Leo's shirt, Jake bouncing on the bed,
ice-cream stains round his chattering mouth. His dark eyes
glowing, he told her about having breakfast with his father,
visiting some park, playing on the swings and falling off the
slide. A trouser leg was rolled up to display a chubby knee
bearing a minuscule plaster, and a replay of the fall was suddenly enacted. Angie caught her over-excited toddler a split
second before he nose-dived off the bed in his enthusiasm.

'Go wash,' he announced importantly, sliding out of her
arms again like an eel to scramble back down onto the carpet
and race back to the door. 'Daddy say go wash.'

Angie sprang out of bed to give chase, but was drawn up at
the bedroom door when she saw Harriet gather him up. 'I'll
see to him,' the older woman said cheerfully. 'He'll need a
change of clothes before he goes out.'

Angie had a shower and put on a slim black wool dress,
scrubbing at her cheeks in the mirror to give herself some
colour. A whole box of cosmetics, that was what she needed,
she decided sunnily.

She walked down the stairs, careful in her high heels, not
yet used to wearing them again. The library door was ajar

and she could hear Leo speaking, so she hung back in case he had someone with him.

'There *is* no risk...' he was murmuring with audible amusement. 'But I still won't feel safe until I get that ring on her finger...no, I can't meet up with you beforehand...I don't want her to suspect what I'm up to.' His dark, deep drawl dropped even lower in pitch. 'Marisa, you're tremendous...'

Transfixed to the spot, Angie strained feverishly close to the door to hear what he was saying next, and distinctly heard a roughened reference to 'any sort of bed at all as long as it takes two', and then, in a very husky, sexy whisper, 'You're embarrassing me'...

Leo...*embarrassed*? Leo who didn't have a self-conscious bone in his body? Angie shuddered, perspiration dampening her upper lip as she jerked away from the door and shot across the hall into the drawing room opposite. He needn't worry about being embarrassed, she thought. He should worry about living to breathe another day!

CHAPTER TEN

SICK with shock at what she had overheard, Angie crept over to a chair and dropped down into it to stare into space. Leo and Marisa Laurence. Only two days before he married Angie, Leo was indulging in the sort of sexually suggestive dialogue which only lovers shared. After last night, how *could* Leo betray her trust to such an extent?

Unable to sit still, her sensitive stomach still turning somersaults, Angie got up again. Her mind was the most terrifying blank. All she was conscious of was the shattering pain of her own disbelief. And then she questioned even that sensation, for where had she ever got the idea that Leo would be faithful? She had been outrageously naive. An awful lot of men—and rich men in particular—were serial adulterers!

She fumbled to recall exactly what she had overheard. Leo wasn't prepared to meet up with Marisa before the wedding in case his bride-to-be got suspicious. He had also said that he wouldn't feel safe until that ring was on her finger. Some chance of that *now*, Angie reflected in agony. But, of course, Leo didn't want to upset the apple cart at present. He had a lot to lose if the wedding didn't go ahead.

When had she allowed herself to forget that Leo was marrying her only to gain legal rights over his son? As she abruptly recalled that pre-nuptial agreement he had mentioned, Angie's blood ran cold. Leo evidently planned to continue his affair with Marisa. Concerned that his extra-marital activities might provoke Angie into demanding a divorce, Leo would naturally seek to safeguard his wealth. Her pounding head ached. She blinked, breathed in deep. Her imagination was getting out of hand...

Leo *loved* Jake. Leo had to know that if there was a divorce and he tried to fight her for custody of their son it would be Jake who would suffer most. No, she wasn't dealing with some Machiavellian plan to steal her son away from her, she decided. Her sagging shoulders straightened. Her beautiful face clenched with sudden fury. She was dealing with a louse who had blithely assumed that he could be an unfaithful husband, a louse who would find out the hard way that if he put one toe out of line she would make him pay for it in spades!

Angie folded her arms, ramming back her pain with fierce determination. Oh, yes, she could confront Leo and refuse to marry him, and where would that leave her and her son? Leo's wealth would still put him in the driver's seat. He would have to support them. She would have to put up with him visiting for Jake's sake. She might even have to tolerate Marisa Laurence as her son's stepmother. No, marrying Leo would give her equality and a certain amount of power. Flouncing off in a huff would only reduce her to the level of being his dependant...wouldn't it?

'What's wrong?' Leo enquired with a startled frown when she pulled away from the light arm he had dropped round her shoulders as they left the town house.

'Nothing,' Angie said flatly.

'Look, there's obviously something wrong,' Leo stated with conviction in Harrods when Angie kept on behaving as if he was stalking them.

'Maybe I'm having a bad hair day,' she said frigidly.

With Harriet in restrictive tow, personal dialogue of any length was all but impossible. While everyone else ate their lunch, Angie enjoyed several glasses of wine on an empty stomach, grimly conscious of Leo's brooding frustration.

They had spent several hours in Harrods. Angie had resisted any suggestion that she might want to look at wedding dresses. But Jake was now in possession of a wardrobe large enough to clothe three little boys because, when it came to his son, Leo had no sense of proportion. He had also fully borne out Angie's every expectation in the toy department, and had gone on to hit Hamleys with unquenched enthusiasm.

But Angie had lurched at frightening speed from rage to misery to the kind of sick, despairing jealousy and pain that pooled like poison inside her. She had reached the stage where one minute she was convinced she could still marry Leo and happily make his life hell by policing his every movement, but the next she was convinced that she couldn't go through with the wedding under any circumstances.

In fact her emotions were in full and very dangerous control of her by the time the helicopter circled over Deveraux Court and made a neat landing on the pad to the west of the house. It was late afternoon, and the icy temperatures had finally borne out their wintry promise. It was starting to snow.

'Snow...' Jake gasped ecstatically as the first fat, fluffy flakes drifted slowly down. He raced across the gravel frontage of the house, twisting and turning like a miniature dervish as he tried to catch them.

Leo surveyed Angie. Angie watched their son as if his innocent wonder and joy were a tragedy of the biggest order. How *could* she deprive Jake of the father he already adored? Security, love, two parents. Those were the things which her son needed most...

The Great Hall was dominated by the Christmas tree. The Scots pine now glittered and glowed with gold and silver decorations and candle-shaped lights.

'I'm the sort of woman who would hack your designer suits

nto tiny shreds if you were ever unfaithful,' Angie delivered chattily to Leo as she slid out of her coat.

Having been momentarily engaged in watching their son rot off with both his grandfathers in keen pursuit, Leo's arrogant dark head whipped back round to her. Angie had the pleasure of seeing him utterly frozen to the spot, bold dark eyes incredulous.

Her smile was colder than the snowy peaks of the Himalayas as she climbed the stairs. 'I'm the sort of woman who would tell the whole story, with the inclusion of every minute and dirty detail, to the Press.'

'Angie—?'

'I'm the sort of woman who would rip you off for every penny you've got if you betrayed me,' Angie slung at him in warning from the minstrel's gallery. 'And I would be the sort of ex-wife who would feature only in your worst nightmares. I would be unreasonable, manipulative, demanding and just downright nasty!'

'What the hell is the matter with you?' Leo demanded not quite steadily as he strode up the stairs after her, taking them two at a time. 'Apart from rather too much wine...'

Angie stiffened, eyes flashing. 'I just thought you should know what you're getting into *before* you marry me. If I ever had cause to doubt your loyalty, I would hold spite and pursue vengeance until the day I died!'

'You're heading in the wrong direction.'

'No, I'm not,' Angie muttered tightly. 'While you are considering your options, I will be sleeping in the Chinese bedroom.'

'So I'll visit,' Leo delivered cheerfully.

In disbelief, Angie focused on the amusement flashing across his lean, strong face, shaken even in the mood she was in by the raw charisma he possessed. 'No way!'

Drew, looking rakish with a patch over one eye, strolled

down the corridor towards them with his arm ostentatiousl
draped round a small, curvaceous brunette with smiling gree
eyes. 'This is Tally,' he announced.

'Hi…I'm Angie,' Angie managed to say, and then sh
walked on, only hesitating long enough to throw over he
shoulder, 'And by the way, Leo, I will not be signing an
pre-nuptial agreement!'

She closed the bedroom door behind her. A split secon
later, Leo thrust it open. No longer did he look amused. 'Dre
and Tally heard that last crack,' he drawled in stark reproo

Embarrassed by the rebuke, Angie shrugged jerkily, tear
thickening her throat. 'Why should that worry you? Mr Ser
sitive you're not,' she condemned. 'As for that agreement,
you expect me to take *you* on trust, I expect you to take *m*
on trust too.'

Lounging back against the door with innate grace, Le
studied her with measuring dark eyes. Infuriatingly he sai
nothing.

'After all, you've already made it clear that this is a ma
riage of convenience for our son's sake,' Angie continue
doggedly. 'And maybe I'm not too sure of the kind of treatmer
I can expect to receive after the wedding.'

'When have I ever given you cause to question my since
ity?' Leo demanded with level bite.

Angie spun away and breathed in deep, hands knottin
together. 'Someone told me that you were heavily involve
with Marisa Laurence until very recently.'

'So *that* is what this is all about…'

Angie turned back to him, very pale and taut.

Exasperation had set Leo's hard facial bones. 'Marisa and
have been close friends for years. In fact, it's Marisa you hav
to thank for the soft toys and the clothes that were acquire
for Jake the day you left the Dicksons'.'

'Close friends?' Angie repeated with tense, frowning uncertainty.

'With never a spark of anything sexual because there was never a spark even to begin with for either of us,' Leo supplied very drily. 'Marisa *is* heavily involved, however—not with me but with an environmental scientist who's been working abroad for the past year. Marisa stayed in the UK because she has a business to run.'

Angie stared at him with wide eyes, and then she reddened fiercely. There was something so very deflating and convincing about Leo's cool, incisive gaze and sardonic intonation.

'The "someone" who talked was Drew, right?' Leo prompted in derisive continuance. 'He doesn't miss a trick when it comes to causing trouble. But it's you I'm disappointed in, Angie. You talk about trust, and yet you couldn't bring yourself to just come right out and ask me about Marisa—'

'You're saying it's a platonic relationship…yet you wouldn't accept that same explanation from me—'

'Drew wanted you. The situation was different.' Leo wasn't yielding an inch. He opened the door again, his strong features harshly set.

Angie nibbled anxiously at her lower lip. 'Leo…I heard you on the phone to Marisa this morning and it didn't sound like a purely friendly conversation—but possibly I misunderstood,' she muttered in an increasing rush. 'Only you were talking about not wanting me to suspect what you were up to, not being willing to meet her before the wedding…'

'You'll understand after the wedding. Until then I'm afraid you'll have to take me on trust,' Leo imparted with distinct irony as he closed the door.

Angie was so worked up she burst into floods of tears. Evidently she had got herself into a state over nothing. But why the reference to a bed? A joke, a flirtatious innuendo between old friends? Leo had been so cool, calm and superior. But she

wondered how he might have reacted had he eavesdroppe
on a similar one-sided dialogue. But she could answer th
question for herself—Leo would have immediately confronte
her. Openly and honestly.

Her luggage arrived and a maid appeared to do the unpac
ing. Angie went off in search of Leo, only to discover that h
had taken Jake down to the stables with him. Her father re
minded her that it was the staff party that evening. That mea
that the family would be dining out and returning late.

A knock sounded on the bedroom door as Angie was tryir
to decide what to wear.

It was Drew. Without invitation, he made himself careless
at home on the side of the bed.

'What do you want?' Angie enquired thinly.

He grimaced. 'I guess I owe you an apology for what I di
two years ago.'

'Fine…is there anything else?'

Drew gave her a reproachful look. 'I was rather nast
the other night, but I wasn't expecting to find you here and
frankly, it was one of the worst nights of my life!'

'Yes,' Angie allowed grudgingly, thinking of the man
shocks Drew had been dealt at the dinner table. 'I suppos
it was. But where *did* you get the strange idea that Leo wa
almost on the brink of marriage with Marisa?'

Drew went red and evaded her eyes. 'So I exaggerated
bit—'

'A *bit*?' Angie derided grimly.

'OK…so I knew they were just friends. It just riled me
seeing you with Leo again,' he admitted rather rawly. 'I hat
the way he always seems to get what he wants. But Tally think
that I did a rotten thing keeping the two of you apart.'

'You didn't keep us apart. Leo had already scrubbed m
out of his life.'

Drew groaned. 'Well, who can say how it would've turne

out? But Leo *did* land back here a few weeks later, expecting you to be sitting waiting like faithful Penelope even though he'd ditched you...and you weren't; you were painting the town red with *me*!'

Angie was frowning. 'What are you talking about?'

'I could've been noble and stepped back and made it clear that there was nothing heavy between us, but I'm not noble and I *didn't*. Actually, I revelled in the knowledge that Leo wanted you back and thought he had missed the boat.'

'That time he visited...he wanted me back?' Angie whispered unevenly. 'Did he tell you that?'

Drew rolled his eyes. 'Angie...can you really see Leo confiding in me?'

'No...but you said—'

'It was obvious that you were the only reason he came here. He flew straight back to Athens first thing the next morning.' Drew sighed as he read the devastated look in her eyes. 'He was his own worst enemy, Angie. He could've put his cards on the table then and given you a chance...'

Angie spun her head defensively away, her throat thickening as she recalled Leo approaching her when she had come home at the end of that evening. 'He did try to talk to me... but I wasn't really paying the right sort of attention.'

'At the time I thought it was hilarious,' Drew confided wryly. 'Everybody *but* Leo knew that you had always been crazy about him.'

The door opened without a warning knock. Leo froze on the threshold. Drew uttered a very rude word in his dismay. Angie's tear-filled eyes encountered a look as aggressive as an attack in Leo's glittering dark gaze.

'This is as close as I ever got to Angie's bed... honest it is,' Drew quipped with a distinctly strained laugh. 'For heaven's sake, Leo...lighten up before you give me a heart attack!'

Leo swung on his heel and strode off down the corridor.

Angie made a move to follow him. Drew stepped in her path
'Give me a chance to get well out of the way first,' he sai
wryly. 'I do not want to be involved in this round. I've go
Tally now, and, although you're still a remarkable eyefu
you're definitely more Leo's style. I'm not into throbbin
passion and high drama, but the pair of you appear to thriv
on them!'

As soon as Drew was gone, Angie splashed her face wit
cold water. Leo had come back specifically to see her on tha
flying visit to the Court two years ago... Dear heaven, coul
that be true? And had she, in her bitter pride and driving nee
to appear untouched by his rejection, been her own wors
enemy too? The suspicion savaged her.

'Your presence has a wondrously enlivening effect on Leo
Wallace remarked when she went to collect Jake from th
drawing room. 'I know my grandson as a serious, rationa
and even-tempered man. You make him do extraordinar
things.'

'Such as?'

Wallace gave her a sardonic smile. 'Sneaking into his ow
home like a cat burglar with roses and pink champagne. H
hates flowers...he hates champagne. Such as storming out lik
a thundercloud, leaping into his Ferrari and driving off...'

Angie had turned pink. 'Leo's gone out?'

His grandfather nodded. Angie swallowed hard and too
Jake to have his tea. Her son's energy level was flagging fast
He was half-asleep when she lifted him out of the high chai
and in no state for a bath. Gently slotting him into his pyjamas
she put him to bed. Drew's girlfriend, Tally, came in to tak
a peek at him.

They parted outside Angie's bedroom door, having share
a thorough discussion of what each of them planned to wea
that night, although the brunette had done most of the talking

Angie was finding it hard to concentrate because all the time she was wondering when Leo would get back, *if* Leo was planning to come back and even if there would be a wedding—for avoiding confrontation was not a characteristic that she was used to Leo displaying.

She owed him a full explanation about Drew. She had never attempted to explain that relationship in a way which would make sense to Leo. So naturally he was still uneasy. His cousin was a part of his family, and likely to be around now on a regular basis. All Leo had ever asked her for was the truth, but she had been too proud to give him it.

Was the intensity of her relief written across her face when she entered the drawing room and found Leo there? He skimmed a narrowed glance over her jade-green dress and light jacket. Angie stared back at him helplessly, her pupils dilating, her breath running out in her throat. His hair still damp and slightly curly from the shower, he was wearing a casual but incredibly elegant dark suit with a silver-grey sweater. He looked devastatingly sexy in the way only a very masculine man could.

'Shall we go?' he suggested to the room at large, and then he flicked a glance at Angie. 'I presume you're putting on your coat?'

She would have a chance to talk to him in the car, she assumed. But it was not to be. All five of them piled into the back of the limousine. It was a short drive to the country house hotel which had the only restaurant in the district Wallace was prepared to patronise. Angie was seething with desperation to get Leo on his own by the time they walked into the hotel. She closed a hand round his sleeve and leant up to whisper, 'Leo—'

'This is not the place, Angie,' he said very drily.

Mortified, Angie withdrew her hand. She watched him

over dinner. Although the winter chill never ebbed from hi
spectacular dark eyes, he laughed and he chatted with an easy
social dexterity she was quite incapable of emulating. Wallace
was the life and soul of the party.

'Leo behaving badly...I love it,' Drew murmured at one
point under cover of the conversation.

Angie looked up as a group of people stopped by their
table to exchange greetings with Leo. A tiny, svelte blonde
with huge blue eyes studied her intently and then smiled at
her. She extended her hand. 'I don't think we've ever been
formally introduced, Angie.'

'Marisa...' Angie's smile was strained as she stood up
towering over the other woman and feeling absolutely huge.

'I'm so pleased for you both,' Marisa confided with the
kind of warm and deep sincerity that even the Wicked Witch
of the West couldn't have doubted.

'Lovely woman,' Wallace commented as she moved off
again. 'It's a mystery to me why she's not married. This career
woman nonsense, I expect...owns one of those twee decorating outfits, doesn't she?'

'An interior design consultancy that's worth several mil-
lion,' Leo responded.

'*Never*...' Wallace ejaculated in healthy astonishment.

Angie was shrinking. Marisa was little, gorgeous to look
at, successful in business and genuinely nice. She was convinced that Leo had to be comparing them to *her* detriment.
Tally and Drew got up to dance. Wallace was hailed by an
old gentleman sitting at a nearby table and he went over to
socialise. Leo lounged back in his chair and surveyed Angie
in silence.

'You're angry with me—'

Leo rose abruptly from his seat. 'Let's get some fresh
air...'

'Leo... Drew came to my room to apologise for all the

things he's done,' she muttered as he fed her into her coat with astonishingly gentle hands in the foyer.

'You were crying,' he gritted.

Angie sucked in a deep, anxious breath. 'I was in love with you two and a half years ago.'

'I know...' Leo said flatly, swinging open the door and walking her into the still white world beyond. 'I am not stupid.'

Silenced by that assurance, Angie bit the soft underside of her lower lip, tasted blood and shivered in the cold, crisp air.

'But you were very young,' Leo murmured in driven addition. 'It was perfectly possible that in the space of a few weeks you had fallen out of love with me and into love with him.'

'But I didn't...and Drew knew right from the start that I loved you—'

'You *told* him?' Leo shot her a startled glance and then he groaned. 'For the first time in my life I feel sorry for my cousin.'

'That's why we were only ever friends.'

'*Cristos*...no wonder he hit the bottle so hard while he was with you! To have you and yet *not* have you,' Leo breathed with a stark shudder. 'I could not have borne a relationship like that.'

'I talked about you all the time as well,' Angie confided guiltily. 'But I honestly *didn't* know how he felt about me. And this evening something he said upset me and that's why I was crying. He said...he said that time you flew over for twenty-four hours—he said that he thought you wanted me back—'

'I *did*,' Leo confirmed, closing a strong arm round her and pulling her close as they walked down the well-lit path under the white, frosted silhouette of the trees.

'So why did you ditch me in the first place, then?' Angie

demanded strickenly, her lovely face convulsing with the strength of her emotions.

Leo stilled and rested his hands on her quivering shoulders. His brilliant dark eyes were full of pain and regret. 'I needed time away from you to work out what was going on inside my own head. I wasn't happy with Petrina, but I *chose* her... how could I have any faith in my own judgement after one weekend with you? What room did I have to even explore my feelings *with* you when both our families would've been justly outraged by the level of intimacy we had already enjoyed?'

'Are you s-saying that you thought you m-might be in love with me then?' Angie framed so shakily she could hardly get the words out.

'I was afraid it was only an infatuation which wouldn't last on my side...and you were so vulnerable. I *had* to leave, and I couldn't make you any promises. I didn't know if I would come back to you.'

'You could've told me the truth,' Angie condemned unevenly. 'You could've asked me to wait—'

Leo vented a harsh laugh. 'I was arrogant enough to believe that I didn't *have* to ask. I wasn't prepared for you to take up with Drew, but I recalled enough of my own teenage experiences to know that nothing is more fickle and fleeting than the emotions of youth. You seemed happy with him—'

'Where were your eyes?' Angie gulped, tears clogging up her throat. 'I was *miserable*.'

'I was very angry... Strange as it may seem, I felt that you were the one who had made a fool out of me. I had spent six weeks wrestling with my desire for you,' he admitted rawly. 'And there you were, prancing about happily with my cousin. I wanted to kill you, but I told myself I had had a narrow escape from making an even bigger ass of myself.'

'I didn't w-want you to know how much you'd hurt me.'

'Ditto...' Leo said roughly half under his breath, and he

gathered her close, crushing her into his arms and then framing her tear-stained face with his hands to look down at her, bold dark eyes intense and possessive. 'And now I've got you back in my arms I'm never letting go of you again.'

His hungry mouth was cool on hers and then hot…hot…hot, the taste and the scent of him and the hard strength of his powerful physique filling her with electrifying excitement. She went pliant and clung. Leo needed no further encouragement. Wallace coughed unnoticed from the hotel steps. That kiss went on and on and on until Drew wolf-whistled from the limousine which had drawn up on the other side of the snowy verge.

Angie didn't remember the drive back to the Court. It meant so much to her that Leo had come back for her after that weekend, and she didn't know whether she was on her head or her heels. She floated back into the house, tucked under Leo's arm, and drank a toast to Christmas with him as the staff gathered in the Great Hall, laughing and chatting and full of seasonal spirit after their own evening of festivities. Leo gave a wonderful speech about how much he appreciated everyone's hard work. Angie watched him with the exclusive attention of a woman in love.

They got one foot towards the stairs. The head groom broke breathlessly through the thinning knots of the departing staff, his wrinkled face troubled. 'I'm afraid that little mare looks like she's going to deliver early, sir. I've phoned for the vet but he's on another call, and with it being her first foal…'

'It's OK…I'll come and take a look at her.' Leo gave Angie a rueful look. 'Don't wait up for me,' he advised.

'I could come with you…'

Leo frowned and shook his head with decision. 'No point in both of us going without a night's sleep.'

Angie went to bed alone, feeling hurt. She might not be as skilled or as experienced as Leo was with horses, but it certainly wouldn't have been the first foal she had helped to deliver. As a teenager she had spent all her free time down at the stables. But then Leo didn't feel any need to have her hovering round him *all* the time, did he? Only a man in love would have welcomed her company.

But two and a half years ago, given the time, the space and the opportunity, Leo *might* have fallen in love with her. That was a bitter pill to swallow. But after he had seen her with Drew any fledgling feelings he had had for her had been destroyed. He had spent almost all the years since believing that she had slept with Drew, become pregnant with his cousin's child…not to mention believing that she was the household thief.

When he had come back into her life again, he had done so on Wallace's behalf alone, and initially he had been anything but pleased to find himself still attracted to her. But, being Leo, he had soon decided that the logical thing to do was to go to bed with her and get her out of his system, and he probably would have managed that feat, she conceded, growing steadily more wretched, had it not been for the fact that she was the mother of his son.

Any treacherous and insidious thought that she might reasonably lodge herself in Leo's bed and wait for his return was now soundly squashed, and even the memory of the thought a source of deep shame. Angie clutched a pillow miserably to herself. She would never throw herself at Leo again.

Angie's father brought her breakfast in bed the next morning. She sat up and practically snatched the tray from him. 'Dad!' she scolded in embarrassment. 'I don't want you waiting on me…it's not right!'

Samuel Brown chuckled. 'There are so many staff here now that I rarely get to lift anything heavier than the morning post. I wanted a word with you. Have you got a wedding dress yet?' he enquired anxiously. 'I suppose I'm a little late asking.'

'No, you're not.'

Smiling with relief at the news, he informed her that that was just as well because it was his duty to buy her one. These days, he told her proudly, he had a very healthy savings account. Before she knew where she was, he had organised her day for her. She was to make a shopping trip into Exeter with her stepmother and buy the best dress she could find. And what about presents? he asked. Had she bought presents for everyone? Her face fell a mile. He shook his greying head. 'So Leo doesn't think of everything.'

'It wouldn't even occur to Leo to suspect that I might be running round with less than five pounds in my purse...he couldn't imagine that level of penury— Gosh!' she exclaimed. 'You actually called him *Leo*!'

'I feel rather idiotic calling my future son-in-law anything else. As Wallace says, we have to move with the times unless we want to be written off as a couple of hidebound old fogies. But it's hard to break the habits of a lifetime.'

Apparently, Leo had spent the night in the stables, appeared for breakfast at seven and then gone to bed. The foal had been delivered successfully. But Angie was deprived of even a view of Leo before she left the house.

It was the most frantic day. But Angie fell in love with a dress in the second shop they visited. It had a stand-up Elizabethan-style beaded collar, a tightly fitting bodice and a lowish neckline, and it was the most beautiful shade of ivory. Angie looked in the mirror and saw a medieval princess gazing romantically back at her, and that was that.

Buying Christmas presents was the greater challenge. A book on modern manners for her father, another book—but a humorous one—for Wallace. For Drew cigars and for Tally a silk scarf. She bought a blouse for Emily while her stepmother was in a coffee shop. And then she came to Leo—Leo, a male who already had everything right down to a solid gold pocket knife and Turnbull and Asser shirts inscribed with his initials. She dragged her stepmother from shop to shop, and then daringly settled for another book—love poems. There was always the hope that inspiration might lead to change.

It was dark when they got back to the Court, but the great house sat with blazing, light-filled and welcoming windows of warmth, surrounded by the snow. A rather unusual snowman now adorned the lawn. He wore a black trilby, a false beard and sunglasses.

Angie, having been deprived of Leo for an entire day, was now indecently eager to see him again. She sped into the Great Hall, attention landing on Drew and Tally, who were standing by the log fire, both of them looking so embarrassingly flushed and tousled that she did the decent thing and pretended not to have noticed them.

'Where's Leo?' she asked her father, who was coming down the stairs.

Samuel Brown frowned in surprise. 'Do you know, I haven't a clue.'

'He said he had some last-minute shopping to do,' Drew delivered surreptitiously, straightening his rumpled sweater.

'Took the hump at you disappearing all day, I shouldn't wonder,' Wallace volunteered when Angie went into the drawing room. 'He got up at lunchtime, built a snowman for Jake and then spent the rest of the afternoon pacing by the window like a great prat! I couldn't get a sensible word out of him.'

'Oh…' Angie had extreme difficulty picturing Leo behaving like a 'great prat', and could only assume that his grandfather was exaggerating. Wallace then went on to complain about Drew and Tally canoodling in every corner like demented turtle doves and, shaking his head, returned to his book. 'Better company to be had between these pages.'

Her father was waiting for her when she emerged. 'Emily and I would like you to spend this last night with us in the flat,' he told her hopefully. 'It'll not be a chance we ever have again. Of course, if you have other plans...'

'No, I haven't.' But Angie turned a deep, guilty pink because she had been ready to lurk in the neighbourhood of the front door to wait for Leo. She bit her lip. 'That's a lovely idea...I'll come down as soon as Jake's settled for the night.'

Yes, you were going to play it cool with Leo, not behave like an adoring, desperate doormat, she scolded herself.

Eleven o'clock found her ensconced in the narrow bed in her father and stepmother's spare room. Even though it was un-recognisable as the room she had once slept in, it was rather touchingly adorned with the childhood mementos and books she had brought to the Court with her at thirteen. They had kept a place for her and that warmed her heart, but it didn't stop her tossing and turning and wishing she were with Leo. Tomorrow was Christmas Eve and her wedding day, and she really couldn't yet believe that. It was also her twenty-second birthday...but, it being so close to Christmas, nobody had ever paid much heed to it, so Angie never had either.

A soft knock sounded on the window-pane. As the bed was right up against the window, Angie almost jumped out of her skin. She rolled over onto her stomach and sat up, and saw Leo in the moonlight. She opened the window without hesitation.

'Are you coming out...or am I coming in?'

Angie scrambled barefoot over the window-sill, only to give a stifled squeal when the soles of her feet hit snow. Leo whipped off his coat, wrapped her in it and lifted her into his arms. She didn't get the chance to ask where they were going because he was so busy kissing her. She clutched at him as if they had been apart a month, head swirling and heat infiltrating every chilled inch of her responsive body.

Leo lowered her carefully down onto the window-ledge and lifted his head, breathing in deep and audibly.

It took Angie longer to recover. 'Why were you pacing the floor when I was out today?' she gasped.

'Because you were in a car…and it was in weather like this that Petrina and Jenny went off the road,' he divulged tautly.

'Oh, hell, Leo…I never even *thought*,' Angie sighed, arms fastening even tighter round him as she hugged him close in consolation.

Broad shoulders shrugged beneath her arms. 'It was stupid of me…but lightning can strike twice in the same place, *pethi mou*. That's why I went out. Waiting for you was driving me crazy.'

Angie rested her head on his shoulder, blissfully drawing in the reassuring scent of him. He had been worried sick about her. A wave of overpowering love engulfed her, and she recalled his miserable marriage and his disillusionment and she decided to be generous. 'I'll sign that pre-nuptial whatsit if you like,' she offered.

Leo groaned in the circle of her arms. 'That was a joke that rebounded on me…I had no intention of demanding that you sign any such agreement. I was simply paying you back for pretending that you were a gold-digger on the make two years ago.'

Angie jerked and lifted her head, eyes wide. 'Paying me back?'

Leo studied her with rueful amusement. 'That very first night I saw you again, you told me that you had been very much in love with your son's father…'

Angie's soft mouth dropped open.

'And you said it with such fire…you threw it in my face

with relish. When I realised Jake was mine, I recalled that conversation and I finally got the answer to a question that had plagued me for a very long time.'

'The problem plagued me even longer,' Angie confided. 'I've had my eye on you since I was thirteen.'

'Angie…Angie,' Leo framed with helpless amusement.

'I set out to get you any way I could…I wanted to make up for Jenny,' she said chokily. 'It was so stupid.'

'No, it wasn't…and you've blessed me with a beautiful child who was conceived in love.' With a ragged sigh, Leo scooped her back off the ledge and planted her firmly back on the bed beyond. 'And since I don't want our next child to be conceived outdoors I think I'll say goodnight, *pethi mou.*'

Dizzily, Angie watched the moonlight twirling little circles on the ceiling. She remembered him saying how tremendous he felt the day he'd asked her to marry him. Now she wondered if that had related to her as well as Jake. She went to sleep with a blitzed smile on her face. He might not be romantic but he was very sexy…

In the little country church in the village, Leo waited at the altar. Drew looked unusually serious in his role of best man, and Angie smiled because she hadn't expected to see Drew in that role. She drifted down the aisle on her father's arm, conscious with every step that Leo's dark golden eyes were welded to her with the most flattering degree of intensity.

Every word of the marriage service which followed seemed to have special meaning for her. When they exchanged rings, Leo retained a grip on her hand. Jake plonked himself between them as they drove back to the Court. Then the lure of the flowers in his mother's hair proved to be too much of a temptation and Leo had to distract him. Angie was incapable of anything other than studying her ring and her new husband.

A smart photographer and his assistant awaited them back

at the Court. After being made to pose just about everywhere but at the top of the Christmas tree alongside the angel, Angie gave Leo a pleading look of frustration.

'I've never had a photograph of you...don't you realise that?' he countered.

'He's going to sit in his big fancy office with lots of photos of you so that he can get through the day without you,' Drew mocked.

Angie's heart blossomed with hope.

'I hope you won't mind that we're leaving you now,' Leo announced at the end of the indoor photographic session, entwining Angie's fingers with his and leading her to the door.

'Where are we going?' Angie demanded.

A gleaming open-topped carriage complete with a coachman and two horses sat outside waiting. Poleaxed by the sight, Angie allowed herself to be hustled out and handed up. Leo curved her up against him. 'Don't ask any more questions. Just wait and see.'

The horses trotted not down the drive but round to the back of the house, and stopped at the stable block. Leo helped her down from the carriage and swept her over to one of the stalls. 'Happy birthday,' he said with quiet pride. 'The mare's called Reba and the filly hasn't got a name yet. They're yours.'

Angie gazed, dumbstruck, at the silver-grey Arab mare and her long-legged, gawky but beautiful baby. 'Nobody bothers about my birthday.'

'I do,' Leo asserted. 'What will you call the filly?'

'Joy,' Angie told him dizzily.

From the stables, the carriage turned down one of the lanes which criss-crossed the estate, passing through the woods and then climbing. Angie was in a daze.

'Close your eyes,' Leo told her.

The horses came to a halt a few minutes later, and this

time Leo simply lifted her up into his arms. Angie tried to peek. He kissed her, and she always closed her eyes when Leo kissed her. When he set her down, she wasn't quite sure she was still earthbound and, when her lashes lifted, she was even less sure because she appeared to be standing inside the Folly, and it had been transformed again.

Only this time the Folly had been transformed with striking warmth, colour and taste. Angie's stunned gaze slowly drifted over the crackling fire in the polished grate, the soft, deep carpet, sofas, rugs and throws, the wonderful little Christmas tree, and a giant lump formed in her throat.

'This is what I didn't want you to suspect I was up to.'

'Oh, Leo,' she gulped.

'Marisa pulled off a miracle for me. This is why I insisted on taking you up to London. I wanted this to be a surprise.'

Marisa and her interior design consultancy. Setting up the Folly for their wedding night had been the subject of that conversation.

'It is…' Angie said hoarsely. 'It's the most wonderful surprise anybody has ever given me.'

Leo turned her slowly round. 'It was the happiest weekend I ever had in my adult life,' he breathed tautly. 'And yet I walked away from what we had shared because I was so damned scared of making another mistake!'

Angie was seeing him through a fog of tears. 'I was only nineteen…I can't blame you for doubting that we could have a future.'

Leo drew her down onto the sofa by the fire. 'I started looking for you three months after you left the Court.'

'But why? At the time you thought I was expecting Drew's baby.'

'And he hadn't looked after you. I wanted to be sure you were all right because I blamed myself for what had happened with him. I had rejected you after giving you every reason

to expect more of me,' Leo breathed with stark regret in hi
deep, dark voice. 'But I couldn't find you. If there was a trai
to follow, it had gone cold by then.'

More tears clouded her vision at the thought of Leo look
ing for her without success when she would have so rejoice
in being found. For a moment, he held her so close she coul
hardly breathe.

'I kept the investigators at work, but more or less gav
up hope,' Leo confessed grimly. 'And then you registered t
vote a couple of months ago and bingo—you were no longe
lost.'

'A couple of months ago?'

'I asked for a full report on you before I informed Wallace.
knew everything down to your shoe size before I came knock
ing on that door. I even made sure that the Dicksons would b
out,' Leo volunteered with raw discomfiture. 'I worked ver
hard at telling myself that finding you didn't mean anythin
personal to me after so long, but...'

'But?' Angie prodded anxiously.

'*Theos*...I was kidding myself. One look and all I wante
to do was gather you up in my arms and take you home wit
me.'

'But Jake stuck in your throat...'

'At first—not by the time we arrived at the Court. And the
Drew arrived and things went haywire...or possibly I was th
one who went haywire. All of a sudden, I didn't know whic
of us you might want, and I was terrified of losing you.'

'Leo...you could never lose me...you idiot,' she said shak
ily, rubbing one blunt cheekbone with caressing fingers. '
love you like mad; don't you know that?'

'And did I wreck your self-esteem so much that you stil
can't tell when a man is wildly in love with you?' Leo en
quired as he raised her upright, passed a long arm below he
legs and carried her up the stone staircase.

'You played games, Leo.'

'You wouldn't admit that you loved me.'

'Why wouldn't *you*?'

'I tried to *show* you in every way I know,' he protested defensively. 'Couldn't you see how happy I was the day I asked you to marry me?'

'You told me, you didn't ask.'

'We'd already wasted so much time apart, and I just couldn't wait to make you mine.'

Angie focused on the candlelit upper room, and, primarily, the most gorgeous bed festooned in lace. 'Definitely big enough for two.'

'You heard that?' Leo exclaimed. '*Cristos*...no wonder you were suspicious! Marisa was teasing the life out of me—what sort of a bed? What sort of sheets did you like? I just gave her a free hand.'

'So what were you doing with Marisa that night until two in the morning?' Angie queried.

'I left her about eleven...then I drove around, thinking about you.'

Angie pushed a proprietorial hand through his thick black hair. 'So who was it you *were* dating? You did say you had a date that first night...'

'Protective fib,' Leo confessed cheerfully as he lowered her to the bed. 'I had a business dinner...I should've known I was a lost cause where you were concerned the minute I lied.'

Angie reached up and kissed him. Leo came down to her with smouldering dark eyes and a tender smile that turned her bones to water. 'I adore you, Mrs Demetrios,' he told her softly. 'And being romantic is no longer a major effort.'

Angie lay back with an ecstatic and quite shameless sigh of invitation. 'More children?' she offered as if she were holding out a lure.

Leo's smile was blinding. 'You're just so perfect for me.'

'I'm making you perfect for me,' Angie whispered blithely.

Clothes melted away like snow off a hot chimney. Sentence became increasingly disjointed and finally ebbed altogether as passion swept the two of them away in a joyous celebration of their love.

At six in the morning, they climbed out of bed and helped themselves to the supper they had ignored the night before. Leo's pre-planning had been so exact that even a change of clothes awaited them both. Arms possessively wrapped round each other, aglow with mutual contentment, they walked up to the Court in the dark and discovered that even Jake was still fast asleep.

Angie's father had ensured that their son's presents were all sitting in readiness below the tree. So Angie and Leo exchanged presents. Angie received a whole host of items, and handed over her single gift in some mortification. When Leo went into whoops on opening that book of love poems, she mock-punched him in the ribs, and he pulled her down beneath him and stole her embarrassment with one passionate kiss that went on and on, and very nearly turned into something quite unsuitable for the Great Hall.

'"How do I love thee? Let me count the ways",' Leo then quoted from the much maligned book, beautiful dark eyes resting with slumbrous hunger and appreciation on Angie as she ripped off wrapping paper to get at her presents. 'Yes... could get into that one.'

He brought Jake down in his pyjamas. Jake took one wide eyed look at the toy car and had not the slightest interest in opening anything as pedestrian as a wrapped present. He careened about the ground floor in noisy ecstasy, and toot tooted his determined way into Wallace's rooms. 'Ganpa... Ganpa!' he called.

Leo loosed a wicked laugh. 'The wonder of a small child at Christmas,' he roared. 'I bet Wallace is putting a pillow over his ears!'

'*Leo*...' Angie's cheeks burned as she tugged out a black lace bustier.

'The spirit of self-indulgence crept in occasionally...and you could model it after lunch.'

'I could put it on for lunch...'

'Put it on *for* lunch?' Leo was aghast.

'This *isn't* lingerie, Leo. This is an outer garment.'

'No way are you showing yourself in public in that!'

Angie laughed and stopped winding him up. 'Relax, Leo. My father would throw a table napkin round me if I exposed that much flesh.'

Ten minutes later she was still piling up gift after gift. Jewellery, the most vast box of cosmetics, another coat, a pile of books, a whole host of cute little things that she just knew Leo secretly considered naff. But he had bought them to please her all the same. 'Oh, Leo...I only got you that one little book,' she moaned.

'Actually I did fantastically well this Christmas, *pethi mou*,' Leo confided with supreme satisfaction as he eased her back possessively into the strong circle of his arms. 'I got you... and I got Jake.'

Angie turned her mouth up blissfully under his. They didn't quite manage to merge.

'If there's likely to be any of that canoodling at this hour of the day, I shall go back to bed!' Wallace threatened.

Garbed in a rather magnificent crimson wool dressing gown, he seated himself in the chair nearest the fire. Angie's father, fully dressed and immaculate, placed himself behind the chair. Wallace twisted his head round and frowned. 'Oh,

sit down, Sam, for heaven's sake! They've bubbled us, an
you don't want to be standing around with that arthritic kne
of yours. Right, where are my pressies?'

* * * * *

◆ HARLEQUIN® A *Romance* FOR EVERY MOOD

If you enjoyed these passionate reads, then you will love other stories from

◆ HARLEQUIN® *Presents*

Glamorous international settings...
unforgettable men...passionate romances—
Harlequin Presents promises you the world!

◆ HARLEQUIN® *Blaze*

Fun, flirtatious and steamy books that tell it
like it is, inside and outside the bedroom.

▼ *Silhouette* *Desire*

Always Powerful, Passionate and Provocative

Six new titles are available every month from each of these lines

Available wherever books are sold

HSCPASS10

HARLEQUIN *Presents*

USA TODAY *bestselling author*

Penny Jordan

*introduces the first installment of
an epic tale of passion and drama!*

The
**PARENTI
DYNASTY**

Power, privilege and passion
The worlds of big business and royalty unite...

Part One:

THE RELUCTANT SURRENDER

When buttoned-up Giselle first meets
the devastatingly handsome Saul Parenti,
the heat between them is explosive....

Available January 2011 from Harlequin Presents.

If you enjoyed this story from
USA TODAY *Bestselling Author*
Penny Jordan,
here is an exclusive excerpt from her upcoming book
THE RELUCTANT SURRENDER
Available January 2011 from Harlequin Presents®.

"LET ME GET THIS STRAIGHT. Are you actually suggesting that I would stoop to that kind of game-playing?"

Saul came out from behind his desk and walked toward her. Giselle could smell the hot male scent of him and it was making her dizzy, igniting a low, dull, pulsing ache that was taking over her whole body.

Giselle defended her suspicions. "You don't want me here."

"No," Saul agreed, "I don't."

And then he did what he had sworn he would not do, cursing himself beneath his breath as he reached for her, pulling her fiercely into his arms and kissing her with all the pent-up fury she had aroused in him from the moment he had first seen her.

Giselle certainly *wanted* to resist him. But the hand she raised to push him away had developed a will of its own and was sliding along his bare arm beneath the sleeve of his shirt, and the body that should have been arching away from him was instead melting into him.

Beneath the pressure of his kiss he could feel and taste her gasp of undeniable response to him. He wanted to devour her, take her and drive them both until they were equally satiated—even while the anger within him that she should make him feel that way roared and burned its resentment of his need.

She was helpless, Giselle recognized, totally unable to

withstand the storm lashing at her, able only to cling to the man who was the cause of it and pray that she would survive.

Somewhere else in the building a door banged. The sound exploded into the sensual tension that had enclosed them, driving them apart. Saul's chest was rising and falling as he fought for control, and Giselle's whole body was trembling.

Without a word, she turned and ran....

Find out what happens when Saul and Giselle
succumb to their irresistible desire in
THE RELUCTANT SURRENDER
Available January 2011 from Harlequin Presents®.

THE PREGNANCY SHOCK

Glamorous international settings…unforgettable men… passionate romances— Harlequin Presents promises you the world!

Save $0.50
on the purchase of 1 or more
Harlequin Presents® books.

REQUEST YOUR FREE BOOKS!

HARLEQUIN *Presents*®

2 FREE NOVELS PLUS
2 FREE GIFTS!

PASSION GUARANTEED SEDUCTION

YES! Please send me 2 FREE Harlequin Presents® novels and my 2 FREE gifts (gifts are worth about $10). After receiving them, if I don't wish to receive any more books, I can return the shipping statement marked "cancel." If I don't cancel, I will receive 6 brand-new novels every month and be billed just $4.05 per book in the U.S. or $4.74 per book in Canada. That's a saving of at least 15% off the cover price! It's quite a bargain! Shipping and handling is just 50¢ per book.* I understand that accepting the 2 free books and gifts places me under no obligation to buy anything. I can always return a shipment and cancel at any time. Even if I never buy another book, the two free books and gifts are mine to keep forever.

106/306 HDN E5M4

Name	(PLEASE PRINT)	
Address		Apt. #
City	State/Prov.	Zip/Postal Code

Signature (if under 18, a parent or guardian must sign)

Mail to the **Harlequin Reader Service:**
IN U.S.A.: P.O. Box 1867, Buffalo, NY 14240-1867
IN CANADA: P.O. Box 609, Fort Erie, Ontario L2A 5X3

Not valid for current subscribers to Harlequin Presents books.

Are you a current subscriber to Harlequin Presents and want to receive the larger-print edition? Call 1-800-873-8635 today!

* Terms and prices subject to change without notice. Prices do not include applicable taxes. N.Y. residents add applicable sales tax. Canadian residents will be charged applicable provincial taxes and GST. Offer not valid in Quebec. This offer is limited to one order per household. All orders subject to approval. Credit or debit balances in a customer's account(s) may be offset by any other outstanding balance owed by or to the customer. Please allow 4 to 6 weeks for delivery. Offer available while quantities last.

Your Privacy: Harlequin Books is committed to protecting your privacy. Our Privacy Policy is available online at www.eHarlequin.com or upon request from the Reader Service. From time to time we make our lists of customers available to reputable third parties who may have a product or service of interest to you. If you would prefer we not share your name and address, please check here. ☐

Help us get it right—We strive for accurate, respectful and relevant communications. To clarify or modify your communication preferences, visit us at www.ReaderService.com/consumerschoice.

HP10R

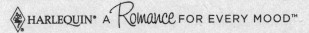

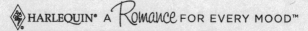